Violet and Peridot

She was dressed in rose . . . the tight bodice and unfashionably tight sleeves showed every curve. Her hair was as tousled as ever, as if it never recovered from a lover's wandering hand.

Violet turned and took in Peridot's companion for the first time. A speculative curiosity joined the laughter in her eyes.

"Who's the gentlemen, Perry?"

Peridot now looked at Marcus Radcliffe. When she saw the look in his eyes as he watched Violet, it was not her intellect that took a blow. It was a quick, sharp jab to the stomach—of envy, of the inevitability of it all.

JILL DOWNIE

AVON
PUBLISHERS OF BARD, CAMELOT, DISCUS AND FLARE BOOKS

TURN OF THE CENTURY is an original publication of Avon Books. This work has never before appeared in book form.

AVON BOOKS
A division of
The Hearst Corporation
959 Eighth Avenue
New York, New York 10019

Published by arrangement with the author
Library of Congress Catalog Card Number: 81-70566
ISBN: 0-380-80861-7

First Avon Printing, September, 1982

Printed in the U.S.A.

WFH 10 9 8 7 6 5 4 3 2 1

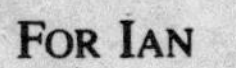
FOR IAN

Chapter One

THE CLINGING, SMOKY FOG that hung over London at the end of 1879 had insinuated itself without pause into the opening of the new decade and poured forth unabated into the January of 1880. With complete disregard for the clearly drawn lines between the classes of society, it encompassed both the slum dwellings of the East End and the stately homes of Belgravia.

The woman moaning and tossing on the wide canopied bed was unaware of it seeping around the tightly closed windows behind the overlapped damask curtains. She was in labor—not too difficult or too complicated, but painful enough to make her fret against circumstances that, for once, her prettiness and charm could not control and turn to her advantage. She clung to her doctor's hand and begged him—aware, even in pain, of the pleasing break in her throaty voice—"Dear *sweet* Dr. Bartlett, is there nothing you can do to hasten this—this process? You promised me it would be easier this time."

Twenty years of catering to the fashionably sick or the fashionably laboring female lay behind the good doctor's response. "My dear Lady Sinclair, you are doing very well—most nobly indeed. Do you wish me to give you something that might jeopardize your child? Would you wish me to take measures to hasten the birth at the risk of tearing that beautiful skin of yours?" He watched the final warning sink into a mind whose thought patterns were shaped completely by the contours of the exquisite body that curved around them.

Outside, darkness had fallen on the shrouded city landscape, and the moan of a rising wind caught in the chimney pots above and echoed into the fire burning in the grate, swirling a little scurry of smoke into the room. The watchers in that silken cocoon of a bedroom shivered to themselves at this reminder of the outside world, half-hidden from the eyes of all since November of the previous year.

When would it all end? A bad summer had preceded this terrible winter; the harvest had been appalling, and the unemployed were crying out in vain for bread to feed their children. Hyde Park was filled not only with the frolickings of the children of the well-to-do, but the gatherings of those who had nothing to do.

Dr. Bartlett crossed to the window and twitched the curtain aside. There was a sudden movement from the bed and a cry from the woman. He moved softly and smoothly across the floor to her.

"I think it is time, my lady. It will soon be over. I think it is time now."

* * *

In her own good time, not her mother's, and into a time that would be far, far removed from her mother's, Sir Rodney and Lady Sinclair's second-born, a daughter, entered the world. (Second-born, and last-born, for the lady decided that one of each gender was enough.)

The second footman was dispatched to fetch the master home, and this news was relayed to his wife, who composed herself and those around her to look as charming as possible in the circumstances. She asked for the child to be placed in her arms, and it was thus that she received him.

Lady Pamela raised a languid and perfectly curved arm from around the child.

"Dear Rodney, do you know what I wish to call her?"

Since her husband had been showered with a list of possible names on and off for the past few months, he had no idea.

"I shall call her Peridot. Yes, I have finally decided it is to be Peridot."

Rodney Sinclair looked puzzled and faintly disturbed. There was something outlandish about this choice of name. "Dearest, I know of no other child in the family called by that name."

Lady Pamela smiled delightedly. "There—you see? How clever of you. That is the reason. I want her to be a jewel. But "Ruby" and "Beryl" are so common, aren't they, nowadays? And then I thought of my peridot and diamond bracelet—and I couldn't call her "Diamond," because that sounded a little odd. So I thought of "Peridot." It has such a *French* air about it and sounds beautiful with my own name. Peridot and Pamela. Pamela and Peridot."

Her husband bent over and kissed her hand. "As you wish, my dearest, as you wish."

Their moment of felicity was broken by the importunate cry of the baby. As a flicker of distaste crossed the features of his wife, Sir Rodney drew back. He took the opportunity by his daughter's intervention to remove himself from the room.

At Brierley Park, on the Sinclairs' country estate, exactly a month after the birth of Peridot Sinclair—February 6, to be precise—the birth of another baby girl took place.

Hers was no uppercrust arrival, tended by white hands and linen sheets. She was born in a cottage on the estate to a maid from the big house: a pretty, sickly young mother who died within hours of the birth of her daughter. The little girl was handed over to the head gardener and his wife, who had no children of their own.

As she was handed over to her foster-father, she appeared to stare directly at him, a focused, concentrated stare from eyes of such color and intensity that he called her Violet.

This apparently unrelated event was to be as important in Peridot's life as anything else that happened to her in the next ten years.

Peridot's earliest, clearest memory went back to when she was three and a half. In later years she could verify the age because the phenomenon that prompted the memory was so well documented. She remembered going to the window with Nanny and watching the sunset. It exploded in golden splendors, streaked with a red so fiery and wondrous that one could almost imagine an accompaniment of the music of the spheres.

With Nanny's arm snugly around her, the little girl would watch the pageant laid on by nature, while the rooks flew cawing home to roost and before the nightingale sang his song, the liquid notes flowing like honey across the night air of the park.

Nanny talked of Jesus and God and how some said he would soon come back and save the good people and punish the wicked. She also told her that Mr. Symes, the butler, had told her that it was because of Krakatoa.

The name, with its heathen-sounding plosives, stuck in Peridot's mind and stayed there for years. In her games, her imaginary villain was always called Krakatoa. It was much later that she discovered Mr. Symes had been talking of the volcanic eruption of that year which had loaded the atmosphere with a myriad of tiny dust particles, each one of which caught the level rays of the setting sun and exploded into glorious color.

The wonder of the sunsets was enhanced by the addition of Mr. Symes's name, for Peridot thought of the butler as being either God himself in disguise or, at the very least, God's emissary on earth.

Say "God" to Peridot and there immediately came into her mind the image of a tall, middle-aged man of mournful demeanor, in a dark suit with a starched wing collar, carrying a silver platter with letters or a decanter on it.

After that year, Peridot's memories became a little more coherent, one following almost on the heels of the other, so that it was possible to string together the months and years of her childhood.

The larger events that touched the outside world

came to her through her parents or the servants. She could remember Gordon at Khartoum. Both Mr. Symes and her father had gone on for a long time about that. Again, there was that same foreign ring about the word *Khartoum* as there had been about *Krakatoa*. She tested it to see how it would sound in her mouth, rolling it off her tongue.

Nanny's musings on the end of the world reached a crescendo with the rash of dynamite explosions that rocked various railway stations during the course of the year and threatened both the safety of Nelson's Column and Scotland Yard. Both Nanny and the head parlormaid, Lily, spent fruitful hours over the household linen and mending, talking of "anarchists" and "the devil's work."

So lurid were the conversations of Peridot's closest companions, so intense was their need for drama to enrich their restricted lives, that four-year-old Peridot had nightmares about this dangerous and threatening world in which she lived. During the day, Belgravia and Brierley Park were calm oases amid the chaos which pressed in on them from outside. At night, however, goblins in the form of anarchists with smoking bombs and sticks of dynamite could easily slip through the mullioned windowpanes or over the area railings to invade her bedroom.

She would wake crying and sweating and calling for her nurse, the unwitting cause of these torments.

The year ended with everyone feeling happy and hopeful that Gordon would be relieved at Khartoum, and the season was very brilliant.

Peridot's happiest memories of her mother at her most accessible were when she played the piano. At such times, her mother actually preferred her to Terence, who found the whole thing rather boring.

His attention would wander, and he would sometimes ask to leave the room on these occasions.

Lady Pamela would be hurt, but she would say, one pretty beringed hand arranged attractively over her bosom, "But then, my darling, he is a man, after all. And they are made to *do.*"

Did this, wondered Peridot, mean that she was meant to *don't?* And what did that mean?

It was around this time that Peridot gradually became aware that she was, in some way, a disappointment to her mother. With her fingertips under Peridot's chin, Lady Pamela had once or twice tilted the little head toward her, looking into her face and shaking her head.

"Where is the delicacy of feature she had when she was born? The lightness of bone? I fear this child will be a *big* woman."

She said it in tones of such tragedy that Peridot would feel compelled to examine herself afterward in the tall, tilting mirror in her bedroom. Staring solemnly back at her was always the same little girl with a round, flattish face framed in slightly frizzy fair hair. She always seemed quite familiar and yet quite strange.

Khartoum fell in 1885, Gordon was lost, the dynamite continued to explode around them and they moved into a summer the like of which had not come in living memory according to Cartwright, the head gardener, who watched his beautiful green lawns wither and die.

Oh, the terrible, awful discomfort of being a small Victorian child in layers and layers of clothes, under which the trapped perspiration prickled and trickled down your body! Nanny was as understanding about it as she could be and propriety would allow. She and Peridot and Terence would go down to the river on the Cotswold property, where they sat under a large weeping willow that cast its shade over both banks. They pulled off their shoes and hose, rolled up petticoats or trousers, and dipped their feet with shrieks of delight into the cool, topaz-tinted water. Terence would leave them after a while, take his fishing rod and go to try for the old trout who lived under the bridge farther upstream. With one eye in his direction, Nanny would tell Peridot stories of what was going on in the outside world.

One of Nanny's favorite topics was the white-slave trade. She showered the government with praise because the practice had been made officially illegal that year. When pressed for details as to what exactly a white-slave trade was, she became rather vague.

"They round up all these poor girls in London—young 'uns, only about fourteen, some of them—and send them over to those foreign cities in foreign parts."

"What for, Nanny?"

"O-o-oh, they make them look after palaces, skivvying and suchlike, for no proper wages."

Since Peridot had always thought from Nanny's conversations with the other servants that this was a big complaint in her own country, she wondered what the difference was. If she had to choose, she thought, she would prefer to skivvy in a palace in a foreign city rather than stay in England and do it.

"Did Gordon have white slaves at Khartoum when he fell?"

Nanny was deeply shocked. "No, no—whatever made you think such a thing. General Gordon was an honorable gentleman. He would never have allowed that for one moment. No, it's more cities like Paris in France, that go in for that sort of carry-on."

From then on, Peridot's villain, Krakatoa, always operated out of Paris, France, the city of carryings-on.

While such exotica were being discussed by the five-year-old and her nanny under the willow tree, the English countryside shimmered and danced around them, creating images of rivers on the dried fields, as if they were in some heathen, far-distant, desert landscape.

In the autumn of that year, Peridot was deprived of her brother. Never very close, they had however been company for each other.

It was that little death of so many seven-year-old English boys—the departure to boarding school—that removed him from her. Not that it ever struck Peridot or Terence as cruel, since it was a completely accepted part of their lives.

Peridot watched Terence leave with her father for the station, his bags piled in the hall, looking dashing and strangely adult in his uniform of top hat and tails. Her mother clung to him, kissing him and wiping his brow with her hand as if he were ill, dabbing attractively at invisible tears with a minute kerchief.

As Terence walked into the outer vestibule, Peridot saw him for a moment in profile. Against the frosted glass of the doors, she saw that his chin was quivering slightly. A phrase of Nanny's came to her: "A lamb to the slaughter."

When father and son had gone, her mother turned from the door and saw Peridot standing there. She put her hand under her chin again and, this time, burst into genuine tears.

"And what shall we do with you, I wonder?" she wailed, leaving the hall rapidly to regain her composure.

Mr. Symes and Lily and Nanny, who were all there for the great departure, looked at each other speechlessly. Then, Mr. Symes did an unusual thing. He bent slightly, took the little girl by the hand and led her downstairs for a cup of weak, deliciously sugary tea and some flapjacks, still warm from the oven. Her little world put itself to rights and moved onward.

It seemed very lonely that autumn and winter without Terence, but Christmas felt more secure because he was there again.

Lady Sinclair was even more preoccupied with her social life, spending many hours wailing and lamenting over her guest lists. Peridot heard an exchange between her father and mother which, though intriguing, threw little light on the subject.

"It always *was* an art to know who to put next to whom, dearest, but now it is impossible. *Why* cannot you men sort out this Home Rule affair? It is *ruining* one's social life."

Her father's retort was unusually caustic. In exchanges with her mother, he tended toward the amused and indulgent approach rather than the critical.

"This 'Home Rule affair,' as you call it, Pamela, is far more important to the nation than a little inconvenience over the dining table arrangements. I tell you, I will not have old Marjoribanks in this house again. He has even been blackballed at the club."

Peridot took her unanswered questions, as always, to Nanny. "Who rules in our home, Nanny?"

Nanny replied without hesitation. "Your papa, of course, my dear. That is the way it should be in every home. He is the master. Mind you"—at this, Nanny winked her eye and looked knowing and wise—"not that there's not moments in every household when a woman gets her own way, if she's clever enough. And your mama is as good at that as any and better than most."

All of which cleared up nothing over Home Rule. It did, however, reinforce the idea of male supremacy in Peridot's head and the desirability of acquiring her mother's characteristics, since she had inescapably been born female.

The year of 1887 was remarkable for the fact that it was the Jubilee of Queen Victoria and that Peridot's governess arrived to join the household. Up to that time, Peridot had done some reading and writing and sums with her cousins' governess, but it was now considered time for her to have a governess of her own.

Miss Boileau arrived one beautiful spring morning and stayed for the next ten years. She was a young woman when she arrived, of a refined but impoverished background. She came highly recommended to the Sinclairs because of the comparative gentility of her parents, who had fallen on hard times. It was Peridot's good fortune that Annie Boileau also possessed a physical toughness, an artistic sensitivity and a keen intelligence to go with that breeding.

It was Nanny who led Peridot into the small sitting room that was to become the schoolroom. Miss Boileau was sitting by the window, looking down into the street below. She turned quickly as her new charge came into the room. There was a sharp, birdlike quality about her movements, and the eyes were alert, searching, examining. She was very slender—her waist is as small as Mama's, thought Peridot—and quite tall. She was plainly dressed in dark brown with a high white collar, the hair severely coiffed above the oval face. Her hands were clasped stiffly in front of her. She wore glasses.

Peridot felt a momentary pang of fear as she confronted this new figure in her life, and she stayed close to Nanny's ample and comforting contours. Then, Miss Boileau smiled and the tension broke. Miss Boileau had a smile that warmed the heart and brought a beauty to her otherwise undistinguished face.

"Peridot, I have heard so much about you. I'm so glad you came with Nanny Williams, for I have heard about her, too. I am Miss Boileau." She turned to Nanny Williams. "Annie Boileau," she said.

The relaxation Peridot felt in Nanny Williams's body was transmitted to her own. From that moment on, the world became a richer, fuller place.

This was a festive summer. On the twentieth of June, the Queen rode to Westminster in triumph in a right Royal procession that boasted three kings—from Belgium, Denmark, the Hellenes. There was also a galaxy of crown princes among whom rode the crown prince of the German Empire—in a silver helmet and a white tunic, his long fair hair streaming in the wind. They lit bonfires on all the hills, and Brocks' fireworks were displayed at the Crystal Palace. A new coinage was struck. England rejoiced, and the warmth of the patriotism that flowed was no more strongly felt by master than by servant. In the midst of it all, Colonel Cody brought his Wild West show to Brompton and gave a new game to generations of small boys.

As November moved a jubilant population toward the hardships of winter, Peridot heard Miss Boileau and Nanny Williams talking about something Nanny called "Bloody Sunday." It was difficult for her to follow who was fighting whom, but it seemed to be the working classes again.

Miss Boileau spoke of Trafalgar Square and the Life Guards called up from Whitehall. Nanny said there were guards standing with fixed bayonets and they were enrolling special constables.

"It's like a revolution," said Miss Boileau, and Peridot had anxiety dreams for Queen Victoria and her family. She and Queen Victoria and Mama and Papa and Terence, all trying to run away, with the working classes hot on their heels.

Colorful gossip from the servants' quarters still continued to lend excitement to Peridot's days and terror to her nights. Louisa the kitchenmaid misguidedly kept her informed of the Whitechapel murders and the activities of the man who became known as Jack the Ripper. She even showed Peridot copies of her penny dreadful, the Penny Illustrated Paper, from which she gleaned her information. The first murder was on August 31 and, from then on, Louisa imparted to Peridot with lugubrious relish the continuing series of horrors in September, October, November and into the new year of 1889.

Nighttime became a torment for Peridot. Finally,

she awoke screaming in terror and disturbed Miss Boileau, whose room was close by.

Annie Boileau calmly analyzed the problem with the little girl. Yes, there was such a man. No, the police had not caught him yet. However, he operated only in the area of Whitechapel, which was a long way from Belgravia, and he only attacked certain poor women, who had to earn their living by walking the streets. She, Peridot, was the last person in the world who would have to fear him.

"How can they earn money by just walking, Miss Boileau?"

"They earn it by selling the only thing they have to offer. Themselves."

For the very first time, Peridot was aware that Miss Boileau was somewhat at a loss, perhaps even being evasive.

"How do you sell yourself, Miss Boileau? What do people use them for?"

Miss Boileau hesitated. "If it were my decision, child, I would tell you. But I feel it would fit in better with the wishes of your mother and father if I left it at that. But rest assured—the world of these poor creatures in no way touches yours."

Louisa was severely reprimanded for her thoughtlessness and crept about the kitchen and the house with red-rimmed eyes for a day or so. There was a gulf between them that Peridot had never felt between herself and the servants before. She began to be aware that, although she personally felt nothing, they themselves were always conscious of it and held her a little apart.

The decade which had brought Peridot into the world was now on its way out and she was into her tenth year. Her life was bounded by Brierley Park on the one hand and Belgravia on the other. There were occasional visits to various cousins and the children of her mother and father's friends. Interspersed with these encounters, the outside world came to her through the eyes of the servants and Miss Boileau. It was hard to reconcile the narrow, ordered world in which she saw her little friends with the rich, complex structure presented to her by her governess and those belowstairs. Douglas sang her street songs about the Shah of Persia's visit to London. Forgetful of Louisa's comeuppance, Emily, one of the parlormaids, regaled Peridot with colorful details of the trial of the notorious Mrs. Maybrick, for poisoning her husband.

"Mind you, I dunno 'ow they can tell. It says in the paper 'e took eighteen different drugs in two weeks. A bloomin' walkin' chemist's shop, 'e was."

Peridot, whose knowledge of drugs was restricted to the various powerful emetics and the ipecacuanha wine that Nanny forced down her periodically, marveled at Mr. Maybrick's willpower.

As usual they left the London house for Brierley Park in June. Some of the staff went first, then she and Miss Boileau and Nanny. Her parents followed when their interests or other travels allowed them, or when the weather became too hot in London.

Peridot loved the time when she and the staff had the house to themselves. She ate her favorite meals, read, talked a great deal and walked with Miss Boileau, or rode with one of the grooms. Then Miss Boileau went for a week's holiday to her parents and Nanny was left in charge.

Peridot wandered about the estate in complete freedom. She did not miss companions, for there were none close enough whose company she would have wanted. Life was perfect.

One golden day she was on her own, down by the river. It was high noon, and the sun was hot on her head because her straw hat lay under the willow with her shoes and stockings. She had pushed up her sleeves and, flat on her stomach, trailed both hands in the water, feeling the tug of the river pull them away from her.

Just at that moment she heard a laugh. Or rather a giggle, moving and rippling like the waters of the stream. She looked up.

Directly across the water sat a girl about her own age, but as different from her as the moon from the sun, as chalk from cheese.

It was the eyes that struck you first, even then when the girls were only ten years old. The expression in them: as fathomless as the eyes of the Mona Lisa, but with a sparkle that led you to feel at first that that was all there was to them. The skin was perfection, polished gold by the sun, a Cox's Orange Pippin of a skin, with the bloom of a peach. The hair was dark, glossy, curling in tendrils over the forehead, pulled back from her face, so that the child could admire in the stream's surface the bunches of cherries hung over her ears. The mouth was not wide or generous, as might have been thought desirable, but it was faultless in its contours—a cameo of a pouting mouth, heightened at the moment by the juices of the cherries which she had smeared on her lips.

She was dressed in a faded blue muslin dress, on which the sprigged white floral pattern could only faintly be seen. It mattered not one jot. In spite of a total lack of ornament, she was perfectly beautiful.

Peridot recognized the slender wrist, the curve of forearm that she saw in her mother. Her first reaction was one of complete, utter envy.

The child spoke: "Want some cherries?"

It seemed strange, a shock, to hear the common country accent from the mouth of such an exquisite being.

"Yes, please. Where did you get them from?"

Again, the laugh. "Oh, don't be thinking I stole them. Me father's your head gardener."

"I didn't think you had stolen them—how do you know who I am?"

"'Course I know who you are. You're Peridot Sinclair." The girl sighed. "Oh, that's a lovely name. You're so lucky, 'aving a name like that."

Peridot said awkwardly, "I don't know. I think it's rather silly. People—well, my friends, always spell it wrong. Why—what's yours?"

The girl pulled a face. "Violet. It'd be all right if they'd say Vi-oh-let." She sounded out the syllables. "But everyone says Vi-lit. That's so *common.*"

"Vi-oh-let," said Peridot.

"There! You see!" The girl was delighted. "Ooh, you make it sound ever so nice. I'm going to sound just like that one day. 'Ere, wait a minute."

Violet sprung up, gathering the bunches of cherries that she had with her. "I'll come over to your side."

Peridot watched in admiration as Violet unerringly hopped and skipped without pause over the uneven rocks that stood out of the running water.

"There." She plumped herself down on the grass by Peridot's side. "'Ave some."

They shared the cherries, throwing the stones into

the stream, and watched as some floated, others sank.

"I wonder why some float and some do not?" said Peridot.

Violet shrugged her shoulders. "Dunno. It's like animals. When they're born, that is. Me dad says plants is like that, too. They're some you can 'elp, some as'll never make it, whatever you do. 'E calls it Mother Nature knowin' best."

"Oh." Peridot digested this. It seemed a little remote from cherry pits, but it was an interesting thought.

"*I'm* going to make it," said Violet.

Peridot looked shocked. "But of course you are. You look quite well to me. You don't have something wrong, do you?"

Violet rolled over onto her back, pulled up her knees to her chest and laughed with the delighted abandon she would never lose.

"Ooh, you are funny. I didn't mean that. I'm just not goin' to live like this"—she waved her arm vaguely in the direction from which she had come—"but like that." She gestured toward the house in which Peridot lived.

This was another challenging idea. As a member of the Church of England, Peridot had been brought up to believe:

> The rich man in his castle
> The poor man at his gate
> God made them high or lowly
> And ordered their estate.

Yet here was this very pretty but undeniably lower-class girl saying that she would alter the status quo. Peridot thought of her conversations with Miss Boileau.

"How will you do it?" she asked. "By a revolution?"

Violet hugged her knees with delight again.

"'Course not, silly. That only 'appens in them foreign parts. You know 'ow I'm goin' to do it?"

She rolled over and looked straight at Peridot. There were honey-gold flecks in her violet eyes, and her lashes were as thick and curly as any Peridot had ever seen.

"No. How?"

"Wiv me looks."

It was said with enormous candor and a total lack of vanity. She was stating a fact, and she did not gloat over it.

"Oh."

There seemed no need of further comment.

Peridot had gleaned enough from belowstairs conversation to know that her mother had "caught" her father by her beauty—although her vague memories of her grandmother did not suggest the humility of background from which this child came.

Violet sat up in one swift, unfolding movement and drew a shoulder up to her cheek, coquettishly, apologetically. It was a gesture Peridot was to see repeated many times, and she alone would know that it was not contrived. It was part of the makeup of a little girl of ten who dreamed dreams, but knew nothing as yet of the calculated gestures of the life she would choose. It was God-given, part of her birthright.

"Now you'll think I'm vain. That's what all them cats in the village say. But I'm not, you know. Really I'm not."

Spontaneously, she clasped Peridot's hands in her

own little brown ones. The fingernails were torn and dirty, infinitely appealing in their contrast to her beauty.

At the warmth of the touch, some of the reserve Peridot always felt with those of her own class and her own age melted away. She smiled back.

"I'm sure you're not. You *are* very pretty, Violet, and it would be ridiculous not to admit it. Miss Boileau—she's my governess—calls that 'false modesty.' Only, with me, she means cleverness at my lessons. Not the way I look," she added.

Violet closed her eyes and sighed deeply. "Oh, I love the way you talk," she said, "All the words 'n everything." She opened her eyes again, picking up the end of what Peridot had been saying. She looked at her, considering. "You're all right, you know. You really don't look 'alf bad. Anyway"—she shrugged her shoulders—"you can't lose. You've got it all made already. So why worry?"

Peridot didn't find this comforting and felt hostile for a moment. But one of Violet's strengths in her ascent was her ability to sense people's moods and to work on them. Both for their good and her own. She laid a hand on Peridot's knee.

"You're *distinguished,* Peridot. See what I mean? 'N that's what I want to be, more 'n anything else. Distinguished. Like your mama."

"You know my mama?"

"I seen her, getting out of her carriage 'n going hunting. I copied the way she walks."

She jumped to her feet. "Come on. You can tell me if I got it right."

Violet began to walk about, swaying exaggeratedly from the waist, her chin held high in the air, a fixed smile on her face. Peridot started to giggle.

She thought she shouldn't, since it was a bit like laughing at Mama, only she didn't mean it to be. She got to her feet.

"No, no, not like that. Like this."

She tried to remember all the instructions in deportment she had received at the dancing lessons she was forced to attend in London. Violet stopped to watch her. Then she too started to laugh. The promenade ended abruptly with the two girls sitting on the grass, giggling together.

In the distance, from the direction of the house, Peridot heard Nanny Williams calling.

"I must go, Violet. That's my nurse."

Violet grabbed her by the shoulders, all laughing now forgotten. She said urgently, "Be my friend, Peridot. You teach me what you know. I'll teach you what I know."

She must have guessed Peridot's thought, because she grinned. "You'd be surprised what I know. Really." And again, urgently, "Be my friend."

Peridot felt a strange sense of commitment as she answered. "I would like to be your friend, Violet."

A flash of the eye, a chuckle, a quick hug.

"I'll see you again here, tomorrow."

She turned and was back across the stream before Peridot had moved. As Peridot started to walk toward the house, she heard Violet call, "'Bye, Perry."

When she turned around again, Violet was already out of sight.

Chapter Two

THE BARN WAS WARM AND DARK. Darker than usual, because of the rain pattering down on the roof. The hay rustled beneath them, pricking at their skin even through the skirts and the petticoats and the bloomers.

The two little girls watched the falling rain through the loading window, high in the front of the barn. They were sharing an apple and a hunk of ripe cheddar cheese and waiting for the rain to stop, so that they could go back outside, in case Nanny Williams called. Peridot did not want to miss hearing her because, if Nanny discovered this precious friendship, it might be taken from her, and with it, some of the freedom that she was enjoying.

She had, in fact, sounded Nanny out on the subject of Violet. Nanny had heard of Violet. She had sniffed, in classic disapproving nannylike way, when talking about her.

"Too pretty for her own good, that one."

"But that's not her fault, Nanny, is it?"

"She's only that pretty because she knows she is. She works on it, that one. Mark my words, she'll end up no better than she should be. Just like her poor mother."

"Why? What happened to Violet's mother?"

"Ah, well, the poor lass is dead now, and I'll not speak ill of the dead. But it was her looks that led to her downfall. You mark my words—no good ever came of looking like that."

"But my mother is said to be very beautiful."

"And that's as it should be, Miss Peridot. It's all very well for those who are born to it. It's a trial and a tribulation for those who are not."

Peridot had now got to the age where she found intriguing Nanny's constant assertions of the rights of the upper classes, as opposed to those of the lower classes, to which she, Nanny, presumably belonged.

"Violet, Nanny told me that your mother is dead and that she was very pretty."

Violet looked at Peridot suspiciously. "Do you talk to her about me?"

"Oh, no, really I don't. I said I had seen you and that you were pretty and who were you. That's all. Honestly, I promise you."

"That's all right. Yes, I know all about me mum. What 'appened to 'er 'n that. It's not going to 'appen to me, I can tell you."

Peridot looked distressed. "Oh, but Violet, we all have to die. It's the will of God."

Violet sat up abruptly. "Oh, Perry, you don't know

nothing about nothing, do you? Oh, you can say all those poems 'n you know all about Latin 'n French 'n that. But you know nothing about *life.*"

"No. No, I don't think I do," said Peridot slowly. "You tell me, then, what you mean."

Violet's natural ebullience had subsided. She was looking out of the window, far, far away. "Me mum had me out of wedlock. She wasn't married. They 'ushed it up and she died 'aving me."

"But your father—"

"Me father isn't me father. 'E's me foster-father. I don't know who me real father is, but 'e's one of your lot. One of the gentry. Took advantage of 'er."

This was an expression that Peridot was familiar with from her belowstairs eavesdroppings. An expression shrouded in mystery, its true meaning hidden behind a curtain of taboos. She looked at Violet helplessly.

"I don't understand what that means, Violet."

It was Mona Lisa in the violet eyes now, eyes that had looked into the future and knew the past, for whom all was known and from whom nothing was hidden.

"No more you wouldn't. 'N neither did me mum. Or, that's what me foster-father says. No 'arm in 'er, 'e says, but a fool to 'erself. She fell for 'im, whoever 'e was. Fell in love, they call it. 'N I'm *never* going to do it. Never, never, never!"

The words rang out and echoed in the wooden beams of the barn, disturbing a pigeon that roosted there, who squawked protestingly and then flew away through the open window. Everything settled and grew silent again.

Peridot repeated, "Falling in love. Took advantage. What do they mean, Violet?"

Mercurial Violet, mood slipping after mood, clouds over the sun. She grinned naughtily.

"Remember the billy goat 'n the nanny goat?"

Peridot's hand flew to her mouth. They had been down by the animal pens on the home farm a day or two earlier, and she had seen one goat mounted on another's back. She had pointed them out to Violet, saying, "Look at the goats playing piggyback, Violet."

And Violet had laughed and said, "That's not piggyback, that's the way of the world. That's what Alfred the cowman calls it."

That was taking advantage? Her mind shied away from the image suddenly presented of Violet's unknown mother and father and then bucked even more violently at the idea of her own parents. And—even more horrifying thought—*this* was 'falling in love'?

"Oh, Violet," she cried, "I think you're teasing me now. That cannot be falling in love. Goats cannot fall in love, can they? Louisa says that falling in love is when you hear music in the air and the man gives you flowers and a ring and will do *anything* for you. She says it's beautiful."

By the window, Violet turned her head back toward Peridot and snorted.

"Huh. She'd better be careful, then, or she'll end up just like me mum. Men lead you on like that, so as they can do what they want. That's what I think."

Peridot looked across at the small cynic.

"There you go again. Do what they want. What do you mean? I don't think you really know," she challenged.

Violet did not smile. "Oh, don't I though! I know

all right. It's making babies, that's what it is, only they don't care about the babies, they only care about the making part." She leaned forward confidentially. "Only I know there's a way of doing it without babies. Look at them actresses 'n that. 'N that is what I'm going to find out."

Somewhere along the way, Peridot had got lost in the convolutions of Violet's logic.

"I still don't understand, Violet. Do what? You cannot mean the goats—what we saw," she ended lamely.

Violet looked at her pityingly. "That's the easiest bit—what to do. It's all the other things I've got to find out 'n I've got to find out before the wrong thing 'appens first."

Peridot looked straight at Violet. "What do they do, Violet?"

Violet told her.

Peridot's first reaction was one of complete disbelief. Surely Violet had her facts wrong. Shock followed closely on the heels of disbelief. It seemed utterly impossible to think of what Violet described in connection with most of the people she knew in the adult world. It concerned a whole area of the body that was unmentionable, unknowable, unviewable.

Peridot began gradually to arrive at the conclusion that there must be a different method for the upper classes. It was the only solution that her mind could accept, and she was to cherish that belief for quite a long while.

It was very quiet in the barn. The rain had ceased its pattering on the roof and some sunshine had begun to filter in across the floor, touching the feet of the little girls. A soft breeze got up the strength to push in through the open window and stirred the dust and wisps of straw on the floor. The scent rose and tickled the nostrils, and Peridot sneezed.

Violet, changeable as ever, leaned over to where Peridot was sitting, caught her by the arm, pulled her alongside herself and hugged her.

"Bless you, bless you, bless you," she said, accompanying each phrase with a swift hug. Peridot, however, was still shaken and solemn.

"How do you know, Violet," she said, "that it is all as important as you think it is? Why should all the things you've told me be going to help you"—she floundered around for the right words that would describe Violet's aims without sounding superior—"get along in the world?" She reverted unconsciously to a phrase of Nanny Williams's.

Violet, however, was getting bored with the subject. The earth outside smelled good after the rain, and she felt restless. The distant murmur of the working world reached her and made her want to stir and move on. She jumped up and pulled Peridot after her.

"Perry, let's get out of 'ere. Look, it's stopped raining, 'n you're all covered with straw. That nanny of yours'll 'ave a fit."

"*H*ave a fit," said Peridot automatically. She had begun, at Violet's request, to correct her speech.

"*H*ave a fit," repeated Violet. "Oh, my Lor', you'd think I'd know that one by now."

Peridot persisted, clinging to her original question. "Yes, yes, I'm coming. But tell me why, how you know it's important?"

Violet was on top of the ladder by now, only her head and shoulders showing above the floor level. Against the pales of the straw and hay and the darknesses in the corners of the barn, her brunette beauty gleamed with the rich, glossy brilliance of an oil painting.

"'Ow do I know? *H*ow do I know?" she corrected herself. She looked down at her hands and then up at Peridot.

"Cos some of 'em already want to do it with me, that's why," she said simply. The head disappeared, and then Peridot heard her laugh and the rustle as she ran across the floor below. Disconcertingly, her voice suddenly came from outside the window behind Peridot. "Come on, you slow coach, let's go to the river!"

Peridot made haste to follow her, pulling straw out of her clothing and hair as she ran.

That night, Peridot lay in bed and thought about Violet and what she had said.

Falling in love, taking advantage, being wanted. The words passed through her mind over and over, accompanied by images that were nonetheless disturbing for being imprecise. The only precise picture was that of the two goats and it seemed totally irrelevant, for some reason. It fact, rather funny.

Peridot giggled and felt a disturbing, but pleasantly warm, feeling rise in an area of her body to which she had given little thought up to that time. She moved her fingers toward this warm, pulsating center and felt an immediate response. Sharply, she removed her hand, overcome with guilt for the pleasure it had given her. For that night, she had conquered the impulse, but something deeper than conscious thought intimated to her that both the sensation and the response would return to her again...for completion of some sort.

And, in that incomplete fulfillment, she would begin to understand the feeling that Violet had tried to explain to her. From herself, she would first sense the power and the beauty of passion, and its hold over human destiny.

The fates were indeed smiling on Peridot that summer. Miss Boileau sent an anxious letter to Nanny and the Sinclairs to say that her mother was ill and could she possibly stay away longer. Nanny Williams, who was undeniably enjoying the freedom of Peridot's apparent independence, as well as the lack of interference from her superiors, warmly assured Peridot's parents that she could, indeed, manage. Peridot returned with a sigh of relief to the fields, the barn, the river and Violet.

Violet was full of questions about Peridot's family. She asked interminably about what Lady Pamela wore, how she had her hair done and what manner of hats she chose. Peridot found it difficult to remember enough detail for Violet, but even she had noticed that Mama's bustle seemed to have disappeared and that the line of her skirts had changed.

Peridot's own need for Violet was difficult to define, but none the less strong for all that. For Peridot, Violet's beauty was of the kind she had been taught, largely by inference, was desirable in a female, in females of her own class above all; she had also been led to believe it was something she did not possess.

Violet took Peridot with her one day when she went to give her father his lunch in the fields. First, they went to Violet's home, one of the cottages on the Brierley estate. It was a picture-book dwelling covered in honeysuckle and ivy, the garden riotous with hollyhocks and sunflowers and gloriously perfumed roses. Peridot was entranced.

"You are lucky, Violet. It's like living in a fairy story."

Violet looked at Peridot, a somber, sideways glance, as they walked together down the path. She said nothing.

Not so pretty inside. It was chill and damp, and the light filtered weakly through the inadequate small-paned windows, so pretty to look at outside.

"Mum!" called Violet. A voice answered from the back, and they went through to the kitchen. Violet's foster-mother was finishing packing her husband's lunch on a well-scrubbed wooden table. It was the only time Peridot was to see her: a small, overweight woman with a jolly expression and a roistering chuckle reminiscent of Violet's. Apart from that they had nothing in common. Even at ten years old, Peridot was struck by the contrast between Violet and her background. In this damp, simple room Violet stood out like a candle burning in some subterranean cave.

There was warmth between foster-mother and foster-daughter. They hugged each other, and the woman bobbed a curtsey to Peridot, much to her embarrassment.

The two girls went along the bridle path to the fields carrying Jacob Cartwright's lunch in a red and white checked napkin, his tea kept hot in a tin mug with a lid on it. The air smelled sweet and heavy with honeysuckle and briar-rose. Along the sides of the path the cow-parsley raised its great, lacy head in profusion, and down among the long grasses were hidden wild violets, white and purple.

Suddenly, a sharp crack split the densely perfumed air of the Cotswold jungle around them.

"What's that?"

"Guns. They're shooting rabbits today. That's why me dad's there. Otherwise, 'e doesn't work in the fields, cos 'e's a gard'ner."

A feeling of dread came over Peridot. She hung back as Violet turned off the bridle path to a stile that led into a large, high meadow.

"C'mon, Perry. We're 'ere. There are the men."

Peridot could see them in the distance, carrying their guns slung over their arms. She could, thank God, see no rabbits, dead or alive. One of the men waved to them.

"Dad! We've got your dinner!"

As Peridot approached the group, they all slowed their walk, wiped their brows and pulled off their hats and caps, if they wore any. Again she felt the burden of her station, saddled with their embarrassed bowing, like a yoke across her shoulders. She had met Mr. Cartwright before in the vast greenhouses close to the house.

"Miss Sinclair, you should not be a'carrying my dinner to me. What is this young 'arum-scarum 'ere up to?"

The words chided, but the arms held Violet tight. Peridot spoke quickly. "Oh, no, Mr. Cartwright. It was I who wanted to come. It was kind of Violet to bring me."

"Well, that's all right then. You'll excuse me, miss, if I sit down and eat? We must get back to work."

The men ate with a natural hunger and enjoyment Peridot had never seen before in an adult. Then one of the men brought out a large stone jug, unstopped it and passed it round. Cartwright filled his now empty mug from it. The laughter grew, the men leaned back into the shade of the hedgerow against which they had grouped themselves.

"What is in the bottle?" whispered Peridot.

"Cider. I'll see if I can tease some out of Len Pershaw for us."

Peridot sat in the grass at a distance from the group and watched Violet approach a youngish man at the far end of the line from her father, who sat talking to two other men. She watched Violet sidling up to him, pulling at his arm and then whispering in his ear. She watched the other men nearby watching Violet and saw something in their eyes she had never seen before and did not recognize. Years later, in London and Paris, she would see it again and know it for what it was.

A moment later, Violet was back with a tin mug full of a golden, bubbly liquid. They shared it between them. It was apples and yet it was not apples. It tasted the way they smelled when they lay in heaps on the ground of a deserted part of the orchards and gave up their ripeness to the autumn air.

The bubbles tickled her nose, caught in her throat and made her hiccup. Violet giggled at her and hiccupped too. Peridot felt the strangest tingling sensation in her shoulders and down her arms, like pins and needles. Her legs felt weak.

"Do they get it from the elves?" she asked. "Is it magic?"

"Me dad says it's magic for good or evil. It can make you happy, or it can steal your mind away, like poor Willy Lowther in the village, who is good for nothing now."

Peridot could well believe it.

The men had started to leave, gathering their belongings together, picking up their guns. Across the space that separated her from them, she heard the words: "We must 'a shot nigh on a thousand of the little buggers today."

She shivered, reminded of the scene of slaughter that must be out there, somewhere beyond the hedgerows. Like the damp darkness behind the pretty walls of Violet's home, the call of the owl in the night as his voice swooped across the nightingale's song, to be echoed by the cry of his victim.

Conqueror and conquered. Vanquisher and victim. Gordon at Khartoum, the women who walked the streets. It would seem to be, as Alfred the cowman would put it, the way of the world. Peridot was in this sober frame of mind when she left Violet at the river and headed for home.

She was greeted as usual by Nanny Williams—who had been out that afternoon, a fact that had allowed Peridot time for her trip to the fields—with the news that Miss Boileau would be returning the day after the next, as her mother had quite recovered.

"Oh."

Nanny looked at her sharply. "Is that all you have to say? There was I, thinking you'd be so pleased to know. It'll be more company for you, till your mama and papa return."

"Of course I am glad," said Peridot slowly. "It's just that I don't feel very well, that is all."

Worriedly, her nurse held up her charge's chin and looked at her. "You do look pale, my little lamb. Where have you been and what have you been doing?"

Peridot closed her eyes. "I think I would like to go to bed," she said.

Distressed at this unusual request, Nanny led her, clucking all the way, to the night nursery, where Peridot heaved up her lunch and the more recent alcoholic beverage that had created the problem.

The local doctor who attended to the Sinclairs when they were at Brierley was called, and diagnosed the ailment as "too much sun, a touch of summer fever."

Accordingly, Peridot spent the next twenty-four hours in her darkened room, the curtains drawn tight, with a cool cloth on her forehead and Nanny at her side, suddenly smitten with anxiety over her neglect of her charge.

Peridot, for her part, fretted about Violet and what she would think when she did not appear again at the stream. She knew that she must make a recovery in time to see her before Miss Boileau returned and their sweet freedom was curtailed. The day after the "fever" was out of the question, but, on the pretext of such growing excitement over Miss Boileau's impending arrival the following day that she needs must wait down the driveway for the carriage, Peridot was able to escape the house.

Running in her anxiety not to be seen by Nanny going in quite the wrong direction for Miss Boileau's carriage, she made her way down to the stream with a feeling of "the last time." It was about the time that she and Violet usually met. She hoped against hope that Violet would not have given up because she had missed the previous day.

Violet was not there.

Peridot waited and waited. Still Violet did not appear. A feeling of utter desolation filled Peridot and a painful sob shook her body. She could not bear it. She must return soon, in case Miss Boileau arrived, and maybe she would never see Violet again. The landscape swam around her through her tears, and she turned round and started for home.

She was halfway up the slope that led to the lower terrace beyond the meadow when she heard her name being called. "Perry! Oh, come back, Perry!"

Swift for once as Violet, she spun around and careened down the hill. Violet had crossed the stream and started up the slope on the far side to reach her friend. They fell into one another's arms, laughing and crying all at once, as they tottered and fell to the ground, hugging and rolling and talking explanations at each other.

"I thought I wouldn't come 'cos you weren't here yesterday 'n then I did and you were!"

"I was ill yesterday—no, the day before—and I had to stay in bed. I worried that you would wonder why and not come. I'm glad you did."

"Come." Violet jumped up. "Let me show you the new kittens in the barn. They are just born 'n I watched 'em. 'Ow I wished you were 'ere yesterday."

Peridot dropped her friend's hand and withdrew a little. "I cannot, Violet."

Such dark desperation in the violet eyes, almost black in their despair.

"Why, Perry? Don't you like me any more?"

"Oh, no, no. Never that, it's nothing like that, Violet. My governess returns today, and I must meet her at the gate. That is where I'm supposed to be, now."

Violet understood the situation. "'N you will not be able to meet me 'n play any more?"

"I don't know. Sometimes, perhaps. But how can I let you know?"

Violet chewed her lip, with characteristic refusal to be beaten by a difficult situation.

"Let's think. There must be a way." She grasped Peridot's hand hard. "Yes, yes, there is. Timothy!"

"Timothy?"

"Aye, Timothy. You won't have seen 'im. 'E runs errands at the big 'ouse—your 'ouse—for Mr. Symes. 'E's from the village. I go to school with 'im and 'e likes me."

She slid a sideways glance at Peridot and giggled. "'E tells me things about the parties 'n such 'n I—let 'im do things."

"What things?"

Violet was evasive now, as if sensing the gap between her ten years and those of her protected companion. "Never mind. I know what I'm doing, although 'e's older 'n me. Fourteen or fifteen, I think. 'E's not too smart at his sums 'n that, but 'e's ever so good-looking. So, I really don't mind."

She giggled again and then grew serious. "'E does the boots 'n shoes in the morning. You could leave a note in your shoes for 'im. I'll tell 'im, warn 'im about it."

"I've got to go, Violet. If they find out, they'll stop it."

Violet let go of her hand. "I know. You'd best be leaving, then."

As Peridot started to move away, she felt Violet tug at the back of her skirt, like a small child begging for attention. When she turned, there were tears in Violet's eyes, brimming over and splashing down her cheeks, onto the faded bodice of her dress.

"You'd not forsake me, would you, Perry? You'd not leave me—to live like them, no way of escaping?"

She pointed her hand back across the stream, in the direction of the village.

Peridot felt the welling-up of a love she had never really felt before at those dramatic words, so reminiscent of a style of literature favored by the maid-servants.

Impulsively, she hugged Violet. "I love you, Violet. You are my good and special friend. I swear that I will see you again."

Violet appeared satisfied. She sniffed loudly and brushed the tears away with the back of her hand.

"That's good. You're bound to me now, by an oath."

But it was no oath that bound the child who walked back up the hill toward Brierley Park. It was love, pure and simple.

Peridot stopped for a moment and looked back across the stream and the meadows. Violet was nowhere in sight now. The only object that moved was a lark spiraling upward into the summer sky. How strange that her prison should be Violet's escape route! In her eyes, she was looking back at freedom and forward to a loss of that freedom. Violet saw it quite the other way around.

With the return of her governess, Peridot's thoughts removed themselves temporarily from the sensual and visited more intellectual realms. They were walking together one day around the small ornamental lake which was fed by the same stream where Peridot had met Violet.

"Supposing you were very poor, Miss Boileau," said Peridot, "and supposing you were very, very beautiful—would you think it right to escape from poverty that way?"

Miss Boileau looked at Peridot guardedly. "Which way?" she asked cautiously.

Peridot looked at her, surprised. "Why, by marriage, perhaps, to someone much richer, who wants to marry you because you are pretty, and for no other reason."

Miss Boileau's reserved response was tempered by knowledge of the circumstances of Lady Sinclair's marriage. She could not know that it was not her mother who was Peridot's concern.

"If you loved him, my dear, then I think it would be quite all right."

"Do you *have* to love them?"

Miss Boileau looked taken aback. "But of course. It would be wrong otherwise. That would be—mercenary."

"What is—what you just said?"

"Mercenary? To do something for the money alone, for financial reasons. And not for the heart, or any other of the good emotions."

"Is it not good to be mercenary?"

"Dear me, no. It is one of the chief troubles of the world."

"Oh... Then, how else can a poor person escape from poverty, if she does not love someone rich?"

Miss Boileau spoke with conviction now. "By education. Knowledge sets you free."

Carefully, Peridot tucked all this wisdom away in her mind for sharing later on with Violet. Only, it must not be too much later, for her parents were to arrive quite soon and then her freedom would be gone altogether.

Fortunately, Miss Boileau decided to take the

pony and trap into the nearby market town later that week. She offered to take Peridot, who said she would rather stay at home. The evening before, she slipped a note into her button boots, tucked well into the toe, and left them, as usual, outside her door. It was now up to the unseen and unknown Timothy to do his part. She would simply have to go to the river in the hope that Violet would be there.

She was. She was already waiting on the far side. She had been crouched down, throwing sticks and pebbles into the water while she waited. Now, on seeing Peridot, she was on her feet, dancing with impatience.

Peridot picked up her skirts and ran down the slope, while Violet danced her usual skip, hop and jump over the stones in the brook to meet her friend. She waved Peridot's now crumpled note in the air.

"See! See! Timothy brought it to me! Told you 'e would! *He* would," she corrected herself. They hopped and skipped around each other, celebrants around an invisible bonfire of happiness.

"C'mon! The kittens are still ever so little. I'll show 'em to you."

It was a good feeling, to be back in the barn again. The kittens were indeed tiny, but their eyes were open, and the more daring among them were already crawling off to leave their mother's side. She, the mother, lay there, apparently still exhausted, her thin flanks moving up and down with her breathing, as her offspring nuzzled and fed from her. Peridot watched, fascinated.

"*This* is how babies feed?"

"Yes, 'course it is. Only, some of the great ladies don't do it. Like your mum. They send their littl'uns out to people who've 'ad babies or 'ad 'em die. They does the feeding."

Violet leaned back in the straw and folded her arms behind her head. "I'm never going to feed no baby, neither."

Peridot paused for a moment and then gave up the thought of changing Violet's convoluted sentence structure.

"Why? Does it hurt?"

"I don't *think* so. But it doesn't make your *things*—you know—look good. Pulls 'em all outer shape. I mean, look at poor Tibby there."

They had named the unnamed barn mother themselves. Peridot looked at her. Her coat had lost its gloss and her ribs showed. Her dugs were stretched and extended by the kittens. She saw what Violet meant. Violet went on. "But then, I'm never going to 'ave children."

There seemed something shocking and unnatural about this. However, when Peridot looked at Tibby, she could not help having a similar response.

"But you will do—what we talked about?"

Violet's eyes opened wide. "Of course. That's one of the ways I can get ahead—if I'm clever enough at it and careful enough. Besides," she giggled, "I think I'm going to like it."

"How can you know that, Violet. It sounds horrible to me."

"Ooh, you're a real goose, Perry. It's not 'ow it sounds. It's 'ow it feels. That's what matters."

She closed her eyes and smiled, a smile heavy with a knowledge that ought to have been beyond her years. "You should 'a seen 'ow I paid Timothy off."

Peridot didn't want to know and yet did want to

know. She said nothing and Violet continued. "I let 'im put 'is 'ands 'ere."

She pointed to that area between her legs that Peridot had felt throb and sing when she had touched it so long ago.

"'E liked it and so did I."

Suddenly her mood changed. She shot forward on the hay and said vehemently, "But I mustn't. I mustn't like it too much. I got to 'old on to it, watch it, or I'll be just like me mum. And that I'll not be."

"Violet," said Peridot, carefully feeling her way through the ideas given to her by Miss Boileau, so that she could convey them clearly, "You could escape another way, you know."

Violet looked at her skeptically. "What other way?" she asked.

"By education. You work at your books and sums and things and become very clever and then you can rise in the world."

When said by her it sounded far less plausible an escape route than when expressed by Miss Boileau. How she wished she could put Violet and Miss Boileau together!

Not surprisingly, Violet was unimpressed.

"Phoo. Where d'you get that idea from? If I work hard at sums 'n things, I could get to work in the village store—summat like that. Mind you, I'll work 'ard at school. Most of your lot can read and write lovely, I know that. Only trouble is, I can't learn piano 'n French and dancin' and that. Good thing is, I'm a quick learner, so maybe I'll pick it up later. I'll 'ave to, at any rate."

Miss Boileau's escape route seemed to have collapsed before it had got anywhere, and there was nothing that Peridot could do about it.

The instinct that she had built up over the weeks of the secret friendship with Violet nudged Peridot when it was time for her to go. A great pang of unhappiness filled her and she hugged Violet hard.

"Somehow, Violet, I will get back to the river before I have to go back to London."

Violet's own unhappiness was laid aside for a moment at Peridot's remark. "Lucky, lucky you, Perry. I'd give anything to go to London, to live there."

Again, Peridot was struck by the wide divergence between her idea of what was desirable in life and Violet's.

"Oh, Violet," she said earnestly, "it's not so nice as here. I cannot go anywhere on my own and it gets foggy and there are crowds and I always get sick in London."

She thought of the long hours she had spent in bed, with colds and coughs of varying degrees of severity.

Violet snorted. "Huh, you've never seen this 'ole in the winter, 'ave you? You only come 'ere when it's summer and you can be outside and it looks pretty 'n that. In the winter, it's cold and wet and dark and there's nothing to do. And everyone gets sick 'ere too, you know. I mean, when your mum and dad come down for the shooting and fishing, they never bring you, do they?"

"No," said Peridot slowly, "that's true."

She realized that Brierley Park only existed for her in a summer landscape, with the flowers all growing and the trees fully dressed in their leaves.

"When I am rich," said Violet, her eyes misty with dreams, "the autumn and the winter will be beautiful too. Just like the summer. The weather'll not matter, because I'll just go from house party, to garden party, to dinner party. And I'll dance all night long and me carriage'll always be waiting by the door, so that the rain'll never bother me no more."

"Perhaps it *will* seem more interesting when I grow up," said Peridot dubiously. The picture that Violet had drawn still held few charms for her. "Maybe I will change and get to like those things."

How strange it was that the dross of her thoughts was purest gold to Violet. It glowed through her every dream and fantasy, coalescing into the stuff of which the future was to be built, brick by shining brick.

The time to part had come. The arrangement with Timothy was reiterated. As Peridot walked back up the slope to the house, she had again that extraordinary feeling of loss.

A great airing and summer cleaning of Brierley Park went on all the following week, due to the impending arrival of the Sinclairs and Terence. All the staff seemed far too busy to spend much time on Peridot, and even Nanny Williams's services were called upon. Peridot, therefore, spent most of her time with Miss Boileau.

The night before her parents' arrival, Peridot was bathed; her hair was washed and tied up in papers—which it hardly needed. Her most becoming dress was washed and starched and laid out for her. Little sacrificial lamb to the slaughter, she put up patiently with the ministrations of her nurse and the reminders about decorum, manners and etiquette from her governess.

It might just be possible for Mama to be pleased by her appearance this time.

In the morning she peered anxiously into her mirror to see if perhaps some of Violet's beauty had rubbed off on her—fairy dust from those magic butterfly wings. It seemed a long, long time since she had really bothered to look in the mirror. The reflection she saw was surprisingly changed. The first real friendship of her life had given Peridot's features a vivacity they had lacked with introspection.

Her mother and father arrived in the afternoon with a panoply of houseguests, a fanfare of carriage wheels and horses' hooves, and much laughter and witty conversation. It was a dislocating experience to be surrounded by perfume, peacocks' feathers, cigar smoke and the swishing of silken skirts after the peaceful, bucolic atmosphere of the past few weeks.

A curtain of rain descended over the English countryside and stayed for a fortnight. Papa sorted out various problems on the estate, Mama went on a round of visits, and Terence and Peridot played endless card games and went horse riding in between the downpours.

It seemed fairly easy to plumb Terence's depths. He saw himself going to University and then going into one of the Guards' Regiments, making the army his career. He did not see himself as merely a gentleman of property like his father, but this alternative was quite acceptable. Pictures of his uniformed ancestors decorated the walls of Brierley Park.

When Peridot asked him, "And what do you think will happen to me, Terence?" he looked at her, surprised.

"You'll be presented at Court and be married some day, like Mama."

"But I'm not like Mama."

"That doesn't matter. You're a girl, that's what matters."

What matters is that I am a girl, which means I don't matter, thought Peridot. She knew that Miss Boileau would counter such thoughts with indignation.

When she had voiced the same thoughts to Nanny Williams, the response had been, "But of course you're important, little Miss P. You're the power behind the throne. Remember, the hand that rocks the cradle rules the world." Nanny had a saying for every eventuality. Sometimes they soothed and sometimes they did not. Mostly, now that she was older, it depended on whether Peridot allowed them to do so.

She decided to plan a return to the river. It would not be very long before her parents left for Scotland for some shooting. They usually headed north at this time of the year for her father's brother's estate, and Terence was to be further instructed in this end-of-summer, early autumn ritual. According to plan, Peridot left a message in her shoes that night and prayed that the rain would stop for the next day.

It did. A watery sun rose over a sodden but velvet green landscape, and the birds greeted it with a glorious burst of morning song. She asked Miss Boileau if she might just walk in the grounds instead of riding that day.

Luck was with Peridot, if not with Miss Boileau. The governess was suffering from an unpleasant summer cold and felt that she should stay indoors and nurse it a little longer.

"Nanny Williams can go with you," she said.

"Yes, of course," said Peridot. She did not ask Nanny Williams. And such was the structure—or lack of it—in this English country-house summer, that Peridot slipped outside its protective, pampering walls without hindrance, escaping through the gap between two areas of responsibility.

No feeling quite like it, that push and thrust of the heart-beat as she escaped, running with unaccustomed abandon as soon as she was beyond the terrace and the cultivated lawn, down the meadow toward the river. The ground grew wetter and wetter as she came down the slope, and the grass squelched beneath the shoes polished by Timothy. The gentle meadow-stream had become a fierce little torrent, and to Peridot's dismay, it was rushing over the tops of all the stepping-stones. There was no sign of Violet in the fields or misty woods beyond the stream.

Peridot shivered with apprehension and wet feet. Perhaps Timothy had not been cleaning the shoes for some reason, and, horror of horrors, perhaps someone else had found her note.

With all these unpleasant possibilities in mind, she worriedly called out Violet's name. She heard her voice catch and echo in the valley opposite, but there was no response. The sun went in behind a cloud, and the place she had come to love so much seemed dark and ominous.

She decided to call once more, then return. She cupped her hands round her mouth and put all she had into her shout.

"Vi-oh-let!"

She heard the sound echo back to her and, from behind her, another voice.

"What *are* you doing, Peridot? You won't half be in trouble if they catch you out here."

It was Terence. He wore his riding clothes and carried a hunting rifle, broken over his arm. He had been out getting some practice with Papa or one of the keepers. The only blessing in the situation was that he had not brought them with him.

Before she had time to reply, the voice she had so longed to hear but now could have done without came eerily toward them from the mists on the far bank.

"Perry! Perry! Are you there? Wait on, it's me. I'm coming."

With a feeling of the inevitability of it all, Peridot watched the little figure dancing through the mist. Terence watched it, too, dumbfounded.

"Who is that?" he finally asked, as the figure stopped on the riverbank, close as could be to the water.

"It's Violet," said Peridot simply. "She's my friend."

Terence took in Violet's appearance. "But she's a village girl," he said. He looked at Peridot, but got no answer. Getting as close as he could to the stream, he called out, "Are you from the village?"

The marvelous husky richness of Violet's chuckle drifted across the water to him. "No—and yes," was the reply.

With dramatic appropriateness, the sun came out again from behind the clouds, and Peridot watched Terence see Violet for the first time. There was no mistaking the jolt she gave even this very young male. She had a dark blue cloak around her, and with a casual glance toward the sun, she unfolded it, pushing it back with her arms and loosening the strings at her throat. The hood fell back, and Terence blinked, whether from sudden sunlight or from Violet it was difficult to say.

Violet addressed Peridot. "Did you bring him?"

"No. He just—arrived."

Violet shrugged. "No matter. He's your brother Terence, isn't he?"

Peridot noticed that Violet's *h*'s were all present and correct in her speech. Had she been practicing or was it Terence's presence?

"Yes. I didn't tell him, Violet."

Terence turned to his sister. "Didn't tell me what?"

Before Peridot had to answer, Violet took up the game.

"If she didn't tell you then, why should she tell you now, silly-billy?" she asked. The teasing coquettishness of the tone turned the childish insult almost into a caress.

Terence's gaze was drawn back. He took up the note in her voice.

"Do you always just stand there and shout across? Is this a barrier over which you are not allowed?"

Their eyes met and held in a duel of personalities that was as old as time itself. Then, Violet tossed her head back and put her hands on her nonexistent hips. The effect, however, was devastating.

"I can cross any barrier I want to, you naughty boy. It's whether I want to or not that's the question."

She looked at the swollen water at her feet, then back at Terence. A slow smile parted her lips.

"But I don't think you can. You wouldn't *dare* to get your pretty boots wet. What would Mama and Papa say? 'Course"—she looked at the river again—"*I* know where all the stepping-stones are. I could get across and wet only the bottom of my feet and the edge of my gown."

"She could, you know," said Peridot.

Terence bristled. "So could I," he said.

Holding his eyes with hers, Violet said, "Show me."

At Terence's hesitant step forward, Peridot said, "Oh, don't, Terence," which only precipitated matters. Boldly, her brother swaggered to the river's edge and set foot on the first stone, still visible under the water. The swagger lasted into mid-stream, where he foolishly glanced up in triumph at Violet.

It was his downfall. With an undignified squawk, he came splashing down. Even after heavy rain, the stream was not very deep in the middle, but the stones were slippery and the water was moving fast. Horrified, hands to her mouth, Peridot watched him clamber onto a rock and slowly negotiate his way backward on all fours to the bank from which he had started.

Terence stood on the bank, water dripping from his jacket and riding britches. He moved his feet, and the sodden squelch from his once beautiful tall leather boots was clearly audible to Peridot. No word had been spoken since he had fallen. With one accord, brother and sister looked at Violet.

She did not laugh. Instead, she bent down slightly and picked up her skirt and petticoats knee-high. Then, without hesitation, but with a kind of deliberate delicacy, she picked her way over the river to where they stood watching her.

Terence spoke first. His teeth chattered a little as he spoke.

"You're a witch," he said. "I looked at you and you *made* me fall in."

Violet arched an eyebrow. She did not deny it.

Then, she flashed a smile, turned and made her way back across the stream. On the far side, she turned around once and called out, "Bye, Perry—I'll see you again," picked up her cloak and ran away toward the village.

On the way back to the house, Terence was full of practical matters, concerning which version of the truth he would present to show his bedraggled appearance in the most favorable light. He finally settled on one in which, called by Peridot, he rescued a village girl from the stream. Peridot agreed willingly.

Having sorted this out, Terence started to justify his failure. "It was much easier for her. I'm quite heavy now, and I had these wretched boots on. They became waterlogged. It was quite unfair. She had small feet."

He paused for a moment. "Yes," he added thoughtfully, "She really had *very* small feet."

Whenever he pestered her for details about her friendship with Violet, Peridot held the threat of the true version of the river-wetting over his head.

"I will say that you *lied,* Terence."

Eventually, he left her alone and asked nothing more about the village girl. They were bound by each other's secrets to silence on the subject.

Terence left with his parents and went to Scotland. Peridot returned to London shortly after, with Nanny and Miss Boileau. She did not see Violet again that summer, but the winter was warmer for her friendship and the promise of its renewal in the summer months to come.

And whenever the wind whistled through the

railings and around the chimneypots of Belgravia that winter, Peridot would think of Violet in the damp, dark little cottage in Brierley village. She would snuggle closer to the fire or pull the blankets farther up around her ears, with a mixture of guilt and pleasure and a longing to see her special friend again.

Chapter Three

IN 1891, the Sinclairs' departure to the country was precipitous; a frightening outbreak of influenza hit London in May and struck belowstairs. Without much time to turn around, Nanny and Miss Boileau packed up and removed themselves with Peridot to the country. Terence was still safely at school. Lady Sinclair persuaded her husband to stay on for two weeks to attend a social function that she had set her heart on, and then fell horrifyingly ill with the disease.

In the country, Peridot guessed at how ill her mother was—not so much from what was told her as from what was not told her and from the appearance and attitude of those who were not saying it. Overcome with remorse for her growing feeling of alienation from her mother, she spent most of her time in silent prayer for her to be saved. She even offered up her friendship with Violet—because it was what she cherished most—as a sacrifice.

"Please, please, God. I will not see Violet again, I will not think of her, if you let Mama live."

Her mama lived. Soon she was well enough to be moved to convalesce at Brierley Park.

Lady Pamela seemed to be a changed woman. She had looked on the face of the Grim Reaper and found herself wanting in his eyes. She wanted Peridot close to her, hugging and kissing her, saying how lucky she was to have such a thoughtful, loving child. Peridot could not do enough for her—fetching and carrying and reading aloud to her, until her voice nearly failed. But it was wonderful to be loved and appreciated.

Like a ball rolling downhill, Lady Pamela's recovery gathered momentum, and she moved on to a full return of her health and spirits with leaps and bounds. And—not surprisingly perhaps—the progress that gave Peridot so much pleasure removed her mother from her again.

Sir Rodney Sinclair was delighted at the return of his wife's health and whisked her off to recuperate in the South of France. Peridot, left alone with the staff of Brierley Park again, not unnaturally found her thoughts turning to Violet.

"Is there a boy called Timothy who works in the kitchen?" she asked Nanny Williams as she got ready for bed one night.

"Yes," said Nanny Williams, a little surprised. "A nice enough lad, but so slow there's times you itch to give him a good shaking up. Why?"

"Oh," said Peridot lightly, "I thought I heard one of the grooms say something about one, that's all."

Fortunately Nanny Williams was not interested

enough to pursue the subject, and Peridot changed it with ease. The next night, she left a message in her shoes and begged the following afternoon off from Miss Boileau.

"I feel so—so *tired* after looking after Mama."

Miss Boileau looked concerned and put a hand on Peridot's forehead. "You are not feeling unwell, are you?"

"Oh, no. I would just like to get out on my own, walk around for a while. Think."

Miss Boileau was a great respecter of thought, and was not unaware of the jolt that Peridot had taken when her mother dropped her again and departed for the delights of the Continent. She looked out of the window. "Yes, well, it's a lovely day, and you have had little fresh air. Give yourself an hour or so in the grounds after lunch."

A ritual was established. Every afternoon after lunch Peridot went out to take the air and, as soon as she was out of the house, took to her heels to see Violet. They met at the river, as they had done the summer before.

The summers that followed moved them together into adolescence and each girl marked the changes in the other when they were together again after the winter and spring separation. They moved toward their fifteenth birthdays and the year of 1895.

Peridot hated being in London and being fourteen. Do what she could, she seemed to be developing in all the wrong places. On top of it all, she wanted to laugh and then, a minute later, to cry. Taking refuge in her books and the calm reassurance of Miss Boileau that "all would come together in due course," she read until her eyes ached. As much as possible she avoided going out and she was grateful for the lack of attention from her parents, who exchanged meaningful glances whenever they saw her. She did not judge their reaction too harshly, since she felt as despairing about herself. She saw herself slated for a life of bluestocking activities, good works and visiting other people's homes and children—a figure to be pitied and laughed at. An Old Maid.

The summer arrived and the return to Brierley Park. Peridot made no effort this time to find out if Timothy were still around, or to contact Violet. The thought of Violet's beauty was too painful, and she dreaded the thought of seeing the changes in her own appearance reflected in Violet's eyes. She kept herself to herself—an unrewarding experience, but nobody else seemed to want her anyway. Her afternoon walks were solitary now, just as she had always led Miss Boileau to believe. She avoided the path that went to the river, taking her walks toward the gatehouse and the far side of the terrace.

The birds sang, the sun shone, the flowers bloomed as they always had, unaware of the heavy heart that walked among them. She found she had to repress a wild notion to hum a tune as she walked along. Sternly she reminded herself of the emptiness of her life.

It was then that she saw Violet waiting for her just before the turning to the main gates, leaning against a wall of the gatehouse. Peridot stopped.

"No," Violet called out. "You'll not escape me, Perry. If you want this to be our last meeting, then that's what it'll be. But a last meeting we must have."

Peridot turned away.

"I'll go on until I see you," Violet called out. "It's

the last time for sure, 'cause I'm going to run away quite soon."

This finally stopped Peridot in her tracks. She turned and walked back to where Violet stood. "Run away, Violet? Oh, why run away? Where will you go?"

She put out her arms and they clung together, both crying for each other and for their own sorrows.

Violet pulled Peridot by the arm. "Come, we can sit in the woods 'ere, 'n you can tell me why you wouldn't see me."

They left the path and moved among the trees out of the sunlight. But, even in the quiet light and shade of the wood, Peridot could see only too well why she had not wanted to see Violet.

Violet was delicious. She had blossomed in all the right places, just as Peridot had overflowed in all the wrong places. Her breasts stood out beneath her sprigged cambric gown as firm as the rounded knobs on a young goat's head before it sprouts horns. Her waist was tiny, wrists and ankles small. Even her ears, visible beneath the roughly upswept mass of hair, were perfection itself—pink and downy and as highly tempting as petits fours.

Above all, Violet still vibrated with the bubbling excitement, the juicy vitality that would make her presence felt before anything else had time to make its mark. It was the sum total of Violet that was so devastating. It was, indeed, greater than her parts, incredible as those parts were.

But the anguish that Peridot expected to feel no sooner manifested itself at the sight of Violet than it disappeared. Here was her friend, her confidante. Before she explained anything, she felt as if a load had been lifted from her.

"Well then," said Violet fiercely, "why wouldn't you see me? Realized I'm not good enough, 'ave you?"

"Oh, *no,* Violet, never that. I'm not good enough for *you,* don't you see. I *hate* myself and I hate the way I look and—and everything."

Violet looked at her critically. "Well, you 'ave put it on a bit, I grant you, but it's still you under there. You'll just 'ave to do something about it, won't you, 'cause no one else can, right? That's if you want to."

"What can I do?"

Violet snorted. "Coo, if you ate like some of the families I know and worked like 'em, you'd just be like a stick, you would. I wish I 'ad your problem and not mine."

Peridot remembered the running away remark. "Yes—what do you mean, you're going to run away? Why? Where to?"

"I got to get to London," said Violet, with intensity. "If I don't go now, I'll 'ave 'ad it. Me mum's dying—I know that, and it won't be long now. I'll wait for that and then I'll leave. See that—" She thrust out her small hands. They were chapped and rough-looking. "That's doing 'er work 'n 'elping me dad. 'N I'm only fifteen! Me dad doesn't understand me at all. 'E wants me either to skivvy up at your place, or to marry some old geyser in the village who's got a bit of money 'n is prepared to take me with no settlement."

She laughed. There was no humor in it. "I bet 'e is. The dirty old maggot paws at me whenever 'e sees me—'n would 'ave 'ad me by now, if I weren't stronger than 'im."

She shot around and took Peridot by the shoulders. "'N if I'm going to be 'ad, by God, it'll be at a price 'n not what the local village 'aberdasher can pay for me."

Peridot shuddered. "Oh, Violet, how awful. About the man and your mother and everything."

A sadness crossed Violet's face. "Yes. She was all right to me, 'n I'll stay till she goes. But me dad'll 'ave to fend for 'imself. I can't waste meself for 'is sake. I got to go."

"But you can't just—take off. With no plans. Nowhere to go. What will you do? London's so big, Violet. You might end up as a white slave."

Violet giggled. "Ooh, Peridot, you're so funny, sometimes. I can think of worse things. At any rate, that's what I am now. But no—I don't really want that. I want you to help me plan."

Peridot felt helpless. "I'll try, Violet, but it's really not something I know a lot about."

Violet answered quite seriously. "No, you don't. But at least you can listen."

Someone to listen, someone to care.

Peridot rediscovered the strength to sort herself out, to alter the image which gave her so much unhappiness. She ate less. With Violet to look forward to in the day, it was really quite easy. She got Miss Boileau to join her in walking tours, and Miss Boileau, relieved at the change in her charge's personality, was only too happy to oblige. In between she rode her pony and ran and ran with Violet through the fields until she was out of breath, exhausted and laughing again.

Through it all she worried about Violet, but she knew deep in her heart that there was nothing she could do. Violet was following her destiny. Peridot resolved that she would be there to help her in any way she could.

Violet's plan was simple. When her foster-mother died, she would go to London, to stay with her foster-mother's brother and family. She had met them before, and they had taken to her. From there, she planned to take her chances. She was unshakably sure that, once in London, those chances would occur.

"What does your uncle do, Violet?"

"'E's got a tavern. It's not really the posh kind 'n the right people don't go there, but it's not one of your dockside taverns, neither. It's very respectable—used by clerks 'n people like your Mr. Symes 'n that."

The thought of Mr. Symes in a tavern seemed almost blasphemous, but the mere mention of his name lent an air of respectability to tavern life.

Violet's companionship had to be foregone when Peridot's parents returned. It was, however, some consolation to see the impact her changed appearance had on them. Peridot was fast learning that when the world judged her more favorably, she felt better about herself.

As always, the summer brought visitors and visiting to Brierley Park. Sir Rodney and Lady Pamela rearranged the affairs of the estate to their satisfaction and then planned one of the biggest garden parties they had had in recent years. Every possible hand would be needed to help, and Peridot found herself roped in to be her mother's aide. She hated the whole business.

This time, however, the Brierley Park garden party was to be, by one of those flukes of chance, a key moment in her life. The reason was one of the prime guests of honor, a man called Marcus Radcliffe.

He was the younger son in an influential family

with much money and no need to do anything for it, a background very much like that of Peridot's father. But Radcliffe was a doer; he was one of the new breed of left-wing doers. Abhorring violence, as scornful of the anarchist's bomb as of the brutality of most worker-master relationships, he used his looks, his gift of eloquence and his money to promote the causes in which he believed.

In spite of himself, he had become a cult figure by his association with the likes of Keir Hardie, the Webbs and George Bernard Shaw—and with the Prince of Wales and his circle. He may not have been a colossus spanning both worlds, but he grasshopped between them with apparent complete ease.

The gossip columns loved him. He combined the intellectual ability of Sidney Webb with the eloquence of David Lloyd George and the amatory success of Edward, Prince of Wales. All this, and money and position too. And he was not married. No wonder he was a hostess's delight.

The wonder was that he had consented to appear at Brierley Park, whose inhabitants were not renowned for their intellectual brilliance, political interests or their links with Royalty, exalted though they considered themselves.

The truth was that he had been trapped into it. He had retired to the home of friends to write a treatise on the trial of Oscar Wilde, his link with the whole fin-de-siècle café society (now being so brilliantly drawn by Beardsley) and the contrast of all this decadence with the rise of middle-class Socialism. His friends brought him along, and he found himself, willy-nilly, headed for the Brierley Park party on a hot August day.

Peridot woke up to a sunny morning on the day

itself. She could hear the hammering and shouting of the workmen erecting a great marquee just below the terrace at the top of the meadow that led to the river and freedom. She had been instructed by her mother to "spend the morning composing yourself and trying to look as presentable as possible."

She sighed and crossed to her bedroom window. She had found enough courage—or else her mother had been too distracted to fight harder—to veto the attempts to clothe her in ruffles and frills, and was wearing a comparatively simple dress in white, trimmed with blue. The blouse was soft, with leg-o-mutton sleeves and a lace collar, tucked into a starched bell-shaped skirt. The outfit was all in white and trimmed with a braid that matched the blue of the sash around her waist. It was not an unpleasing dress, and Peridot had to admit that she quite liked it. Now, if she could only persuade herself to like herself when she got into it!

Miss Boileau and Peridot looked out of the window together at the activity below them.

"Doesn't it all seem so *pointless*, Miss Boileau?" asked Peridot, watching Mr. Symes remonstrating with a luckless servant who had dropped a tray of cutlery en route to the great tent. Again, Peridot was aware of the hesitation that meant that Miss Boileau was balancing her beliefs with expediency.

"Not entirely, my dear. What would happen to all these people if your parents did not have the money or the need to employ them? It will take some very great changes in society to create a purpose for them all. And besides, I must admit that I am quite looking forward to seeing the company today."

Peridot looked in amazement at Miss Boileau. She

appeared to be slightly flushed with excitement. Miss Boileau rarely took any part in their family activities and then, if produced for inspection, appeared with great reluctance and a withdrawn coolness.

"Why, Miss Boileau? What is different about today?"

"My dear, one of your parents' guests is a Mr. Marcus Radcliffe. He is coming with the party from Willowdale Hall. He is a very fascinating and interesting man."

Peridot looked at Miss Boileau with astonishment. This was praise of a kind previously reserved for certain historical figures and the likes of David Lloyd George. "What is special about him? Have you met him?"

"Oh, dear me, no. But I have heard of him, of course. He is a close friend of many influential thinkers—George Bernard Shaw and so on. And he is acquainted with the Royal family." The latter was mentioned on a dismissive note, but seemed to count nonetheless. Miss Boileau went on. "A friend of mine is governess with the Duncan family, with whom he is staying, and she is quite impressed with him. I believe he is every bit as remarkable in person as he is in his writings."

Peridot turned excitedly to Miss Boileau. "Oh, how marvelous," she said. "I have met people who are important by my parents' standards, but never one who is important by yours. This is going to be a much nicer day than I thought."

Annie Boileau felt a lump in her throat as she heard this moving endorsement of the standards and beliefs she had tried to convey to her charge. The implied rejection of the parental standpoint went not unnoticed. She looked at the young woman in front of her, for that was what Miss Boileau saw, she now realized, when she looked at Peridot: a young woman, taller than she was, with a waist that curved softly between breasts and rounded hips and a face that still carried childish curves of flesh over the strong bone structure. The gray eyes had not yet learned to conceal and so revealed all to those who cared to look: diffidence, unsureness, curiosity, enthusiasm.

"Peridot, my dear," she said gently, "I feel that you have the makings of someone very special."

"Thank you, Miss Boileau. You make me feel a little better about all this dressing up."

The moment passed in shared laughter, and Nanny Williams arrived to prepare her little lamb. The finished result was quite striking. This opinion was obviously shared by her parents and Terence when she went down to the blue drawing room to join the family for a light luncheon before the guests' arrivals. Her father looked delighted, her mother surprised, and Terence was congratulatory. Terence himself looked magnificently handsome, as was only to be expected. All the same, it was she who stole the show by being so unprecedentedly presentable.

Like Royalty, they stood together en famille on the steps at the front door of Brierley Park, greeting the local worthies and dignitaries as they arrived. At each new arrival of note, Peridot kept looking for Marcus Radcliffe. His was the only name she was interested in, and she would, she thought, die of disappointment if he did not come.

She need not have worried. He came and took everyone by storm. She knew as soon as he stepped out of the carriage who he was.

He was older than she had expected—about thirty or so, his hair and beard already turning a little gray around the edges—and extremely tall, which Peridot was tall enough to be grateful for in anyone else. But he carried his height with a grace that Lady Pamela was later moved to describe as "almost Italianate, quite un-English in a way. If one did not know that his background was impeccable, one would suspect him of having Latin blood." His coloring was unremarkable, of that English halfway-house variety that is indeterminately fair. He was slimly built—but neither consciously ascetic nor conspicuously athletic.

But what impressed her were the eyes, the smile, the voice. He could probably have been a remarkable actor, or a great criminal lawyer. He had, indeed, thought of both and been vehemently dissuaded by his family. However, they had hardly been comforted by his subsequent espousal of left-wing movements and the underdogs that trail on the heels of such causes.

Apart from his presence the afternoon was much as Peridot expected it to be. She avoided the dancing in the marquee, and would have spent most of her time by Miss Boileau's side if her mother had not gathered her up and forced her to "circulate."

Finally, mercifully, her mother abandoned her, saying she intended to look for Terence who was nowhere to be seen and should be entertaining their guests. Thankfully, Peridot looked around for Miss Boileau.

As she walked back up to the terrace outside the house, she met Mr. Symes, coming in the opposite direction with his habitual silver tray in hand.

Mr. Symes, of godlike perfection, had beads of perspiration on his forehead. His white gloves and wing collar looked painfully warm. "Miss Boileau is over there, Miss Peridot, listening to the gentleman talk." He indicated a shaded corner of the house at the end of the terrace. Thanking him, she moved gratefully into the shade flung across the flagstones by the high walls of the house. A welcome little breeze brought the sound of voices round the corner to her, distinct from the massive murmur below, on the lower lawns.

Her father was there, and her mother, who appeared to have abandoned her search for Terence. Miss Boileau stood at a respectful distance, in the shadow of a large elm, leaning against its trunk. The Duncans were there and some of their house party. And, of course, Marcus Radcliffe. He was sitting on the ground, comfortably relaxed, his hands playing with a stray blade of grass as he addressed the assembled company.

"French she may be, but she is, in a way, a facet of a wider movement toward a new view of woman. There is a freedom about her, a departure from the old style. A welcome breath of fresh air."

At this point, Lady Pamela spoke. "Actresses are surely not the measure of *all* women. At least, I sincerely hope not."

She gave a ripple of silvery laughter, and Peridot felt her skin tingle with embarrassment.

Radcliffe, however, did not put her down. Indeed, he bestowed upon her a smile that Peridot would have loved to have had for herself. "Lady Pamela, they are straws in the wind... beautiful mirrors held up by the playwrights to show us what they foretell for the future."

Sir Rodney appeared nettled by this response. "Good God, man, what a disturbing thought. Not trends for the future, surely. I cannot accept that. Just one of the many whims our womenfolk put themselves—and us—through. All this cycling and running around in totally unsuitable getups for a female. Absolute nonsense and it will pass. Sets a very bad example."

"To whom?"

"Beg pardon, sir?"

Radcliffe was standing up now, lightly brushing down his impeccable trousers. He appeared casual, detached, but Peridot sensed an anger in him. Again, her skin tingled. With embarrassment for her father, certainly, but also with a feeling of excitement. Radcliffe repeated. "To whom?"

Before Sir Rodney had time to respond he went on, to Peridot's utter amazement, "To your daughter, perhaps?" He put out an arm to where Peridot hovered on the edge of the group.

When he saw her hesitating, he went over to her and took her by the arm. His fingers touched her wrist, where the cuff of the blouse revealed the skin. She felt a shock of pleasure run through her.

"Come, Peridot, you look to me like a thinking woman. What do you feel about these new women? Are they absolute nonsense? Are they a bad example?"

Sir Rodney went redder, and Lady Pamela looked dismayed. It was obvious that she was alarmed at how disastrous might be the response of this awkward daughter of hers.

Peridot herself was unaware of these reactions. All she heard were the words "a thinking woman." All she felt was the hand on her wrist. She spoke as she had only ever spoken before to Annie Boileau.

"No. To me, they are neither of these things, because they show me another option in life, another way to be."

She turned to Marcus Radcliffe and addressed the rest of what she said to him, to the warmth in his eyes. "We cannot all of us be ornamental, or love to dance, or want to be mothers and wives—just because we are women. Just being women doesn't make us all alike. What happens to one who cannot fit that pattern? Must she feel worthless because she cannot? Should she not be able to feel she has some purpose in life? I am not saying that to be pretty, and to love to dance—and—and so on, is wrong. I just feel that the second should be as right and proper and—and—unridiculous as the first."

There was a burst of applause from the group. It would indeed have been worth preserving for posterity the expressions on the faces of Sir Rodney and Lady Pamela, where a struggle between amazement, pride and discomfiture took place.

Peridot saw all this but, for that moment, her attention was not even with Marcus Radcliffe. She looked toward the tree where Miss Boileau was standing. The look on Annie Boileau's face was all the confirmation and reward she needed. In her head she thought, "For you, Miss Boileau. For you."

A young man in a boater, whom Marcus Radcliffe had addressed as Tom, jumped to his feet and came across to where Peridot was standing. "I say, jolly good show. I think you stuck up for our generation very well."

Peridot looked helplessly at him. Some girls would have made hay at this point while the sun was shining, she knew that, but she couldn't blush, dissemble and say something charming. "I don't think I was standing up for our generation at all. Most of them don't feel like that. I only said what I felt for myself."

Tom of the boater was not deterred. "Well, I still think it was very well put. You would be very good at speeches and that sort of thing, you know. Look"—he somehow managed by the position of his body to isolate her from Radcliffe, who had rejoined by now a general discussion on the extraordinarily hot weather—"do you think we could walk for a while and discuss some of your ideas?"

Unbelievable. A highly presentable twenty-year-old wanted to discuss ideas with her. Her parents were only too delighted to give their permission. After all, was he not Tom Duncan, an eldest son?

Self-consciously, she detached herself from the group and, for the first time, found herself accompanied by a male other than her father or brother. A momentous occasion.

It was not. Basically, Tom Duncan wanted to talk about himself, about how he didn't always see eye to eye with his father, about his problems at Oxford, about the delights of cycling in Hyde Park—about anything but her ideas. He did, however, keep reassuring himself that she was still there by saying repeatedly, "Do you understand what I mean?" And didn't even notice when she stopped saying "Yes."

Through boredom and disappointment Peridot again became aware of the heat. She became aware that she was taller than her companion. She watched his over-full lips opening and closing and wondered what would happen if she screamed. When they were about to circle the lower lawn for the third time, she made some excuse and escaped, leaving him in mid-sentence, staring after her.

At least it was both cool and quiet in the library.

Her parents would be furious if they knew that she had hidden herself away in here, but it was to be hoped that they were too happily occupied to find out. Remembering the French turn of the earlier conversation, before her intellectual debut into the social world, she found a copy of Racine's plays, ensconced herself in a large, winged chair and started to read.

It could only have been a few minutes later that a voice from behind the high back of the chair startled her into dropping the book onto the carpet in front of her.

"And what are you doing here, Peridot Sinclair? Feeding that original mind of yours—with what, I wonder?"

It was Marcus Radcliffe. He came around the side of the chair and retrieved the book from the floor, glancing at the title before returning it to her.

"Hmmm—Racine. For the passionate intellectual, I always feel. Of course, Sarah Bernhardt is magnificent as Phèdre."

"You have seen her?"

"Oh, yes. The eyes like hot coals, the voice a river of delight."

He took the book back, flicked over the pages and read:

"Ce n'est plus une ardeur dans ma veines cachée,
C'est Vénus toute entière à sa proie attachée."

His voice was like velvet. An indescribable feeling trickled through her.

"You know what that means?"

"I think so."

"Translate for me."

Haltingly out of emotional rather than linguistic confusion, Peridot responded. "It is no longer a passion hidden in my veins. It is the entire Venus—um—Venus's very self, fastened on her prey."

He raised his eyebrows, handed the book back to her. "Good, very good. You have a certain style."

He regarded the girl, sitting in front of him. "But, what am I doing, discussing and translating the likes of Racine with a—how old are you? Fifteen?"

"Yes." She plucked up courage. "What's wrong with that? This is the first interesting conversation I've had all afternoon. Actually, ever except for Miss Boileau."

Radcliffe laughed and leaned forward, intrigued. "Who is Miss Boileau?"

"My governess. She is—very special."

He caught the emotion in her voice.

"Was she out there today? Did she hear your little oration to the assembled gathering?"

"Yes."

He leaned back and folded his arms behind his head. "Hurray. Always nice when people reap their just rewards, and I'm sure that that was, for her."

Such perspicacity. How had he guessed?

A little silence gathered, shared and friendly at first. Then, there was something too penetrating about the eyes that surveyed her. Peridot shifted a little in her chair, wanting to move.

As if sensing it, he jumped up. "Come, it is growing cooler now. Evening will be here soon, and I am sure that it is much more proper that you should show me the grounds in the gathering dusk—filled, as they are, by all the world and his wife—than that you should share a darkening library with me. Filled with all these inflaming thoughts and ideas."

His gesture embraced all the shelves of books. Then, he crooked his arm to hold hers, exactly as if she were truly an adult. "Come, show me these greenhouses I have heard so much about and refused to enter in the heat of the day."

They talked as they went, and Peridot could not have said who saw them together and whether anyone was impressed. She had forgotten to feel impressed herself, so involved had she become in what they were talking about. Mostly, they talked books—what she liked and what he liked. Occasionally, he would suggest one.

The air was, indeed, cooler, and most of the guests had already left. A steady stream of carriages filtered down the main drive to the road outside. The reflection of the setting sun was still on the greenhouses, lending a brilliant rosy glow to the space above their heads that shone down as if through stained glass on the ground beneath. The gardeners had gone, and they had the greenhouses to themselves.

Almost to themselves. As they walked together down the main aisle, talking companionably—he even knew an amazing amount about orchids—they became aware of a movement in the soft shine and shade ahead of them. It was the shifting of two bodies, moving as one, arms around each other, the girl stumbling slightly as the boy pressed against her, laughing quietly, protesting and then silent as the boy's lips met hers.

Marcus Radcliffe was intrigued. He stopped and watched with unconcealed interest the passionate vignette before them. Peridot stopped, too, but with a far more powerful reaction than his, for she knew who the participants were.

At that moment, the couple looked up, and Terence and Violet realized that they were no longer alone.

Violet, as usual, reacted with complete spontaneity. She broke away from Terence and threw herself into Peridot's arms. "Perry, Perry! I am so fortunate—now I have seen you as well!"

She was dressed in rose, as rosy as the light that poured in on her, as sinfully delicious a rose as the heart of a peach, the center of a peony, the secret, sacred places of the body. The tight bodice and unfashionably tight sleeves showed every curve. Her hair was as tousled as ever, as if it never recovered from a lover's wandering hand.

If Violet was rosy, then Terence was scarlet. With one hand, he made snatching gestures at his collar, as if it were too tight for him, and with the other he clutched at the air, as if grasping at straws. Finally, he blurted out, "Peridot, Mama and Papa are not with you."

"No," said Peridot shortly—for she was annoyed at the spoiling of her own tête-à-tête.

Violet turned and took in Peridot's companion for the first time. A speculative curiosity joined the laughter in her eyes. "Who's the gentleman, Perry? Will he tell on Terence and me?"

Peridot now looked at Marcus Radcliffe. When she saw the look in his eyes as he watched Violet, it was not her intellect that took a blow. It was a quick, sharp jab to the stomach—of envy, at the inevitability of it all.

There was a sudden flurry of voices approaching, laughter on the evening air outside. Terence jumped and started to move toward the door of the greenhouse, pushing past Peridot. Radcliffe caught his sleeve. "Wait. The girl can go out that way, and you can walk out with us. Everyone will be only too charmed to see the three of us together."

He pushed brother and sister ahead of him and turned back. Peridot heard his question, "What is your name?" and the whispered reply, "Violet." She lost the rest of the exchange as Terence propelled her with him to the door. Marcus Radcliffe joined them as they reached it, and they presented the charming, united front that he had intended, as the party from the house approached.

The cloud under which Terence's long disappearance had placed him was somewhat mitigated by his reappearance with Marcus Radcliffe. Radcliffe himself bridged the gap by a sudden and dazzling display of rhetoric on the glories of the greenhouses, that fell over the assembled gathering like a burst of shooting stars and startled them into complete silence on the subject of Terence's absence.

When the time came for the Duncans to leave, taking their houseguest along with them, it was with a sense of loss that Peridot watched the carriage depart, taking Radcliffe away.

As she lay in bed that night, the silhouettes of Violet and Terence crossed and recrossed the darkness behind her closed lids. Then came images of the darkening library and Marcus Radcliffe's eyes in the shadows. The two became confused as she drifted slowly into sleep. With the images came sensations of heat, the heady odors of tropical flowers, the pungent smell of orchids.

Peridot awoke the next day without any feeling of anticlimax. In fact, she thought of the phoenix rising from the ashes and thought, "That, at the moment, could be my coat-of-arms." She felt at the beginning of everything, on the threshold of she knew not what. She looked back on the summer, on the year that she had been fourteen, as on a slough from which she had risen.

She thought of Terence and Violet and the scene in the greenhouse and a little of the light went out of the day. Characteristically, she analyzed her feeling. It seemed to be composed of some concern for Terence, who seemed so smitten by Violet, and a lot of envy over the look in Marcus Radcliffe's eyes when he had looked at Violet. What were her feelings about Violet now, she wondered.

At the thought of Violet, however, a smile crossed her face. How could she feel hostile to someone who had given her so much love and companionship? She found that she couldn't, that all she wanted was for Violet not to get hurt.

Terence and her father were already having breakfast when she arrived downstairs. Her father seemed inordinately cheerful and very affectionate, remarking on her achievements of the day before. "You were the unexpected success of the day, m'dear," he told her, and Peridot accepted this as the compliment it was intended to be.

After breakfast, Peridot searched for Miss Boileau and found her in the little drawing room upstairs, writing letters. "Thank you, Miss Boileau."

Miss Boileau looked up from the writing desk at her pupil. Her face seemed grave. The beautiful smile Peridot had expected to see was not there. "Peridot, good morning. Why are you thanking me?"

Peridot was puzzled by the withdrawal she sensed in the woman. At a loss, she started to stammer, "For everything. For making me able to say what

I did, think as I do. For all the things you have shown me. For—for helping me to be me."

There was sadness, not joy, in Annie Boileau, as she heard the words. For all unknowingly the child was speaking of the finishing of a project, of the end of something that had, indeed, been special, but was now over.

"Dear Peridot, I was so proud of you yesterday. You said something of what I feel to a gathering that I, myself, could not have addressed. Most of all, though, you were not merely my mouthpiece. You spoke from your own convictions."

Peridot saw the sadness in the woman's face. There was still no smile, even in the eyes. "Then why do you seem so sad, Miss Boileau? Are you not happy that yesterday happened?"

Miss Boileau bent urgently forward, putting her hands on Peridot's shoulders. "Of course I am, my dear. I am very fortunate that I saw—if you like—the reward for my labors before it was too late."

Chill and foreboding now. "Too late? Why too late? You—you are not *dying*, are you, Miss Boileau?"

"Oh, no, no. No fear of that. I am as strong as a horse." This was said in a light and flippant tone that only served to underline the seriousness of her true emotion. Miss Boileau held up the paper on which she was writing.

"This is an application for a post in another household. Your parents told me—just prior to yesterday—that they would have no further need of me after this year. They plan to send you to school in Switzerland for a year or two."

She paused and added, in the ringing tones of false conviction, "I am sure that it will be a wonderfully *good* experience for you. And your parents have assured me, particularly during the course of yesterday evening, of excellent references. I am really most fortunate."

Peridot felt completely abandoned. All the joy of the day dropped away from her. Instead of rising from the ashes, she felt she was back in them, clothed in sackcloth. She cried out, tears running down her cheeks, "But *I* am not fortunate. Who will give *me* excellent references? They will not see me in Switzerland as you do—as everyone saw me yesterday. They will only care about looking pretty and walking properly, and I'm already pretty good at French, anyway. Oh, Miss Boileau, you can't leave."

Miss Boileau's cool shell of acceptance cracked at once. She bent over and took Peridot's hand in hers. "Oh, Peridot, Peridot, I don't want to, but I have no choice. I must consider it my good fortune that you really wanted to learn, and valued the things I found important."

The fifteen-year-old dissolved back into the child, and she repeated hysterically and pointlessly, "I won't *let* you go, I won't *let* them make me go."

Through her outcry, she heard the voice of Miss Boileau saying, "Hush, hush, someone will come in, and it will be hard to explain all this, so listen. Listen to me, Peridot. There is one chance, just one."

Fighting to control herself, Peridot looked up. "What is it?"

Miss Boileau took her hands and spoke slowly. "Marcus Radcliffe is our only chance."

Surprise now made Peridot forget her grief. "How can he help?"

"By changing your parents' minds about your future. You see, I think you should go to University. It is not such an unheard of thing for a girl of your background to do now. I know there are plans for a return visit to Willowdale Hall, and the Duncans have particularly requested your presence. If, somehow, you could talk to Mr. Radcliffe about your feelings, there might be powerful persuasion from that quarter."

"But how would that help you stay here, Miss Boileau?"

Now, a smile crossed Miss Boileau's face and stayed there. "Because you are too young yet to go, and there would be much work to be done. After all, you would have to pass the entrance examinations."

They laughed together and hugged each other, and the phoenix rose from the ashes again.

There was, indeed, a return visit planned and in quite short order. It was to take the form of a tennis party, with croquet for those who did not play tennis, and conversation for those who preferred to do neither.

Peridot was thus given what was, for her, a unique experience: that of looking forward to a party. But she was apprehensive. Their plan seemed so far-fetched. Miss Boileau, however, was strangely calm. "I feel quite fatalistic about it," she said. "If it is meant to happen, it will happen."

Peridot spent every afternoon, weather permitting, practicing her tennis game, generally with Miss Boileau as her opponent. Her parents approved, for they wished her to make a good showing at Willowdale Hall. Miss Boileau turned out to be surprisingly athletic, and Peridot's game quickly improved. Although the outfits that she wore could hardly be called unrestricting, they were far less constraining than the normal clothes she would have been expected to wear and were, therefore, very welcome.

The more Peridot's physique improved, the more disturbingly she became aware of her body, the sensations it gave her and the demands it made. Grace and agility might not yet be hers, but she felt a new confidence in herself. She became less concerned that, if someone so much as looked at her, she would fall over her own two feet.

At night, she would remember Marcus Radcliffe's eyes, the embrace of Terence and Violet. Then, she would hear her heart beat under her breast, run her hand down the now taut, firm skin over her ribcage and her belly, and shudder with guilt and pleasure at the sensations that ran through her.

Sir Rodney, Lady Pamela, Terence and Peridot went by carriage together to Willowdale Hall. Not surprisingly, Miss Boileau was not with them. How Peridot wished she were! She was sure that she would perform better, if she knew that Annie Boileau were there. Still, she could not do worse than Terence who, for all his handsomeness, sat sulking and long-faced in the corner seat, next to her father. He had answered with a curt yes their solicitous inquiries as to whether he was ill, and then refused to divulge the nature of his malady. Both parents had given up in exasperation and turned to each other and to Peridot for conversation.

The reversal of roles struck Peridot. Who would ever have thought that she would be her parents' comfort on an outing to a grand house, where they hoped to impress and be impressed? A new confidence filled her, and she sat up straighter, clutching her racquet across her knees. Terence had flatly refused to bring one.

Their reception was informal, cordial and confused: a melee of friendly, barking dogs and everyone laughing and greeting everyone else. To her horror, Peridot found herself firmly channeled in the direction of Tom Duncan. Was this why it had been particularly stressed that she should come? In her vanity, she had thought that it had something to do with Marcus Radcliffe.

Despairingly, she found herself led off to play mixed doubles with Tom Duncan as her partner, against two of the other young houseguests, a newly engaged couple who had eyes for no one but each other and were, therefore, boring in the extreme. They made Tom Duncan's repartee seem positively witty by contrast and lost all the games played by an appalling margin and without a care in the world.

Does love always make one moronic? wondered Peridot, as they lost sight of all else—including the tennis ball—in each other's eyes once more.

Tom Duncan kept congratulating her on her game in a condescending manner that made it clear that he felt their success was due to him and him alone. When the engaged couple finally moved off to play croquet, she challenged him to a singles match and took practically every point off him. It gave Peridot a grim pleasure to watch him walk off the court, curtly muttering about rejoining the other guests.

It was turning out to be a truly horrid afternoon. The tennis lawn was higher than the croquet lawn and, down below, she could see Terence—now perfectly happy, apparently—teaching the finer points of croquet to a girl about his own age, who giggled and shrieked in a manner that Terence obviously found highly appealing.

"Terence, you are fickle," she said out loud.

"Such is the nature of young men."

Marcus Radcliffe stood behind her, looking down on the scene below.

"I don't see why that should be."

"Trial and error. Experimentation. The nature of the beast. All is as it should be. Terence only follows his destiny."

"Do you really feel that is all we do? That what will happen, will happen?"

Radcliffe took her by the arm and led her to a bench under a large copper beech by the side of the courts. "Oh, not entirely. Biologically, maybe. But of course we can shape our own destinies. I believe that most firmly. Some do more determining for themselves than others."

Now was the chance, the perfect opportunity. The merciful Fates had, indeed, meant it to be. "I want to determine for myself."

Radcliffe seemed to have reminded himself that she was only fifteen, for he laughed lightly and said, in an almost paternal manner, "And I'm sure that you will. You will not be one to be swept along by circumstance."

Peridot looked at him in desperation. "But that is just what will happen, unless you help me."

The flippancy was gone now. He looked startled. "Me? How can I help you?"

"By persuading my parents, particularly my mother, that I should go to University. That it would be a wise, even a—a fashionable thing to do with me."

Words falling out, one after the other, she told

him about Switzerland and Miss Boileau and their plan to ask him to help their cause.

Marcus Radcliffe was intrigued. "Quite a conspiracy between the two of you. I am fascinated by your tenacity. You will be interesting to see at thirty." He paused. "All right, my dear, I will see what I can do. On one condition."

Peridot felt worried. "Oh, dear, there is so little at my age that I can do, but I will if I possibly can."

"Oh, I am sure that you can fulfill this one. It would have been unfair of me to ask you otherwise." He looked at her. "Can you tell me about the girl in the greenhouse, who seemed so very fond of you. Or, is it a deep, dark secret?"

So, Peridot went through Violet's life history and their relationship for the second time in a few days, all the while wondering at the motivation of the man beside her. Terence she understood. This man was an enigma. In her innocence and inexperience, she could not decide if he was dangerous or not. When she came up to the present in her story, to Violet's decision to leave the village after the death of her foster-mother, to make her way in the world through the good offices of her unsuspecting uncle and aunt, she saw the change in his expression. When she had finished, he leaned back against the bench and paused before he spoke.

"You know," he said, "this has turned into an unexpectedly interesting time for me. I have met two thought-provoking members of the female species. You and Violet."

"Me?" She did not question the mention of Violet.

"Yes. You have the makings of the sort of mind that brings about changes. That is why it would be a pity to see you swallowed up by some Swiss finishing school. And Violet—"

He stopped, as if wondering how to express what he felt, as if for once the words did not come easily.

"Now, Violet has the makings of one of those women who affect the world by the power of their physical attraction alone. A Helen of Troy, a Cleopatra. She is truly extraordinary—and I speak as one who has seen many beautiful women. In her way, she too could shape destinies."

There was no more envy now, mixed in with her love for Violet. For had he not said that she, Peridot, was also extraordinary? An idea came to her.

"Mr. Radcliffe, will you help Violet as well as me?"

He looked at her and smiled.

"Peridot, I had already planned to do just that."

He leaned forward from the bench, staring out across the lawns, hands clasped loosely in front of him. A fine mist threatened to put an end to the sunshine, and a chill had entered the summer afternoon air. She heard him say, half under his breath, "What man, given the chance, would not wish to play Pygmalion?"

Voices were calling them across the grounds, laughter came toward them from the croquet lawn. He stood up, took her by the arm again and, together, they walked back to the house.

He was as good as his word. He returned Peridot to the gathered assembly with warm words, directed toward her parents, on her cleverness and originality. His next move was to isolate Lady Pamela on the pretext of showing her some mementos of a visit to Paris in the company of the Prince of Wales. She needed no persuading, but Radcliffe was exuding charm from every pore as he led her away.

Poor Mama, thought Peridot, so unaware that she is being manipulated, though she is so good at it herself.

When the afternoon finally came to an end and everyone was saying good-bye, Marcus Radcliffe said, as he shook her hand, "It is done."

And done it was. The very next day, she and Miss Boileau were called into her parents' presence in the main drawing room. Lady Pamela opened the conversation. Sir Rodney looked as if he was not yet quite sure what had hit him.

"Peridot darling," her mother began, "your father and I wish to talk to you about your future. As you will see, this will affect you too, Miss Boileau, which is why I asked for you to be present."

Clasping her hands and leaning slightly forward, she said, "We are thinking, my dear, that perhaps it would be better for you to go to University."

Miss Boileau and Peridot looked suitably surprised.

"After all, any girl in your position can go to Switzerland. It is so much the done thing that it is almost outmoded, I feel. So many people in society are sending their daughters to Oxford or Cambridge. Lord and Lady Lethbridge, for example, and—" Here, Lady Pamela ran out of names, but she had already convinced herself, or been convinced, and needed no further proof. "—oh, many more. And, after all, you do not quite fit the normal mold of young girl, my darling. You could still be presented, and you would meet all sorts of interesting and eligible people."

Here, Sir Rodney interjected. "Let the child speak, Pamela. How do you feel, my love, eh?"

Peridot's joy ran through her answer. "Oh, yes, please. I would so love to go."

Thus it was that Peridot found her summer closing with two more years of work ahead of her, Miss Boileau with her for those two years, and the promise of a happiness she had never hoped for.

She knew she must see Violet again to find out what part Marcus Radcliffe intended to play in her life. She waited, very deliberately, for about ten days, so that he would have time to approach Violet, if that was what he intended to do. She wrote out no clandestine messages to be left in shoes. Instead, when she was ready she searched out Timothy herself and told him to let Violet know she would meet her the next day in the usual place.

There was a touch of autumn in the air, and the feeling of the beginning and ending of many things as Peridot walked down to the river and to Violet. The wind was blowing in the tops of the tall elms, and the rooks wheeled wildly overhead, cawing in protest as the gusts of air bore them along.

Violet was already there, on Peridot's side of the river. They clasped each other tightly without speaking, and Peridot felt the old, familiar rush of affection as she hugged Violet close.

"Perry, I love you."

"And I love you, Violet."

They crossed the stream and made for the barn, where they had spent so many happy hours. Tibby, the original barn cat, was long gone—she had simply disappeared one day—but her numerous children and grandchildren still scampered about the place. The two girls had no time for them this day.

The cats and kittens were part of a childhood that was now slipping away from them.

They climbed into the loft and found a comfortable straw-covered patch to sit on, with bales of hay behind their backs. Violet produced two pears from the pocket of her skirt and handed one to Peridot. The skin was firm, russet brown and green, but when Peridot bit into it, the juices squirted into her throat from the soft, white flesh beneath.

"I know about you and the University, Perry. I'm so glad for you."

"So Mr. Radcliffe saw you and spoke to you."

Violet bent over her pear, holding it out to avoid the juice running onto her skirt. Peridot could only see the dark fringe of her lashes shading her eyes. Her expression was hidden.

"Oh, yes, 'e came and saw me. Me mum just died."

"Oh, Violet, Violet, I am so sorry."

She put an arm around Violet's shoulders and was surprised by the reaction, as Violet pulled away from her.

"No, don't, Perry. I know you're sorry. Don't talk about it. It was worse than I thought it would be. I don't want talk about death 'n things like that. I don't want to be frightened. I only want to be happy. Let's just talk about Mr. Radcliffe."

"Of course. What happened? Let's just talk about him."

She saw Violet fight for control, and then watched her look up and smile.

"'E's a cool one, that one. All very open 'n above-board—but is 'e? Came round 'n saw me dad as well, said 'e heard I was going up to London. Said 'e 'ad been impressed by me qualitites. *That's* a laugh.

'E never saw me working that day at your party. Except on Terence, of course."

This made her really laugh. "As it stands at this minute, 'e's going to be looking me out a good position in London. 'E knows where I'm going to be. Me dad's only too pleased to see me settled in a position, and 'e's given 'is permission. Me uncle's going to be told 'n all."

"But I thought you didn't intend to be a servant, Violet."

Violet found this hilarious. She licked her sticky fingers and giggled as she did so. "Oh, Perry, Perry. Whatever makes you think I'm going to be a servant? Not with that one, I'm not."

She sobered up a little. "Mind you, 'e's a good bit older than me, but 'e knows what's what. 'N this way, I'm not likely to get caught out 'aving a baby or nothing like that. And I don't think 'e'd desert me. And 'e can teach me other things."

"You mean—he *loves* you?"

"Na—but 'e wants me. 'N at this stage of the game, it's the same thing."

Peridot did not feel envy, or jealousy. She felt bewildered and frightened. "Violet, you must look after yourself. Oh, I liked him too, but I do hope he is not a Krakatoa."

Violet, hands on hips, stared at Peridot. "'N what's a Krakatoa?"

In spite of her feelings of concern, Peridot started to giggle. "When I was little, Mr. Symes told me about this volcano called Krakatoa that exploded and did a lot of damage. It sounded evil and fascinating, so I called all the villains in my stories 'Krakatoa.'"

In a sudden return to small girlhood they sat and

giggled together. Violet said, "I think 'e's a savior, not a villain. Least, 'e is to me. But I'll remember about Krakatoa. It can be our secret word for villains."

With Marcus Radcliffe pigeonholed as a possible Krakatoa, the subject was dropped by some unspoken mutual consent. They talked on that afternoon of the shared hours of the past rather than of the future. For the future brought separation and the unknown.

"When will I see you again, I wonder?"

"Don't know, Perry, but we will both be very different then, I think."

"Will it be the same? Will we like each other?"

"I'll like you. I always will."

"And I you."

"No. You'll always love me, but you may not like me, sometimes."

Outside the barn, an unripened apple fell too early from its branch, with a soft thud onto the orchard grass. Most of the world was unaware of its descent, but myriad small creatures in the grass were devastated by its fall.

Chapter Four

LONDON WAS ALL that Violet had expected it to be and much that she had not expected. It was dirtier, noisier, more confusing. But it was alive. Oh, how it was alive! The moment that she was deposited in its teeming, grimy streets, she knew that she was born for the city. Even when 'the country' came to mean great estates with ornate gates swinging open for her, she never cared for it again. It was always too reminiscent of where she was from. She would discover and love the seaside, but only when it was composed of the buildings and trappings of expensive civilization—cities, as it were, on the edge of an ocean. Only for a very short period of time would she be able to tolerate the lonely villa on the cliffside, or the castle in the country.

She saw out the year of 1895 in her uncle's tavern, the Lord Nelson, under conditions very little different from the cottage she had left behind. One bright spot was that she was allowed to help her uncle serve in the bar. Indeed, when he saw the effect that Violet had on his customers, he positively encouraged it.

Violet flirted discreetly, learned all the latest songs, listened to all the gossip and kept her distance. She walked out with no one, entertained no gentleman callers. She knew that Mr. Krakatoa would arrive one day and take her away. She never doubted that.

He did. They were into 1896 and she was turning sixteen when he turned up. He appeared in the lounge bar one day.

"Well, here you are, then, like the well-known bad penny."

His strength of personality and his class stood out in those surroundings even more than she had remembered. She watched the eyes and knew she still had him.

"Bad penny, indeed, little Violet. I am your crock of gold, as you very well know."

"Are you, now? I don't see no rainbow anywhere."

"Tut, tut. Living here has not improved your speech, although you are quite as dazzling as ever."

She gave him a mock curtsey. "Thanks and no thanks. You look after the one. I'll take care of the other."

"What a precocious little sixteen-year-old you are. You have known all along, haven't you?"

"'Course I have. Well, you'd better be telling me uncle about this good position you're offering me, show him that letter from me dad. I can't stay here fighting 'em off much longer. I'll have to strike out on me own."

He looked at her, as she turned to lead him through the door into the back.

"No need for that. You have made the strike that matters. You will now be carried along by sheer momentum."

She did not understand the words that he used, but she knew that the life she had chosen had begun.

From the Lord Nelson Public House to the discreet comforts of the area around Brompton Square may not have been far as the crow flies, but the journey could not possibly be measured in those terms. Violet would have used almost any means to make such a journey.

That the one she had was so agreeable was a stroke of luck she intended to exploit as fully as she could. For was that not what he intended to do with her? Each would get what he wanted most from the other, and all would be quite fair and just. And extremely pleasant.

For Violet could not wait to dispose of her virginity. The only reason she had clung to it so long was that she was going to sell this treasure to the highest bidder. She did not despise either herself or the buyer for it. She had enjoyed her brief skirmishes with the likes of Timothy and Terence at Brierley Park and looked forward to Marcus Radcliffe with anticipation.

At this stage of her life, there was no romance in her vision of lovemaking. She thought she would be taken to his bed, that it would be pleasurable, that it would be soon over.

Instead, she found herself being taken to the theater. Not to a play by his acquaintance, Shaw, nor yet to the Music Hall. He took her to a romantic costume play, starring the current toasts of that genre of theater, Fred Terry and Julia Neilson. He told her what he had planned for them as they drove to his rooms.

"You don't need to do this, you know," she said.

In the dimness of the cab's interior, he stared at her. "Violet, if you're going to get anywhere in the world you have chosen, *you* are going to need to do these things. You will have to learn how to dress, how to talk—about the theater, about so many things. You are a very, very beautiful girl, God knows. Look at the way I am behaving, heaven help me. But you must learn to use that beauty, not have it use you."

She looked at him defiantly. "I know all that. If I didn't, I wouldn't be here now. I'd be back home, married to an old man, scrubbing 'is floors 'n doing 'is bidding. For a few quid more than me father 'ad."

"Then why did you tell me I needn't do this?"

There was a softness in her expression as she looked at him. "Because you don't 'ave to go to all this trouble—first. I know how bad you want me. You don't 'ave to take me to the theater 'n that. I'm a bit hungry, 'n I wouldn't mind me dinner. But that's all."

It seemed strange to her, but there were tears in his eyes as he took her hands in his.

"For all the sophistication I may try to give you, Violet, never lose that straightforwardness of yours. It is quite devastating. You might say," he added, "that I am doing this as much for me, as for you. I am feeling very guilty, I must confess."

"Guilt!" He saw the glint of Violet's sharp, white little teeth as she threw back her head and laughed.

"I gave up on that a long time ago. You can afford being moral 'n that when you're nice 'n rich. All those do-gooding ladies who used to come round the village with their bread 'n soup, patting me on the 'ead and saying, 'Be a good girl 'n you'll go to 'eaven.' If it takes what they call being bad to get some rewards right now, then that's what I'll be. 'Ypocrites!"

She caught Radcliffe up in her gaiety, and he pulled her to him, laughing. What he had intended as a simple hug changed as he felt Violet's body against him. She heard the catch in his breath as they touched, and she raised her face. His mouth came down softly on hers at first, then with increasing pressure, until her lips parted. She lay back against the leather upholstery and gave herself up to the sensations that ran through her, allowing them to dictate her moves.

Tongue caressing tongue, hands moving over each other's bodies, they made their first explorations.

"Touch me there."

"No. No, Violet. I'm going to save that."

"Still want to go to the theater?"

"I most certainly do."

"We'll see. What'll I wear, anyway? Can't go like this."

"I have something you can wear. Chose it myself."

Love games temporarily forgotten, she sat up in excitement. "Oooh, lovely. What's it like?"

"Wait and see."

It was beautiful: pink, with a square-cut décolletage, finely pleated bodice, wide velvet sash in a deeper rose than the dress, and suede elbow-length gloves to match. The whole was to be wrapped in a matching cape trimmed with fur. It was all laid out in the bedroom that was to be hers. Her own room. Any room to herself would have been paradise, but this one was splendid—big and airy, all in blues and greens, with a soft carpet, heavy curtains and a fire in the grate.

Radcliffe explained that he had staff in during the day to help run his establishment, but that he had—up to now—employed no one to live in, except one manservant. If she wished to change that, she could.

"I can?" Such power, such unbelievable power.

"Of course."

He watched her walk around the room, taking in her surroundings.

"I hope you won't be bored, Violet. I go to many meetings, do a lot of writing and so on. But you can come with me when I go out, most of the time."

She looked at him, surprised. "I won't be bored. Mistresses are never bored. Besides, I have so much to learn. You are my teacher."

The perfect game. The intellectual and the sexual combined. The two sides of his character united in one goal. Once again, he felt doubt as he wondered what some of his friends would say. If she were only four or five years older, it would be simpler. Was this why he had chosen the kind of theater at which he was unlikely to meet too many critical acquaintances?

Violet did not care about his motivation. She loved the play. Leaning over the edge of the box, exquisite in her rose pink outfit on the bodice of which he had pinned a corsage of pink rosebuds with badly trembling hands, she watched in fascination. As she leaned forward, he saw her waist, pulled in even smaller than usual by the stays underneath, watched the swell of her breasts over the square neckline, longed for it all to be over. But when he saw her pleasure and delight, he was glad that he had done it this way. Besides, there was a certain cerebral pleasure in anticipating the course of events he had planned to follow.

He had not allowed, however, for the unknown quantity that was Violet. She was unkissable in the cab on the way home, as an endless stream of comments on the costumes, the theater, the play, the audience, issued from her perfect lips.

At his rooms, there was a cold collation left by his discreet manservant. It was intended as part of the seduction—a little champagne, a slow buildup to the moment of truth.

Violet flung herself at the food. She drank some champagne, hiccupped, then sneezed, and returned to the chicken, the soft white bread, the fruit. As he watched her eat, he saw what true hunger was. She moaned and gasped with pleasure, as if he were already making love to her. He began to wonder if he ever would that night. It looked as if she would either collapse with a stomach ache or drop off to sleep from sheer exhaustion. He himself was beginning to feel tired from merely watching her. She ate with a gusto that was quite fatiguing to contemplate and that seemed insatiable.

Finally, she dropped the spoon which had returned countless times into the pink blancmange before her and put her hands across her velvet sash.

"Oof—I'll 'ave to get these stays off now, or I'm going to pop out all over. I'll be back."

He said nothing but watched her take herself out of the room, yawning as she went, loudly and with her head thrown back in abandon. Was she hinting that she wanted to sleep, to be left alone? He got up impatiently, stacked all the dishes together on a sidetable and went around, lowering the lights. They had eaten in the drawing room, with Violet and her plate of food hopping from chair to sofa to stool, and then back to the table. He drew the curtains, then held them to one side and contemplated the quiet road in the pools of light beneath the street lamps.

"*That's* better."

Shock upon shock. The visual impact of Violet, in the doorway, naked. So much for the slow uncovering and seduction of this shy and blushing flower. She wore nothing—not shoes, not peignoir, her hair down loose and curling. She put her arms up on the doorposts, and the high breasts jumped higher, their blackberry tips pointing at him.

"Well . . . Mr. Radcliffe?"

It was like being the first astronomer to see a distant star, the first traveler to find the source of the Nile. How to report on the flawless colorings of Violet's apricot beige skin, the length of leg and perfectly turned knee and ankle, the narrow rib cage surmounted by two full, golden, dark-tipped globes, the almost muscular curve of the shoulder into the arm, tapering into the slender wrist.

Flexing herself off the sides of the door, she swung her indescribable thighs at him, with a thrust of her loins that turned his knees to water.

"You are the rainbow *and* the crock of gold, Violet. Journey's end from the beginning of timeless time. Nirvana and Nadir."

"Don't know what you mean, but it sounds lovely. Makes me feel funny inside."

The hands came down from the doorway and clutched her flat belly. Suddenly, she shivered.

"Wrap me up in my cape, Marcus. I'm cold."

He snatched the cape from the sofa, where she had thrown it on seeing the food. She met him by the fireplace, and he wrapped it tightly around her. Her eyes looked trustingly, confidently, into his.

"Carry me to your room. I always hoped that my first man would carry me."

What a revelation in that phrase. The first man. That she was, indeed, a virgin—of that he had not been sure. More significant than that, perhaps, was the underlying implication that he was only the first in a line of conquerors, of men who would vow everything for the possession of that body.

So there was tenderness in the way he carried her, cheek against his neck, laying her down gently on his bed, covering her carefully with the bedcovers.

"Keep warm till I come to you."

When he came back, she seemed to be asleep, lashes brushed against cheeks, only her hands visible above the coverlet. Gently, he pulled back the bedclothes and lowered himself beside her.

With a sudden burst of laughter that hit his eardrums and made his heart lurch with shock, she pressed her body against his, curling one leg high over his naked thigh.

"See! I'm wide awake! You thought I was asleep, didn't you—fooled you!"

"You little—"

Tenderness forgotten, to suit her own mood of abandonment he forced his body between her open legs.

As if it were the most natural thing in the world—which it was—without any preliminaries whatsoever, Violet lost her virginity, to the complete satisfaction of them both.

If Marcus Radcliffe had thought that project Violet would satisfy the dual aspect of his nature, he quickly had to modify that view. Writing went completely out the window. He could not even read. He could think of nothing but Violet's body and his body and what they could do together. Intellectually, he was a desert. Sexually, he was a veritable fountain of never-ending activity and inspiration, in which Violet was his willing partner and in which she quickly learned to become initiator as well. She learned with uncanny speed how to arouse him, how to satisfy him, how to make him cry out for more.

He felt his creative juices overflowing as never before, but they all seemed to overflow into Violet. He felt powerful, but it was a power limited absolutely to the radius of Violet's body.

She went out on her own once or twice shopping for clothes—which were becoming a passion with her—and he sat down to his treatise. It ended up covered with drawings worthy of the Kamasutra. He did not even, at this stage, have the power to worry about his intellectual sterility.

They rarely left his rooms, except to return to the theater and to eat out on a few occasions. For their second visit to the theater, Radcliffe took her to a play by Shaw. He wasn't quite sure why he had done so, but he had been curious about Violet's potential growth in directions other than her phenomenal sexuality. He feared she had been bored. She was silent throughout the play and then silent on the way home.

"I'm sorry, Violet. That was tedious for you."

She turned to him, as if startled to see him, her thoughts obviously elsewhere.

"No. I didn't understand a lot of it, though, I admit it. No, it's not that. It's those women."

"Yes. You would find them difficult to understand. Why they are as they are."

To his surprise, she replied, "Oh, no, I understand them. I understand them because they made me think of Perry."

"Perry? Oh, Peridot Sinclair."

"Yes. She'll be like that. Peridot's different. I love her."

"That's a very strong statement, Violet. Were you two so close?"

"Yes. She meant everything to me, once. When we meet again, even if it's years and years and years, I know we'll be just like *that.*"

She clasped her hands tightly together in the air. Then, the sober mood passed as quickly as it had come, and she bounced onto his knee, making flirtatious and outrageous suggestions into his ear. The thoughts that he had meant to pursue with her about Peridot left him, as he was engulfed in the helpless onrush of his body's response.

They made a highly successful trip to the Haymarket Theatre to see Du Maurier's play, *Trilby,* which was the sensation of the day. It was obvious that Violet identified with the romance between the girl and the man and thrilled with every twist and turn of the plot.

Highly successful was the visit and highly significant was the event afterward. Radcliffe had arranged to meet a group of friends at an after-theater supper at the Café Royal. It was to be Violet's coming-out party, her introduction to society.

The Café Royal was highly fashionable, and it had the advantage of private rooms. Violet would only have the pressure of encountering the group that he had selected, rather than the eyes of the whole world.

He had been struck by the calm with which she had received the news. He had thought she would be apprehensive, perhaps ask him to call it off, or postpone it at least. He had forgotten that, for Violet, this was her destiny unfolding. Things were only progressing as they should.

"You're not worried then, at spreading your wings outside our nest?"

"Oh, no, Marcus. After all, we can't stay in bed *all* the time, can we?"

He was saddened by her answer, suddenly threatened by his own plans for their relationship.

When he watched her on that momentous evening—in the company of a duke and duchess, a couple of honorables, a minor visiting European prince and his lady friend—laughing and smiling and at her ease, he was reminded of Walter Pater's dissertation on the Mona Lisa: "She is older than the rocks among which she sits; like the vampire, she has been dead many times, and learned the secrets of the grave; and has been a diver in deep seas, and keeps their fallen day about her."

This was Violet. At sixteen, she knew it all. It was as if she had been in the situation before, as if nothing could surprise her.

Was this the secret of world-shakingly beautiful women? A knowledge, an art, that defied description and understanding, that melted logic and reason and bowed inspiration to their will. He thought again of Pater. Violet was a living example of his premise that a color sense was more important than a sense of right and wrong. Violet transcended right and wrong with her own shadings, the faultless tones which she selected for each occasion. She was not a chameleon for she was always herself. She was perhaps a diamond, reflecting the light of its surroundings in its prisms and yet always its own greatest glory.

Her entrance into the plush-lined, gilt-chaired dining room had been sensational. Her youth alone would have guaranteed that, but Violet engineered a few surprises herself. As the door was opened by a footman, Violet made some remark to Radcliffe and then gave one of her delicious giggles. The gathered assembly first saw her standing there, in white silk, feathers in her hair, her slim neck encircled with five rows of pearls, her lips parted in laughter. Then, as she saw the company, her eyes widened in interest, the lower lip caught in her little white teeth, the hand dropped, executing a curve down the line of her body. A pause, a flicker of a glance at Radcliffe, showing the profile and turn of throat—all enchanting enough in a twenty-one-year-old coquette, devastating in a girl of sixteen.

During the course of the evening, Radcliffe watched her create her style as she gained in sureness. He watched her try out various techniques on different members of the group, watched her work skillfully on the women, who were understandably hostile at first. How much of it was instinct and how much pure calculation, it was impossible to say, but Radcliffe became uncomfortably aware of his own part as a sounding board, in this part of her development.

When I try out all those wonderful sensual games on her, he thought, it is I who am the guinea pig.

Suddenly, he felt fragile, exploited, as much by the pull of his own desires as by Violet's, the reasoning part of his brain locked away somewhere behind a door whose key he had mislaid. Hastily, he gave his attention to what Prince Raspioli was saying.

"My dear Radcliffe, you are to be congratulated. I had quite thought—since your last visit to Rome with that very *clever* lady—that your tastes were more, er, cerebral is the word I think I am looking for. Where did you find her?"

"On a friend's estate."

The prince contemplated the smoky hollows under the eyes, the slightly swollen lids on the usually ascetic face of the man next to him. "Does she eat you alive, then, my friend?"

"Oh, yes. Not entirely, as yet. But I fear that she will."

"Fear not, fortunate man. Try to survive, though, if you can. For she is on a journey, that one."

Together, they contemplated Violet across the table in the candlelight, doing a harmless child act for the benefit of the duchess, who treated her with indulgent condescension. As the great lady turned to the gentleman on her left, Violet—without missing a beat—turned to the duke on her right and, with a dip of the shoulders, offered up her apple breasts to his fascinated gaze on the honeyed platter of her voice. True, the accent of her humble origins was still there, but it added a certain salacity to her most innocent statements. Violet could make the listener salivate at the dropping of an *h* or the broadening of an *o*.

Ignoring the warnings that were filtering through from some remote but still functioning segment of his brain, Marcus felt the lust in the duke's eyes reawakening a heat in him that he had neither the wit nor the desire to control.

"That was a wonderful, wonderful evening. All that I dreamed an evening like that would be. You are so kind and good to me, Marcus. I hope I didn't let you down."

"You know very well that you didn't let me down."

"I'm so glad. Now—can I meet your other friends?"

"My other friends? What other friends?"

"Oh, you know, Marcus. The ones that go with your writing. With that play we went to see that reminded me of Peridot."

"Oh, those friends. Are you sure they are really part of what you want? May you not find them boring?"

"I shan't know that until I meet them, shall I? And besides—you're not really worrying about me being bored, but about *them* being bored."

He had to laugh at her perspicacity.

"Oh, no, I'm not. They are very rarely bored."

She looked at him, resentment in her eyes. "You know what I mean. You are afraid I will let you down."

He felt very weary all of a sudden, lack of sleep, physical exertion and the evening's drinking catching up with him. "You know, Violet, whether you believe it or not—that is not the case. I am more concerned about how they will judge me than about how they will judge you."

"Is it not the same thing?"

"No, not at all. Not at all the same thing."

"Well, you must either be judged by them in the

end or drop me. I don't think either of us is ready for that yet."

Again, the extraordinary insight. Working from instinct, alone, Violet possessed a mental sharpness which he constantly underestimated.

"Not yet. Not ever, perhaps."

"Ooh—you and your ever and ever. 'I never felt like this' and 'I don't think I have ever—.' I will never talk like that."

He burst out laughing. "Listen to you. You have broken your own rule immediately."

She took it quite seriously. "You're right. I'm beginning to think too much like you. I mustn't. It works for you, but it wouldn't work for me. I must learn more and more, but I must always think like me, and me alone."

Violet set herself the task of doing some reading over the next few weeks. The school run for the children at the Brierley Park estate might not have risen to dancing or French but it did at least endeavor to make them literate. Radcliffe did not always approve of her choice of books. She approved greatly of Mrs. Humphrey Ward.

"I can see why you wouldn't like it, Marcus, but it tells me so much about people in your class. You don't need to know about all that. You're already one of them."

It was mildly disturbing to think of himself as a character from a Mrs. Humphrey Ward novel. Was that how he thought and acted?

She got him to try and describe the circle she would be visiting. Sidney and Beatrice Webb had taken a house in the country and opened it up to friends for weekends of work and intellectual discussion. He decided to take them up on the offer to visit them, but to maintain his independence by staying at a friend's country cottage, which was close by. He could then teach Violet the joys of bicycling and they could cycle over to visit the others. That way, he could judge how much they and Violet could mutually tolerate each other.

Actually, what he dreaded more than introducing Violet to his friends was confessing that he was doing no work at all worth discussing. He hoped the weekend would give him the intellectual stimulus he so badly needed.

Violet shopped with passionate enjoyment for additions to her wardrobe that would be suitable for country life. In cycling knickerbockers, a long overtunic and a small hat with a feather, she looked so enchantingly different that Radcliffe devoured her with renewed passion—if that was possible. Violet, prancing around in knickerbockers and her little hat and nothing else, made any thought of intellectual activity disappear.

The beginnings of their trip were not auspicious. Violet objected to the comparatively light amount of luggage that was all Radcliffe thought necessary. By now, she had a maid of her own and the two of them slipped in extra cases that were not at first noticed, but that caused problems both in the hansom cab and at the station. Violet was also upset that he would not allow the little maid to come with them. She stared out of the carriage window for a long time without saying anything and then declared, "I hate the countryside. Look at it. So untidy and mournful."

"But I thought you wanted to do this, Violet."

"I want to meet these friends of yours, yes. I only wish they lived in some nice, big city. Not among a lot of cows and marshy fields."

"How can you say that? Look at it, it's so beautiful. I wouldn't mind if I had to live here all year round."

"Oh, yes, you would. If you'd really lived here all year round, as I have, you would."

He gave up in exasperation, the first negative feeling he had had for her since their affair had started. He left her to her own thoughts and returned to his. She sat next to him, her head turned away, her neck sunk into her high collar, spine curving against the padded seat. Her desolation, her introspection, seemed genuine. Again, the flash of guilt at what he had done to her. Where would she go from here? Where would he go?

At the small country station, they were met by the caretaker of the cottage, a small, elderly gentleman, who looked askance at the luggage and summoned two porters to move it to the pony trap that he had brought.

It was carefully piled up in a pyramid and stayed there for about ten minutes of the journey, when the top valise fell off, bringing about the dislodging of two other bags. They bounced off into the road, and Radcliffe's carpetbag fell off into a puddle. He and the caretaker redistributed the baggage, and Radcliffe traveled with his feet on the carpetbag, which was, by now, quite wet.

Anger was now added to exasperation. He began to feel exploited again, realizing, as he did so, that this was the last thing he should feel. After all, was he not the exploiter? That is how his friends would view the situation, he felt sure. At the thought of his intellectual acquaintances, he added apprehension to the anger he was feeling.

He glanced sideways at Violet. To his surprise, he saw that she appeared to be laughing. The trap bounced over a rut in the road, and a chuckle escaped her.

"What do you find so amusing in all this?"

"You."

"Me? Why me, pray?"

"Well—that's life, isn't it? When you don't have, it takes away from you. When you have, it gives you more. There you are, barely one valise and wouldn't it be the one to fall in the water. All because of mine. It isn't your just rewards, you know. Life gives you the unjust ones. I'd like to tell that to those lady bountifuls."

"So, you just go on pushing and taking advantage, is that it?"

"Of course you do. Otherwise you just go under. Survival of the fittest. You know, like you told me."

As he had told her. He was teaching this little monster beside him to eat him alive. My God, he was becoming fanciful, morbid. Relentlessly, he turned his attention outward and contemplated the countryside so despised by Violet.

The cottage was isolated in a charming setting, comfortably furnished. The perfect bachelor pied-á-terre, with deep chairs, sporting prints, horse brasses and a rack of beautiful pipes, it bore no signs of female habitation.

Violet's face grew longer as she saw the interior. It brightened a little as a middle-aged woman came through from the kitchen to greet them, with cheering remarks about lit fires, cooked meals and hot water.

When she had left, Radcliffe put his arms around Violet.

"You see, dearest girl, a perfect love nest."

"I only like nests in big city buildings, not perched in the middle of trees."

"You seem determined not to like it."

She looked at him, bewildered. "That's right, I don't like it. But that's not important. All that matters about all this is meeting your friends."

It went surprisingly well. Yet again, Radcliffe had underestimated Violet's charm and adaptability. She had the good sense to lay coquetry aside here. Most of the gathered assembly approved of her, found her intriguing. Fascinated, Radcliffe watched her perfect a new act.

The weather improved and became more summer-like and with the change came a lift in Violet's spirits. In the morning, everyone worked. Radcliffe would rise, leaving Violet abed, and cycle over to join the company. Violet would join them for luncheon. In the afternoon, he taught her the pleasures of cycling. Violet's natural aptitude made her a more able cyclist than he was, to his surprise, for he had thought she might not be at all interested.

They would arrive home in the evening—she, radiant and glowing; he, exhausted. He would collapse into bed for a rest, while Violet bathed and dressed her hair and experimented with her wardrobe, singing all the while. She had a naturally pretty voice, but her choice of songs lacked any lullaby quality. The strains of "Knocked 'em in the Old Kent Road" and "She did the fandango all over the place" pierced the depths of his slumber.

In political discussions at the Rectory in the evening, Violet found her niche. The mixed group that Sidney and Beatrice had assembled listened with more than patience to her accounts of her childhood. They were also interested in her friendship with Peridot and Violet's analysis of her character. It was all going amazingly well. As a consequence there were no harsh judgments of him whatsoever.

Radcliffe himself had actually managed to do some writing—bereft, this time, of erotic illustration. He also found himself able to expound on his views with a return of his customary gift of eloquence. He loved it when he saw Violet watching him admiringly.

He loved it even more when they returned to the cottage at night and invented a new game.

Violet would remove her clothes, while insisting that he repeat the particular thesis he had put forward that evening. She would then lie naked on the bed and watch him undress. Together, they would plan what they would do, in as detached and academic a manner as possible.

The contrast between the intellectual and the sensual inflamed Radcliffe to the point of total engulfment before he had even touched her. The trick was then to control himself, for, as part of the game, he then had to repeat the argument, reaching its conclusion at the moment of climax.

Was this indeed Nirvana, he wondered. His ability to think was returning, and his physical lust for Violet burned more brightly than ever. She herself seemed as happy and passionate as she had ever been, touchingly delighted at the discovery of mental gifts she had not known she had. They stayed on an extra day, buoyed up as Radcliffe was by the unexpected success of the experiment.

On the final morning a fond farewell was said to the housekeeper, the luggage piled up on the trap—more carefully this time—and they returned to the station for the London train.

"Well," said Radcliffe, as the train rattled through the countryside, "that was a surprise, wasn't it? I think some of your loathing for the country has disappeared, am I right?"

They were alone in the carriage. As she turned to him, he noticed that her back was not slumped as it had been on the previous journey. She held herself erect, chin balanced delicately on the tight, high collar that swathed her neck, her eyes staring at the antimacassars on the seat opposite, as if they were a screen across which passed a parade of happy thoughts. She was still smiling when she turned to him.

"You're wrong, quite wrong. I still *loathe* the country. What I liked was that I was accepted by your friends and they didn't judge you."

"Thank you." This was said ironically.

"Oh, no. I know that worried you. I did so well they not only passed me—you passed the test also."

"True. Now our life together will be that much easier. You can share my writing and the friends who are associated with it."

"Oh, no."

It was said quite calmly, in a small voice, but there was tenderness in her eyes for him, the first he had seen. It was as if she looked at a child. Then, she frowned, and put her little hands over his and held them tight.

"I've had a choice to make, Marcus. Now it's made. The nice thing is, I could have decided either way, because of how things went. That world"—she pointed back to where they had been—"is not for me. This one is."

Just a finger pointing in the direction of London, but ahead of it lay power, wealth, jewelry, furs, perfume, scandal; the inconsequential, naughty gaiety of the nineties, which she had chosen for herself.

He knew it all, without her having to explain it to him. He also knew that if he followed her pointing finger, she would swim and he would sink. It was a pleasurable, peripheral part of his own life, but it could never be the core. For her, perhaps it could. He knew he couldn't stop her. She had connections now. Her beauty already intrigued a powerful few. It was the fear of rejection he now felt, for he still wanted her as much as ever. Loved her perhaps. God knew, his thoughts grew confused when he tried to work that one out. So much simpler if it was just passion. Or was it? There was nothing simple about the grinding, gnawing jealousy that engulfed him when he thought of anyone else touching her.

Her pressure on his fingers tightened, and he saw she had tears in her eyes. Tough little Violet, with tears in her eyes.

"Stay with me, Marcus," she said. "Don't let me go yet. I'm not so sure of myself as I sound. I know I shouldn't ask you, but don't give me up yet. Let me stay a little longer. Hold on to me."

As he held her tightly against him, he realized she was the most precious thing at that moment in his life.

As autumn came and the leaves withered and died on the plane trees of the city, Violet flowered. Dressed by Worth in gowns imported from France and fitted by his own fitters, she began to be noticed by a larger circle of people, by those who mattered.

Most evenings would find Violet and Marcus at the Alhambra or maybe the Empire, part of that mixed cosmopolitan crowd that thronged the Promenade behind the stalls. Violet watched the demimondaines in their boas and ostrich feather hats, the beautiful show girls and, most of all, the devotion they inspired on the part of the young men who watched them night after night and waited for them with their horses and carriages after the show. The stage-door johnnies, the mashers, the lady-killers. They went to the Tivoli, the Adelphi and the Gaiety where she first saw the Prince of Wales, in his element, laughing and joking.

Afterward, she would meet them again—marquesses and barons and millionaires who courted and married girls who had started life as merely a Jessie Smithers or a Hilda Harris. Why not a Violet Cartwright? Why not indeed.

At Rules, in Maiden Lane, behind the Strand, Kettners, the Cavour, the Carlton, they ate truite meunière, partridge en casserole, ortolans, and Benedictines rosés. Violet learned not to hiccup over champagne or to turn up her nose at grilled pigs' feet at the American bar of the Criterion. After all, the plebian becomes acceptable when it is chic. When one does not *have* to eat pigs' feet they are a wholly different kettle of fish.

Like that of a pretty little pigeon, Violet's breast filled out, even her hips became more rounded in the fashion desired by Edwardian men. Magically her waist did not expand even when her corsets were removed. Marcus Radcliffe, well into his thirties and used to long periods of ascetic living, watched an incipient paunch start to swell where once there had been hard flesh over muscle. The flecks of gray in his hair increased, even as the hair itself began to recede.

His Violet, his Delilah, was she drawing strength from the very hairs of his head? Should he bring the pillars of their temple, their marvellous treasure-house of pleasures, crashing down? Ah, he could not, he could not. She had him bound by chains stronger than anything he could break. Even his willpower seemed to be hers. She waxed, he waned, but he was happy in his bondage, unwilling to escape.

Their life fell into a pattern now. Violet was a late riser, neutralizing the effect of their late nights by sleeping in until the lunch hour. Marcus would force himself out of bed, contemplate his sunken face in the mirror—strange contrast to his increasing girth—wash and shave with the help of his manservant. Then he would sit at his desk and try to write for three or four hours until Violet appeared, fresh and rose-tipped as a daisy, smiling and smelling delicious.

At last he found himself able to write again. He started making notes for a novel and became obsessed with what had been a diversion. He suspected that he was motivated by a desire for self-exploration, confession. The phrase 'mea culpa' ran through his head, and he became fascinated by the writings of some of the great divines. In poetry he turned to the work of John Donne. The struggles of that great seventeenth-century divine between the sensual and spiritual sides of his nature fitted his own feelings so well. From Donne's poetry he turned to Donne's sermons.

Cleansed and purified by the ascetic, he would see

Violet's seventeen-year-old body and burn again. Better to marry than burn. Ah, Saint Paul, he thought, what can you do when you douse that fire and the mere sight of the girl kindles it again and again?

Violet was struck by how much less she noticed the passing of autumn into winter in the city. One swathed oneself in a few more furs and the fires were lit in the morning, but that was about it. Otherwise, life continued in much the same way. She resisted the country-house weekends to which they were invited, without any pretense or excuse.

"I don't like the country," she would say, but her straightforwardness was so charming that none were insulted. Marcus didn't mind, since he would sooner be in his rooms with Violet. The outside world shared her enough as it was. At least here some elements of the cocoon remained.

For her seventeenth birthday they had planned to visit the Gaiety and then to dine with friends at the Carlton. There were about ten of them: two of Radcliffe's friends from Eton days—one an honorable and one a marquess—and their ladies. One was a wife and one was not. There was a financier whose acquaintance Marcus had made when seeking advice on investments. He was bringing along a friend on a visit from France and ladies for himself and his friend.

As usual, the theater performance set the mood for the evening: light, lilting, not at all taxing of the mind, and as charming as the ladies who filled the stage and the audience. Violet felt quite at home with the Old Etonians, the financier and all the women. It was the wife who was the odd woman out in this gathering and, since she herself was young, rich and attractive, she was undisturbed by the situation. Did not Alexandra herself dine with her husband's mistresses?

Prior to the curtain rising, Teddy Bostock arrived with the Frenchman, Comte Michel d'Aulnay and their ladies for the evening. D'Aulnay's companion was a demimondaine—on the higher end of that particular scale—called Maisie Devere who had, at one time, been on the stage herself, but had given it up.

"Too much like hard work," she said, when asked her reasons, shrugging her plump and pearly shoulders at her new escort, which made her ample bosom jump alarmingly over her boned bodice.

D'Aulnay did not appear either alarmed or charmed. He was looking at Violet, from dark, melting eyes that were totally unlike the piercing English blue ones of Marcus Radcliffe.

He was shorter than Radcliffe but moved with the same athletic grace—or, that which Radcliffe had once had. His dark hair was perfectly groomed, as was his beautifully curled and waxed moustache. His dress was impeccable, his manners smooth and unforced. When he smiled, he had the flashing white teeth of a Spanish hidalgo. Violet could almost imagine a pearl in his ear and a sword by his side, as though he were out of the romantic plays she had seen.

As he helped her into the carriage after the theater, his hand touched hers and she felt a sharp tingle go through her. It took her by surprise. So many other men she had met now, and this had not happened.

Oh, she tingled with Marcus all right. She had

with Terence and Timothy and some others. But only after they did nice things to her and not before anything had happened. She looked at d'Aulnay and saw the predatory, watching eyes. She felt them like a hand on her breasts and her thighs and knew that was where the thoughts behind the eyes lay. Occasionally during the evening she would flick a quick glance sideways and see their gaze intent upon her.

Radcliffe saw it, too. Other men had looked at Violet, flirted with her. It was inevitable, given the society among which they moved, and Violet's beauty. But there was something calculating about this man's stare that sounded a warning bell inside him. It rang even louder when he saw Violet glance at the count under her lashes. She had never dissembled or hidden her reactions before, and she was doing it now.

In a roomful of people, in the pink and cream lounge of the Carlton, two human beings scented and stalked each other, and a third party smelled in the air the hot, heady perfume of sexual attraction. How could he not recognize it, when he had paced that hunting ground himself?

The wine flowed, the champagne bubbled into willing mouths and Marcus drank far more than usual. He was aware that, in the spinning distance, the conversation had turned to music hall and the vogue for suggestive songs that sounded innocent, but were not. Comte Michel d'Aulnay professed his ignorance of them and begged one of the ladies to oblige with a rendering. Maisie Devere maintained them to be beneath the sort of thing she had done on stage. In the midst of her protests and refusals, Marcus heard Violet say, "I know a lovely one. Let me sing it for our visitor."

She stood to scattered applause, in her cream brocade no warmer and richer than the color of her skin, picked up Maisie's feather boa and held it coyly across her breast. The song that she chose to sing was, ostensibly, about a girl on a bus, who would not let the conductor have his way and punch her ticket. The double meanings were easily picked up, even by the Frenchman. Her outrage was perfect, the movements of her body suggestive; the contrast was indescribable. Drunk as he was, Marcus felt the lust rise in him. God, what he would do to her when they got home. Every man in the room was looking at her. Her youth gave an added eroticism to her pretended innocence. Marcus wanted to ravish her all over again.

The applause was prolonged when she finished. Violet sat down, flushed and delighted. There was a chorus of inquiries as to why she did not go on the stage—such talent, such a delightful mimic, such a pretty singing voice. Deliberately, Violet echoed Maisie's remark.

"As Miss Devere says, it's too much like hard work."

She echoed also the gesture that Maisie had given, but with a subtlety that moved one shoulder up in the direction of her ear, bringing the attention to the face rather than to her breast. It marked her out, clearly, as in a class above the other girl, with a style all her own. She refused all further entreaties to sing again with the remark, "I always leave my audience clamoring for more."

Radcliffe leaned forward, refilled his glass and drank the contents down. It was his last memory of the evening as he passed into oblivion.

Violet's senses were even sharper than usual. She

watched Marcus fall from the chair to the floor and saw the count take in the situation. She was aware of events rolling out of control, going in a direction which she had not planned. At that moment she decided to let life take its course. She had dreamed and schemed her way into this blue-lit, palm-filled room. Now, she would allow herself to drift on the current moving her toward the magnetic Frenchman. All she wanted, at that moment, was to feel his hands on her again.

The financier, Teddy Bostock, took control of the situation. He had Marcus carried to a hansom, accompanied by Violet. They got him into the seat and then Bostock turned to her.

"Will you be able to manage at the other end? Perhaps I should come with you."

"Please do, Teddy. It will be difficult. Reynolds is there, but I will have to pay the driver and go and get Reynolds out of bed and—oh dear—"

She made a helpless gesture with her hands. D'Aulnay stepped forward. In his elegant, lightly accented English, he said, "No, no, Teddy. It is better that you escort the other two ladies home. You know what the form is, about such things over here. I will see this lady home and take a cab to my hotel."

Bostock did not protest. He understood what was going on only too well.

It was strange, their first encounter alone or, to all intents and purposes, alone, with the oblivious Marcus wedged into a corner of the hansom.

"You know what I want."

"Hush."

"Do not concern yourself. He has had the good

breeding to make sure he does not hear. I wish to see you again."

"I'm not sure I can. I owe everything—all this"—she indicated her clothes, her jewels—"to him."

A smile curled over the count's mouth, splitting the lips apart over the predatory teeth. "He created you, then? He gave birth to you, made you out of clay, formed that body of yours? He no more created you than I did. We have equal rights. And, as to all that"—he reached across the intervening space and, lightly, touched the tip of one finger to the lace and jewels over her breasts, so that the electric sensation hit her again—"you can return them all if you wish, come to me naked and I will clothe you. Will that make you feel better?"

Violet felt little drops of perspiration on her upper lip. Her heart thumped painfully above her tightly laced waist. Guilt. She had decreed that she would feel none, once.

"I don't know. How will you—will I—?"

A haughty gesture of the hand swept away her questions.

"The details need not concern you. I will make sure I see you again."

Outside, the driver pulled his horse to a halt. The cab lurched and swayed to a standstill. With a movement so swift that it took her by surprise, the count leaned forward from his seat opposite her, hands on each side of her, pressing down hard against the upholstered seat. Eyes were open, staring straight into hers, then lowered, as he deliberately flicked his tongue over her upper lip, licking off the moisture on her skin.

"*Délicieux*. Just a foretaste of more good things to come."

Then, just as suddenly, he was businesslike, organizing the removal of Marcus and herself into the house and himself off again in the same cab, into the night.

Jubilee year. The outside world was celebrating Jubilee Year. Or, the second one, the Diamond Jubilee Year, to be precise. A complacent nation was reminded by Mr. Rudyard Kipling in the rousing poem "Recessional" in the *Times,* to set its face to the future, not merely to rest on the laurels of the past. Rumblings from the Transvaal and from the remote mountain regions between India and Afghanistan reinforced this warning to self-satisfied patriots.

And, as Queen Victoria's light began to dim, so the cohesive structure of Victorian society began to crumble. Traditions and taboos were disappearing; the Prince of Wales gave Sunday dinner parties.

In London, the intellectual world aahed as the Tate Gallery was opened, and the demimonde oohed as William Terris, acclaimed actor of melodrama, was stabbed to death at the stage door of the Adelphi, in a death as violent as any he had ever enacted.

All these were mere superficialities, incidents that lightly peppered the surface of Violet's life. She was aware of them because she lived with an informed man who read the *Times* and had clever friends. There were servants, too, who kept her in touch with what other newspapers and periodicals had to say.

It all came to her secondhand, skimming the surface of her consciousness. Underneath it all was a ferment, for Violet was in love. The one thing she had sworn she would not allow to happen. One meeting, a few superficial caresses, a promise. And she had fallen. Like her mother, like so many of the foolish girls she had known in her village. She raged at herself, cursed herself, mocked herself, all to no avail.

The year passed toward its close, and she heard no more of Comte Michel d'Aulnay. From carefully casual inquiries, she learned he had returned to France for the summer, and no one knew when he would be back.

The feeling, however, did not go away. She had only to remember the lick of his tongue, the flick of his finger, and her lip and breast burned. She felt bound now to Radcliffe, afraid of the power the Frenchman would have over her. If he returned, she would have nothing to do with him. I must not, I must not, she told herself.

But, said a satanic voice somewhere inside her, why not? Why does it matter, as long as you have fallen for a very rich man? It is only if you fall for someone unsuitable that the emotion is dangerous. So, why not?

She didn't know why not, but she was still frightened by the force of her feelings. So, when she hugged and kissed Marcus, she was not pretending to care for him. She needed his warmth and protection as much as she ever had before.

Autumn came around with a summons from Marcus's family to return to the fold for his parents' diamond wedding celebrations, which coincided with the Queen's own Diamond Jubilee year. He offered to take Violet with him, but she refused. He was not sure whether to feel relieved or not.

"Oh, no, Marcus. It could be very difficult for you, and you know how I hate the country."

The Radcliffes senior had almost entirely deserted the town and lived in seclusion on their estate near Brighton.

"But what will you do, here on your own?"

"Why, shop for clothes, of course! My winter wardrobe is so out of style now. And I have Reynolds and the others to look after me."

Thus it was that one rainy morning, she stood on her own at the living room window and watched his cab drive off to the station. Shortly afterward she set out for her dressmaker, leaving Reynolds instructions for a light supper.

She spent a delightful afternoon indulging herself. From the dressmaker she went to the milliner, and then she bought shoes. To spend money without worry or concern was still such a pleasure that she savored every purchase. Violet often thought she preferred adorning herself to eating out, going to the theater or, even, making love. After all, was she not her own work of art? This face and this body were what had brought everything to her in this life; she had no false modesty about them and no small skill at showing them at the peak of perfection.

A message which had been delivered during the afternoon was waiting for her when she returned home. It was from Teddy Bostock, inviting her out to dinner that night, with a group of friends. It added, "Marcus asked me to see that you were all right and to entertain you."

The apparent consent of Marcus put to rest any misgivings she might have had. She sent out her acceptance, delivered by hand to the address shown on the invitation.

Did she know? Did she hope that he would be there? Did she really believe Teddy? Violet kept her mind free of speculation, free from agonizing. After all, if she did that, she could also stop herself thinking about Marcus. She pinned her thoughts to her gown, studying the effect of every detail of her ensemble, planning her appearance as critically as if she were preparing for a performance. Or a battle.

Teddy had arranged to send one of his own carriages to meet her. It arrived at the appointed hour and deposited her at Kettner's, as the letter had said it would. An unctuous footman received her instructions.

"Mr. Bostock's party, if you please."

Up the stairs she had ascended many times before, laughing and talking in the company of Marcus and other friends. This time, all was quiet, her footsteps hardly audible on the thick carpeting, the footman leading the way. Into a room she had been in many times before, with Marcus and Teddy and others.

Teddy, however, was not there. The Comte d'Aulnay sat on a velvet sofa, one leg up along its length, smoking a cigar that perfumed the room with its expensive aroma.

He smiled at her, cigar in hand, curving his arm indolently over the curled end of the sofa. "*Bienvenue, petite fille de joie*. I told you all would be arranged."

The spider at the center of his web, with such honey to catch her that she couldn't turn away.

"Where is Teddy?"

"No one accepted the invitation—but me and you."

"How did you know?"

"Teddy kept me informed."

So much for friends. She made one effort to assert her control over the situation, to keep the reins in her hands. She looked at the table, laid for dinner for two, the candles lit.

"Well, Comte d'Aulnay, I am here, as you wanted. But I'm not hungry, so get them to take the food away. Let's finish what we have started."

She was in front of him now, her leg through the gown touching his leg that rested on the floor. Surely, he must feel the spark she felt, lose control?

A shrug, a spreading of the hands.

"But I am. *Je meurs de faim.* We have all the time in the world."

He stood up abruptly and pulled her against him. "My way," he murmured. "We do it my way. I want you, but we do it my way." With his arms around her like that, she knew that she would do anything in the world he wanted.

The insolence in his manner disappeared over the meal. He was amusing, made her laugh, listened with apparently genuine interest to what she had to say. Above all, he enchanted her with his stories of Paris.

Violet first fell in love with that city through the words of the man with whom she was in love. Always, Paris and love would be confused in her mind. Even when that love had gone its glow would linger over the *ville lumière* that she too would learn to adore.

He talked of its gardens, its buildings, its beautiful river, the theaters, the women called *les grandes horizontales* who formed one of the subcultures that thrived in the Paris of the nineties.

"Are they *very* beautiful, these women?"

"Indeed. They dedicate themselves to it. It is their whole existence, their raison d'être."

Violet felt threatened, insecure. "Then why did you come to me?"

The liquid brown eyes gazed at her over the table. "I don't know yet, do I? Maybe a conquest. But I think not just that." He looked at her slowly, tracing every inch of her with his gaze. "I suspect you have more to offer, that you have something—special. I have seen the greatest of them, but you—ah, you stayed in my mind all summer, *Violette.*"

For the first time, Violet took pleasure in the sound of her name. Violette. That was how she would like to be known. That is what she wanted to be called. She threw back her head and laughed with delight.

"That is the only way I have ever heard my name said and liked it."

"Violette." He reached across the table and held her hands. "I can wait no longer. Let them clear this and then I can see just how beautiful you are."

A waiter with years of training in the virtues of being unseeing, unhearing and unspeaking, wheeled out the ice pail, the dirty dishes, the tablecloth, and discreetly bowed good-night. As he moved out through the door, a maid appeared without being summoned, bobbed a curtsey, crossed the room and pressed a button on the paneling near the small window.

Slowly, a bed descended out of the wall. The count turned to the door and took himself and his after-dinner cigar into the passage outside, as the maid started to pull out a lacquered screen across the room. It was all automatic, each move following on the other, for she had done the same thing many times before.

No feeling of degradation or humiliation arising from the fact that both these human beings had performed these functions so often before—the maid with the bed and the screen, the count with his cigar outside the door—troubled Violet. There was a certain sense of relief that these necessary, unromantic details could be so easily taken care of.

And, besides, it took time and help to undo the work of art that she and her maid had created at home out of whalebone, satin, muslin and lace—not to mention the multiplicity of pins and flowers in her hair alone.

Strange. So strange. The maid worked skillfully and swiftly; Violet felt like a bride being prepared for her wedding night. Her heart thumped as it surely never had before, her fingers shook as she tried to help in her disrobing, slipping on the gleaming slide of white satin that covered her now uncorsetted body.

When the maid brushed her loosened hair, she caught sight of her eyes in the mirror and she hardly recognized them as her own: large, burning pools, almost feverish in her small, heart-shaped face. There was a high color on her cheekbones, and the flickering light burning low in the lamps created huge hollows beneath them.

I am eaten up with wanting him, she thought. I *want* to be devoured by him. I am afraid of it no longer.

He must be back in the room. On the other side of the screen, she heard the maid say good-night and the door close behind her.

His jacket was off, and he was unbuttoning his shirt as he joined her, cursing softly in French as it caught at the back, before he pulled it away. She sat on the bed, holding the satin robe around her, her bare feet tucked under her, solemnly watching him.

His torso and arms were strongly muscled, much more than was apparent when he was clothed, and he was lightly tanned. He tucked his thumbs into his belt and grinned broadly at her. Something about the grin made her realize that he was probably less than a decade older than she was. Still a very young man. His foreignness and smoothness had led her to think of him as about Marcus's age. She saw the dark hair on his chest that ran down in a narrowing band to the flat loins, the slim hips.

"See, *chérie*. I'm quite pretty, too."

He grinned again, and she started to laugh at his unabashed vanity, his male conceit. "Oh, you are. You are very beautiful. Only—what are those?"

He was closer now, and she saw tiny scars, white lines against the brown of his skin, one much longer and twisted than the others.

"Dueling scars."

"Dueling? You don't, do you?" She touched them with her fingertips, fascinated by the romance of those small seams in the fabric of his body.

"Si! I'm very good at it! You should see the marks on my opponents!"

Fear, a feeling of panic, touched her again, the realization that it was not just love that she was afraid of, but love of this particular man. There was a dangerousness about him, outside her realm of experience. She gave a little shiver and saw the pleasure her reaction gave him, in his eyes and his smile. No grinning now, the voice dropped to a low level, a rough note at the edges of it.

"But you, little *poule de luxe*. No scars on you, eh? A different kind of dueling for you, in which everyone wins and no one loses."

Drowning with his mouth on hers, gasping for

breath as he smothered her face with his full lips, luxuriant moustache, hungry teeth. The feel of his hands pulling off the robe, then finding her body, fondling it, transferring his attention from her face to every other inch of her, until she cried aloud, begging him to finish it, she wanted him so.

He was indeed beautiful. The body of a Greek statue, the stamina of a Trojan; the liquid words of that delicious language flowing over her like a honey that would hold her forever.

Later in the evening, he taught her some of them, delighted at her English accent, translating them—sometimes with difficulty. "For they are not, most of them, words that my English tutor taught me. I learned them in bed, with French ladies who do not speak English."

"So, there is one thing at least I do that they cannot," she said defiantly.

He leaned on one elbow, staring seriously down at her. "*Ma chère* Violette, I have a feeling there are many things you could do that they cannot. You are"—he shrugged his shoulders—"*je ne sais pas*, but it is something, some quality. The—ensemble, the whole of you that is different. You could, I think, conquer many with that body, with whatever it is I sense behind it. You have"—he thought a moment for the right word—"allure. I think that is it. I do not think I will be able to have you this once and then do without you, as I thought I would."

It was not "I love you," but, for Violet, it meant there was a future, that she had succeeded, that—somehow—she would be part of his life. For a while, for a long time, maybe, if she put her skills to good use. She was beginning to learn how to use her head to attain the wishes of her heart. In the life which she had set out to make for herself, that was to be desired most of all. All the other things she had, apparently. What she had to work on now was holding them all under control. Especially such a difficult and wayward emotion as love.

"But, you know," he said, "you know what you have that is best—that is better than most, Violette? You really *like* to make love. It is real when you give yourself. You love it. With that, you could hold any man on earth in the palm of your hand. Or, between those exquisite thighs and breasts. You have him snared."

She sat up on the bed, with the silk sheets rumpled around her. A cool, gray dawn started to break outside and filter its flat, chilly fingers of light through the curtains. The lamps in the room burned less brightly, losing their power in even this tentative morning light. There were dark hollows under her eyes, matching the contours beneath the cheekbones, and there was the mark of a love bite on her lower lip. And yet she still shone that remarkable incandescence at him.

"Not the world, Michel. Can I just snare you?"

He reached out and took up her two hands and placed them on his neck. "*Malgré moi,* Violette. I did not mean it to be so, but you are the hunter and I am your fox."

"And the fox then hunts the hare, so both are caught, and catcher. I am a hunter and a hare."

"*Bien entendu.* That is what life is all about. The hunter and the hunted. What one must do is to make sure that one is on the winning side."

Her philosophy exactly. Body and soul, they were surely meant for each other. There would be no guilt, hunting him. What she had to do was to make sure that she was not crushed herself by the relentless force, the egotistical ruthlessness of his drives. She would have to ensure that she stayed on the winning side with him—a Diana, an Amazon. Not a Persephone to be dragged, helpless, into the abyss.

Chapter Five

MARCUS RADCLIFFE WAS A MAN OF CLASS, which meant, as it often does in England, that he was a good loser. He could bow out without losing face and without apparent humiliation. What went on inside was a private matter and had nothing to do with the outside world, who judged only what they saw, as they were intended to do.

It was Teddy Bostock who first told him, in a fit of repentance and, perhaps, with a touch of the envy that had afflicted him after Michel d'Aulnay had raved to him of the remarkable effect of a night with Violet—a night which was repeated before Radcliffe returned to London.

Marcus was glad he had heard from Teddy first, and did not judge him too harshly. Didn't judge him at all, in fact. He didn't seem to have any feelings to waste on Teddy in this situation.

He was, he thought, like a farmhouse he had once seen after fire had swept through it—the exterior remarkably intact, no visible signs of the terrible inferno that had, on closer inspection, excoriated and devastated the interior, leaving it bare of all furnishings and black as a corner of hell.

He maintained the gracefully forgiving facade as he parted from a contrite and blustering Teddy Bostock at the Cosmopolitan Club, refusing his offer of lunch. He stood on the steps for a moment and looked at the well-ordered, well-heeled world of Berkley Square and decided that he was, after all, rather hungry. Perhaps some food and drink inside would ease the terrible burning in his throat and belly.

He hailed a cab and asked the driver to take him to the Wheatsheaf restaurant. It seemed as good a place as any to make a symbolic return to the values of another of his worlds, the one he intended to stick to for the next little while.

As he ate his simple, vegetarian meal, the breaking of the bread seemed to him like a sacrament, an act of contrition. Such an irony that religious sentiments returned to him, the agnostic, in a moment of crisis.

Marcus thought of the novel he had started and felt excited. Some of the pain subsided, and he felt almost optimistic. He pushed back his chair and rose from the table.

How good it felt to leave with something to do awaiting him. As he briskly walked the pavement home, the unaccustomed exercise tugged at his calf muscles and made his heart pound.

"Off with the old and on with the new" was the refrain that marched through his thoughts in time with his step. Not the New Year yet, but it damn well felt like it to him in the dying months of the year.

Difficult to remember one's personal renaissance, though, when faced with Violet again. Violet in Valenciennes lace, a toque perched on top of her head and a tiny spotted veil over her eyes, her lips curving at him, her eyes glinting at him through the net. Stupid, weak mind, that it allowed itself to be so dominated by what seemed to him at that moment to be his baser instincts.

"I bought myself a boater, look!" she called to him, as she deposited her packages in the hall, watching him as he came from the living room and yet not quite meeting his eyes. Amid a rustling of tissue paper, she removed the new straw from its box, pulled off the little toque and popped the boater on her head.

With her hair curled up over her forehead, the wider brim of the new hat perched on top of it, he was reminded of Violet in the country, Violet in knickerbockers prancing around their bedroom, laughing at him, challenging him to catch her, the feel of her naked breasts against his hands, her compliance as he undressed her and made love to her, still in his street clothes.

No, no, no. Off with the old, on with the new. Harshly, forcibly, he supplanted the image of himself with the body of d'Aulnay against her and nearly gagged. It gave him the strength not to plead, to do what he had to do.

"Violet, come. We have to talk. In here."

Obediently, she followed him into the living room. After all, she knew what was to happen. He stood by the mantelpiece. She sat on the sofa, in front of him.

"I know about you and d'Aulnay."

"I know you know."

He was taken aback. "Do you know how I found out?"

"Oh, yes." She seemed quite cool, detached, looking straight at him now. "Michel told Teddy to tell you. He thought it would be easier for you and me. And Teddy felt it was in your best interests, too."

"Good for Teddy." He allowed himself some irony. "What a useful go-between he has proved to be. Your typical bourgeois capitalist financier. Sold to the highest bidder."

Violet made the little moue with the mouth that he had once loved so much, that now seemed more bitter than sweet, taken with the words that followed.

"Not Teddy. Me. I have sold to the highest bidder. Marcus—" She got up and crossed to the mantel. She put out her hand to touch him and then, seeing his eyes, withdrew it. "I will always remember. Always. So kind and clever. Too clever for me. I'm glad it was you who were the first."

It was he who put out a hand now, and it hurt her arm—he, who had never hurt her or raised his voice to her before. "The first of many, I know, Violet. Your choice, I know that too. But remember, many of them will not be kind and considerate. They will hurt. D'Aulnay will hurt you. You haven't said, but I know you've been fool enough to fall for the bastard."

She felt anger and fright—not of Radcliffe, but at being reminded of her vulnerability. "I can look after myself, don't you worry that oh-so-clever brain of yours."

Both of them angry, both of them starting to hurt

each other, which he had not intended. He had to retain control of himself, not vent his feelings on her.

Yes, he could. Yes, he would. Once more. Take her as he never had before, wipe out the memory by wiping out the worship. Holding her by both arms, he pulled her down onto the rug before the fire with him.

"Take off your clothes."

She obeyed him, watching as he stripped himself, pulling off buttons, cursing at his clumsiness, then tearing at her own. Savagely, he was upon her before she was ready, thrusting himself into her, hurting her and then leaving her. Then, as she started to get up from the floor, pulling her down and taking her again.

She made no sound through it all. It was he who roared out in pain and agony as the climax hit him. Crouched against a high-winged armchair, he watched as she collected her clothing, pulled a torn petticoat around her.

His voice, when he spoke, was exhausted, small, as if it had a long way to travel to reach the surface.

"That is how it will be with many of them. That is your career. That is how they will have you, when they have done their wooing and buying."

She looked down at him and an oddly tender smile curved her lips. "That's all right, Marcus. You see, I quite enjoyed it. Who knows? If you had done that earlier, maybe I would have stayed." Even with her clothes in her arms, the torn slip inadequately pulled around her waist, she retained her dignity as she crossed the room, her beautiful buttocks swinging as she went.

Radcliffe turned his head in his hands into the brocade seat of the chair and let his grief subside to a level below tears, so that he could handle it. He had raped her—dear God, he had virtually raped her! So how was it that he was the one who seemed to have been humiliated, abased? Slowly, slowly, he put into operation the process of withdrawal that was to preserve his sanity. He got up, dressed, rang the bell and informed Reynolds that Miss Violet would need Doris to help her pack her belongings, prior to a departure to the Continent. He then asked to have a small valise packed for himself.

In the expressionless, businesslike response of his manservant, he found help for his own self-control. He left a note on the writing table for her, informing her that he would be moving to a hotel for the next week, to give her a chance to make her arrangements for leaving.

Just before he went out, he called Reynolds again.

"Oh, Reynolds—when Miss Violet has left, please would you see that any of her belongings—clothes, ornaments, whatever, that she did not require and that were not here before her arrival—are removed. Give them away, get rid of them as you see fit."

"Of course, sir."

Oh, the supreme convenience of having domestic help, he thought, when one has to dispose of the evidence at the end of an affair. No debris left over, no flotsam to wash up against the shoreline of memory, to remind one of what once had been and never would be again.

The London season of 1897 was extraordinarily brilliant. Violet was not there to notice it, nor could she have cared a jot. Neither did Marcus Radcliffe, who was in the country, revisiting old haunts in an effort to dispose of more recent ghosts, picking up the skeins of a life more or less abandoned for nearly two years, while he had disappeared from the social firmament into another sphere of his personality.

Meanwhile, Violet traveled by steamer to Calais with d'Aulnay, sables on her back and a diamond on her finger as big as the starlight, starbright, first star she saw at night to wish on.

She was never to see England again, but she was not to know that. She would likely not have cared if she had known. She was following her destiny as surely as she had always planned she would.

D'Aulnay was attentive, amusing and passionate. She forgot the dueling scars, the aggressive manner of his acquisition of her, her own doubts and even the bothersome guilt she had sworn she would never feel. She was only too happy to do everything he asked of her, for it was what she wanted, too. He seemed to have no vices, apart from a fondness for drink, but he was so inventive when he was drunk that she found him more amusing—as well as sexually stimulating—than ever.

She started to drink a little more herself, on the journey, and then stopped when she saw what happened to her eyes and skin the morning after. She was only just coming up to eighteen years of age, after all, and had to preserve her assets for a very long time yet.

The progress by train across the French landscape felt more like the start of a new life than anything she had yet experienced. Even the clack of the wheels against the track sounded different, played a Continental rhythm. She was on the Continent. She, Violet, was being born again.

From the beginning everything was different. People treated her differently. They did not look at her askance when she opened her mouth and spoke, spoiling the illusion of her fine clothes with the sounds of the past that still clung to her voice. They could not judge her accent by class, only by the charming effect it had when she tried to speak their language—and Violet's nimble mind and tongue were picking it up quickly, especially when she saw that in speaking French lay another way of escape from her past.

An English accent in French was very fashionable at the moment. The demimonde was suffering from Anglomania, and some even went so far as to copy the appearance of the Princess of Wales. Violet's star could not have risen at a better time.

Perhaps it was because her sensuality had been so strongly aroused by this man she was in love with, perhaps because of the changes in everything around her, that all Violet's senses were awake and aware as never before. The smell and taste of coffee in the early morning, the delectable flaky meltingness of croissants against the tongue, even the garlic and cheap wine on the breath of the porters who handled the luggage—it was all ambrosia to her.

Frenchmen looked at her differently. Oh, yes, in London, men had looked at her, too. But in France, they ate her up with their eyes, sometimes making comments as she passed. She felt herself start to ripen under the hot sun of their admiration and d'Aulnay's pride and pleasure at seeing her admired. It happened once or twice, on the boat to Calais and the train to Paris, that a man tried to approach her; then with a frisson of delight mingled with fear, she was reminded of the dueling scars beneath d'Aulnay's elegant clothing, and of the hardness beneath his velvet voice and skillful, caressing hands.

Paris. Paris first seen from a room in the hotel attached to the Gare St. Lazare, with mansard roofs and chimneys copied from the Tuileries. Elegance and uproar, a panoply of sights and smells and an incredible light that seemed to hang over the city. Its own special sky that changed at night into a myriad of lights extinguishing the stars above. There was an electricity about this *ville lumière,* as if everyone were on the verge of a great holiday, preparing for a birthday party that would outshine all others.

The rococo elegance of the hotel bedroom in which Violet stood was in striking contrast to the cacophony outside: trains shuddering to a halt or roaring into departure, the shriek of whistles, shouting voices struggling to be heard above all the other noises.

As soon as they had arrived, d'Aulnay sent for his personal manservant and a maid for Violet.

"She will do to help you for the time being. When you need more and if she is not satisfactory, you will tell me."

"Why did we not go straight to your house? You said you live alone and that your parents have known of all your mistresses. You told me about your father's own lady friends. Why are we in a hotel?"

He motioned her to a chair in front of the fire. "Come, sit. I have a great deal to explain to you."

He sat for a while, looking her over, examining this new property of his, reassessing her, deciding where to begin to explain the elaborate edifice that he and she would create together.

"I did not bring you here, Violet, just so that we could lie in a bed and make love to each other. Anyone can do that. The bourgeoisie do it all the time.

No—what makes it special for us is that we make of the whole act of love, and we two who partake of it, a work of art. It is what the world sees—what *le tout Paris* sees—that is important. That is why even the choosing of your maidservant is vital, because she will help to create that image."

"Am I not beautiful enough, then?"

He threw up his hands in exasperation. "Come, come, Violette. You must know by now that there are beautiful women everywhere. But you have also that certain *je ne sais quoi* that can, with careful planning, turn you into something above the ordinary. Something extraordinary."

"Why would you do all this for me?"

"You mistake what I say again. It reflects on *my* style, makes me to be envied and talked about among those who matter. Make no mistake about it. I am a selfish man. This is for me."

He paused, took a cigarette from the gold and vermeil box on the table in front of him and lit it. The strong acrid scent of his tobacco, which was to become so much a part of her life for the next few years, filled her nostrils.

"You will be one of the mirrors through which the world will view me. It is not, *ma chère* Violette, the self we are born with that matters. It is the self which we acquire. You can be a supreme example of that. I, at least, was born to be a count. Now"—he became businesslike, precise—"we have a lot to do to achieve this goal, to make you this nonpareil. Let us set about it. First, I have acquired for you a little apartment on the rue St.-Honoré, where we will go tomorrow. Very chic. Decorated, I think, in a style that will enhance you. A good ambience for you. Secondly, your name. Do you wish to change it?"

She was out of her depth again. "Why would I do that? The police don't want me or anything."

"Oh, Violette, Violette!" he called out in irritation, "you would be *agaçante* if your innocence were not so amusing. Today, tonight, you are creating yourself. That is why we hide ourselves here. Tomorrow, *Gil Blas* or *La Vie Parisienne,* or *Paris en amour,* may spot you and put you in their pages—I am very newsworthy—and we must be prepared for them. Many of the great lionesses, the grandes horizontales, have taken names that appealed to them. Emilienne d'Alençon, par exemple. What about you?"

The fear again, some feeling of the essence of herself inside, slipping out of her grasp. The name she had once scorned, she now wanted.

"No. I was born Violet Cartwright and let that be all that remains of my past. Or, if you want, what I heard that man you got angry with call me, when he heard you say my name. On the train—you know, Violette l'Anglaise."

He laughed in delight. "You are beginning to understand. That is perfect. Yes, that will serve very well. English is chic at the moment. Tomorrow, we start to launch you like a beautiful ship. Tomorrow, we organize your wardrobe, and we will talk about your first appearances to the world."

He stood up briskly. "That is enough for now. I want to watch you undress while I have a cognac." He pointed at the rug before the fire. "Take as long as you wish. I will tell you what I wish removed and you will do it. Refill my brandy glass for me."

A beautiful possession. Goods. Chattels. She dismissed the thought, but then was startled to find that it excited her. His eyes watched her, never shifting from her body as he gave his orders, handing over his glass two or three times to be filled. Deliberately, she contorted her body as she bent over him with the cognac; calculatedly, she altered the angles at which she offered her various delights to his eyes and watched the desire spring up and the muscles twitch in his face.

Inside, she smiled in a secret triumph. I am Violet Cartwright. And this owner of mine is owned far more than he bloody well knows. Flex my thigh, curve a hand around my breast, and watch my puppet jerk on the strings that bind him to me.

Outside, the world of arrivals and departures roared, whistled and shrieked all through the night.

Coffee and brioche and fruit in the morning and the strong black smell of Turkish cigarettes. The oddly comforting sight of Michel in his embroidered slippers, feet up on a footstool, reading the paper, no longer imperious.

"Why do we not live together? You're not married."

"It is not done. It is quite acceptable to keep an establishment. In fact, it is *de rigueur,* in my position. Besides, I will, I suppose, have to marry eventually, and I would wish, perhaps, to keep you—on the side, as it were."

"So, you might have a wife and me?"

"That is entirely possible. Only, we try to make sure that the one has the children and the other does not."

For a passionate race—as she had always supposed the French to be—this seemed remarkably logical and sensible. Violet saw how her position was made easier by that coolness, that separation of fact and feeling. She was also aware that she could accept d'Aulnay's position all the more easily, because there was no wife, or prospective wife, around, as far as she knew. She decided to ask no questions on the subject. She was learning fast.

While it was still early, they made their way to the rue St.-Honoré, before anyone who mattered would be out of bed. They took a closed carriage and arrived shrouded in cloaks and capes, like conspirators, giggling and whispering together as the luggage was unloaded.

"You will love your appartement," Michel kept repeating, like an enthusiastic small boy. "Wait until you see it. You will love it."

She did. It was lit by chandeliers, their beautiful crystal droplets splintering light off porcelain, glass and lacquer, the exquisite Louis Quinze furniture. There were table lamps, too, their pink silk shades upheld by pretty plump cherubs and lascivious muscular satyrs in bronze and silver. There were silk cushions everywhere, and white fur rugs thrown over Persian carpets. And, joy of joys, through the far door of the salon, Violet saw a miniature conservatory, filled with palms and statues, the centerpiece of which was a small fountain, with water playing off a marble mermaid whose hard, shining breasts jutted into the spray.

D'Aulnay watched her take it all in. "The perfect ambience for my *petite cocotte anglaise,*" he murmured.

She accepted what he said as a compliment. "You are right. I shall be happy here."

The bedroom was like a tent, the luxurious habitation of some Arabian desert sheik, walls paneled and hung with carpets, the bed canopied in brocade that descended from the ceiling itself. The whole effect was muted and enclosed, lit with the gleam of deep, jewellike colors from the fabrics. All sound was muffled underfoot by more animalskin rugs.

D'Aulnay went over to the bed and pulled a heavy, tasseled rope by its side. It was not a bell. The hangings from the ceiling parted to reveal an enormous mirror, surrounded by more cherubs and satyrs, smiling in at their own reflections, perpetual companions to the scenes that would take place below.

Something about it struck Violet as funny. Perhaps it was because, in her rapid rise from little countrygirl to kept woman, she had never seen a brothel, or a house of pleasure. It seemed incredibly amusing to her to see so much trouble taken to enhance the delights of one act. A temple dedicated to love. It all seemed so solemn that it provoked the opposite response in her.

She collapsed on the ornate, be-cushioned bed, helpless with laughter. "Oh, Michel—it is so funny!"

"I do not see that myself."

D'Aulnay was stiff, as embarrassed as if she were laughing at him. Then, the infectiousness of it reached him, blowing across the gap between them on the gales of her merriment. They rolled together on the bed like two children, now and then catching sight of their contorted faces in the mirror above them, only to collapse again in helpless mirth.

It always seemed to Violet that it should have been a good omen that they had christened that bed with laughter, and not with what passed for love in the half-world she entered that day.

"You will take me to Worth for clothes today?"

"No."

She was hurt. "Why not? If we are to be the very best?"

"He is among the best, and we will go there as well. But, for your dénouement, we start with someone new. Jacques Doucet, he is called. He knows a great deal about the new movements in this city, the new painters, the new engravers. We will use his talent to launch you. He will understand when he sees you. We will use him to make you a fitting frame for your beauty."

Again, d'Aulnay did not use his own carriage with his family coat-of-arms on the door. They went anonymously by hired cab to the new dressmaker's establishment.

As d'Aulnay had foreseen, Jacques Doucet understood perfectly. As soon as Violet walked into his atelier, he saw that here was a very special showcase for his designs. That she was an unknown made the situation all the more challenging.

"And where will you be launching her, Monsieur le Comte? The first ensemble will, of course, be very important."

"I have given much thought to that and have decided in favor of the Opéra, instead of, say, the Moulin-Rouge, or even the Comédie Française. It has more grandeur, is more—remote. She will keep some mystery a little longer."

"An excellent choice. We will go, then, for a contrast. The untouchable simplicity of white—in keeping with her extreme youth—plus elaborate ornamentation and high style. Diamonds in her hair, not flowers, par exemple. Feathers on the gown, not ribbons. A fan of feathers, too. If she wears a corsage, make sure that it is an orchid or, possibly, a gardenia. For the Moulin-Rouge, I suggest the innocence of pink, with roses. And, for the Comédie Française, scarlet with black lace. The contrast will be devastating. For riding in the Bois, we sheathe her in dove-gray satin with accents of lilac."

She was examined from head to toe, spun round and round on the tips of fingers, measured and murmured over and marveled at by the cutters, the fitters, Doucet himself.

Back at the rue St.-Honoré, she collapsed onto a sofa, quite worn out. Who would have thought that being fitted for clothes could be such an exhausting affair? She was not sorry to hear that her white outfit would take quite a while to complete, even though work was to start on it that day. It gave her some respite before her first night. Violet's thoughts strayed momentarily to the gray-faced young girls, briefly glimpsed in a backroom, as they worked at their benches. Quickly, she whisked the image away. She had made her choices. Let them make theirs.

D'Aulnay absented himself from her apartment that afternoon and late into the evening on "family matters." He had to visit his home, deal with some financial affairs. Marie, her new maid, unlaced her, bathed her forehead and prepared a tisane that Violet found very soothing. Finally, she drifted off to sleep on the great, soft bed, swathed in the brocade coverlet.

When she awoke, it was quite dark, apart from a faint light burning in a hanging lantern of faceted, colored crystals. Michel's face was above hers and, as her eyes opened, his mouth came down hard on her lips, his moustache bruising her skin.

"Close your eyes again."

She felt the coverlet pulled back, her limbs straightened. He was laying objects of some kind which were light in weight, but cool and hard, against her neck, her arms and her breasts, balanced in the navel of her belly, in the warm cleft between her thighs. His fingers lingered in each place, and she moaned lightly, wanting him.

"Lie still. You can open your eyes now."

She was looking up at herself in the mirror overhead, spread-eagled on the bed, naked. Naked, that is, except for a king's ransom in jewels that covered the warm translucence of her skin with their incredible fire.

Black pearls around her neck, deepening the color of her eyes, creaming the skin by contrast. Magnificent emeralds over her breasts, a long string of rosy pearls winding down her arms. One enormous diamond in her navel, which was the center stone in the superb necklace that stretched along her waist. And, glimpsed in the secret, dark cleft of her body, the burning spendor of a giant ruby.

This d'Aulnay removed first, to reveal the gold band of the ring to which it was attached. He kissed where it had been, picked up her hand and put the ruby on.

"A sample of what I will adorn you with, *chérie."*

"Michel—what can I say? They're—oh, they're more than I can say. You must be very rich."

"Yes, I am. Some of these I bought for you at Cartier this afternoon. Some are in the family. Now, we make love."

Afterward, they played more slowly with each other and the gems, watching the light catching their brilliance in the mirrored ceiling above them.

The next day, a woman came to the house to give her a massage, exclaiming all the while at the perfection of her client's body. She manicured Violet's nails to perfect, pointed ovals and buffed them pink. She arched her eyebrows to give a more startled and feline look to her violet cat's eyes. As she left, Violet heard her congratulating Monsieur le Comte on his magnificent conquest.

Yes, she supposed that was what she was, but she felt more like a conqueror, with her spoils around her. All that lay ahead was to take Paris by storm and, with these weapons at her disposal, she did not see how she could fail. One thing that she had to do herself was to work at her French, so that she could communicate with this new world.

She made Marie speak French to her. Marie could not read, so Violet persuaded Michel to read to her, pointing out the words and correcting her accent as she said them.

There was a vogue at that moment for mildly erotic novels, written, in many cases, by the women in whose company Violet now belonged. Michel brought some to her and, together, they read and translated into action many of the scenes.

In this way, the days passed until Doucet's designs were ready for her.

On the morning of the day she was to make her debut at the Opéra, d'Aulnay arrived, newspaper under his arm, vibrating with excitement. "Look, Violette! It could not be going better, if I had planned this part of it myself."

He unfolded the paper, pulled her down on the sofa beside him and read:

> The new mystery that everyone is talking about—who is it that le Comte d'Aulnay visits so frequently in the rue St.-Honoré, and with whom he spends so many of his nights? Who is the mysterious woman with whom he has been seen to leave this apartment, to visit the great Doucet?

For whom did he buy a magnificent parure of diamonds at Cartier's? Why does he hide his unknown companion in the depths of an anonymous carriage, forsaking his own equipage? Our perspicacious reporter has done her best to uncover the identity of this lady of mystery and will continue to do so, until we can put her name on these pages for you, our faithful readers."

Violet took the sheet from his hands and followed the words. She could pick out without difficulty "*femme mystérieuse*" and said it aloud.

She had become "*une femme mystérieuse.*" In a newspaper, in Paris, someone was talking about her. Someone wanted to know who she was.

"And that," said d'Aulnay. "is nothing. By tomorrow, Violette, your name will be on everyone's lips, and you will see it on the printed page. It has all begun."

Paris by night. The first time that she had seen it, really. A vault of clear, cold sky over the magnificent facade of the Opéra and the throng of carriages on the boulevards leading to it. She felt no fear, no stage fright. She longed to show them who the mysterious woman was, how beautiful she was. For she had taken her own breath away when she had seen herself as Doucet's creation in the mirror: white silk tussore clinging to the exaggerated laced curves of her body, her beautiful shoulders bared but edged with a riot of ruffles and feathers that dipped in the middle so that the soft down of the feathers tickled the valley between her breasts. The skirt was trimmed with a flounce of ruffles and the whole was embroidered with seed pearls. She wore diamonds on her neck and in her ears, and her hair was dressed up with a network of diamonds and feathers. For the journey she was totally wrapped in glorious white fox, from her chin to her toes.

D'Aulnay was elated.

"Doucet has excelled himself," he crowed. "It will be an entrée like no other."

Entrances like no other can only be achieved if the human factor is like no other; they cannot occur on the strength of beautiful clothes alone. D'Aulnay knew that, knew that the unknown quantity was Violet. This "unknown companion" of his would have to achieve a great deal of the success herself. He looked at Violet as she looked at herself in the long mirrors and knew that he had, indeed, found himself a star.

They descended from the landau—his own, this time, with the coat-of-arms on the door—and it seemed to him as if all eyes were on his young, white-clad love goddess. As she moved, the eyes followed her. Violet had perfected a walk that suggested with every step the free, firm, undulating body beneath the restricting whalebone. She could move her legs against the fabric of a skirt in a way that seemed to make their long line obvious, all the way from the tiny ankle up to the bifurcation at the hip.

Many would try to copy it. Few, if any, would succeed. Talk of Violet's "allure"—*l'allure de la Violette anglaise*—which, in French means so much more than just attraction, but the whole comportment, behavior, the sum of a human being, would use up much ink on the gossip sheets in the years to come.

That night, at the Opéra, when she unveiled that walk for the world, she started to create her legend.

When she removed the encompassing fox furs, standing near the front of their loge at the theater, she did so with such voluptuousness, such a consciousness of the body beneath, that men imagined the undressing of Violet—as if she would soon remove all, as if this were a sort of promise of more. Thus, sang the society sheets, the gossip columns, the boulevardiers, must Salome have removed her veils for Herod, to get a man's head on a platter. To have all men at her mercy.

As she looked into the eyes of the men and women who looked at her, Violet knew she was where she had always intended she should be.

In that moment, as she looked down from the box and the curtains on stage drew back, she thought of Peridot. Peridot, the only "have" she had ever really known. And loved. At that moment, she wished Peridot were here with her, or could see her. If Perry did not entirely understand her dream, she would still rejoice that it had all come to pass for her. Violet wanted someone to feel glad for her. The moment of arrival was not quite what it should be without another human being there who shared it with the little creature, Violet Cartwright, who still lived under all these trappings. And the only one who had shared those dreams was Peridot.

At that moment, Violet decided to try to write to Perry, to share her triumph. She suddenly wanted to know what Perry's life was like, what was happening to her. In her present apparent security, she had the time to remember the feeling she had for her childhood friend.

She spared not one thought for Marcus Radcliffe. He simply did not enter her mind.

In the intervals and at the end of the performance,

she could hear the murmurs around her. Some, she understood.

"A true jewel—*un vrai bijou.*" "*Quelle femme!*" "That d'Aulnay, he has done it again."

With whom had he done it before, she wondered. And quickly banished the thought. Such must be the philosophy of her kind: live in the present, forget the past, ignore the future.

She really could not remember the performance or the players at all, but she did commit to memory the names of the people to whom she was introduced, for this inventory of names would be useful for her: Baron Armagnac, le Maréchal de Villiers, the Marquis de la Costa Grada. And then, the women—Liane de Pougy, la belle Otero—incredible, beautiful women, with a repertoire of wiles that Violet at once perceived as far beyond her own. Once her newness, her novelty, had gone, she had a great deal more to do if she were to surpass—not just equal—these legendary lionesses.

Her French still let her down; there was a lot of work to be done there. She grasped the gist of the conversation, but could only manage short and faltering replies, which she imbued with a detached and mysterious quality, hiding her inadequacies behind a display of youthful innocence and her feathered fan. The latter was a barrier that enabled her to use her eyes and to watch, watch, watch: who were rivals, who loved whom, which people mattered.

One conversation she did have. A very tall, willowy woman, with strikingly pale hair and dark eyebrows, dressed in a deep blue that emphasized the color of her piercing eyes, bore down upon them, with a much smaller man in tow.

"Michel! Where have you been hiding? Introduce

me to the mysterious lady friend who has kept you out of circulation so long!"

D'Aulnay seemed amused and delighted to see her.

"Elise, I would be charmed to introduce you to Violette, my companion." Almost as an afterthought, he added, "Oh, and this is the Duc de Malvert, my dear."

The tall blond woman examined Violet from head to toe with unabashed frankness. "Charming, dear Michel, but has she no last name?"

"Unpronouncably English, *chérie.*"

"Ah! *Elle est anglaise.*"

"Yes. One might almost call her Violette l'Anglaise. Simpler, I feel."

Thus, through means of a careful introduction to one of Gil Blas's chief informants, a christening took place.

Elise Damien was approaching thirty—a milestone that most women in her milieu found frightening. She was not unmoved by the rush of time, but had taken care to exploit her other talents, one of which was writing. She provided columns and information for a couple of the more popular papers and had even written two or three novels of the type that Violet and Michel had read together. The Duc de Malvert was said to be devoted to her and had been so for a number of years.

Elise had tempered devotion with common sense by salting away many of her jewels and cash gifts in a private vault in a Paris bank, the existence of which was known only to a very few.

In the early years of her career, she had had extended exposure—of many kinds—to members of the English nobility and had retained a knowledge of their language, since most of them had made little effort to speak hers. Besides, it was another skill that could be useful at any time.

She addressed Violet in English, and the two women talked animatedly together, each examining the other carefully all the while, as rivals in any profession generally will.

There was, however, something about this woman that appealed to Violet. There was a strength, a gutsiness about her, a warmth in her manner. It could also have been that she was fair and tall, like Peridot. There, however, any resemblance ended. Elise had no more to do with Peridot than this visit to the Opéra had to do with musical appreciation.

They said their farewells—for Michel had turned down all offers to dine or to go on to any cabarets—with promises from Elise to call on Violet. The thought pleased Violet.

"Do you mind if Elise Damien visits me?" she said to d'Aulnay in the carriage, as they returned to the rue St.-Honoré.

He was still reverberating with pleasure, expansive at the success of their debut together.

"*Pas du tout*. She is a clever woman, that one. She can teach you much. But keep in mind—she uses her eyes and ears for money, too. Anything worth selling, and all Paris will read about it the day after you tell her. Just remember that, if you tell her anything. But remember also that there is nothing wrong with the right piece of information, carefully placed."

In this half-world, thought Violet, one appears to live on love and dreams, and sentiment and flowers. But it is all as meticulously planned as my dad's vegetable garden: which would come up before what,

what needed shade, which needed sun. The unseen calculations behind the beautiful, finished result. Nothing left to chance.

Yet chance had a nasty way of creating its own situations, as Violet knew well. Unless, of course, one loaded the dice. I will load mine, thought Violet, load them so they do what I want. I will make sure that I throw sixes forever.

Her new life had begun in earnest. D'Aulnay would spend a varying number of hours each day with her, many of them under the damask canopy, departing for his other home when he felt like it. In between, she was left on her own. On her own, that is, except for a small staff of servants, who never questioned her way of life, did what she told them to, and were visible only when necessary.

After that first evening, she lay in bed awake for a long time, on her own, and watched the dawn filter slowly through the shutters, hearing the sound of the rest of the world outside starting to go about its business again. Finally she slept, until Marie brought her in hot chocolate and biscuits in the middle of the day, and a note, written in English. It was from Elise Damien, asking if she could visit her that week.

Violet's spirits lifted, a fact that she observed with surprise. She had not even realized, before, that she was lonely. Marie brought her pen and paper, and she immediately wrote a reply, to be sent to Elise's town house near the boulevard Malesherbes.

That night, she and d'Aulnay dined at the Moulin Rouge restaurant in the Chaussée d' Antin, and then went on to the show itself. With that and similar festivities on successive evenings, she passed the first glorious week of her French début: gasping at the belly dancers, the elaborate stage sets, the risqué songs, the dancing of la Goulue; and being gasped at, whether she wore her froth of pink with ribbons of satin, and real rosebuds, the giant ruby on her finger, rosy pearls at her throat, or her wicked-woman outfit of scarlet and black, black pearls circling her slim throat.

After the night at the Moulin Rouge, she showed d'Aulnay how well she had begun to master the art of belly dancing, fascinated as she was by its uninhibited sensuality. The effect on him was such that he stayed all night with her, leaving only at noon the following day. Late that afternoon, an exquisitely decorated piano was delivered to her apartment. When she opened the lid, she found a sapphire and diamond brooch, attached to a note that read:

> "Chère Violette, so that you may learn to play and sing the songs of Yvette, as well as you dance the dances of the Moulin Rouge."

Perhaps her most favorite visit of all was to the Nouveau Cirque, where she became a child again, laughing at the antics of Footit and Chocolat, adoring the unabashed vulgarity of the costumes, the vitality of the atmosphere. The language barrier mattered little here.

Like some nocturnal creature, she had known Paris only during the hours of darkness. One afternoon, however, d'Aulnay took her to visit the Jardin des Plantes. It was cold, but dry and sunny, and she felt happier than she ever had before, she was sure. Swathed in a long chinchilla stole and encased in a dark green wool serge street dress, she felt the warm sun on her face and breathed in the cool, fresh air.

Entranced by the exotic foliage, the wonderfully strange wild animals that she had never seen before, she felt the cloud of—she wasn't sure quite what—lifting from her, and her full, bubbling gaiety returned, springing from a source deep inside herself. With Michel's arm around her in the carriage going home and the sound of affectionate laughter, rather than lust, in his voice, she felt secure.

Curling her arm around his neck, she turned and kissed him hard and long on the mouth, with a love that she had tried to suppress over the past few weeks. He was so good to her, so loving to her, why should she deny herself the luxury of loving him from the heart?

The following week, Elise Damien arrived for her promised visit, in the afternoon. Marie had advised Violet on what she should wear, what refreshments she should offer her first guest.

But there was really no need for concern. Elise Damien had not come to criticize, but to communicate. She adored new people, new experiences, as she told Violet.

"They help to stave off *ennui*—what you call 'boredom,' darling."

As Violet gleaned from the conversation that afternoon and over the course of her friendship with Elise, her background was unusual for a woman of her profession. She had opted for the life, rather than having it thrust upon her. This much, she and Violet had in common. Elise, however, was born into comfortable circumstances, of a family that was as well placed in the commercial world as the Heriot family, who owned the Grands Magasins du Louvre.

She had explored her budding sensuality while very young, when she had had an illegitimate child and had been rejected by her family for refusing to name her lover. He had been a close friend of her own father. An older brother who was a député (Violet gathered that this was a member of parliament) had taken pity on her and taken her into his home. There, she had formed a liaison with a senior government official, much older than herself, who had set her up in a little private house on the Plaine Monceau. He had died, leaving her some money. Elise had promptly moved on to aristocratic pastures.

"Could you not have married?" Violet asked her.

"Oh, my dear, I discovered long ago that I am a *fille de joie,* not a marrying woman."

Over tea, and cakes that Elise had brought with her from Rebattet's, the older woman skillfully pumped the girl about her own background, while talking of her own. Violet, forewarned by Michel, was well aware of what was happening and chose her snippets of information carefully. She played down her foster-family, played up the mystery of her birth: "My mother was very beautiful and died in childbed. My father was a lord." She spoke of her discovery "by a very intellectual gentleman, a *close* friend of the Prince of Wales" and her meeting with d'Aulnay.

When she mentioned d'Aulnay, Elise Damien looked up quickly, to catch the expression on the girl's face. She put down her teacup and put a long-boned, beringed hand on Violet's lap.

"*Attention, ma petite.* You break one of the few laws we have."

Violet looked at her in alarm. "Which is—?"

"Do not fall in love. Never, never fall in love too much. Oh—your count is a handsome, darling man;

very experienced, very attentive, very wealthy. Quite a catch. But let him remain that. Let him be the catch, not you. He is beautiful, but he is also a very naughty man."

Violet moved further away from Elise on the sofa, eyes sparkling with annoyance, her spine rigid. "I wish to hear no criticism of Michel. What is in his past, is in his past. I live only for the present. I do not wish to look back."

The other woman sighed. "Oh, you are right, so right. That should be your philosophy. But never, never ignore the future. It is our great enemy. Plan for it, be prepared for it. Do not let circumstances ever catch you unawares."

She changed the subject abruptly.

"The beautiful jewels you have worn the past week—they are yours? His family's?"

"Some he bought for me. The emeralds and some of the pearls are his family's, I think."

"Then, those you must view as only on loan. Take my advice, whatever money he gives you—and he will have to give you some soon, for he cannot always go with you to the couturier's, or pay for every carriage and food bill and servant's wages—put as much of it away as you can. Always ask for a little more than you need, for he is a gentleman, and will never query the amount."

"You feel that I really need to do this?"

"Oh, my dear, you may not. But—every love nest, however perfect, needs a nest egg. I can recommend you to a bank here in Paris with the most discreet and charming manager. If you mention my name, he will be only too happy to help you. Oh, and when the profusion of jewelry becomes such that he will not notice the disappearance of the odd brooch or ring—put them away, too. Besides, why lay too much temptation in the way of your servants? Profusion leads to petty thievery. I know."

A struggle between loving trust and practicality was going on in Violet's mind. In the end, the memory of her childhood made practicality win. Besides, had not Michel himself said that Elise was a woman whose advice was worth taking?

"When can we go to your bank? I have a lot of money that I was given yesterday. Also, I did not like two of the hats from the milliners that came today and I intended to exchange them, but I will send them back instead. Michel will never notice."

Elise approved of the speed of Violet's decision.

"Splendid! It will do to open your account. I can take you there the day after tomorrow, if you like. Tell Michel that I am taking you to visit a new shoemaker I have discovered—we will do that, too. He will agree, I am sure."

Linked now by a feeling of conspiracy, they laughed together, and Violet put her guilt behind her.

Elise jumped up, unfolding the long length of her like a jack-in-the-box.

"Tiens! Something else that might interest you. It is another form of investment, if you like, but one out of which I get so much pleasure. Ask your maid to bring us the flat package that I left in the hall when I arrived."

Marie duly brought in a large, rectangular package tied, with no thought of decoration, in plain paper and string. Elise laid it carefully on the table before them and opened it.

It was a painting of a commedia dell'arte Harlequin. Violet recognized the costume from some books of Marcus's that she had leafed through in London. The style in which it was painted, however—that was something the like of which she had not seen before.

The background was in blues and oranges, with strange daubs of color that looked, at first, as if they had been accidentally dropped on the surface of the work. The Harlequin himself, however, fairly shot off the painted surface as his eyes stared sadly and cynically into hers. He was flat and yet not flat. His hands and fingers seemed incorrect, and yet the distortion caught the attention as no perfect likeness could have done.

"What do you think of it?"

Violet said, slowly, "Strange. I haven't seen anything before like this. It is sad, and strong. I like it better than trees that look like trees and brooks that look like running water. But then, I hate the country. He's from the theater, isn't he?"

"Indeed he is. And he is different—the painter, I mean. They call him the wild man. Cézanne. There are quite a few of them. Impressionists. They laugh at this man's talent, most of the people I know. But listen to me, little Violet. Buy him. Buy Manet, the others. I will show you how and where."

There was something about the sharing of the painting that seemed like a sharing of Elise's soul. Violet's eyes filled with unaccustomed tears.

"You are kind."

Elise turned from the painting of the sad harlequin to the emotional Columbine by her side. "I like you. You're a fighter. Do not think that I will write of this part of our conversation. It is between you and me. And I would never tell Michel anything that you did not wish him to know. I would never tell a man what a woman told me. Mostly, I tell on the men."

"Why?"

"It is women who are important to me, a discovery I have made in the last few years. Men are a necessity, but women are a luxury without which I would not want to live."

Elise seemed about to say something, but abruptly changed her mind. "You like the little harlequin? Well, the wild man is painting another. He told me so. I will get it for you. It will not be quite the same as mine, because the harlequin changes as the man changes. The same, but different."

"Peridot would like that. She would understand that."

Elise looked up from rewrapping the canvas in its rough covering. "Peridot? She is a close friend?"

"She was my only friend," said Violet simply. "As I was hers. I haven't seen her for—oh, ever so long. Maybe two years now. But she will always be my special friend. I love her."

Impetuously, Elise clasped the girl's hands. "*Merveilleux*. You will understand, then, will understand when I tell you that it is women whom I really love, would never betray. I care for them—*passionnément*. I sleep with men because it is my profession. It is how I live. No—'exist' is a better word. It is for women I *live*."

For all the sexual knowledge that Violet had acquired at a precocious age amid the uncomplicated basics of farm and village life, she had never seen or heard of the love that dares not speak its name. It had not arisen in her brief exposure to upper-class life in England, under Marcus's protection, and the Oscar Wilde scandal had passed her by. It had never occurred to her that her looks would be of any interest to a woman—except as a possible rival—and she had never been approached by one. It was men who had laid siege to her from an early age.

"I sleep with men because I like it, because it was a good way to get where I wanted to be in the world. And I love Peridot, and will have, I hope, other women as friends. But I don't understand what it is you're saying."

Elise threw out her arms in amazement and amusement. "Oh, Violette, you are so charming, so innocent. You must drive d'Aulnay wild with desire. From your instincts, you know so much. And yet, of the world you know so little."

Elise hesitated, then looked straight at Violet.

"What I have to do with men, I love to do with women. That is why I am happy with my Duc. His drives are not—excessive. Mostly, he wants to be cuddled, to feel secure. He was so starved of affection as a child. I am like his mother. I satisfy my other needs elsewhere."

Horror. Shock. That was Violet's first reaction. And to think that this *wicked* woman thought that she and Peridot—oh, no, it was too much! She withdrew physically from Elise, recoiling as far from her as she could go on the couch.

"How could you think that Perry—she was my *friend*. You don't do—that—with *friends!*"

Elise did not try to approach her. There was a sadness in the dark, blue eyes, as she felt the other woman's rejection and disgust.

"Men are not friends, then?"

"Oh, no! They are, well, men. They are lovers, or husbands, or brothers."

Elise smiled, a hard rictus of a smile that did not

reach the eyes. "Then we are not as far apart as you think. We are only separated by one act. And I know that, for me, it is not the most important part of my feelings for other women. You have your friendships. So do I, my '*amitiés particulières,*' as they are called here. They are my solace, my warmth, the light of my life."

Could a truly wicked woman say that, have feelings like that? A whole reevaluation of her instinctive reaction and feelings began to take place in Violet's head.

"There are others like you?"

Elise laughed quietly. "Oh, yes. I am not so special. There are many of us. We are very close, a society of our own. A world of our own in this demiworld."

She laughed again, with more amusement in the sound this time. "*Chère petite* Violette, do not huddle so against the arm of the sofa. I will not touch you, you know, force myself upon you. Don't you understand? That would be to force upon you the very bondage we wish to avoid in our friendships. It is of our free will that some of us choose this way of loving. Many of my friends have been so terribly humiliated by men, so terribly subjugated. Why would a woman add to that coercion, that abasement?"

There was defiance, now, from Violet. "*I* am not forced to do this. I *want* to."

She stood up and swung around the room, touching the gleaming furniture, the priceless ornaments.

"I love it here. I love making love with Michel, and he loves it with me. I love going out to dinner, to the theater, not having to take care of anything I don't want to take care of. If this is humiliation, then—let it go on and on!"

It was like a clarion call ringing out from the soft, red mouth, the remembrance of her feelings of sensuality for d'Aulnay bringing a flush to her cheeks.

"Long may it last, little one. Long may it last. You will be much happier in this life if you really feel this way. It is better so."

Then, she clapped her hands abruptly. "Let us change the subject. You still wish to buy shoes, visit my bank with me—perhaps, visit me? Or are you now afraid of me?" She said this, smiling wickedly at Violet, who started to laugh.

"Elise, I am afraid of no one. Of course I would like to do all those things."

"*Bon*. Then it is settled. Tell Michel and send me a note when it is convenient."

As Elise pulled on her long gloves, preparing to leave, she turned to Violet and said, "Listen, *ma petite*. I may have led you astray. Not all these women will be your friends. Some of them would steal your man and slit your throat at the drop of a petticoat. Always remember that. Reserve your judgment for a long, long while. Even make reservations about my judgment, until you can form your own. Sometimes, I am led astray by those—particular—feelings of which I spoke."

Violet's answer reflected a wisdom that Elise Damien realized she had seriously underestimated. "I will, Elise. I think I am probably less trusting, in many ways, than you are. You see, I have come from farther down the line than you and still have some distance to go. I intend to get there in one piece."

That night, as Violet and d'Aulnay dined together at Maxim's—Violet in violet shot silk, a new solitaire on her finger—Michel said to her, "Well, did

Elise Damien teach you many things? Were you careful in what you chose to say to her?"

Violet's smile was worthy of the Mona Lisa. "Oh, yes, Michel, I learned a great deal. And I think she told me more than I told her. She opened up a whole new world to me."

And as d'Aulnay chuckled and patted her hand, saying, "Wonderful, wonderful," Violet had a little giggle inside at his probable outrage if he knew the particular field of human experience that Elise Damien had tried—however lightly—to introduce her to.

Through the enthusiastic gossip of Elise and the careful planning of Michel, "Violette l'Anglaise" became a name as well-known as any other in their milieu. Her circle of acquaintances grew and, at the same time, so did her command of French. Her occasional idiomatic and grammatical errors and her accent only added to the charm and seductive quality of what she had to say.

While her star gained the ascendant, she had no fear of losing d'Aulnay, for an object coveted by others is always much desired. And desire her he did. Violet had become too skillful to allow familiarity to breed contempt, and there was nothing haphazard about her journey through this world she had chosen. She learned, as none of his other mistresses had learned, the secret springs, the trigger points of d'Aulnay's particular erotic fantasies and sexual desires, and she wielded these weapons with unerring skill in the battle to hold him to her.

And battle it was. There were many rivals for his money and his looks, and Michel always liked something new and fresh. Or new and corrupt.

There was the night of the apache dancer. She appeared one night while they were slumming at the Moulin de la Galette. Not a stage version of those street fighters of the Paris netherworld, but the woman of a real apache, dancing onstage. Her man stood and watched her by the side of the stage, in his peak cap, tight-fitting trousers, his hair in side-burns down his swarthy cheeks.

The girl was gypsylike and rather dirty. But in her narrow, shiny silk skirt, which she lifted to put the money that was thrown to her in the tops of her stockings, she exuded an animal carnality that had nothing to do with frills and ruffles and corsets of whalebone. She danced like a dervish and shook her loose breasts and magnificent buttocks practically in d'Aulnay's face. When she allowed him to put the money he offered in the tops of her stockings himself, there were roars of approval from the crowd.

Violet felt a seething hatred unlike anything she had ever known before, which frightened her almost as much as the fear of losing Michel. She might not lose him to one night—or one hour—with this slut, but the dancer represented all the fears Violet had to contend with.

So Violet did the only thing that she could. She found just enough strength to smile and watch what was happening and appear amused and untouched by it. She did not compete with the apache girl's raw eroticism. She became more of a lady, more encased within her whalebone than ever before.

At the end of the performance, the crowd danced in the two giant sheds constructed around the two old windmills. D'Aulnay partnered the girl, his eyes glued to the enormous breasts that pressed against him. In her seat, Violet saw the eyes of the girl's apache turn to her. She crooked a finger at him, and he came over.

"Can you dance, monsieur?"

"Better than the girl."

"Then dance with me."

It had been no idle boast. He was, indeed, a superb dancer, better than any man she had ever danced with. Violet momentarily forgot her anguish in the beautiful, fluid movement with which he guided the two of them around the floor together. He held her very close and transmitted his movements to her by the pivoting of his hips against her pelvis.

The tension went out of her, and she remembered again the joy of moving her body rhythmically, athletically. Running, jumping, skipping—these were all pleasures lost to her and for which she had once had a talent.

The apache sensed a change in her and responded by sweeping her around the room, as the couples stood back and let them pass.

"*Tiens,* madame! You dance well for a lady!"

"I am no lady, monsieur. I am no better than you, no worse."

He laughed, revealing his far from perfect teeth. "You do not mind if my *poule* takes your man for a *miché?"*

"Why should I? It is her business. Let him be her client. He will pay well."

"And you, madame?"

She laughed, seeing a source of irritation for Michel that she could tap, for she knew that she was being watched. "I need no business of that kind. I am already in the trade, but I will pay you well for dancing. You have truly a gift for it. Here—"

An idea had occurred to her. It would probably

mean the apache girl would lose her *miché* but—*tant pis*. She would pay this man well instead. She pulled slightly away from him, indicating a small silver mesh purse, tucked into her wide sash. He pulled it out for her, and she opened it, extracting all the money in it.

"Tuck it back into my belt, and I will put all this into your beautiful tight trousers."

Holding the coins up with the hand that was over his shoulder, she exerted all the magnetism in her brilliant eyes. "Do a working girl a favor, monsieur. Move us toward my man, so that your right side faces him."

The apache grinned and, with a swift tack, changed course toward Michel and his girl. As they drew parallel, Violet brought her hand down from his shoulder, caressing his arm all the way. She then felt for the side pocket in the tight pants and, slowly, very slowly, pushed her hand with the money inside. She allowed it to linger there for a moment, watching her partner's shaggy eyebrows shoot up under his peaked cap, with the contact of her fingers.

"*Faites attention, mam'selle.* You could bite off more than you can chew."

Deliberately, she looked into his eyes and bared her sharp little teeth at him. "As you can see, m'sieu, I could chew almost anything you cared to show me."

Before the apache could respond to her audacity, there was a disturbance in the surrounding dancers, and d'Aulnay shot through them and between Violet and her partner, nearly knocking them both over.

"Get your hands off the lady!"

The apache protested, "But, m'sieu, it was the lady who had her hands all over me!" Shrugging his shoulders, he added, "Not that I objected. It felt very good."

A motley crowd of apaches, manual workers, shopgirls, and the group that d'Aulnay and Violet had come with had gathered around, and they broke into laughter at this riposte.

D'Aulnay went white with rage, his eyes glittering black in his pale face. He brought up his fists at the apache, who made a movement so swift that the knife seemed to materialize in his hands.

There was a murmur of fear and anticipation from the crowd, and they stepped back, leaving the two combatants in a natural arena on the rough dance floor. None of Michel's friends tried to interfere. Some, indeed, deciding that discretion was the better part of valor, were making a hasty exit from the room.

The apache was very still now, watching the count, the knife held ready in front of him. His woman had moved away from d'Aulnay behind her man, and from the look on her face, Violet knew that the apache was well able to protect himself with the knife.

"Don't risk it, m'sieu. You have a woman. I have a woman. *On n'a pas besoin de deux.*"

The crowd gathered round laughed again, began to take sides. They did not want to be cheated out of some free entertainment. Violet's pleasure in the situation had long since evaporated. It had got out of hand. She knew that Michel would not back down in front of those friends who had stayed behind, and that he carried no weapon. She had created this drama, she must put an end to it.

With a coolness that she did not feel inside, she walked between the two men, with her back very deliberately toward the apache's knife and facing Michel.

Undramatically, matter-of-factly, she said, "Michel, this is no longer amusing. I am bored. Take me home."

Je m'ennuie. I am bored. Magic words. So unfashionable to do something boring. So without style, so much to be feared. More to be feared than an apache knife.

She watched d'Aulnay put his fists down and shrug his shoulders. She took him by the arm and moved away toward their friends. The apache melted quickly into the crowd, into the shadows, taking his woman and his money with him.

They could leave without losing face now. She had made it the chic thing to do. Without a word to anyone, they made their way to their carriage that waited outside, with a coachman who was only too glad to leave such sinister and threatening surroundings.

Inside, huddled under the fur rugs, not talking, Violet listened to her driving heartbeat in the quiet, dark night. How she wanted to swear at him, shake him, hit him. Out of jealousy, relief, love. She remembered, however, her lessons. Calculate, always calculate.

With a flicker of a glance at him in the darkness, slumped there nursing his still injured pride—however much she had helped salvage it in the end—she gave a great, big sigh.

"Oh, Michel, what a lovely evening. One of the most fascinating evenings I have ever had. Such fun."

Flummoxed, he turned to look at her. No, she

wasn't laughing. She was staring up at the roof of the carriage, a blissful smile on her face.

As his eye caught hers, he started, helplessly, to laugh. "Violette, Violette, you are an outrageous, wicked girl. How can you make me laugh at a time like this, when my honor has been so damaged?"

She tutted and shook a finger at him. "What honor damaged? In a knife fight with some petty thief? It was beneath you, Michel. Where you wanted his woman to be."

She took care not to let jealousy creep into her answer and was rewarded by a slightly sheepish look.

"Not really. Merely *nostalgie de la boue.*"

"And what's *that,* when it's at 'ome?"

"Oh, an expression we have for what we did this evening. Seeking out the haunts of vice and corruption, of those lower than ourselves. Part of us is longing for it."

Violet shuddered. "Never me. That's what I came from, remember?"

However, she had stored up yet another piece of information about d'Aulnay and what excited him. She used it to good effect that night by regaling him in whispers in the scented semidarkness of the Moorish bedroom with exaggerated tales of her encounters with stableboys, footmen and farmhands in the imaginary fields and barns of her youth.

As if driven by a thousand demons from that mud he hankered after, d'Aulnay sated his desires upon her until, exhausted, he fell asleep in the early morning light.

Before he slept, he had murmured, "*Quand même,* if I had had my sword, that scum would have lost his sideburns and his masculinity, as well, for laying a finger on you!"

And Violet saw in her mind's eye the scars on his body and slept an uneasy sleep herself, disturbed by dreams of knives and satin skirts, and a man-demon hissing and crawling toward her and calling himself Mr. Krakatoa.

The apache episode reached the scandal sheets in various forms, d'Aulnay appearing as more heroic in some, less so in others, but Violet invariably featured as the star performer who "averted tragedy by her coolness and '*ses yeux violettes d'une beauté incomparable.*'"

D'Aulnay's pique was assuaged by the fact that he had more compliments showered on him for his ownership of Violet than he did remarks about his cowardice or lack of form. And no one described the incident as "in poor taste" or "boring."

One of the outstanding theatrical events of 1898 was the performance of Sarah Bernhardt as the youth in *Lorenzaccio*, with Lucien Guitry as one of her lead actors. It was given a lavish production, and everyone who was anyone was there. Which meant, of course, that le Comte d'Aulnay was in attendance with Violette l'Anglaise.

Whereas Violet had enjoyed the theater in London, it was as nothing compared with her response to *la divine* Sarah. She was always moved when she saw star quality in another woman, and she was thunderstruck by Bernhardt.

It was not merely idle admiration. She saw how skillfully Bernhardt used her remarkable voice and knew that here again was something she could work on. She persuaded Michel to take her frequently when Bernhardt was playing and would afterward practice the cadence of her own voice in the privacy of her apartment.

To be sure, Sarah could wind herself down a staircase like a serpent in the Garden of Eden, but Violet felt that she moved quite as well. No, it was the voice that she worked on now. What she actually said could take care of itself. The secret of success in this life was all in the way things were done, the appearance, the outer form.

In 1899, because she needed some money, Bernhardt again brought out and polished up *La Dame aux Camélias*. It was always a surefire success. Violet saw it again and again.

She would drive home afterward and say over and over to herself, "Oh, let me never fall in love like that. Let me never lose control. Self-sacrifice is so boring, so pointless. But when I die"—and she would surreptitiously touch the wood on the sides of the cabriolet or landau, or whatever she was in—"let it be like that. Pretty and poetic and—and with *style,* to the end."

And she would drive from her mind the tortured, ravaged face of her foster-mother and thoughts of the young girl whose own life had been lost in bringing Violet herself into the world.

Would she be proud of me? she wondered. She did not know.

"One thing is for sure. At least she wouldn't have to feel pity or sorrow over me. For I am so happy. So happy."

She would pull up the sables around her and hold out a be-ringed, pink-tipped hand in front of her, controlling the tremor that fluttered her fingertips in the air in front of her face.

She never saw Paris in the summer. It was always a cool, fur-clad city for her. At the end of June, she and Michel would leave for the Côte d'Azur, closing up their various establishments in town, but taking some of the servants with them.

There, on the palm-tree-studded slopes and between the bronze lamp standards, she and d'Aulnay would see and be seen. From their flower-decked balustrade, they would watch the flotillas of yachts in the bay. In the casinos of Cannes and Deauville, Violet would learn to play baccarat and trente-et-quarante. She would gamble away Michel's money to her heart's content, in a way totally at odds with her calculated, studied life.

As they moved back to Paris at the end of the prosperous, exuberant, extravagant decade that led into the twentieth century, there was a feeling of Indian summer in the air of the capital. War, or rumors of war, seemed far away, and it looked as if the new century would arrive in an atmosphere of peace and hope.

That, too, was Violet's mood. She had been with Michel, now, for almost two years, and she wanted for nothing. On the dawning of the new century, d'Aulnay gave her something beautiful and new for her collection of jewels: an exotic jewel-studded dragonfly brooch, which had been made by a man called René Lalique. It was her first piece of Art Nouveau, and she became instantly enamored of its swirling curves and intricate lines.

She bought herself a small, elaborate table lamp in the same style and, in complete contrast, a lush, but disjointed still life by Cézanne.

In the light of the Art Nouveau lamp, with the

painting propped in front of her, she finally sat down at her desk and wrote to Peridot.

It is hard to believe, *chère* Peridot, that the century that gave us birth and in which we had our shared childhood, is passing. I wonder about you, and I think about you, very often.

I am happy. Michel gives me all I want. I will tell you about Marcus Radcliffe some time, and more about my life. Why do you not come and see me? I am now looking at a painting that I have bought and that I think you would like.

Forgive me for writing in French, *chère* Peridot, *amie de mon enfance*. It is far better, now, than my English.

But then, my English was never very good, was it!

Has life been good to you? I pray so, for you were good to me and deserve good things, if any woman does.

Come and see me, Peridot *chérie*. There is good horseback riding and theater here, and we would amuse ourselves together so well.

Believe it or not, I think you would like some of my friends. They think you sound very interesting and *sympathique*. I understand you better now myself for having talked to them about you.

Mind you, I have no regrets. This is what I want, what I always wanted.

Ever with affectionate thoughts,

Your tender and loving, Violette l'Anglaise.

Do you like my name? Isn't it *amusing!*"

When she read it through afterward, her mind caught glimpses of that shared past of which she had written. Peridot, square and fair and ten years old, standing uncertainly on the other side of the stream, the great bulk of that magnificent old house framing her in the background beyond the sloping fields and terraces. Peridot's face, once she saw past the shaggy prettiness of the hollyhocks outside and the quaintness of the thatched roof to the inside of Violet's own home. Peridot, glowing and handsome in the warm humidity of the greenhouse, Radcliffe at her side.

As this scene shifted into focus, Violet felt a pricking behind the eyes. I am tired, she thought. So unhealthy, to sit thinking late at night. So unhealthy to think at all, sometimes.

She swiveled round in her chair and filled her eyes with the silk-paneled walls, the satin-upholstered furniture, the greenery glimpsed through the conservatory door, reestablishing in her mind all the solid, tangible, beautiful things in her perfect life.

Chapter Six

> Cuckoo-echoing, bell-swarmèd, lark-charmèd, rook-
> racked, river-rounded.

IT WAS TO A CITY that Peridot had pinned her thoughts and dreams. It became as magic as the poet's description of it. Her Avalon, her Utopia, a whole world, complete unto itself, toward which she was fighting with the sword of her mind, and Miss Boileau at her side: Oxford. And Somerville College.

Peridot was tempted sometimes to work all day and evening, never seeing what the weather was like outside her study window, whether the sun rose or whether it set.

However, "*Mens sana in corpore sano,*" said Miss Boileau. "Remember what the Greeks believed, Peridot, that the mind functions best in a healthy body. Besides, you would not want to become too narrow-minded. Narrow minds are prone to intellectual snobbery and bigotry."

So Peridot rode her horse, cycled, played tennis and learned to fence while she was in London. When she was sixteen, she went on a walking tour in the Lake District with Miss Boileau and would remember it as one of the happiest times of her life. Her thoughts were clear, unfettered and content.

There was time to think of Violet. Whenever she wanted to share a thought and Miss Boileau would not do, the laughter of a dark-haired girl briefly glimpsed in their Lake District boarding house, the walk by the river at Brierley Park, brought Violet to mind. There was some sadness in remembering her, but she knew that Violet was, indeed, following her own chosen destiny, so why should Peridot grieve for her? Besides, Peridot was increasingly busy mapping out her own route to happiness.

It was Terence who brought her the first news of Violet in her new life. He had been out with a group of friends to the Lyceum during the winter of 1897, and, after he returned home, he had gone straight up to Peridot's room and knocked on the door. She was wakened from a sound sleep to hear him whispering through the keyhole.

"Quick, Perry! I've something very important to tell you. It's Terence!"

Hastily pulling on a wrapper, she went and opened the door.

He looked incongruous standing there, top hat in hand, his tailcoat unbuttoned, his hair dishevelled.

"What are you doing, Terence? It's three o'clock in the morning."

He pushed into the room and closed the door, then took her by the arm and sat her in a chair by the dying embers of the fire. "Let's sit, for I am just a bit squiffy, dear girl. You will never guess who I saw tonight!"

"The Prince of Wales."

"Lord, one sees old tum-tum all the time. No, much more interesting. Violet."

Peridot shot out of her chair with a cry and was hushed by her brother.

"Shh! I don't want Mama coming down and finding me like this."

"Are you sure?"

"Positively certain. I'd know those eyes anywhere. Even dressed as she was, I couldn't be wrong about Violet."

"Did she see you? How was she dressed?"

"In frills and furbelows, dear sister of mine, that almost certainly came from Paris. My companions commented on her, and the ladies said it was so—her dress, I mean. As to your first question—no, she didn't see me. She had eyes only for the gentleman she was with. And you'll never guess who *he* was!"

"Marcus Radcliffe."

Terence looked taken aback. "Right first time. From the way it looked to me, she was *acting* adoring, and *he* is totally besotted."

"Poor Mr. Radcliffe. And to think that I feared he would be a Krakatoa and was worried for Violet."

"Be a *what?*"

"It's just a joke Violet and I had," said Peridot wearily, "and it would take too long to explain. I think you are too tipsy to take in too much, anyway. Really, Terence, you shouldn't drink so much."

"Oh, fiddlesticks," said Terence, yawning and getting out of the chair opposite her. "Everyone does it, little protected sister of mine. We call this the naughty nineties, you know."

"A very suitable description for the sort of childish nonsense that you and your friends indulge in."

Terence grinned at her. "Perry, don't be such a little prig. Remember, your precious Violet is indulging in it, too. Aren't you just the least bit jealous of her?"

Peridot looked up at the bleary young face of her brother. "Believe it or not, Terence, I wouldn't be Violet for anything in this world."

The summer before she went up to Oxford—for she had passed the examination, giving her and Miss Boileau a great, shared joy—Peridot made her first visit to the Continent. She went accompanied by her parents and Miss Boileau, for whom she was more delighted than she was for herself. She was sure it was her father's doing, for he had developed a strong admiration for her governess.

Through Sir Rodney's good offices and her success with Peridot, Miss Boileau would be tutoring the twin son and daughter of close friends of the Sinclair family for their entrance to Oxford. For the son, it was a foregone conclusion, given his family's position, but ill health had meant his not returning to Eton for the coming year and Miss Boileau's services were therefore required.

Peridot ached when she thought of parting from her governess, but she knew that things had turned out well from Miss Boileau's point of view. She was, in fact, moving into a far more intellectual household and would therefore, be happy and valued.

Their tour of the Continent was concentrated, hectic and mind-boggling. Miss Boileau and her parents had worked out an itinerary that would have given intellectual indigestion to the toughest academic. They appeared to cover every major cultural achievement of four European countries in a frenzied sweep that Peridot found breathtakingly superficial. However, she did not let it concern her too much. Miss Boileau was ecstatically happy.

On the boat going home at the end of the summer, she, her father and Miss Boileau stood together at the rail and watched the coast of France fade into the mist. Miss Boileau turned to Sir Rodney.

"I never in my life," she said, "thought that I would see St. Peter's in Rome, Mozart's birthplace, the Arc de Triomphe. I cannot thank you enough for this gift."

There were tears in her eyes as she spoke.

A revelation, then, for Peridot, as she heard her unimaginative, narrow-minded father stumble over the few words of his response. "It was a pleasure, Miss Boileau, a pleasure. And now"—he cleared his throat and turned from the rail—"I had better go below and see if Lady Sinclair has her customary seasickness yet."

Peridot watched him vigorously blowing his nose as he walked off into the distance.

How I oversimplify people, she thought. They are really much more complex than I give them credit for. I must try to remember that.

As they stood together on the Belgravia doorstep, waiting for the cab that would take Miss Boileau and her few belongings to her new home, they said pointless, unimportant things, laughed awkwardly together. Suddenly, Peridot wanted desperately to say something worthwhile, something that would let this woman know how incredibly important she had been in her life.

"Miss Boileau," she said, struggling to retain control of her voice, "I have wondered, sometimes, if there is a plan to things, or if it was just chance that brought you to me when I was a little girl." Her voice faltered.

A brisk wind blew around the corner of the street, carrying an early fallen leaf between them. She put up a hand and touched Peridot's cheek.

"Hush, child. I have been a very lucky woman."

The cab had arrived, the luggage had been loaded and Miss Boileau had got inside, when the portly figure of Sir Rodney Sinclair emerged through the front door of the house and hurried down the steps toward them.

"Just a moment, driver," he called out, "I have something I wish to give to the lady."

The object was unwrapped, and he shoved it unceremoniously through the open door at her. "Here," he said, "saw you admiring them and thought you'd like one."

It was a small, alabaster jar, dating from the Roman Empire, that had been part of a private collection offered up for sale at a palace in Rome, when they had been there. They had all attended the sale preview of these art treasures, but Peridot had been unaware that her father had bought anything, let alone noticed Miss Boileau's reactions. Again, she was shaken by this revelation of an unguessed-at sensitivity, hidden beneath her father's bluff, Toby-jug exterior.

Miss Boileau sat in the cab, the little jar cradled in her hands, her head bowed as she looked at it, so the expression on her face could not be seen. As she looked up and opened her mouth to speak, Sir Rodney slammed the cab door shut.

"Well, come on, driver," he snapped at the bewildered cabbie, "can't stand here all day."

As the cab moved off, Annie Boileau leaned out of the window and called, "Write to me, Peridot!"

Sir Rodney turned almost angrily to his daughter."You heard what she said. And mind that you do."

As he went back up the steps to the house, she heard him muttering, "Played a damn good hand of Whist, too."

Peridot had thought about Oxford as the rainbow's end, the achieving of a dream. But for her it was to be a transitional period.

There were many firsts, of course. It was the first time in her life that she formed friendships with girls who were her equals and betters, who shared her enthusiasm for the things of the mind. It was the first time she had had to look after herself entirely. She had not realized before how much she relied for her day-to-day existence on the servant infrastructure over which her class ruled. The same structure existed at Oxford, but in a less elaborate form. Oxford also brought her her first exposure to males en masse, and in a relatively free atmosphere, although the two sexes were kept well apart.

What a revelation it was. Peridot had to agree with the celebrated bishop who had said that the universities were a sort of lunatic asylum for keeping young men out of mischief. It seemed that for most of the men the social advantages of Oxford far outweighed the academic. They talked a great deal, and discussed each other's papers, that was true, but they always seemed to be drunk whenever they did so.

The public school boy ruled supreme. The scholar, far from being respected for the intelligence that had got him there, was looked down upon. The scholar might be lower than the aristocrat, the 'tuft,' as he was called (a suitably silly name, she felt), but lower than all these was herself: the female. Women had their colleges, yes, but they were not really part of University society. They played no real part in the general social life. The males drank together, discussed together—and allowed the women to appear at Eights Week.

Peridot had little contact with the male world at Oxford. It was the norm of the female society which she joined. Many of the women with whom she was now associating would never marry.

It was the mind that flowered. The events of those years up to the end of the century that were so peripheral to Violet were fundamentally important to Peridot. She too went to Shaw's plays. It never occurred to her, as it had to Violet, that she resembled any of the women on the stage.

She visited the newly opened Tate Gallery, filed past the bier of Gladstone with thousands of others, went to hear Elgar's *Enigma Variations* at the Queen's Hall, dipped into the *History of Trade Unionism* by Sidney and Beatrice Webb. She read the first installments of Frazer's *Golden Bough*. She read the poetry in the *Yellow Book* and gazed, fascinated, somewhat horrified, at Beardsley's erotic drawings, with their decadent elegance.

She discussed the Fabian Society, the Marxist Social Democratic Foundation, and the Ibsen Club, where women smoked and talked about free love. She watched with dismay the events in South Africa.

So—while Violet did, Peridot talked. And talked and talked her way through to the ending of the century and of the second decade of her life. She was in a ferment of ideas, a seedbed of opinions. Her contacts were all intellectual and her friendships a kinship of ideas rather than an association with people. However, she had many acquaintances, unlike the lonely little girl who had loved Violet Cartwright.

Gradually, Violet slipped out of her mind, to be replaced by an intellectual passion for social reform. Peridot's nineties were far from naughty. They were nothing like the ones through which Violet had moved, and in which she now lived, in France.

Unlike France, Peridot's country moved into the twentieth century on a shock wave, with the outbreak of war in South Africa. It was difficult to talk coolly and academically of that week in December when casualty lists appeared with a thousand names on them and even women waited with men in the streets, to buy newspapers hot from the presses.

After pointless debate, the Astronomer Royal fixed the beginning of the twentieth century as January the first, 1900. And Peridot ceased to cogitate over how many angels could dance on the head of a pin and started to agitate about reality.

What should she do about the rest of her life—that was what it all boiled down to, really. She could stay at Oxford, taking a further degree, tutoring, teaching. She was, after all, still younger than most of the women up at Oxford, many of whom were in their late twenties. She could come back home and be presented at Court, which she had firmly resisted up to now. This was what her parents wanted. She had exams coming up, a few more months at Oxford and then, that was it.

Before she returned to Oxford for the spring term, Violet's letter arrived from France. It lay on the silver salver—still borne by the godlike Mr. Symes—among other letters for her from friends in the country and abroad, so the shock when she opened it was even greater.

It was so totally unlike her other correspondence, so totally Violet—albeit a French-speaking Violet—that she was knocked sideways. There were so many unanswered questions, so many reminders of the uncertain, half-formed girl she had been when Violet had been part of her life. She was suddenly reminded of whole areas of human exploration that she had closed off from herself up to now.

Curiosity, however, came first. What had happened to Mr. Radcliffe? Who was this count she spoke of? How could Violet feel that she understood her, Peridot, more thoroughly because of her association with a group of women who, surely, could have nothing in common with her?

To think of Violet writing French like this, Violet buying paintings! Somehow, she must find out more.

Over the next few weeks, she was struck by a longing for—she knew not what. She remembered again how her feelings had been stirred by Marcus Radcliffe, her sensual nature brought into consciousness by certain explicit conversations with Violet. As the winter passed into spring, the longing grew even stronger, and she threw herself more desperately into the enclosed intellectual world of Somerville, drawing the reassuring blanket of her daily routine around her.

She could still, however, feel the stirrings inside. It was not so simple as a case of the frustrations of spinsterhood—a subject of some amusement in Victorian society. It was far more complicated than that. There was greatness all around her: the town was full of names to conjure with in scientific and literary worlds, and Peridot was made more conscious of a feeling of inadequacy.

There was also the inescapable class structure around her. She worked at a Play Center for a while, in a poorer part of Oxford, and did hospital visiting on Sundays. It made her feel more of a dilettante, more aware of her wealth and advantages. She took a certain masochistic pleasure in joining a University society called "The Associated Prigs" and enjoyed poking guilty fun at her favored position.

Toward the end of that final Somerville summer, she sat in the window seat of her oriel-windowed room in the West Buildings and looked out on the privileged, independent—and yet protected—world she was about to leave.

Maybe I am only playing at being melancholy, she thought, like the droopy women in Burne-Jones paintings. Maybe I no longer truly feel anymore, and it is all in the mind. I am one big, convoluted brain, nothing more than curls and swirls of gray matter. Will I just wither away after all this? Her parents had resisted strenuously the idea of her continuing at Somerville. At least, her mother had, and her father had gone along with her. Teaching, after all, was for such as Miss Boileau.

On an impulse, she went over to the top drawer of her dressing table and extracted Violet's letter from a pile of correspondence from her parents and Miss Boileau. She had not replied to it. What was there to say, after all? Books, and lectures, and hockey—what could they mean to Violet?

To read it in these surroundings was to be made even more aware of the contrast in their lives. As she turned the paper over in her hands, a faint fragrance arose from it: patchouli, and gardenia, the secret emanations of a female fragrant with clothing from sachet-scented drawers and cedar closets, that had lain on satin-upholstered sofas and held a Havana-scented, India-spiced body in her arms.

The image hit her with all the force of a fist in the solar plexus, followed by a great wash of longing to see Violet. At least, that was what she presumed the longing was for. She folded the letter carefully and put it away in the drawer again, where its disturbing, exotic scent mingled with the carbolicky smell of her own handkerchiefs and stockings.

For her country, at least, things were going well. In February, Ladysmith was relieved and, in May, Mafeking. The mafficking spirit hit Great Britain, and then there was a slackening of interest in South Africa. The *Times* preened itself with phrases like, "Proud, tenacious, unconquered and unconquerable," or, "A glimpse of the fundamental grit of the breed."

Isadora Duncan danced her way through London—too much ahead of her time to be called a hit. Ruskin died. Life went on.

For Peridot, it temporarily stopped.

Summer for the Sinclairs that year was as it always had been: a brief visit to Brierley Park and a visit to Nice or Biarritz. The only addition was to take the waters somewhere. Aix-les-Bains, Lake Geneva, Baden-Baden. Having wanted not to have her daughter around for most of her childhood, Lady Sinclair now found her an indispensable companion. After all, what other purpose was there for an unmarried daughter over twenty?

It was a summer of boredom, torment and humiliation. To become respectful and obedient again in the manner of a small child, after her young womanhood at Oxford, was sheer torture. In her precious spare time, Peridot wrote to her friends, but found she had little to say. She still had not written to Violet and had heard no more. As they passed through Biarritz, Aix-les-Bains, a deserted summer Paris, she looked for her. She saw many women who looked as she imagined Violet now looked, but she never saw Violet herself.

She looked at the flirting eyes, the provocative bodies, the accomplished femininity of these females and then would go to her hotel bedroom and look at her pale, washed-out face in the mirror.

What else is there for me? she would wonder out loud to her reflection. I look like a spinster. It is what I was meant to be. And she would wonder also: why should that matter? Why should that seem—a belittlement?

She knew the answer, though. Oh, how well she knew it. It was not the lack of marriage that mattered, it was the carnal knowledge that went with it.

Violet, after all, was still a spinster—technically. And yet, who would call her that? It was a comic thought. The difference was—that she was a virgin and Violet was not. There, that was what mattered.

Oh, if only, she thought, if only I could find out what it is like, without any of the consequences.

All alone, in the silence of her room, she would

blush with horror at herself and turn away from witnessing the shameful creature who stood reflected in the glass.

They returned from the Continent directly to their London home, and her parents resumed their lives as they had done for the last quarter of a century. Terence was away with his regiment, of course, and it looked as if he would be sent to India. Only Peridot was left, and she was often included now in the invitations sent to her parents.

Life staggered on from one dinner party to the next card party; to afternoon visiting, leaving their calling cards with a corner turned down to show they had left them in person; or, far worse, finding someone actually at home with whom to share an unwanted cup of tea and interminable small talk.

Peridot felt her wonderfully stretched and expanded mind begin to shrink. She felt strangely old, because many of the people with whom she associated were twice her age. Most dangerous of all, instead of fighting against it, she began to accept it.

The *deus ex machina* that was to drive her out of this apathy came in a most unexpected form: her father.

They had arrived back, fairly late at night, from a particularly stuffy dinner party with old family friends. The friendship was mainly between her mother and the lady of the house, a woman somewhat older than Lady Sinclair, with an unmarried daughter of her own still at home.

"A much more interesting evening for you, dear," her mother had said. "There will be someone like yourself to talk to."

Someone like herself? Someone like she would be

in ten years time, perhaps, for the girl—or was she a woman; could one really call her a woman?—was about thirty. All the little lines in her face led downward, where the hopes and dreams of her young womanhood lay in pieces on the ground. And she herself lay groveling at the feet of her mama. "Yes, Mama," "Of course, Mama," "No, Mama." And fetched and carried and smiled timidly in the face of that terrible maternal contempt.

Her father did not even seem aware of her existence. He walked clean through this insubstantial ghost-daughter who stood in the path of his life, whose hungry eyes had not quite given up crying for recognition.

Peridot was frightened. She sat in her room, still dressed, and watched the fire burning, as if she could pull from this primal element the secret of what to do with her life.

There was a knock on the door and, without waiting for a reply, her father came in. He had on his slippers and a silk smoking jacket, but had obviously remained in his dressing room only long enough to don them before coming to speak to her.

"Papa! Is there some problem? Is Mama all right?"

At these innocuous questions, he went brick red and started to stutter at her, his hands clenching and unclenching in his rage, in his desire to express himself forcibly.

"Is Mama all right?" he mimicked her voice. "Is your mother all right? Of course she's all right. She will always be all right. Stop sounding like that pathetic clinging vine of a wet blanket of a girl tonight and start thinking about yourself. Look at you—slouching over there in that chair, moping around the house. Maybe I should've encouraged you to stay on at Oxford, but I allowed your mother to have her way, because I wasn't sure it was what you really wanted, either. However, I did not send you to that Somerville place so that you could sit around here and wait on your mother and grow old before my eyes. Good God, girl, I am beginning to think of you as—as— *mediocre!*" He spat it out as if the sound of the word would burn the inside of his mouth.

Oh, how right he was! She felt like crying on his shoulder, but she sensed that this would make him more apoplectic than ever. Instead, she pulled her spine upright in the chair and said simply, "I agree with you. What shall I do?"

As if deflated, everything about Sir Rodney subsided. The anger and the air went out of him, and he collapsed heavily into the chair opposite her.

"Should really make you do it yourself, but I know that's hard. Not too many precedents, are there, eh?"

He leaned across and patted her hand.

"Got you a job, how would that be?"

"A job?"

She could hardly believe what she was hearing."What sort of a job?"

"Friend of mine. Known him for years. We were at school together. Your mother doesn't like him, but then, she has no time for bachelors. Thinks they're an insult to her sex. One of these chaps who has corresponded with all sorts of writers and so on. Right up your street. Needs to catalogue his library, straighten out his papers. Wants to see you. Thought about it before, but that gel tonight finally decided me. Will you see him tomorrow?"

He sat there, looking absurdly pleased with himself, leaning forward toward her, hands on knees.

Then, she was smiling and laughing and hugging him, as she hadn't since she was a very small girl.

"Tell me more about him. He is about your age, I suppose? Where does he live? He knows about me?"

"Of course he knows about you. Your years at Oxford interest him, because you read English Language and Literature. Yes, he's my age, and he lives in Bayswater. Your mother doesn't approve of the area too much, but I like it. He looks over the Broad Walk and Kensington Gardens. It's—nice."

This was the highest compliment her father ever gave to a good book, theatrical performances or scenic beauty.

"Could I really see him tomorrow?"

"Certainly. I will telephone myself. Now"—he stood up and yawned—"I'm damned tired. Always am when it's a borin' evening. Get your sleep, for I want him to see someone who looks half-alive tomorrow. Not the sort of drooping female you have been over the past few months."

As he went through the door, he whispered piercingly at her, "By the way, his name is Thomas Barroway."

Her father was right. It was a pleasant neighborhood. Not as smart or up-in-the-world as her own, but the houses were big and solid and comfortable looking, breathing middle-class affluence and a sort of happy bourgeois respectability.

Thomas Barroway's was a good example in a pleasant road, the brickwork well maintained, the front door newly painted, the brass knocker shining.

It was obviously Barroway himself who opened the door. There was too much authority in his air, too much eccentricity in his dress for him to be a servant. He was no taller than she, in his late fifties, and sported a magnificent bushy gray beard, with eyebrows to match. None of this hirsute growth, however, could obscure the almost fanatical gleam in the eyes, like jet-black beads. They darted over her person with disconcerting frankness.

"Hmphm, harrum," he said, "So ye came. In looks," he said, "ye'll do."

Peridot wondered what it was about her looks that would do.

What Barroway saw before him was a girl of above average height, who looked strong enough to do the physical work involved in carrying and stacking a great number of heavy books. She also looked him straight in the eye with her own clear gray eyes and was not outwardly thrown by his frank examination of her. She carried no extra fat that might have suggested laziness, but neither did she look the type who would faint away if a spider scuttled out from a shelf at her.

He liked the thick blond hair piled up under her straw hat, with the faint suggestion of frizziness in the ends that had come loose about her face. With the peculiarly perceptive eye that many intellectual men have about the things of the senses, he was not deceived by the plain line, the drab color of her clothes. He saw the full bosom, the firm waist, guessed at the strong hips and legs that lay beneath the princess line of her skirt. A woman not too plain, not too distracting. She would be a welcome change in his life.

"But first things first," he said out loud, in answer to her thoughts. "Let us see what you understand about a library, what you know about the papers I will show you."

The room he led her into was at odds with the rest of the house through which they passed to reach it. The vestibule, the hall, the living room off it, all were spotless, organized, well kept. But when he swung open a door in the back of the hall, it was chaos that met her eyes. Every color was muted by what appeared to be a patina of dust. There were papers, books strewn over every available surface including the floor.

Barroway looked at her, expecting an instant reaction. Instead, she walked into the room and around it, examining the shelving space, looking through a very grimy French window into the garden beyond. At random, she picked up one or two of the books, noting that they were in good condition. It was just that there was no order and a lot of dust.

A stack of papers lay on one of the two desks, and she picked one up. It was a letter from John Stuart Mill. On the pile next to it, she found what appeared to be a scientific dissertation. It was signed by Darwin.

"What richness. What incredible, marvelous richness," she murmured out loud.

Barroway listened to the deep voice from the strong throat and felt a frisson—of what he did not know—pass through him.

"No wonder you need help."

Her hands rose in front of her, and she let them drop at the enormity, the delight, of the task ahead of her.

"You'll come, then?"

"Don't you want to ask me questions about my qualifications and so on?"

"No, no, I know them already. I needed to see you.

I have now, and you'll do. That is, if you want to take it on, now you've seen it."

She looked at him, gray eyes luminous with delight, lips suddenly fuller and less pinched than they had felt in months. "Oh, yes, please, Mr. Barroway."

At this point, there was a knock at the door.

"That'll be my housekeeper, Mrs. Calderwood."

Mrs. Calderwood was also in her fifties, smaller than both of them, but with a jawline of steel and a spine of a ramrod. She looked disapprovingly at the room, speculatively at Peridot.

"Mrs. Calderwood, this is Miss Peridot Sinclair. Mrs. Calderwood will be here to apologize to you for the room and to say that it is none of her doing."

"Indeed, Mr. Barroway, that I am. He won't let me near it, Miss Sinclair, and that is why you see—what you do see."

"Oh," said Peridot, "that much is perfectly clear, Mrs. Calderwood. I was wondering who was the guiding spirit behind the rest of the house."

Mrs. Calderwood looked mollified, and slightly relaxed the set of her facial muscles. Her master added, "Miss Sinclair has agreed to work on this, you will be glad to hear."

"I'm glad to hear it indeed. I would have done it for him, miss, but I once threw out some old scrap of paper in here, and he has not allowed me in since."

"Old scrap of paper, indeed. A stanza by Browning it was, in his own hand." Barroway's beard shook with emotion at the remembrance of it.

Mrs. Calderwood was unrepentant. "Well, it was very messy. Shall I put you some tea in the drawing room, sir?"

There it was that they discussed her hours—he wanted her in every day, except the weekend—and her salary: £50 a year. To Peridot—wealthy, well-provided-for Peridot—the sound of those £50 was music to her ears. Her very own money, that she herself would earn. And doing something that she was actually looking forward to.

Over tea, Barroway said suddenly, "Curious. I never imagined Roddy producing a daughter like you. Not with Pamela by his side."

Peridot felt a little defensive at this. "Are you criticizing them? Or me?"

Thomas Barroway put his cup down on its saucer with a firmness that threatened to break the delicate china. "Let us get this clear, Peridot. I am a free thinker. I believe we should all find and follow our own path. Roddy wanted a pretty wife, an easy, socially successful and busy life. He got it all, and I am deuced glad for him. He's been a good and generous friend to me, your father. But you, my dear" he looked her over, as if assessing her again, "you do not want an easy, socially successful life, do you? Or a pretty husband?"

Peridot felt the annoying, stupid blush that rose to her cheeks. She avoided his eyes and looked down at her cup.

"I don't know," was all she could find to say, "I really don't know."

"Well," said Barroway comfortably, settling back into his chair, "maybe ye'll be able to find out while you're here."

Abruptly, he switched the conversation back to his library and its contents.

Lady Sinclair found herself in battle against the united front of her husband and daughter. She was, indeed, presented with a *fait accompli*. She tried horror and hysteria as her first reactions, then passed through tears and "What will my friends think" to a scornful, hurt acceptance—which she stayed with. It did not help matters that it was Thomas Barroway by whom her daughter was employed. She might have conceivably managed to boast about a daughter who was helping a peer of the realm or a member of Parliament—Conservative, of course. There was no saving grace about this situation that she could see.

"You will not even meet any young men, Peridot!"

"Well, none from Debrett's or Burke's Peerage, Mother."

"That's what I *mean.*" And she tried: "But my dear, it's not proper. After all, he is a bachelor and you are a young, unmarried girl."

Mrs. Calderwood's constant, upright presence was stressed at this point, and Lady Sinclair retreated into reluctant acceptance, casting hurt and surprised glances at Sir Rodney, who remained unflinching.

Chapter Seven

THE NEW ROUTINE OF PERIDOT'S LIFE BEGAN. She would arrive in Bayswater at about nine o'clock, be let in by Mrs. Calderwood, who took her coat and hat, and would go straight through to the library. Thomas Barroway would be waiting for her, already working at his desk, although he discouraged her from arriving earlier. He was working on a critical commentary of Trollope's work, he said, and needed some time on his own.

Peridot had her own desk, set up by the French window—which had now been cleaned by her. The only area that she was not supposed to touch was Barroway's desk and a narrow set of shelves behind it.

She worked steadily and thoroughly. She did not gossip or indulge in small talk, and she could see that Thomas Barroway and his housekeeper approved of her.

They were not always silent together. Often, they would both stop what they were doing to discuss some oddity or rarity she had found, and Barroway's beard would shiver and wag with excitement as he told her of its literary merits or the circumstances of the purchase. When he talked like that, his love of literature oozed from every pore, like some tangible secretion, filling the room with its headiness. Peridot felt her mind start to expand again.

She did not work nonstop all day. They would break off for luncheon, and Peridot would read for an hour, taking the opportunity to read authors who might not have been found acceptable in her own home, but were far from morally reprehensible. She read in French also: Flaubert, Maupassant, Balzac.

For exercise, she would walk along the Broad Walk, into Kensington Gardens and through Hyde Park, watching the nannies and their small charges there and remembering her own restricted, lonely childhood. Once or twice, Barroway had visitors to the house, other academics. He would send her out for a breath of fresh air, while they retired to the library for their discussions. Sometimes he told her what they came for, sometimes he did not. She didn't care, didn't inquire. She was perfectly, blissfully happy.

She acquired a bicycle to keep there and explored the neighborhood further. Sometimes, as she returned, she would see Barroway waiting for her in the front window and would join him, breathless, pink-cheeked with her exercise.

"I am so sorry, Mr. Barroway. Did I take too long?"

"No, no," he would say, studying the flushed

young face before him, fair hair fluffed up in its irrepressible halo, "I was admiring your energy and your youth."

One January evening in the year 1901—6:30 P.M. on Tuesday, the twenty-second of January to be precise—Peridot, like all her compatriots, stopped being a Victorian and became an Edwardian. With the kaiser holding her in his arms, Queen Victoria died at Osborne and Edward VII ascended the throne for what were to be called nine Golden Years.

London turned out en masse for the funeral procession, and the great queen was attended by kings to her grave: the German emperor, the kings of Belgium, Portugal, the Hellenes. Grand dukes, too, were there: from Russia; Archduke Franz Ferdinand of Austria; crown princes of Germany, Denmark, Norway, Sweden and Siam.

The horses were draped in purple and white. Laurel wreaths swung from pillar to pillar.

They laid her to rest at Frogmore, beside her beloved consort. And the King of Great Britain and Ireland and of all the British Dominions beyond the sea started his reign.

Britain moved into an unusually hot summer and the Sinclairs departed for Brierley Park. Miss Boileau arrived in London to stay with Peridot during her parents' absence. In Bayswater, Peridot took a table and some of her work out into the garden behind the house and worked there whenever she could. Barroway grumbled at her, telling her that the house was cooler, and he was probably right. But the smell of the lilac was delicious and the feel of her sun-warmed hair against her neck was so good that she smiled at him and remained outside. There he would join her for a substantial tea provided by Mrs. Calderwood, for whom Peridot could do no wrong.

One glorious late afternoon, Peridot was copying out her rough notes onto cards. It was not as interesting as the original research required for the task, and she felt her eyes beginning to close.

Mr. Barroway is right, she thought. It is hotter out here, and I am becoming sleepy."

She turned once more to the notes in front of her, only to feel them start to blur again.

"Um—excuse me, so sorry to disturb your forty winks, but could you send that back, please?"

She awoke, this time, with a start. A young man, in his early twenties perhaps, was leaning over the garden wall with the support of a branch from an apple tree. All she could see of him was his arms and his face, topped by dark, curly hair. He looked like a cheerful Lord Byron, bereft of that poet's brooding, sultry stare.

"Send what back?"

"The cricket ball. It's in the laurels, over there."

She crossed over and found it for him, half-buried in the longer grass at the back of the garden. She was about to walk toward him with it, when she changed her mind. The forty winks remark still rankled a bit.

"Catch!" She threw it high and hard, watching his expression of surprise change to dismay as he raised a hand to catch it and disappeared from view.

"Ouch!"

The exclamation changed her amusement to concern, and she ran across to the wall, trying in vain to jump up and see what had happened.

"Oh, dear, I'm so sorry. Are you all right?"

After a short interval, there was a sound of creaking branches and the head reappeared.

"Good heavens, that's quite a throw you have there—took me by surprise! Yes, I'm fine. You're Mr. Barroway's secretary, aren't you?"

"Well—yes. I'm cataloguing his library. My name is Peridot Sinclair."

"A pretty precious name." But he said it with a grin, so that it came out jokingly. "I'm Clive Fairley, son of the house. Well—this house."

"How do you do."

"I've seen you in the garden from up there." He pointed back at a window in the house next door. "When I've come back early."

"From where?"

"The Slade," said the young man, mentioning the most famous art school in London.

Peridot was fascinated. "How marvelous. Do you work with Professor Tonks?"

A look of respect crossed Clive Fairley's face. "Yes, yes, I do. Do you know of him?"

"I've heard of him. Are you a painter?"

"Hope to be. But I've sometimes a feeling that I'm better commenting on other people's paintings than doing my own. Still, at least I'm doing what I want to do."

It was all said with enormous cheerfulness, a childlike, open vitality. Peridot warmed to his last remark.

"That's what I am doing too. It is a very good feeling, I know."

"Look," he said, slipping awkwardly on his perch, "this isn't too comfortable. Did I see you cycling yesterday?"

"Yes—you might have."

"Perhaps we could go together, tomorrow. After teatime, when it's cooler? How would that be?"

She was delighted to accept. She felt easy with this smiling young man with the open countenance. Maybe it was just her newfound independence that made things easier.

As she returned through the French windows, Peridot almost bumped into Barroway in the gloom, unable to see him with her sun-dazzled eyes. He made no mention of whether he had seen or heard what had happened, but she sensed a withdrawal in him, as though something had changed. In the glow of the sunlight and the encounter, she did not think to ask what was wrong. It was only later that she recalled noticing.

Clive Fairley was a charming, humorous young man with greater originality of mind and more talent than he gave himself credit for. His father was a doctor, comfortably situated in serving the upper and middle classes of the area. Fairley was the only child left at home, having two sisters older than he, who were married. He was spoiled—he freely admitted it—and was being indulged in his desire to paint. He was, however, as serious about doing well at it as if he had chosen to be a lawyer, or a doctor like his father.

He made Peridot laugh. For a rather solemn girl, she did a considerable amount of laughing over the next few weeks of the summer. She met Dr. and Mrs. Fairley, joining them for supper on one occasion. One of the delights of the relationship was that she did not have to explain it to her parents. She simply told them that she was working later for Mr. Barroway, and the explanation was accepted.

There came a point, however, at which Dr. and Mrs. Fairley started asking questions. After all, Clive was spending a great deal of his spare time with this girl, who came and went like a mystery. She told them her last name readily enough, the area of London in which she lived, and about Somerville and Oxford. However, when Mrs. Fairley saw the glances they exchanged, the shared jokes, she decided to do a little more research into Peridot's background. After all, why did she not introduce Clive to her parents, as any properly brought-up young lady should?

For a long while, their outings were strictly after Clive finished at the Slade for the day, and Peridot finished her work for Barroway. They would bicycle or walk together and talk of everything under the sun. They asked no more of each other, content with this relaxation, this being together at the end of the working day. They had never kissed. Occasionally, Clive would throw an arm around her shoulders or compliment her on her dress. There was nothing more.

They were walking home one day, talking about socialism and the Fabians, when Clive discovered that Peridot had not been to the theater in many months.

"Ridiculous," he said, stopping and looking at her with a tenderness that took the bite out of the word. "We must remedy that. There's a Shaw play on at the Court Theater. Let's go."

Peridot had no difficulty obtaining a release from home, where she was virtually considered a lost cause by her mother, but was readily given her freedom by her father. She did not, however, mention Clive.

Clive, though, told his mother about the evening's excursion on his way out the door. It was at this point that Mrs. Fairley decided to find out more about Peridot Sinclair. Accordingly, she buttonholed Mrs. Calderwood, who was only too happy to supply all the information that she required. After all, she was fond of Peridot and shocked to find that the Fairleys thought her the daughter of an impoverished clergyman or someone in trade. In consequence, she perhaps overstressed Peridot's exalted background.

"But—why should she work?" asked a puzzled Mrs. Fairley—by now horrified to discover that her son was escorting a daughter of the aristocracy, without her parents' permission.

"Why should she *not?*" countered Mrs. Calderwood, covering in one short query a premise which was to change women's lives in the new century.

Deeply disturbed, Mrs. Fairley settled down to await her son's return from the theater. Meanwhile, oblivious to the confusion into which she had been thrown, Clive and Peridot were spending their first evening together.

For all the talking and the odd tender look, it had honestly never occurred to Peridot that Clive liked her for anything but her mind. Immured by her innocence, by her conviction that she was plain, not a "man's woman"—whatever that may be—she could not think of their companionship as anything but platonic. She did not see, as the artist (and the man) in Clive did, the translucence of her complexion, the swell of her full breasts, the beautiful strength of her hands, the powerful thrust of her legs when she cycled with him. She would have been staggered if she had known just how much she had disturbed his dreams on hot summer nights in his bedroom.

When they left the theater, Clive had insisted on escorting her home in a cab.

"No, no," Peridot had protested. "Just see me into one here, and I can go by myself."

Clive Fairley was not solely concerned with her safety, but on being with her a little longer, sharing the intimate darkness of the cab's interior. Peridot, for her part, did not want him to see her home, to associate him with that side of her life. He belonged to Bayswater, and Barroway, and books. And bliss.

Clive won out by simply jumping into the cab with her as it started to depart. There was a tremendous jolt, a curse from the driver, and there he was, beside her, grinning at her. "I'm coming with you and stop fussing," he told her.

Peridot found that she took great pleasure in accepting the *fait accompli,* settling back in the seat and feeling his arm go around her shoulders. She hoped that he could not hear her heart, for it seemed to be thumping ridiculously loudly in the quiet interior of the cab. To distract him from the uproar, she started to talk about the play. Clive was quiet, as if listening to her. Suddenly, he said, "How well he understands the life force. How well he understands it."

Peridot said primly, "I suppose it is what the French call 'the élan vital.'"

Clive turned to her and said simply, "This is what it is." He kissed her. He put both arms gently around her and kissed her on the lips. The mere touching of their mouths evoked a response, an aching delight in the whole of the body. Peridot felt as if honey and wine ran through her veins.

"There," he said unsteadily, his voice a little thick and blurry through the blanket of his emotions. "Oh, how I have wanted to kiss you, Peridot."

Surprise, joy, confusion. "Me? You wanted to kiss *me?* Why?"

"Because you are so beautiful, of course."

In disbelief and delight, she put up her face to be kissed again.

Clive Fairley was not an inexperienced man. Although coming from a Victorian, upper-middle-class home, he had touched, in his career at the Slade, on the fringes of that Bohemianism which is associated with the artistic world. A few years earlier, he had lost his virginity to one of the young models who came in to pose for the students, and the experience had been repeated since. He would have denied that he looked down on the women with whom he had slept, but there was no doubt that he thought of them in a different way from a girl like Peridot. His sexual feelings toward her were confusedly mixed with respect and worship, and he would never have pressed any advantage he might have had. In an age when so little could enflame so much—the glimpse of the smooth swell of a calf above a slim ankle, the rise and fall of a breast beneath a lace blouse—the feel of their bodies side by side in the cab was ecstasy enough.

When they heard the cabby slow down his horse and felt the wheels stop turning on the road beneath them, Peridot moved to the door and Clive took her hand.

"Let me see you to your door."

"No, no." She put out a hand to his chest and pushed him gently back into the seat. "I would rather you stayed here. Please stay. Just take the cab home."

Touched and puzzled, he obeyed her, simply helping her with the door. When he saw the grand, terraced houses and the wide street, he thought, "Very grand for a clergyman. Out of the question for someone in trade. I really must find out what her father does for a living."

All this passed from his mind as he settled back in the cab, to enjoy reliving the strength and softness of Peridot's lips against his own.

It did not, however, pass from his mind for long. Reality, in the form of a mother armed with a list of facts, was waiting for him in the doorway on his return home.

Mrs. Fairley revealed all. She elaborated on the distinction of Peridot's background, adding, "They are *very* wealthy. Why she is working in Mr. Barroway's library is beyond my understanding, but it certainly has absolutely nothing to do with money. Even with an older brother, I am told she will inherit quite a fortune."

For the moment, the bottom dropped out of Clive Fairley's world. The girl his mother was describing would seem to be beyond his reach.

In her Belgravia bedroom, Peridot lay awake for a long time, unwilling to part with the sensations that filled her, seeing before her eyes in the darkness the cheerful tenderness of her love's young face. She flexed her hands on the pillow and felt again the curly springiness of his dark hair beneath her fingers. Undisturbed by thoughts of class or conscience, she drifted into sleep.

Thomas Barroway was an early riser. He had long ago made it clear to Mrs. Calderwood that he preferred to be on his own during the early morning hours, when the gray dawn light still clung to his books and papers. Winter and summer alike, he would wrap himself in a velvet dressing gown, put a tasseled cap on his head, some old brocade slippers on his feet, pick up the spectacles that he wore for close work and go down to his desk in the library. There he would light up one of his four pipes of the day before he started any work. Two hours later Mrs. Calderwood would bring in his breakfast, which he would eat at his desk, after which he would dress and turn to a different set of books and papers.

He had long loved this routine, and regretted how the two hours winged by. But now that those wings carried him toward Peridot's arrival, he found the flight of time more pleasurable, less to be regretted than to be wished for. He would look up from his Trollope—or whatever his daylight work was—and see the halo of her fair hair, the shy smile, the handsome figure, and his fingers would tremble a little on the pen he was holding.

There was nothing to be done about it. A man in his fifties, a-tremble over a young girl. A subject fit for ridicule, for farce. Or the subject matter, sometimes, of those books which he catalogued and researched by himself in the hours before Peridot's arrival. Books whose contents were so—curious—that they must remain concealed behind locked sliding doors except during the dark, lonely morning hours, when he could read them undisturbed.

Now that Peridot shared the library with him, he sometimes fancied that the essence of his secret books would seep through the locked doors into the room, where her virginal freshness, not yet dulled by the ways of the world, would catch a whiff of the sweat and tears in those tales of lechery and despair. But he could not remove the books. They were necessary to him, even more so since she was there.

This morning he sat, as on so many other mornings, pulling on his pipe, a book propped up before him.

Suddenly there was a sharp tapping on the glass of the window, and Barroway jumped violently. The *Index Librorum Prohibitorum* dropped from his hands onto the desk top as he swung around in the direction of the sound. Forgotten, it lay there as he crossed to the window to pull back the heavy curtains.

It was that young fool from next door who had been hanging around Peridot, the young dog, wagging his tail and panting for her, only she did not seem to see it. His mop of hair and cheeky young face were clearly outlined against the window, the sun coming in behind him, like a painting by some religious primitive.

"What do you want—at this hour?"

The young man looked tired. His eyes were heavy, and he had cut himself shaving. "I had to come this early, I'm sorry, sir. I have to get to the Slade. Could I speak to you a moment?"

"What about, for God's sake?"

"Peridot Sinclair."

Her name made the French windows open for Clive Fairley. "Just a minute, and I'll be with you."

Clive looked around the room he had just entered and watched as Barroway carried an enormous book from his desk to the case behind him, which he then closed and locked.

"Now," he said, putting the key down on the desk, "what is it about Miss Sinclair that requires such an early morning visit?"

Clive came straight to the point. "Sir, is it true that Miss Sinclair is the daughter of Sir Rodney and Lady Sinclair?"

"To the best of my knowledge," said Barroway wryly, "she is. Rodney and I have been acquainted for years, and that is what he has always maintained."

"I see, I see. So she would be wealthy, then. An heiress."

At this, Barroway appeared to become angry. "I cannot see what business that is of yours, nor do I know the details of her parents' finances."

Clive withdrew, moving back toward the window. "I understand, sir. It is just that—I didn't know. I should have asked her parents. I should not have taken her out."

"I do not feel a bicycle ride will do any harm."

The words "bicycle ride" were said as if he were describing some truly infantile activity.

"No, sir. Last night. I should not have taken her to the theater. But thank you, sir. I'm sorry that I disturbed you. Please forgive me."

Clive stumbled out and was gone.

"So you took her to the theater, eh?" said Barroway out loud, his hands pulling the cord of his robe, as if he wished to strip the tassel of every thread. "I'll warrant her papa and mama knew nothing of that. And why was the event such a watershed, I wonder?"

His concentration was broken, his early morning mood gone. Grumbling to himself, he returned to his desk, but he did not unlock the secret shelves again, for Mrs. Calderwood would soon be upon him.

Peridot was late arriving. This added insult to the unnamed injury Barroway was already feeling. When she came, she flew into the house as if the wings of time had indeed carried her there. Breathless, laughing. "I am so sorry, Mr. Barroway, I overslept this morning."

Smile fading, as she saw the face of stone.

"I am not entirely taken by surprise. The reason for your late arrival was here earlier this morning, with bags under his eyes and a cut upon his chin."

"Clive was here?"

"Yes. He cost me my early morning's work and a late employee. I would be grateful if you would not allow your private life to intrude upon mine again. If you must have gentlemen callers, let them not call here, to ask me details of your background and wealth."

It was as if he had slapped her in the face. The blood left it, except for little patches high on the cheekbones.

"It will not happen again. I'll work later tonight. I am sorry for the inconvenience."

"Your apology is accepted. Whether you work late or not is up to you. I intend to go out this afternoon. Please make sure that your parents are aware of your plans this time. I would not wish them to feel it is a secret life that you live here, with my connivance."

"I will see to it, Mr. Barroway."

"Good. So let us forget the whole matter and do some work."

She did not leave the room for the sunlight that

day. They both stayed there, working in an estranged silence, broken only by lunch and by Barroway's departure late in the afternoon.

Peridot stayed as she had said she would. Mrs. Calderwood brought her tea and then a light supper on a tray, begging her not to work too late and spoil her eyes.

On the contrary, Peridot worked as if her life depended on it. Her joy had gone, evaporating under Barroway's disapproval.

At the thought of Barroway, she looked toward his desk and noticed the key on it, then looked up at the locked doors behind. Suddenly she was overwhelmed by curiosity.

What is it that he owns, she wondered, that is so precious he must hide it behind locks? There are so many valuable things he has allowed me to handle. Surely, he wouldn't mind me seeing these. I would not damage them.

It was growing dark in the library. The sun was well round to the other side of the house now and was going down. She lit the gas lamp, which he still liked to read by when he was at his desk, and picked up the key. It turned easily in the lock. The shelves revealed were deep, the books on them packed in two layers. Some did, indeed, look very old and valuable: leather-bound, with gold-tooled writing. Some were not so grand, bound in a sort of cardboard not much different from paper. Peridot pulled some out at random.

At first, she got the impression that they were all by foreign authors. She saw Latin and French: *Pisanus Fraxi, la Rose d'Amour*. There was one large, heavy book lying on its side that she didn't remove, with an incredibly long title: *Index Librorum Pro-*

hibitorum: being Notes Bio-Icono-Graphical and Critical, on Curious and Uncommon books.

Librorum Prohibitorum—prohibited books, that meant. Curious books? Was this some sort of list like the Index which the Roman Catholics followed?

Then she saw another title: *A Discourse on the Worship of Priapus.*

A religious book? Why lock it away? She picked up two of the books that she had pulled out, and, gradually, the innocence that had protected her, that had made discovery so slow, parted like a curtain and she looked through a window the existence of which she had never imagined.

What she saw made her legs weaken and tremble under her as she sat curled up in Barroway's large, wing chair. She gasped out loud as she read. Driven by a curiosity that she had not known she possessed, she continued to look.

Love's Tell-tale; or, the Decameron of Pleasure; The new Epicurean; or, The Delights of Sex, Facetiously and Philosophically Considered, in Graphic Letters Addressed to Young Ladies of Quality.

Some had titles brief and to the point: *A Romance of Lust. The Lustful Turk. Randiana.*

"Ah, my child, my child. Why did you have to do that?"

She turned so violently on the chair that her nerveless legs failed her, and she half fell out of it, grabbing the edge of the desk to save herself, but dropping the book in her hand.

"Carefully, carefully. Some of these are quite rare."

Peridot in the soft lamplight, hair untidy around her face, skin flushed with shame and shock and—

who knew what else? She couldn't move, couldn't speak.

Barroway stood in the doorway of the library, which was almost dark. He still had on his cloak and hat and carried a cane in his hands. She saw him now as a satyr, or a centaur—his strong, bull-like stance, the full beard, the hair pulled up almost like horns where he had ripped his hat from his head upon seeing her.

He came over to the desk. Still, she did not move, but her eyes never left him, a complexity of emotions passing through them as she stared at him.

"Do not look at me like that, Peridot. As I value your opinion, I hope you will not change your judgment of me. They are, after all, beautiful things. See?" He pulled out another book from the shelf.

"*My Secret Life,*" he read from the spine, "Eleven uniform volumes, in small crown Octavo, and printed on handmade, ribbed paper. You, who appreciate beautiful books, you must see how fine this is."

"But you do not just collect them for their appearance. You like them for their contents."

She finally managed to speak, her voice surprisingly firm and clear. He put a finger to his lips. Peridot noticed how full and red they were, the lips of a sensualist, hidden in that academic forest of beard.

"Hush, remember Mrs. Calderwood. Oh, yes, oh, yes. I cannot pretend otherwise. It has become—a hobby of mine."

"An obsession."

Anger was reaching her now, not revulsion, anger at the self he had hidden from her.

"That's probably true. I have been obsessed by the body and the delights it can bring, but that obsession has become more and more academic with my middle age. The desires are still there, it's true, but I find now that I can better satisfy them with what lies between these sheets, than between bedsheets."

He said this calmly, objectively, as though he were discussing theories only, not the driving passions that had once mastered him and still possessed him.

It gave Peridot enough detachment to ask, "But why did you not get married, then? Surely, that's the answer."

A sad, terrible smile on the face of the satyr. He sat down in the large chair, and she moved to the other side of the desk.

"Marriage as the answer? Ah, Peridot, Peridot. Easy, maybe, for most men. But I am not like most men. I would have made a wife suffer, quite outrageously. I do not have the virtue of faithfulness in me. But I like women and would not like to see anyone suffer because of me."

She spoke with vehemence now, with passion in her voice.

"You cannot like women. How can you say that? With all these dreadful books, how can you say that? You must hate them very much, or be frightened of them, or..."

Her voice faltered as she saw his reaction to her anger. He was aroused, coming slowly to his feet, leaning toward her over the desk.

"Maybe so. *You* frighten me, certainly. With your cleverness and your virginal righteousness. But I do not hate you. Oh—I hated you when you laughed with that young idiot next door."

"Why? Why?"

He held her wrists on the desk, his face close to hers.

"Why? Because, dammit, I am half in love with you myself. Oh"—he withdrew quickly when he saw the fear in her eyes—"don't be afraid. I won't force my middle-aged self on you. Ridiculous, isn't it? To be obsessed with one of the baser of the instincts and then—to fall in love, like some raw adolescent, with a girl young enough to be one's daughter. My God, what a fool I must look to you!"

From the safety of the far side of the desk, Peridot felt pity fill her.

"Oh, no, not a fool. And—what you call one of the baser instincts isn't, you know. Only you have made it so. I suppose part of me is flattered that someone I respect so much should express love for me."

She had hoped to comfort, to heal, maybe to convert a little. Barroway lowered his face into his hands and gave a groan that was like the tearing of a human soul. Forgetting her earlier fear, she ran around the desk to comfort him, as she would have done any creature in distress.

"Don't, oh, don't. I wish to heaven I'd never looked in those shelves of yours. It started out as a desire to help you. I felt so guilty about my lateness this morning."

As her arm came around his shoulder, he looked up at her and a rueful smile crossed his face.

"You know—you could have been as late as you wanted, if Fairley had not been the cause. And—great heavens, what a lot he has to answer for—the key was left out because I had to lock away the book I was reading when he arrived at that window. Then I forgot it."

What signal then passed between them she would never know, but there was a change in their breathing, a stillness between them. He stood and turned to her, very close. She sensed, in a sudden moment of impact, his strength, his virility. His desire communicated itself to her.

Peridot was also, herself, in an awakening state. Her hidden desires had been triggered by the kiss of a young man in a hansom cab. To her amazement, she found herself moving toward Barroway, responding. Eye meeting eye, their bodies almost touching, the musty, musky darkness of the library closing around them.

To his eternal credit, Barroway stood his ground. He lowered his eyes from hers, turned his head, broke the magnetic field.

"Go home, Peridot Sinclair. Go home. A summer night like this can lead to encounters between maidens and monsters that are bitterly regretted in the cold light of dawn."

She left him, standing there amid his books, the secret shelves open behind him.

It only occurred to her in the cab—she decided against public transport that night—that Clive had not been round to see her during the day. She had not thought of it before.

So confusing, so confusing, she thought. I *wanted* something to happen. At that moment, I wanted something to happen.

The new light that this shed on herself was disturbing, but she didn't feel unduly alarmed or ashamed. Instead, she sat in the hansom and held up all the new facts of her life before her, considering them as calmly as if she were a scientist dissecting a rare specimen in which she had found many things to surprise her.

Bertha, out scrubbing the step a little more lethargically than she would have done if the Sir and his Lady were home, watched with interest the handsome young man who hung around the railings of the house next to theirs. Unhappy in love, she decided. You could see it in his eyes—all soulful and dark. Buckets of tears he'd probably shed in the night. He was a gentleman all right, you could see that, but there was something unkempt in his appearance: a collar sitting crooked, his hair all ruffled, that suggestion of absentmindedness brought about by unrequited love.

Suddenly the young man seemed to make up his mind, turned on his heel and sprinted up the steps to her.

"Is Miss Peridot Sinclair at home?"

Bertha was thoroughly startled. Miss Peridot was not one for gentlemen callers, and this one was certainly calling at an odd hour, and in an odd way.

"Well, yes, sir, but I think she's only just getting her breakfast."

"I wish to speak to her. Would you be so good as to tell her that Clive Fairley is calling."

Bertha hesitated, the chamois in her hand, then went in through the front door, where she came face to face with an outraged Mr. Symes.

"What are you doing, girl? You should be outside, cleaning the brass and then returning down to the kitchen. You know that."

Flustered, Bertha broke in on his words. "Well, yes, I know that, Mr. Symes, but there's a gentleman outside, for Miss Peridot. Says 'e wants to see her."

Mr. Symes straightened his lapels and put on an even more forbidding face than his usual one. "Very well, Bertha. Return to your work. I will deal with this."

Majestically, he strode forward to deal with the intruder and to repel him, if necessary.

He found that Clive Fairley did not take to repelling easily, not after having waited an hour already in the street before finally plucking up the courage to call at the door.

A few minutes later, he was waiting in the hall and an unusually ruffled Mr. Symes was making his way upstairs to the morning room. Clive Fairley, standing in the hall, turned round and saw the little maid peering at him round the door. His triumph over authority had lifted his spirits, and he gave her a delighted smile.

"'E's lovely, 'e really is," she told them downstairs. "Miss P. may not 'ave many beaus, but she can certainly pick 'em. E's a reg'lar Prince Charmin'."

Clive watched Peridot come down the curved staircase toward him, Mr. Symes protectively in tow.

"It's all right, Mr. Symes."

The butler hesitated a moment, then bowed and disappeared beyond a door in the hallway.

"Why didn't you tell me? About all this?"

She shrugged her shoulders helplessly.

"Why, Clive? It wasn't important to us."

"It is, now."

Peridot looked distressed, held out her hands toward him. He wasn't sure if it was to repulse him or to touch him.

"Not yet, Clive, not too fast. I am only just beginning."

Exasperation hit him. "Perry, I *cannot* go on seeing you and taking you out without sorting the matter out with your parents. In case you are wondering why I didn't see you yesterday—oh, yesterday of all days—it was because of my mother."

He told her what had transpired after their visit to the theater.

Peridot smiled sadly. "How complicated things have become, when they were so straightforward and simple."

At this moment, there was a voice from the top of the stairs."Peridot, are you all right?"

Peridot turned. "Of course, Miss Boileau. Come and meet Clive Fairley, whom I have told you about. See that he is fed, Miss Boileau, will you? I'm sure he hasn't eaten this morning. Tell him why I am behaving like this, why I cannot give up work yet, why I cannot make those decisions he might like me to."

Before they could protest, she was gone, snatching up her hat from where it waited for her on the hall table and running out the door.

He was there where she had left him, slumped in the winged chair, in the half-darkness, curtains still tight together over the French windows, as if he had not moved, as if time had stood still.

"You came."

"Of course I came, Mr. Barroway. I am employed here."

"You are on time, this morning."

"I told you it wouldn't happen again."

She went across to the window and drew back the curtains. The garden looked fresh and still dewy, not yet dried out by the sun. She glanced sideways at the old apple tree in the next garden and thought confusedly of Adam and Eve and temptation and the apple of knowledge. Hastily she pushed the thoughts away.

When she turned back, he was writing busily, as though nothing had happened, taking his own mood from the tone of her voice.

It was indeed as if nothing had happened. The routine of the day passed as it always did, and she achieved as much in that day as she had ever done. When she got home that night, it was a letter—and not the conversation between Clive and Annie Boileau, or the events that had passed between her and Barroway—that changed the course of the next few months of her life.

Chapter Eight

Peridot *chérie,* I never heard from you, never knew if you got my last letter, but I wrote to you, to tell you about my life, to ask if sometime we might see each other again.

I need you now. I am so alone. Something terrible has happened, and I am so alone. I have money, but I am alone.

A little bird tells me that you have some freedom. Could you use some of it to come to me? I have an apartment. You would not have to be in a hotel on your own. And I have servants, or you could bring your own maid.

Please come. There are so many Krakatoas. Come and be cool and logical for me.

My address is on the letter. Simply telegraph me. That is all.

It would be good, you know. The two of us together—how good that sounds!

J'ai besoin de toi, chère amie. Je suis si solitaire.

Violette

VIOLET ALONE, AFRAID, CALLING TO HER. There was no question about it. She would go.

It was a good time for her to get away. She could give herself a breathing space, stand back and look at her own life while helping Violet with hers. It could be arranged. Yes, it could. The summer was at an end, her parents were returning, Miss Boileau would be leaving in a day or two, and she was sure that Tom Barroway would release her temporarily. After all, if necessary, he had little choice, for she had terrible weapons to wield. Love and blackmail.

She marveled at her ruthlessness. No, it wouldn't come to that. She would tell Clive that she must have time to think—a traditional response to her dilemma, one he would have to accept, however reluctantly.

How to find out more about Violet? Peridot didn't know a soul in Paris. She didn't count any of her parents' friends. Then she thought, There is someone who might know. Marcus Radcliffe.

With so much arranging to do, there would be little time to think of her own problems over the next few days. As she planned out her moves, she started to return to the cool logicality that Violet expected of her.

That night, with Mr. Symes's help, she set about finding out Marcus Radcliffe's address and had a brief note delivered to him by hand.

Dear Mr. Radcliffe,

I should be grateful for some information. You remember, I am sure, that we met a few years ago at Brierley Park and Willowdale Hall. Violet has written to me, asking for my help. Before I go to see her, I would like to find out what I can about her present situation. Trusting you can help me in this,

Peridot Sinclair

When she went to Bayswater the next morning, she took Violet's letter with her and buttonholed Tom Barroway about it straightaway on entering the library.

First, he read it in silence and then handed it back to her.

"A *cri de coeur*. She says 'alone' three times. Explain to me. Who is she, this friend who writes in French and English? What is a Krakatoa—other than a volcano? And why do you show this to me?"

Peridot sighed. "Where to begin? It goes back so far."

Barroway leaned back in his chair and folded his hands across his chest. "Then, go back—as far as you need. We have time. Tell me from the start."

So she did. When she got up to the present, she could only tell him of her brother's encounter at the theater and guess at the rest. She saw his bushy eyebrows shoot up as she mentioned Radcliffe.

"Hmm—I know him, very slightly. I remember hearing of some liaison with a beautiful and very young girl that's over now and that tore him apart for a while. I understand all the background. Now, tell me what it is you plan to do, for that's where I come in, I think. Am I right?"

She told him her plan, as far as it went. Then she frowned as, disconcertingly, he started to laugh.

"No, no, don't be hurt. It's just that you are quite an amazing young woman. You discover that you are working—and that you are working at all in the first place is unusual—that you are working for a collector of pornography, who has a penchant for you. And yet, you stay on. You conceal a relationship with an aspiring young artist from your parents. Finally, you tell me of your plan to visit in Paris the daughter of a gardener, who now appears to be what the French so delightfully call "une grande horizontale." You speak French. I don't think I need translate that."

Peridot replied quietly, "Summed up like that, it doesn't sound very pretty, nor does it make me sound very prepossessing."

"Ah, that's where you are wrong. So far, you have passed through these events and retained your innocence and integrity. Which is why I call you an amazing young woman, and I will indeed help you with this plan of yours."

The laughter ceased and he became businesslike. "Her address—it is expensive, probably an apartment she has been given. It should be a respectable neighborhood, so there'll be no problem there. But your parents will not allow you to travel on your own, and you should have someone over there, whom you can turn to for help if need be."

"Are you offering to accompany me?"

He looked at her wryly. "I'll not pretend that I did not, briefly, think of it—but you have explained a

Krakatoa to me, and I would rate as one, would I not? No, I have a highly respectable clergyman acquaintance who makes many visits to Paris, to the Bibliothèque Sainte Geneviève to do research. He would, I'm sure, be happy to accompany you sometime soon."

Peridot was filled with an immense sense of relief. "I'm so grateful to you. I'll telegraph Violet and tell her I am coming. If Mr. Radcliffe will see me, I'll try to visit him tomorrow, if you can excuse me from work."

"By all means. Meanwhile, I'll contact the Reverend Anscombe and find out when next he crosses the Channel."

When she returned home she found that her hopes had been answered; there was a note from Marcus Radcliffe. She ran upstairs to her room and tore it open. It was, like hers, very brief.

"A voice from the past. I would prefer to meet you in other circumstances, but could call on you tomorrow. Or you could come here. Marcus Radcliffe."

She sent Drummond straight out with the reply.

"I will see you tomorrow morning at your home, at about nine o'clock. Peridot Sinclair."

Better to avoid alerting Miss Boileau to anything out of the ordinary; this way she would presume that Peridot was setting out for Bayswater in the morning, and when she left the Sinclair home after her summer of chaperoning Peridot, she could do so with the feeling of having performed her duties responsibly.

Next day, Peridot took a cab to Brompton Square, telling Miss Boileau that she would return in the afternoon to spend the half day before her departure with her. Marcus Radcliffe met her at the door, and instantly she was taken back to the child of fifteen that she had been, overwhelmed by his sophistication and his interest in her. She owed him a great deal, she suddenly remembered, and she had never thanked him.

He had changed. She supposed that he must be now approaching forty, but it was not just that. Some of the gaiety of spirit seemed to have gone out of him.

"I never thanked you."

"For what, my dear? I've done nothing yet."

He, in his turn, was looking at her. A blond Diana she had become. An academic Artemis. So different from— He turned his mind again to the present.

"No," she was saying, "for what you did that enabled me to go to Somerville."

"One of my better deeds. Reward me for it, Peridot, by doing something good for this wicked world."

Peridot looked over at the desk and table that dominated the living room, littered with papers. Was it merely long hours at that desk that had stooped those wide shoulders? If Violet were the cause, then her visit would hurt.

As if reading her thoughts, he sighed and said, "Sit down and start away. Let's get it over with. Tell me why you need to know whatever I know about Violet." It was the first time he had said that name out loud in many a moon. A little thrust of pain around the ribs perhaps, but nothing too terrible.

She told him, as succinctly as she could. His ribs hurt a little more at the thought of Violet suffering. He pinned his mind to the few facts that he had been able to gather from friends since receiving Peridot's letter. He spoke with detachment.

"She has been living with a Comte d'Aulnay. To

be more precise—he has set her up at the address you see here. It has gone quite long, as these affairs go—about three years. I think she was in love with him. I know nothing of his emotions, apart from the obvious ones. He is very wealthy, and this sort of arrangement is quite acceptable in his circle. I've discovered that he has suffered an injury of some sort during the course of a duel. More than that I do not know, except that the duel was *not* over Violet. There seems to have been some other woman. My friends tell me, though, that this other woman was merely an excuse to pick a fight with the man in question. My friends called d'Aulnay a madman. *Un vrai fou.*"

Peridot closed her eyes. It all sounded so alien, so foreign. "It's like something from *The Three Musketeers*.

"Yes, I know. But that's d'Aulnay for you. A swashbuckler, taking what he wants. Setting his own rules. Society runs for him, not him for society."

A terrible bitterness crossed his face, as if the memory suddenly hit hard. "What fools we are when we are in love. What utter fools."

"But sometimes we think more clearly when we are fools. Or just after becoming one. It humbles you."

He looked at her in surprise. "Perhaps so. Are you in love, Peridot Sinclair?"

He leaned forward, and there was a return to the bantering tone, the mischievous smile.

She answered him seriously. "I really don't know. Maybe I'll find out in the course of the next month or so."

"I had forgotten how I liked your solemnity. I'd forgotten how I liked you."

She suddenly smiled at him. "I haven't forgotten anything. I was a little in love with you, when I was fifteen. And I was jealous of Violet, even though nothing had happened between you."

He smiled in his turn. "Ah, but Violet knew it would. I was part of her great scheme."

"Yes, you were. And I thought it was you that Violet would have to beware of."

"Not as it turned out. But, in her chosen career, it is better to be wary of us all. To have no heart if possible."

"What a frightening thought. Her letter would seem to prove that Violet didn't master that skill."

He changed the subject abruptly at this point. "What are you doing now?"

She told him what she thought she decently could of Tom Barroway, the library and the research, and the help he was giving her over Violet and Paris.

"And your projects?" She indicated the cluttered desk.

"Mine? Well, since—Violet, I have turned from fact to fiction. Not such a long journey. I am writing a novel."

"That's wonderful! Will you sign a copy for me when it's published, Mr. Radcliffe?"

He felt cheered by her excitement, lifted by her ingenuous pleasure. "Of course. Maybe you had better wait and see if it is successful. If it's any good."

"Oh, I know it will be."

The balm of her calm reassurance soothed his still-bruised ego, made him feel like indulging in confidences. He crossed to the window and looked out.

"You know, Peridot, you are the first woman, apart from my housekeeper, who has been in these rooms since Violet. I've had no relationships with women—not even of the most superficial kind, since she left me."

Her voice reached him gently from where she was sitting. "She must have hurt you very badly. I'm sorry."

Suddenly, there was the wonderful flashing smile that crinkled the eyes and had touched her fifteen-year-old heart.

"You know, I am so very glad you came. I had forgotten how much I liked talking to women—forgotten how much I just *liked* women." He put out a hand and rested it lightly on her shoulder.

"Thank you, Peridot, for coming. You've done a great deal for me."

She put up her hand and patted his, almost maternally. There was, for a second, one of those moments of pure communication between them that have no need of words.

As planned, Peridot spent the rest of that afternoon with Miss Boileau, who would depart in the evening for the country estate of a recently widowed woman who had engaged her services as companion. Peridot was sorry to see her go, but she could see that Miss Boileau was eager to go where she felt needed. In Miss Boileau's life—and Peridot recognized this, though she regretted that she was powerless to alter the circumstances of that life—that was one of the things most to be wished for.

The next morning, as Peridot arrived at her Bayswater stop, Clive was waiting for her, curious about where she had been the day before. The sight of his curly dark head inspired in her a mixture of pleasure and anxiety. How could she best tell him of her imminent visit to Paris?

When she got down out of the bus and felt his hand on her arm, she decided, quite simply, on the truth. He listened gravely and then said, "I'll see you again, before you go?"

"I don't know. I don't know when I'm going, but quite soon, I hope. Let's leave things as they are for now, Clive."

He leaned toward her, but Peridot saw a curtain move in the Fairley house, gestured toward it and was gone.

Barroway was waiting for her with news.

"All is arranged on my side with the Reverend Anscombe," he said.

She was to leave in a week's time. Tom Barroway proposed to call on her parents as soon as they returned to London, present the plans they had made together, and extend the credentials of the Reverend Anscombe. They agreed on a three-week stay in Paris, since that would be the length of her escort's visit.

Sir Rodney and Lady Pamela's reaction was unexpected. Her father appeared to be proud of her. Her mother obviously felt there was something socially acceptable about a daughter who was traveling to Europe, especially when she was being chaperoned by a well-known cleric.

She was given a great deal of money with the rider that some of it be spent "on a decent wardrobe. Get this friend of yours you are staying with—Violette, is it?—to help you. I gather from Mr. Barroway she is much admired on the fashion scene." Violet had been transformed into a Somerville friend.

There only remained to meet the Reverend Anscombe, and this took place on the day she left, at Tom Barroway's. He turned out to be a little like a tortoise in appearance, with a sleepy-eyed small face and head peeping out over his high, starched collar. When it became necessary, however, Cecil Anscombe dealt with the public, Peridot, and ship and train porters with economy of words and great efficiency.

Once the mechanics of travel had been sorted out, he retreated behind his collar as if into some sort of meditative state, leaving Peridot to her own thoughts. Thankfully she abandoned the attempt to be sociable, and they traveled together for the rest of the journey in an easy silence.

He deposited her at Violet's Paris door without comment, and with his address. They would not meet again until the day of their departure.

Even to Peridot's eyes, which were not that experienced in things European, the street breathed chic and exclusivity. The buildings, the way they were maintained, the carriages and people that passed while she waited for the door to open, spoke of wealth.

It was a youngish woman who answered the bell, dressed in a maid's uniform but looking rather untidy by what would have been Mr. Symes's standards. "Is this where Violet Cartwright lives? I'm Peridot Sinclair."

The woman's face lifted in a smile, and she opened the door wide. "Oh, *Dieu merci!* Thank God you have come."

She called out, and a valet appeared who, after a rapid introduction, started to bring in her luggage off the street as the maid took her into the apartment.

Strange, this introduction to Violet's world, the

place that was her home. So different from Peridot's own surroundings, redolent with an air of outright luxury, rather than the expensive comfort of Peridot's own home. It was satin that shone in the light of chandeliers, and everywhere there was the gentle sound of trickling water, the glitter of crystal, the sheen of lacquer, and a faint echo of the perfume that had wafted from Violet's first letter, written in her time of happiness.

"Where is she? Where is your mistress?"

"Through here, mademoiselle."

They were in a bedroom as unlike the staid, rather austere bedrooms of Peridot's childhood and young womanhood as anything could be, looking at a confusion of cushions, wall-hangings, quilts and satin sheets in the midst of which lay a slender, motionless figure.

Dark, curling hair across the pillow (shades of Clive—was that, she thought confusedly, why she felt warm toward him?), dark, curling lashes against colorless cheeks, beautifully manicured nails, pale as almonds, atop the red and gold satin quilt.

Peridot's heart gave a terrible, violent lurch. She ran forward and dropped on her knees beside the bed. Before she could speak, a smile flickered across the heart-shaped face, which turned toward her.

"It's Perry. I know it's Perry. I knew you would come."

"It's I, Violet. I am here. I said I would be and here I am."

The eyes opened, with a curious contraction and movement of the pupils as they focused on her. Then, both women were laughing and crying and hugging each other, as Violet struggled to sit up in the bed.

"Violet, you're ill. I thought something had happened to—someone else, not you."

"Oh, yes, that's why I wanted you. But I will be well now, you'll see. I just went to bed when I didn't want to think about it any more."

"How long have you been here?"

A shrug of her shoulders, very French, like the accent in her English.

"I don't know."

Peridot looked back questioningly at the maid still standing in the doorway, still smiling.

"About two weeks, mademoiselle."

"But that is disgraceful, Violet. You—who never give up! Come, come, you must get up now and, slowly, we will get you going again."

"Listen to you! Oh, how good it is to hear your voice—and to see you! Look at you! Such a fine figure of a woman you are now. No, do not blush. I do not like your ensemble, but, that we will remedy."

For her part, what Peridot saw before her was a young woman who, though pale and weak, was truly amazing in looks. The eyes were as incredible as ever, apart from a strange lack of focus. The cheekbones were more beautifully delineated than ever. Although obviously naked beneath the light silk shift she wore, the waist was only a handspan even without corseting, the breasts jutted out as if supported by art. But it was nature that did it all, and nature had done Violet proud.

"*Tiens,* Peridot, I will get dressed, and we will talk. How long will you be with me?"

"About three weeks, I think."

"Ah, *c'est merveilleux!*"

On a little low table near the bed, there was a collection of bottles and dirty glasses. Peridot crossed over and started to pick them up. "You need some housekeeping done. Some of these are empty, and some should be removed."

As she picked up the bottles, she glanced at the labels and the remaining contents. She held them out to Violet.

"How long have you been taking these?"

"Oh, I don't know. It is all so confusing, and they helped a little."

"I'm not surprised you're confused. While I am here, you must try to do without laudanum and opium. Certainly, without wine taken with them." She reprovingly indicated a half-empty wineglass.

"Now you are here, I won't need them, you'll see."

As Violet dressed herself, the maid showed Peridot to a smaller, simpler bedroom, which obviously had been used rarely and was unprepared for visitors. In the schoolgirl French which was to become more fluent as the weeks passed, Peridot started to explain to the maid what needed doing in the room before she used it and what needed attending to immediately in the rest of the apartment. The girl seemed only too delighted to take orders again, as though all the accustomed pieces in her world were once again falling into place.

Violet reappeared shortly after, dressed in a rose silk tea gown. She had obviously put some color on her cheeks and had brushed out her hair. Already, she looked very different from the lifeless figure in the satin sheets. The maid brought in the tray, and Violet obediently drank the hot milk that Peridot poured out for her. The tea that Peridot drank was not what she was used to, but it was refreshing and cleared the head wonderfully.

She let Violet finish the second cup of milk and said, "Now. Start at the beginning."

"The beginning is a long time ago."

And, as Thomas Barroway had said to her, Peridot replied, "We have time. Tell me from the start."

It did, indeed, take a long time in the telling. In her charmingly broken English—pausing now and then to find the words that no longer came readily to her—Violet revealed to Peridot a world as unknown, a land as strange as the interior of the dark continent of Africa, or the hidden side of the moon.

In this exotic setting, however, where every scent that reached her awoke the senses, it was more credible than it would have been in Bayswater or Belgravia. It was a world ruled entirely by passion, by appearances; a world where beautiful women were the supreme ornament, worn to decorate a man as much as his tailcoat, or the horses in his stables.

It made her sad, made her angry, fascinated her. As the story neared the present, the cool, sweet modulation of Violet's pretty voice began to lose its pitch, began to tremble.

At this point, Violet stood up, crossed over to a small lacquer cabinet and took up a silver-gilt box from the top. From it, she withdrew a slim, dark cigarette with a gold tip, which she placed between her lips. She pulled a long lucifer from another box on the cabinet and lit her cigarette with it.

"No laudanum, no opium, *chérie,* I promise you. But you must allow me this one vice, so that I can get through what I have to tell you."

"It's all right, Violet. Hold my hand. I'm here. Hold my hand and tell me."

Her hand in Peridot's, drawing deeply now and then on the pungent cigarette which she balanced on a porcelain dish by her side, Violet talked of Michel d'Aulnay.

"You must understand, Perry, that many of my friends have protectors, but few love their protectors, who can therefore be left—or can leave them—without hurt. That is where I made my mistake."

"I know, Violet. Marcus Radcliffe told me as much."

Violet looked sharply at Peridot. "He spoke to you of me?"

"Only because I went to see him, to find out as much as I could about your present life."

"Dear Perry, always doing your homework. Does he hate me, I wonder?"

"No. I think that part of him still loves you—not that he would welcome your return, though. You are part of the past for him, on which he has deliberately turned his back."

"Sensible Marcus. I should do that now."

"Where is Michel? Has he left you?"

Violet shook her head vehemently.

"Not of his own free will, I am sure of that. No—it is his family. He is with them, recovering from a gunshot wound. It was very bad, his second told me, very bad. And they would not let me see him! *Cochons!*"

When the paroxysm of tears had passed, she seemed calmer than when she had started talking, as if the grief had been stored and needed that release. She stubbed out the end of her cigarette and placed both her hands in Peridot's.

"Michel was always wild. It was one of his charms for me. Oh, he had fought another duel about two years ago, with swords. A friend of his had arrived here and—importuned me. Michel found him, and they fought. But it was one of those silly things. The other man was scratched, and honor was satisfied. This time, though, it went further."

Violet could sit still no longer. She stood up, disengaging her hands, and started to pace the room.

"The other man is a Spanish nobleman, a prince. He brought his mistress with him—she is, I must admit, beautiful in a full-blown way. A rarity, a Spanish blond. I could see that Michel felt drawn. I also know that he felt drawn because he hated the prince. It was a kind of challenge to him, to take his woman."

Peridot was bewildered.

"But you say that he loved you."

"Oh, Perry, Perry, I had forgotten. You must still be so innocent. So innocent. Michel has been brought up to believe that women are his natural prey. I knew that. But always before, he came back to me. I gave him what no one else could. I made sure of that."

In those final words, in the hoarse, purring quality that entered Violet's voice, Peridot sensed a world of carnality of which she had not the slightest knowledge.

"Being Michel," Violet went on, "he succeeded. And then, being Michel, he could not leave it at that. He boasted of his success and then boasted of my—attributes, compared with Graziana's. Manuel heard—he was meant to, of course—and they fought. Michel's father, who *taught* his son to be like this, has now decided that Michel too nearly risked dying and must now marry and become respectable. Normally, in our society, I could still be his mistress, but his parents have decided I have too great a hold over Michel. If he defies them, he will lose everything: his family, his position, his wealth. He is engaged now, I have read in the papers."

"And what happens to all this? The apartment and so on?"

Violet shrugged her shoulders. "I have been careful. I have money and jewels in the bank. And this place is mine. All I have to do is choose another protector. There are at least three who are possibilities. But I don't want them—I want Michel!"

The tears were all gone. All she could do was cry out as the pain hit her.

"My friends don't understand me. Ah, Perry, they don't know what it is to love."

"I thought I did, but I'm not sure I do, either," said Peridot. "I can understand you not wanting any of these other men. But why don't you sell everything and come back to England?"

Violet looked at first blankly, then pityingly at Peridot.

"*Mon amie bien-aimée, tu tombes de la lune!* I shall never go back to England. Life is not possible for me there anymore. I love Paris, you know. Besides, I must stay. Just in case Michel cannot live without me and the family change their minds."

"Oh, Violet," said Peridot helplessly, "you must know that you are clutching at straws. If I am to help you at all, you will have to face up to reality."

"A little correction, *chérie,*" said Violet, coming back to sit by Peridot. "You and I must face up together to *my* reality. You must see what is real for me, what is possible for *my* life. That is where I need your logic."

"I am lost. Explain to me."

There was a glimmer of the old mischief in Violet's eyes, a flicker of her lips.

"I want you to give your honest opinion of the chief suitor I have in mind."

"You said that there were three."

"Oh, yes. But, at the moment, I favor one above the others."

"Why? Tell me first, before I meet him."

"He is, I think, *un honnête homme*. He is rich. He is kind. And he is no longer young. Also, he is crazy for me."

Violet giggled, and Peridot was reminded of a little girl describing how she got whatever she wanted out of Timothy the boot-boy.

"Plus ça change, plus c'est la même chose," she murmured.

"Why do you say that?"

"A saying of your adopted country. The more things change, the more they stay the same, sometimes. I mean you, by that."

"Me? *Au fond,* underneath it all, I suppose I am."

The momentary mood of seriousness gone, Violet grasped Peridot's hands and pulled her to her feet.

"Tiens, Perry, it is going to be so *amusant*. Tomorrow, we will go shopping for you. In the evening, I will take you to visit some of my friends."

Peridot withdrew a little from the latter suggestion.

"Now, Violet—"

"Ooh, don't look like that! I am not taking you to a bordello, or some risqué party! This will be a reunion of many of my women friends. Very respectable. Well," she amended, raising one shoulder in that gesture that Peridot remembered from childhood, "as respectable as we can get in this funny half-world of mine."

And she threw her head back and laughed as heartily as she had in many a long day.

"By the way," added Peridot, as they said their good-nights later that evening, "what little bird told you that I had some freedom?"

Violet grinned mischievously.

"We are a close-knit circle. The *petite amie* of a friend of Terence's found out about you for me. I have—at a distance—followed your career."

She turned in the door of her bedroom and looked back over her shoulder at Peridot.

"For your information—look some time in the locked shelves in Monsieur Barroway's library. They will surprise you."

"I have," said Peridot calmly, "and they did." She laughed at the surprised expression on Violet's face.

Before she retired, she sat down at the desk in the salon and wrote to Tom Barroway by the light of the same Art Nouveau lamp that had shone on Violet's letters to her.

They did indeed buy clothes the next day: an altogether more fascinating experience than Peridot had thought it would be. She had never before encountered people so dedicated to the art of embellishment, the adornment of the human form. There was a frankness about their flattering remarks on her figure that was almost embarrassing, as they evaluated how best to display it.

"But," she said in bewilderment, after one such compliment, "I always just thought I was—big."

Shrieks of horror arose at this suggestion.

"Mais, mademoiselle," said the head fitter, *"vous êtes Vénus—Vénus toute entière!"*

The quotation, conscious or unconscious, from

Racine, took her back to a library and to Marcus Radcliffe and the first flutterings of her heart. Libraries, she thought, seem to be very significant in my life—and not just in an academic sense.

She liked Doucet's clothes. He had the taste not to drape her in too many frills and furbelows, and she enjoyed his sense of color. What a different experience it all seemed to be from buying clothes in England. Everyone got a lot of fun out of it, but she felt that they actually took it more seriously than an announcement from the Chambre des Députés.

The clothes that Peridot ordered had to be made, but they somehow put together something for that first evening that she and Violet were to spend in company together: a gored skirt beautifully cut in a dark blue silk, an exquisite blouse and a stiffly embroidered bolero that was a work of art in itself.

"When your maid dresses her hair," said Doucet to Violet, "let her leave the ends that try to come free around the face. That will contrast so well with the severity of the ensemble. And lend her one of your clips—a sapphire, perhaps—to put in it. Do not overload her with anything else. Her style is so different from yours. *Ca va très bien ensemble.*"

He looked approvingly at the two women, who set each other off so well.

Violet was regaining her form with amazing speed. She sparkled and chattered as she and Peridot returned to her apartment, pointing out the various scenic beauties of the city and peppering her comments with gossipy anecdotes from her own life. Gradually, a picture of her life began to emerge in greater detail. The name which was repeated more often than any other was that of Elise Damien. It became clear that, had it not been for her, Violet would probably have been financially, as well as emotionally, destitute at this point in her life.

"You say so much about Elise Damien. I would like to meet her."

"You shall. It is to her house that we go tonight."

"Her house?"

"*Oui*. The Duc de Malvert has given her one. On the Plaine Monceau. Small, but very private, in exquisite taste."

"Who else will be there?"

Violet smiled and patted Peridot's cheek.

"*Ne t'inquiète pas*. It will just be women."

"In *your* world? Just women? It sounds like Somerville College."

Violet really enjoyed that. She roared with laughter.

"Oh, Perry, you are so funny. And yet—and yet, in its way, I suppose one could call it '*une école des femmes*.'"

"As long as it's not a school for scandal."

Violet missed the literary allusion that Peridot was making and answered seriously.

"Oh, no—only if one wants it to be."

Nothing quite like one's first glimpse of Paris by night. A chill in the clear autumn air, a feeling of suppressed excitement: of secret rendezvous, clandestine meetings, brilliant soirées and theatrical presentations. Such a different city from the hot, deserted summer city that Peridot had passed through with her parents.

It was quite a long ride to the house on the Plaine Monceau. Peridot was in no hurry for it to end. She realized that she felt as happy and free as she ever had in her life. She looked across at Violet, who was entrancing in primrose yellow frills, and smiled.

"No cherries, no cats, no barn."

"No, Perry, just us."

And there was complicity in their laughter, as if they shared a hidden spring of happiness.

Elise Damien's house was different from what Peridot had been expecting, which was a larger version of Violet's apartment. The lines of the furniture and decorations were cleaner, sparer, although no less expensive for all that. There were exquisite examples of Chinese painting and porcelain in the spacious hall, which had a central staircase and a gallery above it. The room into which they were taken, which led off that gallery, was somewhat different in style, with larger areas of bolder color and some extraordinary paintings on the walls. The one nearest to Peridot caught her eye, pulled her in by the impact of its color, the life that sprang from its surface.

"But it's you, Violet!"

Three girls on a bench, laughing, surrounded by men, an impression of people enjoying themselves in the background in a sunlit garden. The girl in the center is turned toward the painter, her shoulder up toward the chin, the eyes like a cat's, the mouth parted over white teeth. Everything seems to be focused on her, on the incredible *joie-de-vivre* that springs from her.

"Yes, that is Violette. Renoir saw her in the Tuileries, asked to paint her. And I bought it."

She was being addressed by a woman even taller than herself, with coloring quite like her own, but very thin, almost gaunt. She was dressed as Peridot had never seen a woman dressed before, in an extremely narrow skirt topped by a wrap-over jacket in a heavy, figured satin with velvet lapels. Her fair hair was pulled back severely from the fine bone structure of her face. She wore no jewelry at all, and was smoking a sweetish, bitter-smelling tobacco in a miniature silver pipe. There was a worldliness, a knowing quality about her, that Peridot had never before seen in a woman.

"*Tiens,* Elise, you are not wearing your trousers tonight."

"No, but I think your good friend is disconcerted enough already. Peridot, I have heard so much about you. You are welcome in my home."

The words were warm and sincere, and Peridot started to relax again. So this was Elise Damien, of whom Violet spoke so much.

"Your paintings are remarkable. I have never seen anything quite like them."

"Come, let me give you a tour of my collection."

Violet pouted. "I have seen them before so many times. I think I will go and find some champagne."

She departed in a frou-frou of yellow frills toward the bottles of Piper-Heidsieck in their silver buckets.

"Good," said Elise, "I can talk to you alone. I am so glad you came. I cannot believe this is the same Violette I visited a week ago. You have worked miracles."

"I've done nothing as yet, really."

"Your presence is enough, *évidemment*. She trusts you, as she does not even trust me. She is better off without d'Aulnay. Without love. For us, it is a fatal disease. See if you can encourage her to take Léon Costals."

"Costals. Violet has said no names, but there is someone she wants me to meet, to see if I approve."

"Thank God. I am sure it is Costals, and I am sure you will. Now, let me show you my Lautrec, my Manet, my Matisse."

Elise turned and looked directly at Peridot.

"We are a strange society here, we women that you will see tonight. But remember one thing. We really care for each other. Some love with the body as well as with the mind and heart, but, above all, we care for each other. I sense that this is all new to you, that Violet has explained nothing. She never does, she just plunges in and takes everyone along with her. It is one of her charms and one of her weaknesses. This is our world, Peridot, where we can live by our rules, and not the uses and abuses of men."

Shock upon shock. Even in her protected life, Peridot knew more of what Elise was talking about than Violet had when she had first seen it. To read, however, is one thing; to experience another. Peridot looked around.

The room was gradually filling up with an assortment of women. Most approached Elise, greeted her and were introduced to Peridot. Some did not bother with such formalities. It appeared this was Liberty Hall: that they did, indeed, abide by their own rules.

Peridot forgot about social niceties as she talked with Elise Damien about the paintings. She found her amazingly acute. Amazingly, because she had assumed that women in her profession would be shallow, informed only to the extent that they could carry on a conversation on whatever was in vogue on a flippant, amusing level. This woman was often trenchant in her views, well and widely informed. Her French was beautiful—clearly enunciated and therefore easy to understand. Many of the women who approached Elise, embraced her and drifted in and out of their conversation were obviously not of the same class, but Peridot never saw any change in Elise's attitude toward them.

They ended their tour of the room and the outer gallery by a large grand piano. Elise brought Peridot a glass of champagne. It was cold and dry, and the bubbles hit the roof of her mouth and exploded into the most delicious flavor. Elise smiled as she saw the English girl's enjoyment of it.

"I am so glad to see that you enjoy a good champagne; within reason it is really one of the cultivated delights of life. It is the downfall, however, of many of my friends."

She indicated a small, overweight brunette, heavily made-up, who was sitting on a couch near them in silent contemplation of her glass.

"A few more months, that one, and I think she will either die or commit suicide."

"But that's terrible! Is there nothing you can do?"

The fine line of Elise's mouth drew an even thinner outline across her face.

"Only so much. Then, it is up to oneself to survive. In the end, it is always up to oneself. But for us, Roxanne would be dead already."

The voice was cold, but there was anger in the eyes, a terrible grief. Peridot felt a chill of fear for Violet. She looked over to where she was—talking animatedly to a group of women.

"Yes—you may well worry about her. One hopes that she will take up with Costals and remain sane."

At this point, it dawned on Peridot that there was

a man—in fact, more than one—in the room. Then, she realized that they were not men. Complete in beautifully tailored jackets and trousers, highly polished boots, hair sleeked back like Elise Damien's, these women talked and laughed without anyone giving them so much as a second glance. As if suddenly aware of her interest, one of them turned and walked toward Peridot and Elise. He/she sported a monocle in the right eye and was smoking a stubby cheroot. A striking redhead, dressed in white, came over as well, clinging to the impeccably jacketed arm. She looked up at her escort with what was unmistakably the gleam of love in her eyes.

"Diane tells me that she promised to sing for you and your friends tonight, Elise. But first, introduce us to Violette's English friend."

The introductions were made. The woman in the superbly fitting *tailleur* was a baroness, the girl who accompanied her a musical comedy star, Diane Lavallière.

"Ah, Peridot? *Charmante, tout à fait charmante.*" The baroness adjusted her monocle and surveyed Peridot with admiration.

Peridot felt appalled, disconcerted. All her usual references had been swept away. She realized now she automatically responded differently to a man or a woman. Class and cultural distinctions came next. She was lost, dislocated. She did not know how to greet this creature of two sexes that stood before her.

No response was necessary, for Diane Lavallière was already at the piano, running her fingers up and down the keys. The scattered crowd in the room began to drift in her direction, still murmuring and laughing together, borne toward her on the sibilant rustle of their silks and chiffons.

Diane sang Strauss waltzes, light opera, the songs of the Paris streets. Her voice was delightful, trained well enough for the operatic numbers, and her acting skills showed in the rough, tough, little street songs.

Suddenly, she changed moods, breaking into an old French folksong which she sang in almost a flamenco style:

Si le roi m'avait donné
Paris sa grande ville
Et il eut fallu quitter
L'amour de ma mie
J'aurais dit au roi Henri
'Reprenez votre Paris'
J'aime mieux ma mie au gai
J'aime mieux ma mie.

As the last chord died away, the beautiful girl turned and looked up at the baroness. There was as much love in her eyes as Peridot had seen in the eyes of any woman. Or man, for that matter.

Violet, by her side, said quietly, "And she has, too—turned down kings for *la Baronne*. She has found her happiness."

"You can accept it, Violet?"

"Oh, yes. At first, no. I felt disgust, rejection. Now, I think that it is love itself that matters. If with it go trust and happiness, then one is very lucky. Both those women have suffered. They deserve to reach some peace together."

This was another new Violet. In her voice, Peridot heard echoes, she felt sure, of Elise Damien. "You could not feel this way, Violet, or could you?"

"No, I don't think so but I wish I could. It might be simpler. Not in your society, Perry, but in ours.

Elise, *par exemple.* She would be better for me than most men."

Peridot could think of no reply. She looked across the room and caught the hungry eyes of Elise Damien upon them. There was no doubt as to how she felt about Violet. It said something for this society of women, that the friendship of these two could continue, without coercion or emotional blackmail on Elise's part. "She has not tried to persuade you?"

"Of course not. That would, in her eyes, make her no better than the men she so despises."

"Do you despise men, Violet?"

Violet looked at Peridot and giggled. "*Mais non! Au contraire,* I like them far too much."

It occurred to Peridot that, in this world of buying and selling, that would probably be one of Violet's most prized qualities in the marketplace. In the midst of satiety and staleness, her sexuality could still bubble up fresh from every pore of her body. Until a few weeks ago, every rivulet from that spring had led to Michel d'Aulnay. Then, deprived of its destination, the spring had temporarily dried up. Now, as it freed and redirected itself with Peridot's visit, Violet started to come to life. Perhaps, now that she felt its pull again, Monsieur Costals stood a chance.

"Dance for us, Marie-Ange."

A strong-looking, dark girl jumped up, snatched some castanets off the piano, a shawl off another woman's shoulders, and broke, almost immediately, into a Spanish dance such as Peridot had never seen before, her skirt switching and flying as her feet spun in and out, her hands clicking castanets. The tempo of the room speeded up again, the noise level rose, as the women's voices called out in appreciation over the clapping of hands and the stamping of feet.

"*Quel merveil!* The movement of a woman's body." Elise had joined them, looking more haggard than ever, a different sort of pipe in her fingers, with a strange and different smell rising from it. She saw Peridot's eyes move to it.

"Violet, does your friend use this?"

"No. What's more, she has made me promise not to, while she is here."

"*Dommage.*" Elise Damien shrugged her shoulders, turned and wafted away to another room, the door to which had now been opened up. Through it, Peridot glimpsed a large, bare, shuttered antechamber, with what looked like incense burning and thin mattresses scattered on the floor. There were a few reclining figures visible, strangely inanimate, as though they slept, propped on one elbow. The Spanish dancer had ceased her wild performance, and, somewhere, someone was playing a flute, its thin, pure notes cutting the heavy air around them. Peridot suddenly felt afraid. "I'm tired, Violet. Would you mind if we went home?"

"'Course I wouldn't. We will not see Elise anymore now. Often, I would have joined her in there."

"But you said she never—"

"Oh, Perry! The only thing they do in there is smoke opium. That may make this a house of ill-repute, but lovemaking is the furthest thing from their minds. They will be as in a trance. It is very peaceful."

"It sounds like the grave."

"Then, if it is, maybe dying will not be so bad, after all."

Violet giggled, which Peridot was beginning to

learn was a sign that she was deliberately changing her mood.

"But, I will postpone that, for a while. You and I will have another day together tomorrow, and then, soon, Costals will be back from his business trip and you shall meet him."

So, Costals it was.

The excitement had gone from the night air outside. There was a cold mist, and the city seemed deserted. But as they crossed the Pont Neuf, a flicker of light sprang up from beneath it. Huddled around this small point of warmth, the *clochards* struggled to drive out the damp, unfriendly night of the *ville lumière*.

Violet leaned forward in the carriage to see what had attracted Peridot's attention. "The have-nots," she murmured. "As Elise says, it is all too easy to be one of them." She shivered and pulled her furs around her, against the bleak thoughts that sprang to her mind.

"She is your Pygmalion, Violet?"

"I know what that means. Yes—in a line of which you were the first and Marcus the second."

A sobering thought. It had never crossed Peridot's mind that she had been one of the catalysts that had started Violet out on her journey to this enchanted and benighted land.

Oh, the delightful freedom of the days that followed, strung one after another in glistening succession! So divorced was Peridot from her normal reality that the sense of being utterly without strings was as great as it would ever again be in her life. They would get up very early, or very late, as the mood took them—whoever woke first going in to wake the other. It was agreed between them that they would do this, so as not to waste a moment together. They would eat lightly and then go out to explore the city. Violet knew it well, and the most interesting things that she knew about it she had learned through Elise Damien.

They visited the *ateliers* of many of the painters that Elise and Violet favored, losing themselves in the bold colors, the freedom of expression—even visiting the dealers who mixed their color for them in Pigalle. To her delight, Peridot acquired another little Harlequin like Violet's—and yet, not like Violet's. This one was more gaunt, more frightening, and yet he touched her in some strange way.

They looked in the smart shops on the rue de la Paix, and Peridot was struck by Violet's ability to discard that which she considered *toc*—trashy. Elise again, perhaps, but also Violet's natural talent for presenting herself.

Sometimes, they would lunch very simply, in a little *crémerie,* which provided four or five tables for its customers, and whose proprietors would pop next door for a bottle of wine to go with the *plat du jour,* perhaps just some *picuolo,* the harsh wine of the Parisian hills. With a superb Brie for dessert, it was a feast fit for a king—or a courtesan and her English friend. Violet would point out the various "types" who passed by.

"See—he's a *maquereau.* A pimp, you know? That's a *miché* he has just picked up for his girl."

Peridot learned fast about life in the streets of Paris.

They saw puppet shows in the Champs-Elysées and Grand Guignol in the Tuileries Gardens, laughing together like children.

They picked up copies of French newspapers and periodicals, which both women devoured—everything from *le Figaro* to *Charivari,* a satirical magazine. And it was Violet who had to help Peridot with the written French. They saw Violet's beloved Bernhardt together, and Peridot thought of Marcus Radcliffe, long, long ago in the gardens of Brierley Park, and of Shaw's life force. And Clive. She had not mentioned him to Violet, yet.

And, everywhere, there were the men. Watching, commenting, sometimes advancing and asking to be recognized, to be rebuffed either wittily or pungently by Violet, as the occasion demanded. That their interest embraced the two of them—*"Voilà la blonde et la brune"*—did untold wonders for Peridot's morale, although she firmly kept telling herself that she despised that sort of admiration.

They talked about that, about Peridot's attitudes, about everything. They talked till their jaws ached and their throats felt dry.

"Why should you think it wrong to be admired for your looks, Perry? Whether you like it or not, we are this flesh that's around us. It's what we walk around in, here on earth. One might as well feel good about it. The French understand that. They call it being at ease in your skin."

"I know, but they mean being mentally and emotionally comfortable with oneself."

"Ah—but notice that they accept, *surtout,* that it has to be done in this body. *N'est-ce pas?"*

Peridot talked about her parents. She never had, to anyone before. She discussed her own inferiority complex, so closely linked to her mother's reactions to her. Again, Violet was surprising.

"You judge your mother too harshly, Perry."

"How can you say that? She rejected me!"

"Not really. She tried to make you turn out in what she thought was the only way for a woman to succeed, the way she herself had succeeded. Her mistake was being too out-of-date, too narrow. She couldn't see the other possibilities. But, after all, she really felt that she was doing what was best for you. She was wrong, but she acted according to her lights."

"How can you be so tolerant?"

"She has let you go now, hasn't she, the way you want to go? She could have fought. Many of your class would have done so, I know."

Gradually, Peridot began to accept, for the first time, that there might be a way of reconciling herself to her mother.

They exercised their feet as well as their tongues. Peridot discovered the sheer pleasure of merely ambling, wandering—*flâner*. The *boulevards* of the *Bois* were made for it, as were the banks of the Seine. The river Seine, in fact, had become much more a part of her emotional life than the river Thames ever had—so separated had she been by her protected class background from the life of London.

Once, they took the train out from the city to the station at Chaton Bridge, only twenty minutes from Paris, on the river. The area had become a sort of boating club, with grassy banks and poplar trees and a charming restaurant called La Grenouillère, where they ate lunch, surrounded by middle-class people and fashionable ladies and gentlemen. Quite a few knew Violet and stopped at their table.

"What does *La Grenouillère* mean, Violet?"

"Oh, you know. Not a *bad* girl, but not a good girl, either. More a good-*time* girl!" Violet giggled at Peridot's discomfiture. "Oh, Perry, you don't have to be one to eat here! We'll allow you in! Look, it's full of very respectable people, just like you!"

Then, Peridot would laugh at herself.

"Dear me, Violet, I really am still such a prig."

"Protected people often are, and you have been protected all your life. Open your eyes and look around the London streets when you get home. You'll see hundreds of people who can't afford to be prigs."

But she would smile and touch Peridot's hand on the table as she spoke, so that her friend would know that no attack on her was intended.

They rode together, too, in the *Bois,* borrowing horses from the Duc de Malvert's stables. For, as Violet explained, "I am between stables, as you might say, and will have to borrow. I cannot really call on Costals's horses yet!"

Again, that heady sensation of freedom, cantering along with the cool autumn wind in their faces and the leaves tangling in their hair. Violet was an amazingly good horsewoman. But then, Peridot remembered the natural athleticism and daring of the child that leapt the stepping-stones of the river at Brierley Park and realized she shouldn't be surprised.

"Is there anything you cannot do, Violet?"

"I don't know. I always assume I can do anything and then see how it goes from there on."

What a philosophy. Except, of course, that it required some sticking out of one's neck, thought Peridot. So far, Violet had stuck out her pretty neck to great effect. She crossed her fingers on her horse's reins as she thought that, looking at the slim body just ahead of her on the narrow path. People's backs always looked so vulnerable. From here, there seemed to be so little of Violet.

They talked about sex. Or, rather, Violet talked about Sex and Peridot talked about Love. It was the one area where there were constraints between them. Violet's wealth of experience in that field and Peridot's Victorian upper-class childhood and still untried womanhood made it inevitable. It was one point where things were not as they had been when they were children.

"Are you still a virgin, Perry?"

"Of *course* I am, Violet. How could you even ask?"

"I'm sorry, don't be upset. It's just that—being away at Oxford and now with a job with M. Barroway. It crossed my mind that maybe—"

"No. Somerville was mostly women and Bayswater is mostly Barroway. And you are not, surely, suggesting—?"

"Oh là, là! Of course not!"

They both started to giggle, and harmony was restored. Guiltily, Peridot thought, as she laughed, of the moment that night at Bayswater, in the library. She also thought of Clive Fairley, the first time she had thought of him in ages.

Was it, then, love? Could love be so easily pushed aside? She felt no need of it now, with Violet and Paris and freedom. Perhaps she only felt like falling in love when she needed love. Maybe the object was unimportant. Finally, she brought herself to talk to Violet about Clive Fairley. "There is someone, though. I'm not sure how significant he is, but there is someone I felt for. I feel for."

"Felt? Or feel?"

"I really don't know. That is what is so peculiar. I seem to have forgotten him, here."

"Hmmm. That does not sound too passionate, ma chère. Tell me about him."

She told Violet everything—the walks, the cycle rides, their kiss—and she tried to put her response to it in words.

"Describe him to me. Make me see him."

Violet listened intently as Peridot described Clive's looks, and then the more intangible things about him: his sense of fun, his grin, the charm of his youth, his painting talent.

"*Tiens,* you must take him back a painting, that is for sure. The other thing that is for sure is that he sounds charming. I'm not surprised that you like being with him, kissing him. As for love—can you imagine spending the rest of your life with him—or without him?"

"I can imagine surviving either."

"Oof. That sounds more like indifference than love."

"Oh, no, not indifference, Violet. His company was—is—very important to me. But I am enjoying so much being here with you that I can forget him, I find, quite easily."

Violet's mood suddenly changed.

"That is not love. You know nothing of love. That is the trouble with you virgins. How can I possibly describe to you the incredible feeling of making love with someone you love? Oh, I'm not like some of my friends who don't like it at all. They act it out and then get up and walk away, unmoved. Relieved, in fact. I just *love* it. But, when you love—aaah."

The sound caught in her throat, and Peridot again glimpsed a world beyond a veil—some dimension where the flesh becomes the soul, and desire and will are as one. Once, she would have envied Violet. Now, she did not. She wanted to avoid that pain and suffering. She wanted to be happy. That kind of love seemed to make one wretched.

"That's the trouble with pain. It makes one suffer so much."

At this truism, the anguish left Violet and she burst into laughter.

"You know what Bernhardt's favorite saying is? '*Quand même.*'"

"Which is—?"

"Almost untranslatable, even by clever me. I think one would have to convey it in English by—'Oh, what the hell, let's just keep going'!"

"How true. Sometimes it's just best to do that with life and see what happens."

"Yes, but I like also to give life a little nudge now and then—in the right direction."

That night they went to the theater together to see Edouard de Max as Aeschylus in *The Persians*. With his posturing, heavy Rumanian accent, and being carried on stage in a sedan chair lit by electric lights, he was worlds, light-years apart from George Bernard Shaw.

Violet said, "You know what they call him, Perry? *Le Monsieur aux Camëllias!*"

Only here in Paris, in this brief interlude in her life, could Peridot have laughed so immoderately at a joke like that.

The next day, they went to the Galérie Vallard, on the rue Lafitte, and bought a painting by a new man—a Spaniard called Pablo Picasso—on Violet's insistence.

"Clive will love it, you wait and see."

With some misgivings Peridot bought it and put it carefully away.

"And we will buy something by Toulouse-Lautrec for you to take back. It will remind you so much of Paris. My naughty Paris. Besides, he has just died, *le pauvre homme,* and they will soar in value, his works. That is the way life is so often, for such brilliant men."

For her mother, Peridot bought some Art Nouveau jewelry designed by René Lalique and for her father some cloisonné. Before his gift to Annie Boileau, she would never have thought of something like that for him.

In a bookstore on the Left Bank she picked up a copy of *Claudine à l'école,* by Willy, with a cover by Ollendorf of a young schoolgirl, in a Red-Riding-Hood cape, yellow sabots and striped stockings.

Violet found it enchanting. "*Tiens, c'est charmant, ça.* I would love to dress like that...And bought for herself Willy's newest, *Claudine à Paris.*

That night, there was a noticeable change in Violet's mood. She was more serious, did not join in so readily with Peridot's jokes. They seemed to have reversed characteristics.

"Is something the matter, Violet?"

"No, no, *chérie.* Not really. But there is a note from Costals. He is back. It is down to business now. The time to be inconsequential is over. I must be logical again."

Logic. Love. A week ago, Peridot would not have hesitated to reverse the sequence, if asked their order of importance in French society.

As they drove out together in the direction of Fontainebleau in the landau that had arrived at their door, she pondered this new discovery. It was only now that she realized how often she had heard Violet say, "That is not practical," or, "Logically speaking." Often she said it about things of the emotions. That she, Peridot—with her muddled and blurry approach to life and love, as she now saw it was—had been called over here to lend her cool logic to Violet's situation seemed exquisite irony.

She looked across at Violet, at the discrepancy between her appearance and her expression. She was dressed in a purply blue that exaggerated to unbelievability the color of her eyes. Her heart-shaped face rose like a flower from its calyx of ruffles.

The expression on that heart-shaped face, however, was one of great solemnity: the President of the Board, about to attend the most important shareholders' meeting of the year. This, then, was how a society devoted to pleasure set about the business of love?

Out of the blue, the face of Roxanne, the brunette at Elise Damien's soirée, came into her mind. She thought of the announcement of a suicide in one of the gossip columns that Violet had commented on: a girl she had been slightly acquainted with, approaching thirty.

"*Zut,* she must have miscalculated this time. She really did it."

"You mean, she tried before?"

"Oh, yes. It is quite *à la mode.* But before, she failed—as she intended to—and he came back to her."

Had Roxanne and the poor suicide deserted logic, or had logic deserted them, wondered Peridot.

"We are nearly there."

They were really in the countryside now, a countryside on a larger scale than that in Britain. It was hardly a wood that lay outside the carriage windows. It was a forest. Violet suddenly shivered.

"Ooh, how I hate the country. It's so *murky.*"

"Then why are we going all the way out here, Violet? Isn't this a bad start to a logical plan?"

"Oh, no. His house is very *civilisée.* One can quite forget that one is in the country. And besides, he has a beautiful town house as well, near the Etoile."

As they were driven through enormous gates, Peridot saw what Violet meant about forgetting the countryside around. This was not a house, this was a château, set in a formal garden that Peridot would hardly have called a garden, for everything had been cut, tamed and controlled: short green turf contained by gravel paths with white edges, clipped trees, statuary and fountains. It made Brierley Park look like a gatehouse.

"Bien civilisé, n'est-ce pas?" said Violet, as she watched Peridot's face.

"Civilized? Tamed, is more the word I would have used."

"And a good one. *Dompté.* Nothing wild, nothing left to chance. Nothing—*sauvage.*"

"Heaven help the weed that dares to show its face in here."

But she had lost Violet's attention. She was leaning forward, looking out of the carriage window.

"Dieu! He is waiting for us himself!"

There was, indeed, a figure standing at the top of the imposing stone steps that led to the front doors.

"Costals? Does he know I am with you? Who I am?"

"No to both those questions. I would like to see him a little—off guard. It gives me the advantage."

"Violet—are you playing games?"

A surprised look, a shrug of the shoulders.

"But of course, Perry. The most important game of all. It is good I have some trump card of my own, when Costals has—all this."

She indicated the formidable edifice ahead of them.

"I'm not sure that I like being described as a trump card, nor that I really want to be one."

The serious look was gone now from Violet's face. It was as if a lamp had suddenly been illuminated, the brilliance with which she instantly shone.

"Oh, Perry, my lovely favorite trump card! *Mon amie chérie!*"

A hug and a kiss as the carriage drew to a halt. Oh, Violet meant it all right, but Peridot had the feeling that the curtain had gone up. The performance had begun.

Peridot had not watched Violet at work before. For that, of course, was what it was. She had seen her with Terence, playing off him to affect Radcliffe. But Violet had been a mere child then, playing out of instinct. Now her instinct and beauty were combined with a skill that took the breath away.

The object of this bombardment, Léon Costals, was a man in his late fifties who looked as if he had once been an athletic and striking man but had let the passage of time run him to seed. The large, muscular build was now paunchy and heavy, and the hair receded atop a face heavily trimmed with beard. He had, however, an excellent tailor, and his appearance breathed money, class and privilege. These, Peridot had gathered from Violet, were acquired, like the château. Costals's money lay in the tin and copper mines of the New World, rather than in the rich aristocratic veins of Old France.

This background gave him what Peridot was to find one of his most attractive characteristics: a vigor and forthrightness without the languor and arrogance of many of the long-established nobility. Not surprisingly, he looked startled as she emerged from the carriage, but recovered his composure quickly enough to save Peridot from feeling like an unwelcome third. It was also obvious that he absorbed with commendable speed that Peridot was not "*une fille de joie*" but "*une jeune fille bien elevée.*"

She liked him. Surprisingly enough, she liked him. He had a wife somewhere else, two fully-grown and long-gone children—she should be shocked—but she liked him. He was obviously, helplessly, in love with Violet. His eyes rarely left her.

The civilized forms, however, of the conversation of the society to which Costals and Peridot belonged, which Violet had so successfully acquired, carried them across the awkwardnesses of the first moments. Costals showed them around the château, which was furnished in a manner worthy of the Sun King himself. It seemed incredible that all this should be lived in by one man alone, although he was surrounded by a regiment of servants, and entertained on a vast scale.

In spite of his lingering, longing eyes, his exchanges with Violet were perfectly correct, even formal, and there was nothing for Peridot to feel embarrassed about. They lunched together—an elaborate affair, with a servant behind each chair. Peridot couldn't help thinking how impressed her mother would be.

"Violet tells me that you have wonderful stables."

"I love horses, love to hunt. It is one of my favorite relaxations."

He looked at them both.

"Maybe you would like to ride this afternoon?"

Violet looked at him over the rim of her glass.

"Costals, how could I ride in this?"

"Ah, you are right of course."

"What a shame."

Peridot meant it sincerely. From the window, she could see the stable buildings behind the house, the stretch of field and wood beyond.

"Unless—mademoiselle, you look about my daughter's size. Her riding habit is here."

Rapidly, he called over one of the womenservants, gave her some instructions and turned smilingly to Peridot.

"Yes, my staff will help you. That is, if you would like to ride. I have an excellent groom who would accompany you and a fine bay that would suit you well."

There was no suggestion of Violet accompanying her.

"Yes, Peridot, go. Costals's land is magnificent to ride over. I've already done so. Go. Enjoy yourself. He and I have many details to discuss."

It was the first direct mention of why they were there. It made Peridot perfectly happy to accept his offer.

As she excused herself and left the vast, mirrored dining room, she saw the two of them reflected in one of the glass panels at her side. Her glance cut into a look between them so intimate, so heated, that she felt briefly as she had when she had opened the books of Barroway's secret cache.

A landscape of mellow beauty. Lines that stretched to the horizon over gently curving fields, bordered by tall trees, deciduous and evergreen. A mauve mist in the distance, where the field met the sky. The sound of the horses' hooves on the hard, autumn ground, echoing on the crust formed by the first frost. And a dampness in the air that day that fell deliciously on her skin.

The groom rode a little behind her, a silent shadow. She had enjoyed riding in the *Bois* with Violet, but there was a vastness, a loneliness about this that fed the soul. She could almost feel whatever it was being pulled in with her breath, through her nostrils and mouth, into her lungs and then out along her limbs.

I am in France, she thought, hit by the unreality of it, galloping across the estate of a great château, on my own.

For a moment she wondered what strange scene was being played out behind the elegant walls she could still see on her left. What was the correct form for a contract of this nature? Was there indeed a written contract or was it instead a verbal agreement, sealed with what one might call euphemistically a kiss?

A little pang for a moment, for Violet, so she wrenched herself away from that particular thought and turned her attention outward again to the fields and the sky.

Not love this time, so one's timing could be perfect. Logic could rule the moves that one made. Not that Costals was unattractive to her. There was something about his brooding heaviness, the heat with which he looked at her, that brought forth a response. And there was, of course, the undeniable piquancy of new territory to be charted, the delightfully erotic feelings aroused by a fresh body, even an imperfect one.

How would he play this? Let him make the first move. Discussion or seduction. She knew that her earlier reluctance of some weeks ago had whetted his appetite. She would not fall, this afternoon, too easily. Well—she could hold out for thirty minutes or so, give or take a few seconds, and then give in with a good grace. Good grace? What was she thinking—it would be with matchless grace, with incredible eroticism, with unbelievable sexual energy. Poor, dear Costals would not know what hit him.

He will remember this, she thought grimly. He will remember this. I may be for sale, Léon Costals, but it will be the sale of the century. I will decorate this house as it has never been decorated before. Not with new paintings or carpets, but with my body. *Le tout-Paris* talked of me when I was with Michel, but I will stop the world as Costals's woman. That will be how I will reward myself. And him.

"I thought of you, Violette. In Genoa, in Rio, I thought of you."

Voice murmuring like a dove, pushing away the hand that felt her breast. "*Cher* Costals. You thought of me, yes. But you had other women."

"Only once. It did not work out well. Your eyes got in the way."

"Ah, you are so romantic, so sweet to me."

"I would be more than that. I will look after you, Violette. I am a generous man. You will be well protected. See, I have already opened an account in your name. Here. And you could live in my Paris house. It would suit you well."

"You are a darling man. Like a father, a kind uncle to me."

"Of course I am. I would look after my little girl."

Words twisting between them, chains binding them one to another, a complexity of financial and business arrangements intertwined with endearments, caresses, the slow removal of clothes. Finally, his triumph over her seeming reluctance, that triumph ending in what was to be Costals's total enslavement to the beautiful body beneath him: the captor far more captivated then the captive.

"I am yours, my darling," murmured the mistress to her slave as Costals, lost in a trough of sensuality, rose suddenly to the crest of a wave and shouted in helpless ecstasy. Through the thundering of his own blood, he heard with delight Violet's answering call—genuine, to her surprise, not simulated, as she had thought it might have to be.

In a sea of tumbled bedclothes, they reached quieter waters together, floating in silence side by side.

Violet contemplated the plaster caryatids on the ceiling above her. For just a fraction of a second, she thought she saw a mirror there and the hard-muscled body of a young mustachioed man, with his hand on her thigh. With the twitch of an eyelid, she erased the image, consigning it to some deep-buried mausoleum of the mind where it could disturb her no more.

His little girl. She thought of Claudine's costume on the cover of the book that Peridot had bought. She would have one made. That game would amuse Costals so much.

No more pain, no more suffering. She was free now to live the life she had chosen. No young man's scars to wound her any more.

Like any good housewife, she began to turn over

in her mind the arrangements for the removal of her establishment.

Costals snored happily on beside her. It had been a hard trip, back from Rio.

"*C'est tout arrangé*. The Paris house is mine. *Tiens,* imagine, Perry. I own a whole house! *Epatant!* I think I shall let the apartment, not sell it. I fancy being a woman of property."

"It will suit you. You know, business apart, I liked him, Violet. He seems kind."

"I think he really is. It is so difficult to tell. However, I have his kindness on paper, as well, and that is what matters, *surtout*. No—don't look at me like that, Perry. I made a mess of things before, because I did not think and talk like that. Without Elise, it would have been even worse. I'll not do it now."

"For a mess, it was a pretty lucrative mess."

"Oh, yes—as money goes. But it tore me up inside and not in the way some nice, expensive doctor could mend. This way, nothing gets torn."

"I'm glad—really I am, Violet. When will you move?"

"As soon as possible. Oh, Perry, stay and set up my new house with me. It will be such fun!"

But they both knew the answer to that. The emergency was over. Besides, both of them had a sense of Violet belonging now in part to someone else. The harmony was not broken, but its exclusiveness was gone. Léon Costals now hovered, bewitched, on the edge of the charmed circle.

Peridot contacted her silent and invisible chaperone. The message she received in reply said—yes, he was still in Paris and would be leaving in three days. He would expect to see her at the boat-train.

He gave her the time, the day, the station and left the rest to her. That night, Peridot sat down and wrote brief notes to her parents and to Tom Barroway, which she sent off right away.

"Now that that is all set up, Perry, we put it behind us and think of it no more. All we do for the next three days is—enjoy! Then, we both go back to our duties."

Violet pulled a face of mock-disgust and then hugged Peridot.

"*Eh bien,* what shall we do tonight? The Comédie Française? Or—your education is not complete. Let's go to the Moulin-Rouge. Come on, say yes!"

"No, Violet. I feel no need for that sort of completion of my education. It wouldn't interest me, you know."

"Oof, you are such a prig, *chérie!* All right, then, the Comédie Française it shall be."

And it was. It was Bernhardt doing *Phèdre,* and Peridot heard those lines again: *"C'est Vénus toute entière à sa proie attachée."*

And watched the divine Sarah twist and glitter and shiver like an aspen, splinters of glass in the voice and the soul. She thought of Marcus Radcliffe and trembled a little herself, as she glanced at Violet's profile, serene and happy beside her.

Three perfect days. That was what they managed to make of them. Arm in arm with Violet, walking along the banks of the Seine, browsing at the stalls of the bouquinistes, drinking tiny glasses of anisette and Pernod, and large bowls of milky coffee. Trying Violet's slender cigarettes and choking, while Violet rolled on the sofa, helpless with laughter.

Finally, they managed to talk intimately together.

"But at least you know how it happens, *chérie?*"

"Of course I do, you silly. *You* told me when I was ten—remember?"

"So I did. And you have learned nothing new since, Peridot *chérie?*"

"Theoretically, yes. But I also know—have felt—how strong that feeling is. How much I want, sometimes, to share it with someone else."

"You want to make love?"

"Yes. But, Violet, I could never feel quite about it like you do."

"I know. That's why it is just as well I am a kept lady and you are not. I like it, anyway, but you—I think you will always have to think it through a little more. You will always mix it up with your mind. I can give my body and still respect myself. You could not."

"It's all so confusing."

"For you, yes. For me, no. You couldn't be me, Perry, but often I'm glad I'm not you!"

"Yes. The sad thing is when I myself am sorry that I am me."

"Never, never, never, Perry. In this life, you have to learn to live with yourself. It is the only way to happiness. Then, all the rest falls into place."

"You are a natural philosopher, Violet. This started off as a conversation about love."

"About sex. Everything starts off with sex and most things end with it. That is my philosophy."

"So far, nothing has led me to believe that you are not right."

"Dear Perry, only you could use two negatives in a remark about such a positive thing!"

"Now she questions my grammar, this English girl who speaks with a French accent!"

"A paradox, *c'est moi*. That's why they call me Violette l'Anglaise!"

A paradox indeed. Not a paragon, perhaps, in the eyes of the world but, in Peridot's view, the perfect, paradoxical paragon of a friend.

Elise Damien called unexpectedly on their last night together. She didn't stay very long, but she came to confirm rumors she had heard that Violet was to move into Costals's Paris home that weekend.

When Violet left the room at one point, Elise turned to Peridot and said, "I am truly delighted for her. It's a step up from d'Aulnay, and that is all to the good in one's twenties. This relationship should hold for a few years, for Costals is quite *épris,* and Violet knows how to play her cards. Whatever happens, she should be well set financially by the time she is thirty."

"But she is still so young—she is only just in her twenties!"

"A time when the pattern is set for the future. Ours is usually such a short career, Peridot."

Just before she left, Elise said, "You remember Roxanne?"

"The one you said—would—?"

"Yes. She died this week. Slashed her wrists. She was depressed, you see. Even we could not sustain her forever."

They both looked up as Violet came back into the room, glowing, vibrant, the life-image of the beautiful girl that Renoir had painted on the Tuileries park bench.

"Don't worry," Elise said, as she put on her gloves, "I will look after this one. You will hear of her. You wait and see. She will yet give me plenty of material for my little journalistic efforts."

As did Peridot herself. For, the next day, she made her first ever appearance in a gossip column:

> "*Adieu* to Peridot Sinclair, the beautiful blond English Diana, who departs our fair city for the shores of Albion once more. Seen around town with Violette l'Anglaise, the striking couple now come to a parting of the ways—Peridot to London and her *famille aristocrate,* and Violette, we hear, to the arms of Léon Costals. Fitting partnership, indeed, between one of the lions of the business world and one of our city's great lionesses!"

Violet insisted that Peridot cut out the column and keep it.

"Who knows when your name will be linked with a demi-mondaine again? It's so amusing. Keep it and show your friends. Not your mama and papa, of course!"

Peridot looked at it.

"I could almost show papa. I think he would understand."

"*Peut-être.* But do not give him a secret to keep against your mother, *chérie*. That is not fair."

"How wise you are, sometimes, Violet."

They were sitting together for the last few moments in the little salon. A fire flickered in the grate and reflected off the shot silk of Violet's *eau-de-nil* skirt.

"Yes, I am becoming wiser, aren't I? Not gooder, but wiser! That is what I want to be when I grow old. A little white-haired old lady, smelling of patchouli and lavender, smoking the occasional Turkish cigarette in a lace-mittened hand, dispensing wisdom to the young—about money, about property and, above all, about love."

"Like the oracle at Delphi."

"To be an oracle in Paris will suit me well."

"Violet, I love you."

"I know. I'll always know that. It will help me be strong. And remember, when in doubt about love, come to this wise-woman friend of yours, *chère amie de mon enfance.*"

Words failing them now, they stopped pretending and clung to each other, tears falling against each other's faces.

"He's not a Krakatoa, Violet. You'll be all right."

"I know, I know. I'm glad to hear you say that. It gives me more faith in him."

Then why, if Violet had succeeded beyond her wildest dreams in this life she had chosen, did Peridot feel only the terrible fragility of this beautiful child-woman? After all, in a world where women were objects—to be chased after, attained and collected—was not Violet the hottest, most select piece of property of all?

Paris in the autumn sunshine, moving away from her eyes into the cloud cuckoo land of her memories, to return in flashes with the smell of a certain cigarette, a certain perfume, a certain blend of coffee. Chilled, dry champagne on her tongue and it would return, the sight of petits fours on a plate, a snatch of waltz music. And, in the center of it all, Violet, queen bee, dripping honey to catch the men who buzzed about her.

Dear friend of my childhood, how you have filled

my senses with memories to draw on, thought Peridot.

A tear dropped onto the yellow sabots of *Claudine à l'école,* which lay unread in her lap. Across the aisle, the Reverend Anscombe, safely ensconced in his own private world, read on, oblivious.

Chapter Nine

PERIDOT WAS GLAD it was her father who greeted her at home, so that she didn't have to face her mother's endless questions. Her mother was "visiting."

"You look different, Peridot. Paris has changed you."

Her father was looking at her as if it were indeed not the scent of the Sorbonne and the Bibliothèque Sainte Geneviève that reached his nostrils but the far more heady air of the Faubourg St.-Honoré and of Violet.

"In so short a time? It must be my new outfit, Papa."

"Maybe. I don't understand these things."

But he understood better than he knew, as Peridot confirmed for herself in her bedroom mirror.

Although her image had been reflected back to her in many mirrors in Paris, it was only here—in this looking glass that had known her from childhood—that she could see the change. Difficult to be precise about what it was. The outfit certainly was far more elegant and well cut than anything she had bothered to own before, but it only served to set off the difference. Then it struck her. It was not that she was taller, shorter, thinner or fatter—but that she looked as if she knew where she was going. She looked self-possessed.

Strange, she thought, because I know less than ever at this moment in which direction I should go.

Live minute by minute. Go back to Barroway, complete the job there. Then—and only then—would it be time to make decisions.

Her mother raved over her. It was easy to fend off the interminable questions by producing new gowns and the presents she had brought them. They were both genuinely delighted. The cloisonné remained on the small table by her father's favorite chair always, after that.

Her mother would like to have spent all the following day happily interrogating her, and it was only against a background of protests that Peridot was able to make arrangements to go to Bayswater the next day.

"But my darling, you must have a rest after that tiring journey."

"Why, Mama? I didn't have to lift a finger the whole time. Besides, I owe it to Mr. Barroway, who gave me this time off." She felt guilty as she watched her mother's pretty face droop and heard her hurt protests.

Nothing had changed. It was as if the three weeks had never been.

"Ah, so you are returned. I hope all went well."

"As well as could be expected in the circumstances."

At the sound of her voice, he looked up from his books.

"Hmm. Paris has changed you."

So Barroway thought so too. Briefly she sketched out for him Violet's collapse, her recovery, her choice of Léon Costals, and her own qualified approval of him.

"I'm glad for your friend. No rich gentleman materialized for you?"

"No. I saw mostly women. And mostly Violet."

"You surprise me. Paris is more a city for love than friendship."

Exasperated, she replied, "Friendship *is* love. Why does love always have to be associated with that one, brief act?"

He leaned back in his chair, the strong hands still holding the desk surface.

"Ah, Peridot, to answer that for you, I would have to make love to you."

Three weeks ago, she would have been at a total loss. And even now, maddeningly, she blushed, but replied, "That is no explanation. That is only to admit that words have failed you. I think you lose the argument."

There was a sudden, tremendous roar, and she realized he was laughing. She had never heard him even murmur a laugh before, so this was all the more disconcerting.

"Ah, but what a way that would be to lose an argument. What a way!"

"I've something for you," said Peridot. "You can add them to your collection, although you will not need to lock them away behind closed doors. They are what I would call 'silly' books."

She produced the copy of *Claudine à l'école* and its companion volume, which Violet had given to her after she had read it, and watched his eyes twinkle at the red-caped schoolgirl on the cover.

"Fascinating. The French do the precocious little-girl theme so well. This is new to me."

"That's because it *is* new. Violet's friends tell me that the author is really a young girl married to this Willy who claims authorship, and that she is something to watch. Her name is Colette."

"Sign it for me."

She did so. "To Mr. Barroway. Thank you for the three weeks. From Peridot Sinclair."

He placed them on the side of the desk and let his hand rest there for a moment. Then, he said brusquely, "I think, now, we will do some catching up on those three weeks—myself and this absentee employee of mine."

It was almost dark when she left the house that night. She had come down the steps and turned to the right, when someone stepped from behind the hedge and put his arms around her so tight that the breath was knocked out of her with fright and she stumbled in mid-step.

"It's only me. Perry, you're back!"

It was Clive. She had forgotten the impact of being touched by a man—or was it the impact of being touched by Clive? Little furry caterpillars of pleasure looped and twisted their way up her neck and down her arms and into the secret parts of her body.

So this was how she felt. Since her return she had refused to allow herself to think about Clive and the decisions that had to be made. It was as if her ability to think logically had disappeared in Paris. With Clive's arms about her, she decided to go with whatever fate would bring about between them. In the end Paris had solved nothing about Clive. Only she and Clive together could do that.

Between kisses, he said, "My God, how I missed you! Will you meet me, Perry, tomorrow evening? I'll find a place where we can talk—properly, not like this. Not hiding away in hedges or hansom cabs."

"Of course."

At her unqualified response, he gave a whoop of delight, his hands around her waist, looking into her face. "Come on—let's get you a cab home, so I can go on kissing you."

"I thought you had just expressed dissatisfaction with hiding away in hansom cabs?"

"Pedantic woman, so I did. But you must admit, it's better than nothing, and nothing is all we have at the moment."

But it was quite a nothing, that nothing they shared from Bayswater to Belgravia. It lacked the solemnity, the overawed quality of their earlier cab encounter. I want to laugh, thought Peridot, awash with kisses and hugs. No wearisome burden of guilt and longing, all mixed up together. Suddenly this all seems right and proper.

The thought amused her. How wonderfully convenient when something so—so outrageously, wickedly pleasurable felt right and proper!

She lay in bed that night and burned with wanting him. Again, she was unsure if it was Clive she wanted or the experience. The sleep that finally came was disturbed by heated dreams none the less erotic for the vagueness her inexperience gave to them.

Clive was waiting for her again at the end of the next day behind the same hedgerow, taking her arm quietly this time as she passed.

"Where can we go?"

"To Fitzroy Square. A friend at the Slade has lent me his flat there. We can be alone."

The details of the apartment were to escape her whenever she tried to recall them in the future, almost certainly because they escaped her then. Clive took her coat and hat and put them with his own over the back of a chair. Peridot crossed to the window. Incredibly, a few snowflakes were fluttering down. The end of the year seemed very near. She felt the light touch of Clive's hand on her shoulder. She turned to him and, finally, found herself saying the words that had failed her before.

"Clive, dearest Clive. I'm so gauche, so shy about words that show how I feel. I'm sorry, truly sorry, because I love you—oh, I love you so much."

Just before he kissed her, he said, "Strange. I thought that, if I loved a girl like you, I would show it by not making love to her. Now I find myself only wanting to make love to you if you love me in return. I don't understand it at all."

"It's all crystal clear to me." She was laughing, softly, delighted with herself, delighted at the expression she saw in his eyes. Laughing together, arms around each other, they found their way into the little bedroom at the back. They fell, entangled, onto the bed.

Laughter gone now, breath enough only for the words and acts of love. Each step seemed to lead with great naturalness to the next, so that she felt no shyness, until he uncovered her breasts. Briefly, then, she raised her hands as if to cover them.

"No, no need for that. You are so, so lovely. Aphrodite. Look at the cream and red of you. Besides, I can't unfasten this damn petticoat of yours."

She started to giggle as she put down her hands to unfasten the hooks, then stopped, thinking perhaps it was a nervous reaction out of place with his intensity. In the dim light, fading away outside the window, she saw his smile, as he propped his head up on an elbow.

"No, giggle often, my love. It's such a delightful contrast. That little chuckle out of such a tall, statuesque woman."

"My size again. You will give me a complex, Clive. Besides, you are tall yourself."

"No complexes. Look at you, the Venus de Milo."

He pulled a blanket up over her and started to pull off all his own clothes, sure and supple even in his haste. Words, jokes forgotten, breath quickening again, then the sight of his beautiful body: chest of soft dark down, slim hips, flat stomach, the hidden flower of his maleness blooming between his thighs.

And then love—gentle, tender hands freeing her from the coverlet and touching her so that she, too, blossomed, nipples hard; the choking marvel of his hand between her thighs as her sap flowed with the discovery of love.

Soothed by the constant stream of his paeans of praise to her beauty, the hurt was sharp but brief. Her cry rose to meet his, and she lay, arms around his neck, feeling the damp tendrils of his curly hair, her tears wetting his chest.

"Peridot, I love you. I'm sorry if I hurt you."

"I love you. That's not why I'm crying. You are beautiful. I did not know a man's body could be so beautiful."

He smiled, his head on the pillow close to hers. Cat-eating-cream smile, a strange triumph in it. "I never, never thought I would be making love to you, holding you naked tonight."

"Surprise, surprise."

"Of my life, my love."

They talked later, as they had originally planned to, after making love again. The second time, her cry was from pleasure.

"Darling Peridot, you're such a warm, responsive woman."

"Oh, I'm so glad. But maybe it's because of you."

"So am I, and maybe it is me. Or both of us, together."

He asked her to marry him.

"You don't have to, you know, because of this."

"My love, I wanted to marry you before this. You know that."

She sat up in bed, pulling a blanket around her shoulders. Carefully, she tried to explain to him her search for freedom to express herself, how marriage at this stage would be a constraint against her voyage of self-discovery.

Somehow there grew out of this a solution. A solution that, a few weeks ago, Peridot could not have imagined herself contemplating. Now, it seemed so natural that she was surprised it hadn't occurred to her sooner. But she had not then been sure of her feelings for Clive Fairley.

On her way home she thought, Violet would understand.

Then it struck her that Violet would not. Clive

was less well off than she was, less socially elevated, by no means assured of a brilliant career. No, Violet would not understand. She would, in fact, be very puzzled by it all.

And Miss Boileau? She might understand part of it, for it was financial independence that freed Peridot to make this decision, to live now as she thought fit. The decision was easier because Peridot had come into an annuity on her twenty-first birthday. Though everything had always been provided for her that was thought necessary, now she could take charge of her own income. She intended to put it to good use, to forward Clive's and her own career. She had not yet told this to Clive. It touched her to think he was prepared to try to support her himself.

She knew what Violet would say to that. "Touched? Yes, you're that all right. The two of you have gone completely potty."

Violet's reaction, she knew, would have nothing on her parents'. She would have to get it over with as quickly and painlessly as possible. She would leave the house, but first she would tell them.

At the thought of finding a place of her own, she smiled blissfully to herself. On her own. Answering to herself and for herself. Her own mistress.

The irony of it, the paradox, did not hit her then: that if she were not now Clive's mistress, she would not have made the decision to leave her parents' home to be on her own. It would have disturbed her if she had thought of it.

What was difficult with her parents was made bearable by the extraordinary calm that seemed to have enveloped her at the loss of her virginity. She was not sure whether she had become stronger or more selfish.

Her parents were quite sure. *Selfish* was a word that they used a great deal. That and *shameful, self-indulgent,* and *immature.*

If anything was a surprise, it was her father's reaction. Peridot realized there was a world of difference to him between her working for someone and living with someone. His ability to change and see her with new eyes, indeed to catapult her into that new life, stopped at this point. It was obvious he felt she had betrayed him, and this made his feeling of outrage all the greater.

"You are exploiting our kindness, our understanding of how different your needs were."

"I hate exploitation, so I will free you of that. And my needs are those of any other human being. I just want to be loved—for myself. Not for any plan I may or may not fit into. The answer to that appears to be Clive at the moment."

Her father almost had an apoplectic fit.

"At the *moment?* My God, child, are you telling me that this is just a—a—*phase?* That you will pass on—to others?"

"I don't know, Father. It seems impossible, at the moment."

His speechlessness gave her space in which to leave the room.

She and Clive had found a small house in Chelsea. She packed her bags and left. Her father's loss of words was to be the end of their last exchange for many months.

They closed off the attics and cellars, and lived on the middle two floors. A girl came in every day, found for her by Mrs. Fairley. Clive's parents had proved to be quite extraordinary. They had faced the inevitable with distress at first, and then with an exemplary acceptance of reality. As Mrs. Fairley said, "We love you and we do not want to lose touch with you."

Even with Peridot's annuity and her small salary from Tom Barroway, they were living on far less money than Peridot was used to.

She wrote to Violet. She had heard nothing from her, and so much had happened to them both.

But Violet had temporarily faded in importance. For Peridot, life at this stage was completely dominated by her awakened sexuality; apart from eating and sleeping, she and Clive thought of little else. Where she had wondered about it and even, perhaps, longed for it before, Peridot found, now the discovery was made, that she was obsessed by it. She wondered how she could ever have hesitated over her feelings for Clive. She would see his springy dark hair, see his grin, watch his now familiar long legs striding toward her when he returned from the Slade and feel weak with wanting him.

The obsession was mutual. They could hardly get inside the house and close the door before they were clinging together and making love.

She was sometimes shocked by the things she felt a desperate urge to say, about how she felt about his body and what he did to her. But she took pleasure in them, anyway.

She felt frightened occasionally by the force that dominated her, but that was only when Clive wasn't there and she was thinking with some degree of detachment. Most of the time, she did not think at all.

She did find time and space for other things. Life started, very slowly, to expand on other fronts. She wrote an article on the Arthurian legend—Mr. Barroway's library contained a great deal on myth and legend—and it was accepted by a small literary quarterly. It was noticed, and she received requests from others to write on similar themes. The money she earned from her articles gave her more pleasure even than the salary paid to her by Mr. Barroway.

While she was looking for outlets for her writing, she started to come across references to Violet in various society columns. Her life, too, had expanded. She was seen on board the yachts of kings and princes and at fashionable watering places in Europe. She was variously described as "the constant and beautiful companion of the business magnate, Léon Costals," or "that incomparable and dazzling trend setter of the international set."

Peridot wrote to her again, sending the clippings, and this time got a reply. It was the beginning of a steady stream of letters between the two women, written every two months or so. Peridot poured out her love for Clive and spoke of her modest literary achievements. Violet's letters read like the society columns that her name now so frequently adorned, apart from the bit at the end where she always responded to Peridot's news and thoughts in her own letters.

Peridot was surprised at first by Violet's response to her relationship with Clive. Unexpectedly, Violet approved, even of the financial side.

"You have found the perfect solution to both your passionate and puritan nature," she wrote. "You have found the most *respectable,* middle-class way of living in sin. *Tellement pratique, ma chérie.* So clever of you."

Peridot was not entirely sure what Violet meant. Did she mean that she might as well be married?

Gradually, imperceptibly, she slipped toward a certain Bohemianism in her appearance and her manner of speech. Where once she had expressed her views shyly, she now stated them with a bluntness and brilliance that went down well in the circle that surrounded her. She adopted the casual, carelessly dressed hairstyles of the young women of the Slade and the intelligentsia, and some of their brightness and color crept into her dress. Clive approved.

"Very titillating," he said, "having this respectable girl who looks like a gypsy."

He bought her a pair of gold hoop earrings for their second Christmas together and then christened them by making love to her while she wore them and nothing else.

It seemed to Peridot to be the perfect life. The cataloguing for Tom Barroway was finished, but she continued to go there, to help him with the book he was now writing—a massive work of reference on English nonconformist religions.

As he had promised, Barroway never once asked her about her private life, and that suited her very well. She continued to write her own articles. She and Clive entertained and were entertained several evenings a week. And then there was the lovemaking.

Out of the blue, in the spring of 1903, there came a letter from her father. She had not seen her parents for about eighteen months. Terence was getting married, and they wished her to attend the wedding. She had a feeling that they had done it merely because they felt that they ought to, so she replied saying that it might be better not. Since she heard nothing further from them or from Terence himself, she presumed she had done the right thing. She saw the engagement announced in the social columns. The girl had been one of the most beautiful debutantes of her year and came from a titled family.

Peridot was glad for her parents that one of their children had met their expectations. It would be some consolation to them. She wrote and told Violet, who made much the same sort of comment when she replied, adding, "It is strange to think how *naughty* and *drunk* and *immoral* Terence has almost certainly been over the last few years—and that it does not matter one jot for him!"

The next event that occurred without warning was in the late autumn of that same year. When she looked back at her life, Peridot was to see it as the first of many seeds of change. She arrived at Tom Barroway's as usual one morning, to find him in conversation in the library with a rather striking-looking woman. A certain resoluteness of character shone from her face and was apparent in the very way she moved.

The woman was obviously on the point of leaving and hastened her departure as she saw Peridot arrive. They smiled and nodded at each other, and she left.

"She would interest you, Peridot."

"She looked interesting. Who is she?"

"Her name is Eva Gore-Booth. You have probably heard of her."

"I have, but I can't think in what connection."

"Women's suffrage. Politics generally. She was just back from a visit to a woman she feels we'll hear a great deal about in the future. Emmeline Pankhurst."

"Also to do with suffrage?"

"Oh, indeed. She has just formed an organization that she calls the Women's Social and Political Union. They are allied, apparently, to the Independent Labour Party. Keir Hardie has given them much encouragement."

There was a momentary pause, as if he were not sure whether to say what came next, but decided to go ahead. "She would interest you in another way, too. When she and her husband were thinking of marriage, she wanted what she called a "free union," instead of the normally accepted form of marriage. She did, however, marry him finally—I'm sure that you can guess at some of the pressures she was under. He died about five years ago, and since then she has brought up four children on her own. Yes," he added in a more thoughtful tone, "I feel we shall hear more of her—quite forcibly—before very long."

It was the first time that Barroway had mentioned, even indirectly, her own relationship with Clive Fairley. Peridot looked at him, sitting behind the familiar desk. He had not changed at all in the two years she had known him. If anything, she was even more aware of the sensuality that emanated from this apparent bookworm. She was not sure if this was because of her own new experience.

One thing was sure—she could not see how he managed to live the apparently celibate life that he did. Did he console himself entirely with those strange volumes that lay locked behind him? It seemed hard to believe.

"Of the three maxims of the Labour Party, I have

a feeling that it will be the middle one that will most preoccupy Mrs. Pankhurst."

"And what are they?"

"Educate, agitate, organize."

All that day, Peridot kept thinking about their conversation.

I have no agitation in my life, she thought. Oh, I talk radical ideas with Clive and our friends nineteen to the dozen, but I don't *do* anything about them. Even my nonmarried state is no reason for courage in our set. It is accepted. We are not the only ones.

In fact, quite a few of their friends were living together or "having relationships," often with parental opposition.

Besides, there seemed to be a wildness, a dissolute quality developing in their circle. There had been a peculiarly clean-living flavor to their Bohemian radicalism in the beginning. A preoccupation with health, exercise, wholesome food—and sex, of course. But now the talk at many of the parties was less coherent because so many of the people at them became drunk earlier and earlier in the evening. And with the drinking and the smoking and the increasingly exotic and unusual comestibles, there was still sex, but more indiscriminate now, as if it were not the relationship that counted any more, but the sensations.

Peridot began to have a feeling of déjà vu. For a while she could not put her finger on it. Then it came to her. "My God, we are all becoming like Violet's Parisian half-world. We've created our own *demi-monde.*"

That realization, on looking back, was yet another seed of change.

Clive, too, had taken a major step. Or, rather, it

had been taken for him. Whether as part of a natural process or, more specifically, because of his love affair with Peridot, he had developed new strengths as a painter. Peridot, delighted, saw them quite clearly. As did someone else.

In the spring of 1904, there moved into the neighborhood of Fitzroy Square—where Peridot and Clive had first made love—the daughter of an earl. Her name was Pandora Glossop—she refused to use her title—and, at the time she set up house in Fitzroy Square, she was in her late forties and recently widowed.

Peridot and Clive had first met her through Clive's paintings. Pandora had seen some on exhibition at a small gallery near the Slade, and as she considered it her main mission in life to support and befriend young artists, she sent the young couple an invitation to an at-home in Fitzroy Square. Clive and Peridot were elated, for they had heard something of Pandora Glossop and her interests.

Clive, long finished at the Slade as a student, badly needed the backing for an exhibition, and recognition of his own. It had been a source of unspoken friction between them—not serious, but definitely there—that Peridot was making a name for herself, even in a small way.

Peridot pressed his arm warmly. "If she was impressed by your paintings, my darling, she will be even more impressed by you."

Never were truer or more prophetic words spoken.

There was already a crowd when they got there: poets, painters, writers, all young and unknown. Their hostess bore down on them or, to be more precise, on Clive.

She was an immensely striking woman. There was a gauntness about her that reminded Peridot in some way of Elise Damien. This woman, however, had long, thick hair, dyed black as a raven's wing, with a blue sheen when it caught the light. She wore purple, with a black, fringed silk shawl loosely knotted on one shoulder and gigantic rings on every finger. Her hands were beautiful, and she used them constantly.

Her face might once, in her youth, have been conventionally lovely, but as age had pared away the soft flesh, the strong bones had become too distinct, too hard. With Pandora, one was aware of the skeleton beneath the flesh all the time. And of her breasts. She was very proud of them and usually revealed half of their perfect globes, especially striking on that gaunt figure.

"Clive Fairley. Dominic tells me *you* are Clive Fairley. Just as I hoped and imagined you would look—but life so often lets one down, doesn't it? I am Pandora Glossop. And you will call me Panda, as all my friends do."

Suddenly, she shot out one of her beringed hands and bounced it off Clive's mop of dark, curly hair.

"Delightful. Utterly delightful. Curly Fairley. Curly, curlicued Clive."

She laughed, inordinately pleased with her own joke, and the group around her laughed in echoing chorus. Peridot looked at Clive, smothering a cross between irritation and laughter at what seemed to her a ludicrous statement. To her surprise, Clive seemed to be enjoying it.

She looked back at Pandora Glossop and caught a glimpse of something glittering, acquisitive, in the eyes. Not a Panda, she thought. More like a Predator.

The evening reeked of money and sycophancy. Everyone being nice to Pandora and then giggling behind her back more often than not. The food was delicious: great mounds of the best caviar, smoked salmon, superb salad vegetables, crisp giant shrimp and capered trout.

"As you see, my darlings," said Pandora, "no meat. I despise animals. So coarse. Nothing but seafood. Besides," here she broke off and pointedly eyed Clive, "seafood does such delicious things to the *gonads,* darling."

She adjusted her shawl as the laughter rose around her, hands lightly touching her breasts. Then, she moved away to another part of the room. By this time, Peridot did not know whether to be annoyed, disgusted or simply amused.

Going home, she settled on the last. But Clive's response was devastating—not because what he said outraged her, but because she couldn't believe that she had so badly misjudged what his reaction would be.

"But, Clive, she was suggestive—sexually—toward you."

"Honestly, Peridot, just because Panda is in her forties, you don't think that means all her interest in these things should stop, do you?"

Peridot thought of Thomas Barroway.

"No, I know it doesn't. But I would have thought you would be—well—amused, certainly, if nothing else, at advances being made toward you by someone twice your age."

"Not at all. I found it rather touching."

Annoyance now replaced amusement.

"And I found it disgusting."

"Ah but then, Perry, you're really such a bourgeois, respectable girl, aren't you?"

Suddenly, a quality of hers that he had found endearing, enchanting, had become a flaw. Something to be thrown up at her as an insult. A black cloud passed over her sunny life. Clive, whom she had always trusted, had brought out the insecure young girl that lay never far from the surface.

Slowly but very surely Pandora Glossop made herself part of their lives until it seemed that they were forever doomed to spin around in her orbit. It all began in quite a businesslike way, as she arranged to set up a solo exhibition for Clive.

But the next step was Clive's physical removal. One day when Peridot came back from Bayswater and opened the front door, she heard voices. She knew immediately who it was, for the familiar strident and imperious tones reached the bottom of the stairs without losing any of their impact.

It was irritating enough to return and find the woman in her home, but it really jarred to hear the joint laughter that echoed down the stairs. Clive's sounded as genuine and unforced as Pandora's.

They were in Clive's studio, Panda lounging on the sofa that Peridot herself had often used when watching him work. Pandora's sloe eyes darted to Peridot as she entered the room, but from the comfortable slouch of the body in the chair one would have thought it was Peridot who was the intruder.

Clive, however, was welcoming.

"Perry! So glad you came home in good time, before Pandora left."

"So am I. How do you do, Pandora."

"I do very well, dear girl. I have persuaded your man to abandon the far from perfect light of this room and take up residence in the sun-room that looks on to my garden."

"Take up residence?"

Clive's enthusiasm blinded him to Peridot's cool withdrawal.

"To paint, my love. You know how often we've said the light in here is not ideal. Well, Panda absolutely agrees and has offered me this marvelous alternative. I shall move my things tomorrow morning."

"Wonderful."

There seemed no point in saying anything else. He had not asked her what she thought about it. It had been decided.

Slowly, Pandora Glossop unwound herself from the sofa and coiled her way to the door. Peridot wondered how she could ever have seen her as angular. She was the snake itself, predator eating the egg from the nest. *Predata Glossop.*

"Well, must be going now, darlings. I will see you tomorrow morning, Clive. Manders will be round with the car for you. Nine o'clock sharp."

"I thought you never got up before midday, Panda," said Clive, in coy, playful tones that Peridot had never heard before.

"Sweetie, there are some things I can always get up for."

On that note, she sailed out the door, saying as she went, "I'll see myself out. Don't disturb that little maid-of-all-work of yours."

"I presume she didn't mean me by that."

"Of course she didn't, Perry. Why does Panda make you so insecure?"

Peridot felt like drumming her fists against his chest and screaming. Instead, she said, "Because that is what she intends to make me feel—and she succeeds, beautifully. Just as she is succeeding in her gradual encroachment on you."

"Perry, honestly. You make me sound like a—a shoreline that's being inundated."

"You are, Clive. You are. Can't you see it?"

Clive looked at her and saw the anger. He took her hands and said, "Sweetheart, it's nothing, honestly. Panda flirts with everyone, even the boot-boy."

"Is she getting up at nine sharp for him, too, and giving him the sun-room?"

Clive withdrew his hands abruptly and said, "Flippancy doesn't suit you, Perry."

"And sycophancy," she replied, "doesn't suit you."

His anger now matched hers.

"Panda is my patron. She will help my career. You have a patron—that old goat of a Thomas Barroway. I'll have mine and you have yours."

She felt as if he had hit her. Old goat? She had never told Clive about the books, so he had heard something from someone else.

"What are you suggesting?"

"As much or as little as you want, Peridot."

Through her tears now, she said, "How could you, Clive—oh, how could you even suggest such a thing?"

He had started to look embarrassed, ashamed.

"I'm sorry. I was suggesting nothing. I was just angry."

The damage was too much to repair that night. Peridot turned and left the room. She went to bed early, and he joined her hours later. As she felt him slide between the sheets, she turned her back on him, and he did the same to her.

* * *

She had expected to find the house empty when she returned home the following night. She was wrong, though. Clive was waiting for her at the foot of the stairs, contrite, loving. He put out his arms, and her anger and hurt melted away.

He had arranged a special meal, bought a favorite bottle of red wine. Afterward, they made love.

There was only one flaw. They had not once discussed the problems that were besetting them.

The year moved on.

Clive arrived and departed when Peridot did and was careful to keep Pandora Glossop out of their shared life. They appeared to be going along as merrily as they had before, talking and sharing and loving. Peridot, however, started to turn outward a little more from her Chelsea cocoon to the world around her.

Since she had been with Clive, a king had been crowned, Britain's relations with France had mightily improved—and women's clothing had started to become a little less rigid. Less whalebone, no more wasp waists.

Peridot broke away from the literary trend of her writing and did an article on the need for women to assert themselves more in the movement for women's suffrage. She learned what it was like to receive abusive mail, and she had a letter of thanks from Emmeline Pankhurst. She kept the letter.

Feeling calmer and more logical about Pandora Glossop, she wrote and told Violet about her. She had not been able to bring herself to do so before. She was surprised when she got a letter back from Violet, written immediately on receiving hers.

Perry, *ma chère amie,*

Lovely to hear from you, but did not like the sound of your new acquaintance. A woman who calls herself Panda and then declares that animals are coarse is not to be trusted. The world is full of women like that, but what is your Clive doing, allowing himself to be involved like this?

As soon as I write that, though, I know the answer. Career. Fame and fortune. Remember, *chérie,* when it comes to a choice, that is the one that most men make. All one doesn't know here is whether la Glossop will force him to make that choice. Ah, the vulnerability of us unmarried women!

Do not think from my words or from the address at the top of this page that I have repented my ways and withdrawn from the world of men. Well—temporarily I have. I have been a little unwell and am recuperating here at a nursing home run by the Sisters of Sainte Marie de la Famille. I have a lovely private room, and they are so good to me. I was at a sanatorium for a while at Boulogne-sur-Seine, but am much better now.

Do not worry about me, dear Peridot. If I myself were really worried, I am selfish enough to call you over again. I am only a little tired, and you know me—I bounce, I bounce! And I will bounce right back.

Léon is still so good to me. I think the dear man really loves me. He offered to divorce his wife for me, but that whole business is so tiresome, *tellement ennuyeux,* that the mere thought of it exhausted me.

You worry me at the moment more than *I* worry me. Keep in touch.

Friendship and love,

Violet.

The letter alarmed Peridot deeply, in spite of Violet's attempt to make light of her illness. She knew only too well what it was. Consumption. Thank God Violet could afford the best attention and had a man who loved her and would look after her.

What was also alarming was that Violet seemed to view Pandora Glossop as a serious threat, when she herself had tried to underplay the whole thing.

Things quieted down during the summer when Pandora departed for Italy. Clive and Peridot left London and went to stay in the Fairleys' summer cottage in the West Country for a few weeks. The Fairleys were abroad, they were alone, and it was a return to the idyllic life of their early months together, in the pre-Pandora days.

Peridot had cheering news of Violet, redirected from Chelsea. She was glowing with health again, summering in Biarritz and Aix-les-Bains—"But only because it's *à la mode,* darling, not because I *need* to take the waters!"

Happy and relieved that Violet was better and that she herself could send good news, Peridot wrote off to her immediately about her perfect summer.

They returned to London when the Fairleys came back to the cottage, with the end of summer still ahead of them. The house in Chelsea, the hot London streets, were still heaven to Peridot, for she and Clive were alone.

Inevitably—*fatalement,* as the French and Violet

would have said—Pandora returned. She descended on them without warning at about eight o'clock one morning, admitted by their surprised maid to the dining room where they were finishing breakfast.

She stood, arms akimbo, in the doorway, her eyes unequivocally fixed on Clive. She was dressed completely in white, from which her sun-tinted face and arms burst in unsubtle contrast.

"See," she boomed, "I said that there were some things that I would always get out of bed for."

The change in Clive was immediate. It was as if some hypnotist had snapped a finger and put him under again. He pushed his chair back and flung his own arms wide.

"Panda, you're back!"

He said it as if it were the one thing he had been waiting for all those weeks. All those weeks which Peridot had thought of as being among the happiest of their life together.

Once more, Clive departed on his day-long sojourns to Pandora Glossop, and Peridot departed for Thomas Barroway's library. There, she could at least make herself think of other things.

When she did allow herself to think of her situation, her one consolation was that the showing was almost upon them and after it, the necessary link with Pandora would be over.

Pandora had decided on a costume party for the opening night of Clive's exhibition. Not too originally or surprisingly, she was planning to go as a gypsy and had firmly decreed that Clive go as an Elizabethan. She had made no suggestions at all about Peridot.

"I shall go as I am."

"But you can't possibly, Perry. Oh, come on, love. This is my big night. Let the world see what a pretty little wife I have."

"I am *not* pretty. I am *not* little. And I am not your wife."

The look he gave her was straight and clear and cold.

"I'd forgotten. You're not, are you?" he said.

The costume of the Elizabethan nobleman arrived, complete with tights, shoes and one earring, from Pandora's own costumier. Peridot had to admit that Clive looked incredibly handsome in it. Pandora had chosen well. With the earring glistening beneath the dark curls and the tights sheathing his long legs, his well-bred, middle-class good looks became sensuous and piratical.

Peridot had decided to bend with the wind. "Panda is clever. That's absolutely right for you."

Clive was childlike in his delight. "Then you'll dress up, Perry? Come on, let's order you an Elizabethan costume."

She smiled maternally at his enthusiasm. "No, no. That's not my period. It would be all wrong. No. I shall go as a Puritan. I think Pandora would prefer that, to us arriving as an obvious couple."

He saw her point only too well and did not disagree.

Peridot had the dressmaker she sometimes used sew her a perfectly plain black dress, with a white collar and cuffs and a plain white bonnet. It looked good on her, with her fair hair and pearly skin. Besides, the contrast with Clive was perfect.

The contrast with Pandora was perfect, too. She greeted them at the door, a tambourine streaming ribbons in one hand and a pair of castanets clicking away inexpertly in the other. She was dressed uncompromisingly in scarlet, with ruffles that never seemed to end. Her skirt reached to her ankles only, and her feet were bare, the nails painted scarlet to match her clothes. She had gold coins and earrings and bangles on forehead, ears, neck, arms—wherever there was a surface to adorn. There was scarlet on her lips and cheeks, and her eyes were rimmed with kohl. Bangles around each ankle knocked together as she walked. With every movement, Pandora crashed and tinkled like a one-woman band.

She led them in to the large living room on the first floor, past Greek gods, Roman centurions, Chinese mandarins, dancing girls. A gypsy orchestra played uncontrollably loudly, amid palms.

In front of them in the living room, a gentleman in full armor was being fed through a chink in his helmet by a shrieking girl, who seemed to be wearing mostly feathers. A vastly pregnant woman bore down upon Peridot, Clive and Pandora. As she spoke to them, Peridot realized it was a man in costume.

"Welcome, welcome! Silence, everyone! Panda is going to present her latest lion!"

There was a roar and a round of applause, and then Pandora addressed the crowd:

"Ladies and gentlemen, this handsome adventurer is Clive Fairley. Remember that name—Clive Fairley! It will be a name with which to conjure one day!"

More applause greeted this bold prediction. Clive stood there, beaming, self-possessed, loving it.

The evening progressed through a blur of uproar, excess and back-slapping. At midnight, a monster cake was wheeled in, and Clive was summoned forth to cut it. He made a great show of insisting on slicing it with Pandora, who was only too happy to cooperate.

They stood together, very much like newlyweds, Pandora's beruffled hip resting firmly against Clive's doublet and hose. As the knife descended, Pandora suddenly shrieked, *"Now!"*

What appeared to be an iced top flew off the cake, and a well-endowed and scantily clad girl leapt out onto the table, landing in the salmon aspic with her bare feet and slipping onto her ample rear with a squeal. A gentleman dressed as a court jester grabbed one of her feet and started to lick the jelly off it. This caused a brief skirmish, as two or three other inebriates fought over the other available foot.

At this point, Peridot realized that Clive and Pandora were nowhere to be seen. She turned away, walked back through the rooms to the hall and found a manservant to locate her cloak and flag down a cab.

When she got home, she took off her cloak and Puritan dress and bonnet, folding them neatly away. Then she got into bed and fell almost immediately into an exhausted sleep.

She did not know how much later it was that she heard Clive. She heard him because he was vomiting noisily in the kitchen.

When she got up in the morning, he was sleeping in his clothes on the sofa in the old studio, an enamel basin on the floor by his side. Looking down at him, she felt no anger, no disgust, no jealousy. And no love.

The showing was a success. Clive started to sell. Whether it was genuine public response or Pandora's large circle of friends and acquaintances, only time would tell.

Peridot and Clive drifted on together, buoyed up by the enthusiasm engendered by this success. They never once mentioned the night of the party. They behaved as if it had never happened. Clive, however, was still working in the sun-room at Fitzroy Square.

There was another party over Christmas which Peridot did not attend. She told Clive that she didn't feel well, and, after a brief show of wishing to stay and care for her, he went on his own, at her insistence. He spent the whole of the following day in bed, having crept in at dawn.

Again, neither of them mentioned it. A pattern of shared separation had started to develop between them.

In the spring of the new year, Peridot received an anonymous letter. She had had some before, about her views on the women's suffrage movement. This one, however, was brief, to the point and on a different subject.

"Why don't you find out what your fancy man paints in the sun-room? Give you two guesses—twin guesses."

It was a shock, but she thought herself lucky that the language was so restrained, almost coy, unlike some of the vitriol she had received over her feminist views. "Why not?" she said out loud. "Maybe I *should* find out what my fancy man is doing."

She asked Thomas Barroway for the following morning off.

"Something important to see to?"

"Yes. I think it may be a rendezvous with destiny."

"Intriguing. Will you tell me about it?"

"Yes. Yes, I think I may."

* * *

Peridot stepped firmly past the stunned butler who greeted her at Pandora's door.

"It's all right. I know where I am going. And I shan't be staying long, so I will keep my coat and hat, thank you."

"But Lady Glossop has left strict orders that she is not to be disturbed for the next four hours, madam."

"Then I'll be sure to tell her that you did your best to stop me."

What a tableau greeted her. She had half expected it, but the shock was still great. After all, she had thought herself in love with and loved by the young man who stood at the easel, paints in hand, furry chest bare, wearing just his trousers over bare feet.

He was facing Pandora Glossop, who had also bared her chest for the occasion and also wore trousers—a pair of diaphanous harem pants that bagged over her bare feet. And nothing else. The large, white breasts shouted across the room, the nipples apparently painted gold. She had been lying, legs splayed, on a chaise longue, a goblet in her hand, but she shot up when she saw Peridot standing there. Snatching a piece of chiffon from the floor, she tried, futilely, to cover her breasts with it.

Clive merely stood, transfixed, palette and brush in hand. The painting on the easel was only too obviously Pandora à la Turque.

Peridot spoke first.

"I promised your butler that I would tell you that he did his best to stop me. Which he did. Aren't you going to cover up your nipples, too, Clive?"

White-faced, Clive replied, "Perry! I was working on—on—"

"So I see."

Peridot turned and looked at Pandora again. She now saw something in the eyes that surprised her. It was pleasure, satisfaction. And then it dawned on her. I am supposed to be here. It was her missive I got yesterday and I obeyed it. She wants this. Well, I had better give as little satisfaction as I can. Let's see how grossly I can make this thing misfire.

Again, Clive spoke. Pandora had not moved, had even let the chiffon drop again; she watched them both, as if she were the voyeur.

"Why did you come?" he asked.

Peridot was amazed at her calm. Raising her eyebrows in exaggerated surprise, she said, "Because I received a note from Panda, telling me to."

She saw the complacent face redden, watched the anger in Clive's glance as he looked across the room in the direction of the chaise longue.

"So nice of you to ask me, Panda. Did you want an audience? I'm happy to oblige."

And she broke into seemingly unforced, helpless laughter, doubling over in her mirth.

"You know," she gasped, "It's really too cold for this sort of thing—you both have goose pimples. Oh, dear, oh, dear, everyone will find this so *funny!*"

She watched as the pleasure in Pandora Glossop's eyes mutated into an embarrassed anger. Clive was looking desperate by now. He snatched up his shirt, started to put it on.

"Look, Perry—don't be angry."

"Oh, but I'm not. I haven't laughed like this for ages. It has taken me so long to cultivate a sense of the ridiculous and you have given me a perfect scene on which to practice it."

She walked swiftly over to the easel.

"Not good enough, Clive dear. Are you sure your heart is in it? Here, let me help you start again."

Before he realized what she was doing, she had the painting off the easel and was across the room, where she brought the canvas down neatly over Pandora's head. There was a satisfying, tearing sound from the canvas and, finally, a sound from Pandora. A roar of outrage.

Clive still stood, glued to the spot, his shirt half on. He gaped at Peridot in sheer disbelief. "Peridot! What are you doing? This isn't like you!"

"Nor is this."

She picked up the paint palette and found herself just tall enough to lay it fairly and squarely over his head. Rivulets of cadmium yellow, burnt umber and white trickled over his face, as the palette fell to the floor.

It was all done quickly, calmly, efficiently. She left the room swiftly, running through to the hall, where the butler still stood, looking as if he had been hopping from one foot to the other since she had swept past him earlier.

"Quick, quickly—Lady Glossop needs you immediately. You are to go right away to the sun-room and to go *straight* in."

The last she saw was his hastily receding back disappearing through the salon. It would probably be one of his more interesting butling experiences. One to dine out on, certainly. And it was most unlikely that he would be dismissed for bursting in, since it would provide him with such delicate information.

Peridot returned to Chelsea. She gave the maid a month's wages in advance and explained that, after that week, they would no longer be needing her services. She then sat down and wrote out excellent references for the startled girl. Next, she packed all her clothes—not rushing, but carefully folding them and putting them away in two big trunks in the bedroom. She made a list of the furniture and belongings which she wished to keep and a copy of it for Clive. It was not a very long list, and she made arrangements for it all to be put into storage. She contacted their landlord by letter, enclosed the rent up to the end of their lease, and added this information to the note for Clive.

There were no children, no pets, none of the encumbrances which make these partings even more difficult. Three years of loving and living were brought to an end in a day's work. She put on her coat and hat, said good-bye to the maid and left for Thomas Barroway's, one small valise in hand.

She had not yet cried.

Mr. Barroway was waiting for her in the living room when she arrived: a change in routine almost as momentous as what had happened that morning.

"Come in. Sit down. Mrs. Calderwood is fetching us some tea and something to eat. I would suspect that you have not eaten today."

"You know."

"Some of it. Fairley has been here. I'm supposed to be reasoning with you. Would you like me to?"

"No, thank you. Please feel free to do so if you wish. But it would be a waste of time."

"I thought so. Anyway, Fairley's idea of what would constitute reasoning is different from mine. Ah, here is Mrs. Calderwood with the tea."

When she had put the trolley in front of them,

Mrs. Calderwood went across and put a hand on Peridot's shoulder.

"Eat up, dear. Troubles always seem worse on an empty stomach."

These trite, kindly words did what all the morning's events had failed to do. Peridot clutched Mrs. Calderwood's skirt and sobbed out three years gone, gone, washed away down some estuary and out to sea.

Mrs. Calderwood tutted and clucked and patted and said, "There, there." Thomas Barroway said nothing. He sat quietly and waited. At a break in the tears, he poured her some tea and handed it to her.

"Do you want me to try to prepare the way for you to go home?"

"Oh, no. I'll never do that. I was going to ask if I could board here."

Barroway was taken aback.

"What about the proprieties, my girl? Won't people talk?"

This made her smile.

"After my last three years, do you think I would worry about the proprieties? Or is it your own reputation you're worrying about?"

At this point Mrs. Calderwood stepped firmly into the breach.

"Miss Peridot is more than welcome here, sir, as far as I am concerned. It seems the most sensible idea, for the moment."

Thus it was arranged. Peridot became a boarder. She insisted on paying Mrs. Calderwood for her keep, as Barroway would have nothing of it. She arranged for her two large trunks to be delivered.

In the early evening, Clive's mother came calling.

It was a distressing interview. She begged Peridot to take Clive back, to marry him.

"But I don't think Clive would want that."

"Oh, yes, my dear, he would. It's what he has always wanted. I think that none of—this—would have happened if you had married him three years ago."

Peridot looked at the distraught woman and felt a great sadness for her.

"Not only would it have happened, Mrs. Fairley, but it would have been far, far more painful to extricate ourselves at this time, if we had been married. Tell Clive I wish him fame and fortune."

Mrs. Fairley was crying as she was ushered out.

Peridot found that she had cried out all her tears.

They sat up late in the little study that night—she and Thomas Barroway. It was a cool night, and Mrs. Calderwood had lit the fire for them.

Peridot sat on a low stool close to it, arms around her knees. Looking at the flames, she found herself able to tell Tom Barroway of the course of events and the final scene that she had interrupted that morning. When she had finished, she looked up at him.

"Like something from your collection of *curiosa,* is it not?"

"With one very important difference."

"What is that?"

"In real life people get hurt by lust and love. In books, no one gets hurt. Or, if they do, it is generally of their own choosing. They can exchange partners, stage orgies, deflower virgins, have brief, erotic encounters on the side of a road, in a strange room, at any time. That is why I prefer my books."

"Ah, I wondered. You were hurt, once."

"Once. Oh, yes. Never more now."

"Do you think I will be like that—sublimate it all in my own little curious collection?"

Barroway bent forward and placed a finger on her lips—the first time he had ever touched her.

"Don't laugh, cruel girl. You will sublimate, yes. But I do not think it will be with curiosa. I think that history and your need for fulfillment are going to place themselves side by side, quite appropriately."

Tom Barroway lay on his bed that night and watched the spring night sky outside the window. A bird called somewhere. Lonely, warning. "Ah, Peridot," he said out loud, "curiosa and sublimation do not, however, stop the wanting."

No, the wanting did not stop. So humiliating to find that she still wanted that young, hard body against her, after all that he had done to her. And it wasn't just the body. It was the laughing and sharing and companionship. She missed it all terribly.

She never cried again in front of Mr. Barroway and Mrs. Calderwood. They conducted themselves perfectly with her: supportive but never fussing; companionable but respectful of her privacy. She realized how lucky she was even as she grieved over her ill fortune.

Her father wrote to her, offering to have her back. She knew that Mr. Barroway must have spoken to him. She thanked him politely, told him that she loved him, needed a breathing space and would then make her decisions.

She wrote to Violet, hiding nothing.

Violet wrote back, almost immediately. She wrote

from a sanatorium called Valmont. She had had "a slight return of my ill-health—nothing to concern yourself about. I will soon be myself again, am off to Cabourg to recuperate. It is not too difficult a journey, and there one can be as quiet or as noisy as one wishes. There is such a charming ladies' brass band that plays on the beach, and I have taken up golf. Or, I hope to take it up again, when I am stronger.

"Please, Perry, come to me. For you, not for me, this time. If not Cabourg, then join me in Marienbad, in August. You will love it. Léon has to leave me alone then, for a while, and he fusses so. Come. It will be such fun."

Thank God for money. She would to go Marienbad. Cure herself and Violet. Both of them so much more frail than they had thought.

"Violet—I come, I come. I will be with you in Marienbad."

Chapter Ten

IN MIDSUMMER, time of fairy tales and dreams, Peridot traveled to a place as close to being fairyland as real life will allow: Marienbad, in the Eger valley of Bohemia. A scene from a ballet, a snatch of light opera—Marienbad was all this and more. The king of England, Uncle of Europe, had made Marienbad, in August, the unofficial capital of Europe by making it his own for three weeks every year.

There was laughter and song and sunlight dappling through the trees on the Kreuzbrunner promenade, where the breezes caught in the women's soft summer dresses and ruffled the frills of their delectable parasols, so that the light and shade flirted across their laughing faces. There was the magnificent Weimar Hotel, where the king himself stayed, and where Peridot also was to stay. And there was Violet.

Violet, at the station, waiting for her, with Léon Costals at her side. Violet, up on tiptoes in impatience, waiting to catch her first glimpse of Peridot in—was it *really* four years?

Violet was beautiful. Violet had always been beautiful, but the mid-twenties, or illness, had honed away any surplus flesh, anything that was redundant. The perfection of the bone structure shone through transparent white skin, a flush of rose decorating the high cheekbones. The liquid flow of the walk was still there—no angularity here—as she ran to Peridot. Men and women turned to look at her. The dark curls brushed her cheeks and revealed her ears, diamonds catching the light on the shell-pink lobes. Her waistline took the breath away. She was a Dresden figurine, a pearl of the Orient. She was at her zenith.

Words failed them both. Peridot felt Violet's heart beating against hers, as they held each other tight, tight. Little girls again, these two women who had now attained their first quarter century. A world of complicity, of closeness between them, that only a shared childhood can bring. They looked at each other, holding each other at arm's length, observing the changes that life had wrought.

"Peridot, you look thin."

"Thank you, Violet, what a delightful thing to hear."

"No, no, *chérie*. Thin in the wrong way. The light has gone out of you. *Pas de quoi*. You will light up again."

"But you're thin, too. How are you?"

"Gorgeous, am I not? And, you must admit, thin in the *right* way!"

Violet laughed, wrinkling her nose, stretching out her arm for Léon, who now came toward them.

Léon looked good. Corpulent as ever, but with a happiness in the face that had not been there before. Four years of Violet had suited him well.

"Pappa, my good friend Perry needs our loving care, does she not?"

"And she will get it, *petite fille*. Peridot—delightful to see you again."

They traveled in Léon's gorgeous silver Mercedes to the hotel, where Peridot was immediately swallowed up in a luxury that she had not experienced for some time. Like salve on a wound it felt unbelievably good to her bruised ego.

They talked the next two days away, with Léon as an amused and indulgent audience. Peridot noticed that Violet tired easily in the early evenings. Costals watched her all the time, trying to ration out her exuberance in the mornings, so that it would see her through to nightfall. She never said anything about her fatigue herself, but there were blue shadows beneath the violet eyes as though the skin had bruised. Peridot felt the pain of anxiety clutch at her heart. She determined to speak to Léon privately.

Her opportunity came the morning before his departure for Geneva. He was leaving them together for a couple of weeks, returning before Peridot left for England. They had all stayed up rather late the night before, and Violet was sleeping late. Peridot found Costals in the hall, making arrangements with a liveried footman about some luggage.

"Léon, may I speak to you alone about Violet?"

His response was warm, eager.

"Good. I would so like that. Let us walk in the rose garden and talk."

Few people were about. There was a freshness in the early morning air. The scent of the roses seemed more delicate than the perfumed heaviness of the late afternoon and evening hours. Peridot and Léon Costals walked slowly together, as if their pace was affected by the gravity of their conversation.

"Is it consumption?"

"Yes, it is. Or, it was. We are hoping—oh, how I hope— that she is cured now. It can happen. She has had the very best of care. She is still, as you can see, a little weak, but she's improving all the time. You are a tonic for her."

"Violet has a great—a supreme—will to survive. At least, she always had."

"Of course. It is one of the delights about her. But she burns too fast sometimes. It is difficult to slow her down. Her tenderness, her caring about you, give her a gentler quality, a breathing space. This, she needs so much."

"I'm glad. Don't worry when you go away. I'll take good care of her."

"I know you will. It is a great relief to me."

Léon hesitated and looked at Peridot. "I wish to marry Violet, you know, but she won't discuss it. She says she cannot endure the thought of the divorce proceedings, finds it all too tiring."

"She told me as much herself in a letter."

Peridot could see the pain in Costals's eyes as he said, "If I could be entirely convinced that is the true reason, I would be happier. But maybe—"

The shadow of Michel d'Aulnay passed, for an instant, across the rose garden.

They saw Costals off at the station the next day, and there was a lightness about the departure that would not have been possible for Peridot without the conversation in the rose garden. Both girls hugged and kissed him, as if he were family. Costals remarked on it. "*Tiens,* it is like being seen off by two fond nieces."

Violet, coquette to the last moment, tickled his chin, as he leaned out of the train window. "*Tut, tut, mon oncle.* What naughty games you play with one of them."

His exclamation of protest reached them, as the train started to move away. "What an inflammatory remark to make to a man who has to leave you for two weeks, *chérie!*"

Two weeks. Precious as the Paris weeks they had had together. Different, in many ways. For one thing, the specter of Violet's illness hovered over them, although she became stronger and more vibrant day by day.

For another thing, as Violet said—"*Tiens,* Perry, how nice that you're not a virgin any more. We can talk about so many more things."

Peridot, in exaggerated outrage, rejoined, "So many more things, indeed—about sex, you mean!"

Violet spread her hands.

"But of course. What else would I mean?"

They went to the konditorei and ate too many cakes, drank too much coffee and chocolate with whipped cream, giggled too much for twenty-five-year-olds. When Violet was feeling stronger, she introduced Peridot to the game of golf on Marienbad's beautiful greens. Peridot loved it, and they usually managed a few holes a day. The Mercedes and its chauffeur were at their disposal, and they drove around the countryside, picnicking at a local beauty spot, the Podhornberg.

Violet enjoyed the Bohemian countryside.

"There is something unreal about it. As if it had been specially *built*. I like that—that maybe it was planned, not accidental."

They saw King Edward with his entourage many times. He saw them, and Peridot watched him twinkle at Violet, with his *bon vivant*'s eye. She smiled demurely back, sketching a curtsey.

"Have you met him? Does he know you?"

"Well, yes, vaguely."

She said no more, and Peridot did not ask. At what stage in her life had Violet met this merry monarch? Was it before, or during, the Costals period of her life and did Costals know? It was to remain an unanswered question.

One night, as they drank chilled champagne in Violet's suite, in loose, comfortable houserobes, their shoes off, after a game of golf, Peridot asked, "Doesn't Costals mind you calling him 'pappa'? Why do you, Violet? Does it not remind him that he is so much older than you?"

Violet giggled and ran her tongue around the rim of her champagne glass.

"But of course. That is the whole point of it. He loves to be reminded. I am his little girl."

"His little girl? Oh, yes, he liked the uncle remark at the station, as well."

"He *loved* it. Here, let me show you something."

Violet went over to a chest near the window and pulled out from one of the drawers a pile of photographs. They were all of her. In among them were a large number of her dressed like the Claudine on the book that Peridot had brought back to England and Tom Barroway all those years ago. She sat, smiling out in the relaxed, loose-limbed poses of a child, hair up in bows. In some, she held a flower or a doll in her arms.

"Costals took them himself. He has taken the ones he likes most with him. They excite him so."

"Oh, I see. It's a game you play together."

Violet poured her more champagne and handed her glass to her. "Drink, Perry. *Je vais m'enivrer ce soir—un peu.* And you must, too. It is so boring to be tipsy alone."

They drank. Violet said, "Come, come. You must have played games with Clive, as well. Did you not?"

Clive viewed through a screen of champagne bubbles did not hurt, Peridot discovered. He acquired a misty unreality. On the strength of the discovery, she poured herself some more. "We-e-ll, yes. But you tell first."

Bobbing along like corks on a river of champagne, they exchanged intimacies. Looking back afterward, Peridot would realize it was at that moment that she knew her feeling for Clive was over. She would never be able to reveal, as Violet could, her love life with someone she truly cared for.

"*Avec plaisir,*" Violet began. She looked at Peridot over the top of her glass.

"Léon likes to play ride-a-cock-horse."

"Charming, but infantile, Violet. What is so—well, *you* know—about that?"

"Perry, Perry, you're still so innocent. Do you really not understand?"

"Oooh. You are undressed."

"Ooooh *no.* We are fully dressed. That is what he likes—except one very important item, *tu comprends?* I am on his lap, and he *really* plays ride-a-*cock*-horse. Sitting in a chair. We can't do it on the bed, because he always falls backward when the climax comes!"

Shrieks of laughter.

"Go on. Your turn."

"Hold on. I'll need another glass of champagne. I don't find this as easy as you do."

"Oh, come on, Perry. You know you are dying to tell me."

"Clive liked it best when I was at my most correct and genteel and respectable. I think he got an excitement at triumphing over my middle-class morality. He once bought me gypsy earrings. So unsuitable—that's why he liked them."

"He made love to you and you wore them, eh? Them and nothing else?"

"How did you guess?"

"Easy. It's a well-known game. It gives them the feeling of seduction—see, the conquering hero comes."

"Yes. He loved it if I resisted, said it wasn't a suitable time or place. It happened in the hallway, once, when I hadn't taken off my hat and coat."

They both tittered, tickled by wine and memories.

"Yes, I know. So silly, really. My head banged against the wall, and I kept thinking the maid might come upon us. But I liked it."

"Good for you. I only play games if I like them. Otherwise, I won't."

"Have there been any you haven't liked?"

"Yes. Violence—though not with Léon. That is not for him, *Dieu merci*. Beatings, whippings. *La vice anglaise*, did you know it is called?"

Peridot shuddered. "How horrible. No, I didn't know. I have only heard about that sort of thing. But how awful."

"Let's change the subject."

They talked about Pandora Glossop. Peridot described her to Violet, who was scabrously funny about her. Oh, the wonderful therapy it was to be able to laugh at the stupidity of the human race—including one's own folly. Violet was delighted to hear how Peridot had handled the scene of discovery in the sun-room.

"*Merveilleux, chérie.* How satisfyingly, infuriatingly unlike-you, you behaved."

And then—because, by now, caution was out the window—Peridot told Violet more about Thomas Barroway's secret library and his feelings about her. When she had finished, Violet said, "And you are sleeping under his roof? You must be driving the poor man mad with desire, darling."

Peridot was taken aback. "You think so? He says he prefers such things in books. It works out better."

"Aha," said Violet knowingly. "So he says. You know—" A fresh thought struck her. "You could do worse than sleep with him, Perry."

Peridot was aghast, even through a haze of Dom Pérignon.

"Violet, how could you? He is old enough to be my father, and I am not in love with him."

With champagne-induced solemnity, Violet responded, "Your first excuse is a red herring—Léon is old enough to be my father and *look* what fun we have. As for your second—I think that part of you has been tempted. Go on, admit it."

Peridot's reply was as respectable and genteel as Clive could have desired had he been there.

"Once, maybe. But that would be surrendering to my baser instincts, Violet."

Violet threw up her arms in abandon. The points

of her breasts stood out in relief against the satin robe.

"Ah yes, I know. But what fun to do it, Perry. What fun!"

They did not feel that anything was fun the next day. Peridot experienced the first and last hangover of her life, and Violet slept, unmoving, until the evening.

As dusk fell, she crawled out of bed, and they looked at each other.

"What did we say and do last night, Perry?"

"I don't know. I just know that I am never going to do anything like that again." Peridot was filled with remorse as well as hangover. "And I told Léon I would look after you. We will drink nothing but spa water for the next week, Violet."

The thought was too much for Violet. She clapped her hand over her mouth and fled to the bathroom.

They did not drink again. They filled the nights with sleep and the days with gentle activity. Mostly, they just were together, and they did not even have to talk much any more. Each took pleasure in the presence of the other. They held hands and hugged a lot and cared not how the world interpreted those acts—the private coinage of love that had nothing to do with sex and yet everything to do with it.

Two weeks is not long. Costals returned, it seemed, in no time at all. He looked at them both, standing there together on the station platform, and said, "I think that you have cured each other."

It was the way they both felt.

From Marienbad, Peridot took away with her the essence of Violet in a bottle. Costals had brought back, from a brief stop in Paris, a new perfume. English Violet, it was called, named for Violette l'Anglaise. There was the rich innocence of Violet and beneath it, the musk and ambergris of her haunting sexuality. It seemed strange and wonderful to be able to dab a little drop of Violet behind each ear.

"Perry, it must not be four years again."

"It will not be, dear Violet."

Man proposes, life disposes.

Back in England, Peridot went to see her father and mother. It seemed to her that the time was right. The condition which had separated them before no longer existed, for Clive was gone from her life. Peridot felt a longing to see her father again, talk to him, share some of her new feelings and plans for the future. She found that her father had remained much the same. Her mother had aged. There was a sadness in seeing the gradual fading of her beauty. Perhaps it would not have mattered if there had been other things as important to Lady Sinclair, but her beauty was all she was and all she had ever wanted to be.

It was not a difficult meeting, surprisingly. There was so much trivia to be caught up with after so many years that it carried them over the first awkward moments. Terence was the father of a son. Her mother wanted to hear all about Marienbad.

"And did you see the dear king?"

"Oh, yes. He knows Violet."

Her mother could not have been more pleased if Peridot had been one of the Royal party herself.

Virtually nothing was said about Clive and those

events of the past connected with him. They wanted only to know her plans for the future.

Her mother said, "You are, after all, in your twenty-sixth year, dear. Are you thinking of settling down?"

"Oh, yes, I think so. I will continue to board, I think, at Mr. Barroway's. But, what's past is past. I feel more resolution in me, more need to face the world."

"That is absolutely wonderful. What do you intend to do? Continue your writing? It would be so nice if you could write for *The Lady,* dear."

"I shall continue to write. But I shall do something I have been interested in for some time. Mrs. Emmeline Pankhurst—Have you heard of her? No?—well, she is moving the base of her Women's Social and Political Union to London soon, I believe. I intend to join her in her work and fight for the right of women to vote."

Once again she had rendered them speechless.

Out of her cocoon she came to join the world. Or, that was the way she saw it. She elected, however, to close herself off from the society of men, except for a chosen few. Men, in fact, became the enemy.

And many women. It was, after all, a woman—another writer, Marie Corelli—who said, "One never sees any pretty women among those who clamor for their rights."

Nonsense, but hurtful nonsense, for it reflected the values that Peridot had felt threatened by all her life. Equally nonsensical was the view expressed by Member of Parliament Henry Labouchère, who spoke of the appalling chances for immorality, if a woman had to canvass a man in his own home. Nonsensical, but few laughed.

Fuel to the fire. In Manchester, Christabel Pankhurst and Annie Kenney, the mill-girl, were arrested and charged with causing a disturbance at a political meeting. They chose imprisonment.

Then, in December, Balfour resigned.

By January of 1906, the Liberals had swept into power. On election day, the results were projected by magic lantern onto huge sheets in front of the National Liberal Club at Trafalgar Square. Crowds gathered on a large piece of waste ground in Aldwych, under the glare of colored lights and magic lantern beams, to watch the names and figures appearing on the sheets. From rooftops, blue and red rockets exploded; blue and red Bengal fires burned at various locations elsewhere in the city.

It was a time of great elation for Peridot. She thought that it was the beginning of a new era. The whole of England seemed to feel the same way. Emmeline Pankhurst moved to London. Peridot joined her, as she said she would. They called themselves "militants."

It would be truer, though, to say that Peridot was a "hesitant." The outrageous behavior of the militants simultaneously appalled and fascinated her. During 1906, she gradually moved, however, from hesitancy to militancy through the example of others. She marched and carried banners. Then, she shouted. She heckled the chancellor of the exchequer in the Commons. She marched from Boadicea's statue to Downing Street, where Annie Kenney rang the prime minister's doorbell long enough to be arrested. Someone slapped a policeman's face. Peridot felt as if she were in a state of continual shock.

Was this what it took? It appeared that it was, that there was more to come. She felt herself driven on by a force that was changing from one of social fervor to a kind of chauvinistic hatred.

Back in Bayswater, Thomas Barroway watched and listened.

"You are becoming hard, Peridot," he said.

She glared at him, the light of battle in her eyes.

"Good. I have to," she said. "I could not endure this if I were as I was before."

"Do you have to endure it?"

"How can you, of all people, ask such a thing? Is this not some part of what you wanted for me?"

"No. I have always thought the pen to be mightier than the sword."

"I can no longer live at one step removed from reality. That's what writing is—and does to you."

Violet, quite simply, did not understand at all. For her, the most important things in the world were the clothes of the new genius, Paul Poiret, and a strange young girl who designed marvelous hats and was called Coco Chanel.

"She has such style, darling. I am *seriously* thinking of changing mine."

For once, Peridot felt impatient with Violet.

To Barroway she quoted Mrs. Pethwick-Lawrence, from the pages of *The Evening News*. "We look to none but ourselves. We are not sorry for ourselves—but what we are going to get is a great revolt of women against their subjection of body and mind to men."

They were in the study. It was evening, and they were talking together, as they still liked to do. Barroway put down his pipe, stretched out a hand as if he would touch her, and then withdrew.

"Peridot, Peridot, you still have such a long way to go. There is a frightening, violent development going on in your organization. I fear that you, and others, will be hurt before this is over. Consider carefully. Do not lose your reasoning faculties. Not just—is the end right? Of course it is. But are the very best means being used to attain that end?"

Peridot hesitated, then put into words some of the fears she had been trying to deny to herself.

"I wonder, sometimes, if I have the moral fortitude of my companions. I marvel at their courage. But these means are the only ones—the only ones."

Barroway knew that, at this moment, there was no point in arguing any more. All he said was, "Sometimes it is braver to withdraw when one sees one cannot take it or that one has been mistaken. Just remember that, when you are screwing up your courage to the sticking point."

For a second, she placed her cheek against his hand and then got up quickly and left the room.

Peridot made many more women friends, but they were comrades of the mind and spirit, not the heart. Only Violet touched that. Violet and Clive Fairley, once. She had friends—men and women—who were artists, writers, actors. She had friends who were wanted by the police, whose whole aim in life was to be wanted by the police—who broke plate-glass windows in department stores and one of whom slashed the Rokeby "Venus" in the National Gallery. Women who had to adopt disguises to evade the law; who dressed as waitresses, messenger boys. Women who would even go so far as to attack Asquith and Churchill with dog whips.

Peridot could not do that, as yet. But she did not disapprove of these friends of hers. She despised herself for not being able to do as they did.

"I can write as a revolutionary, but I cannot act as one," she said despondently to Barroway.

"Thank God for that," was his reply. "They need some brains as well as the brawn."

She glared at him, and he stared back at her, unrepentant.

Her preoccupation with the movement drove Peridot straight through the years of 1907 and 1908 without looking to the right or the left, and without a backward glance. No thoughts of Clive disturbed her.

She really did not care to know about him now. He was part of the trivia of her past.

I lost my virginity at twenty-one, only to regain it again at twenty-four, she thought. I shall probably remain from now on a reconstructed old maid.

She found the thought not in the least disturbing, even lightly amusing.

Her father wrote that Terence now had another son.

"Come and see us," the letter added. "I grow old, and I love you."

Touched, she wrote back, promising to find the time.

Violet wrote, "Come and see me, Perry. No, nothing is wrong. I just want to see you again." She, too, wrote, "I love you, you know. Besides, Perry, how I *dread* being thirty. And it creeps up, it creeps. Come and see me before I wither away!"

"I will come, Violet, I promise," she wrote back.

"Things are very busy at the moment, but I feel that we are on the verge of a breakthrough. Then, the clouds will clear and I will be free."

The year moved on to 1909. Violet and Peridot entered the thirtieth year of their lives.

A sort of desperation came over Peridot. She told herself it was because all the violence and suffering and agitation of the past two years did not seem to have gotten them anywhere.

She also knew that, unless they got somewhere, she herself would seem to be aimless, without a personal goal. She had driven all her energies—emotional, creative, sexual—into this one channel, and it seemed to be getting nowhere. She decided to make one last effort.

All or nothing, she thought, all or nothing.

From Paris, meanwhile, Violet wrote in ecstasies of Les Ballets Russes at the Châtelet Theatre, of Pavlova's dancing and Bakst's decor.

"The world is changing," wrote Violet. "It is all becoming so exciting, so *free*. And—by the way—hold on to those paintings. The rest of the world is beginning to recognize the talents of those artists, at last! Oh, how I wish I were twenty again and entering this new world!"

Peridot, too, felt old. But she felt lost, afraid of the future. She could not look at it through eyes filled with the paintings of the Fauves or the decor of Bakst.

"All or nothing," she reminded herself.

So it was a deliberate act, springing as much from a need to prove her courage and commitment to herself, as from any deep philosophical belief.

It was not on a march, but at a political meeting held by a Liberal minister, that Peridot had her personal baptism of violence. She had by now joined the Women's Freedom League to escape the autocracy of Emmeline Pankhurst. It was none the less militant. The League wanted the meeting interrupted, using hecklers in the crowd and someone hidden under the platform. These were common techniques to attract notice—childish, perhaps, but they certainly drew the attention of the crowd.

Peridot volunteered for the platform assignment. She said nothing to Thomas Barroway or even to Mrs. Calderwood. She was aware of the probable consequences. They were, after all, part of the exercise. They brought publicity to the cause.

From the beginning, things misfired. The platform that had been constructed by loyal party workers of the minister—or, most probably, by labor brought in for the occasion—was unusually low, and Peridot was above average height. She arrived in good time and had no difficulty making her initial move of concealment.

Underneath the platform, however, it was agony. It was dark, hot, and messy, and she had to lie almost flat. This, she had not expected. She also felt incredibly stupid. She had expected to feel heroic, even if afraid, fired with the zeal of revolution.

It had been agreed that there would be a first interruption from supporters in the audience. Peridot would then jump out onto the platform and address the minister and the crowd. She had prepared a short speech, most of which she hoped to complete before the police removed her. But it seemed an interminably long time before Peridot heard the well-known fruity tones of the politician whose speech she had come to destroy. She listened carefully, only anxious now to get out, hoping that her cramped limbs would still be able to move.

Finally, the planned interruption came. She heard Isobel Mullen call out, "Votes for women!" and a cry of "An end to male tyranny!" from Rebecca Miller. She pulled herself out by holding on to the side of the platform and, with difficulty and a distinct lack of speed, pulled herself onto it.

A sea of faces looked up at her. The minister had turned his head in her direction. She had her audience. She hesitated for a moment and heard a male voice shout "Get her off!"

"No! I will not get off—I will say what I want to say!"

And that was it. Two officers had her by the arms and started to drag her off the platform, her feet skidding across the planks. One of her shoes caught and pulled off. As they dragged her, she screamed, "And you think this is a free country! But it's a country of haves and have-nots and women are among the have-nots—we suffer—"

In the confusion at the back of the platform, one of the policemen hit her across the mouth and she tasted her own blood, flowing from her lip. A tooth felt loose. The fight rose in her. She pulled an arm free and hit the man who had struck her across the head, knocking off his helmet. The other officer grabbed her free arm and wrenched it behind her with such force that she cried out with pain.

The paddy wagon. The holding cell. Court and the guilty charge. The course of events that Annie Kenney and the Pankhursts had been through so many times. It was all new to her.

Later, she did not know how she had gone on. She seemed to have become an automaton, obeying a set of reflexes over which she had no control. She remembered Thomas Barroway there. She remembered refusing to be bailed out. She remembered telling him not to let her father see her. She remembered the shock on his face when he saw her swollen lip, her arm in a rough sling.

Above all, she remembered Holloway. It was like one of Dante's circles, with all those women trapped in such appallingly ugly misery. And it was the ugliness that seemed worst of all: the ugly surroundings, clothing, food; the harshness of those who guarded them.

For all her advanced thoughts and her bohemian ways, Peridot had led a protected existence. Indeed, her freedom to live as she chose had only been possible because she was cushioned by money. In prison, she learned what it was like to eat the bitter gruel of deprivation and despair.

And she learned that she was not a revolutionary.

She fought it for a while. When she felt herself weakening in her resolve, she went on a hunger strike. Annie Kenney and Christabel Pankhurst were doing the same thing.

It was very near the end of her sentence. She was not in for very long for she was, after all, a first offender. Tom Barroway came to visit her when he was informed by the authorities of what she was doing. He begged her to break her strike.

She was released into his custody in a state of collapse.

For two weeks, Peridot remained in a semiconscious state, which the doctors said was as much mentally as physically caused. She remembered only broken fragments from that time: her parents, bending over her, her father saying, "I love you, Peridot, and I am proud of you." The constant, calm voice of Mrs. Calderwood, looking after her every need as if she were a baby again, but with an efficient compassion far removed from sentimentality.

Above all, there was Thomas Barroway. She would surface through her dreams at night, in the lost expanses of the days, and he would be sitting there. When he saw she was looking at him, he would smile, and she would see his eyes join the smile, if she smiled back. So she smiled back more and more often.

Gradually, the pieces began to fit together again, and she began to regroup her shattered personality. Sitting up, eating by herself, taking her first few steps around the room.

When she was strong enough, her father took her to Brierley Park. It was her first visit there in many years.

Unlike her, it had not changed a bit. Even many of the servants were the same. It was a journey back into the past, back into that other age of uncertainty, the time of her childhood. And back to Violet.

She would walk down to the river and sit, well-wrapped against the cool autumn air, looking at the stepping-stones and the other bank. She never crossed the stream. Why should she? There was no Violet on the other side. Violet was in Paris, at journey's end, where the stepping-stones had led her. Violet's father never knew that part of the story. He had died shortly after she had left her uncle's public house.

One day, her father found her thus, sitting close to the water, pulling grass and floating it down the stream. He crouched down beside her, grunting a little with the effort.

"You love this stream, don't you? Is that why you spend so much time here?"

She hesitated, then made her decision.

"Sit down on the rug I brought, Papa. Let me tell you a story. It begins, like all good stories, with—once upon a time."

She told him about Violet. Everything—her visits to her in Paris and Marienbad. Sinclair did not interrupt. He listened, until Peridot reached the end of her account. A moment's silence and then he said: "My God. Great thundering, jumping Jehosophat." It was not quite the reaction expected. Anger perhaps, or merely acceptance. But not that kind of amazement. He went on, "She told you that she was probably the daughter of a lord?"

"Yes. Why? I have always assumed that was Violet's imagination, her love of the mysterious and dramatic."

"And she may have thought she was making it up, too. May only have been dropped the odd hint by her foster-father, because he would have been sworn to silence."

Peridot was sitting bolt upright now.

"You are beginning to sound uncannily like Violet, Papa. What *do* you mean?"

"I mean, my love, that Violet is almost certainly your cousin—half cousin, I should say. I think she could be my elder brother's natural child."

He then told her what he knew of the story. About a year or so before Peridot's birth, there had been a liaison between his brother and some servant. It was, of course, all hushed up. The mother had died, and the child been brought to Brierley Park, to Cartwright, the gardener, he thought.

He knew no more than that and doubted that his

brother knew more than that. Like most stories of that nature, it was not supposed to be pursued.

"I could probably find out more, if you like."

A great, serene warmth enveloped Peridot. That her kinship with Violet should be one of blood, even if only half-blood, gave her the final impetus she needed to reenter the world.

"No need," she said to her father. "I don't need to know any more. That much is more than enough."

Peridot improved by leaps and bounds, put on weight, started to ride again. And, joy of joys, Annie Boileau came to join her for a week. She was living now in semi-retirement with an old girlhood friend near Brierley Park. They talked the hours away, and Peridot sorted out some of her own thoughts in the way she had done, with Miss Boileau's help, all those years ago.

There came the point at which her mother and father had to return to London. Thomas Barroway came to see her. There was an uncertainty and constraint between him and the Sinclairs at first, but it soon passed. He asked her her plans.

"I don't really know. My parents want me to return to London with them."

"That, of course, is up to you. But—if you could give me a little of your time first—I have to go to the Lake District, to sort out details of a property of mine I am selling up there. Mrs. Calderwood will be with me. Why don't you take another short break, before you return to London?"

"I didn't know you had a place elsewhere."

"It is named after my family—or, my family is named for it. On Lake Barrowater. I have no further use for it, so I have decided to sell."

"I would love it. To see it, I mean."

"Then, with your parents' permission, that's settled."

She raised a quizzical eyebrow at him.

"Come, come, Mr. Barroway—my parents' permission? I am nearly thirty. I shall go with you."

They arrived at Barrowater on a misty autumn evening, when a light breeze rippled the lake water and brought down the leaves on their heads as they walked its shores. The weeping willows on the banks shivered with anticipation of the winter to come. Ducks scudded the surface of the white-capped wavelets, uttering their harsh warning cries. It was wild and wonderful, even further removed from the confined space of a Holloway cell than Brierley Park.

Barroway cottage was only a short path's length back from the edge of the little lake; built strongly of local stone, its four-square shape was softened by the semicircle of evergreens surrounding it and the creeper climbing its walls. Thomas Barroway had not lived in it—or stayed there—for years, but had rented it to a local schoolmaster, who had recently retired and moved back to the town. It had been kept in excellent condition. Mrs. Calderwood had gone ahead of them, so it was warm and welcoming when they arrived.

As they walked the lakeshore together that evening in the last of the light, with a very light rain falling on them, Peridot said, "It's at moments such as these that I realize I am a very lucky and privileged person."

"Yes, you are. So am I. We were both born into good fortune."

"Have you ever stopped to wonder why, Mr. Barroway?"

He shrugged his shoulders.

"Sheer, utter chance."

"You really think so? That there is no plan? No plan at all?"

"The longer I live, the more random I think the whole thing is."

"The longer I live, the more I think that there is some sort of overall plan. That some things are predestined. Preordained."

"Ah, but then you are not yet thirty."

"I think I shall get less cynical, not more, as I grow older."

He gave her his one-sided, wry smile. "You find me, then, very cynical."

"Incredibly so. You're the most knowing and the most cynical man I have ever met."

Barroway bent to pick up a smooth, purply-colored stone from the shoreline. "Peridot Sinclair, I am the most impressionable, the most naïve, the most unsophisticated of men. Your knowledge of my sex is lamentably, calamitously limited."

With uncharacteristic verve of movement, he flipped the stone across the choppy lake surface, his body swaying like a boy's behind the thrust of the arm. The stone hopped and darted many times, from wave to wave to wave, until it finally sank beneath the waters.

"There's a nice, apt metaphor for you. We should skip and hold on to the crest of every wave, every peak in life. Grasp as many as you can before you finally sink into oblivion."

Again, the same sarcasm in the voice, but there was a brightness in his eyes, a pinkness in his cheeks, that belied the world-weary tones.

Peridot replied, "Not only a rather contrived metaphor, but a very strange one for a scholar like you. One who experiences everything through books."

He looked straight at her now, and again she was reminded of the satyr, the centaur, the great god Pan.

"Dear girl, you have only known me in my latter years. Whatever made you think that I have sat all my life surrounded by library shelves?"

They walked back in silence toward the glow of the lamp that Mrs. Calderwood had lit and hung against the window facing the lake. In the distance, a dog barked and was answered by the cry of a night-bird that rose from the woods beyond them. Peridot felt surrounded and yet alone, enmeshed in the security that only the best sort of solitude can bring.

An Indian summer fell upon Barrowater. The sun shone, the temperature rose and they decided to do some hill walking. They planned their trip the night before, spending hours looking over possible routes on the local maps. Mrs. Calderwood was accompanying a friend to market the next day.

Peridot felt like a teenaged girl again, transported back to the hill walking she had done with Annie Boileau. She had brought her hiking boots with her when she came, and it was wonderful to know she felt fit enough to use them once more.

The autumn colors sang from the ground, and there were subtle changes in lichen and moss and heather. Few trees to carry the autumn tints of the leaves, but they were not necessary in the sweet clarity of the air against the curve where hill line joined sky line.

They ate when the sun was at its highest, for even in an Indian summer, it was still too chill higher up

and toweled it vigorously, leaving it falling over her shoulders. The dampness had gathered it into its customary mass of curls. She pulled a lock of it loose and straightened it. As soon as she let go, it snapped back like a spring. She shrugged her shoulders. It was part of her—like her height, her deep bosom, the size of her hips.

When she called him, they cleared everything away together, then lit the stove and heated the casserole of stew that Mrs. Calderwood had left ready.

Peridot wiped her plate clean with the last piece of bread, leaned back in her chair and sighed. "Food for the gods."

"Indeed. Now, let me give you the drink of the gods. Here, you carry the glasses. I will bring it through to the living room and the fire."

He came back with an old, green bottle in his hand, from which he was wiping dust and cobwebs with a cloth.

"What is it?"

"Mead. Made in this part of the world from a secret recipe that has been handed down from father to son since, they say, the time of the Druids and beyond. It may, indeed, be the drink of the Titans."

It poured like liquid honey and tasted as sweet, with a fire beneath it that blazed a trail down her throat into her belly. She felt the warmth spreading across her shoulderblades, down her arms, touching even the tips of her breasts, so that they tingled. She was reminded of cider in a field with Violet—drink of the fairies, she had thought it. This, then, was the drink of the gods.

"Extraordinary. It is quite delicious. May I have some more?"

"One more, I think, would do no harm—but it's an insidious potion. One is pure pleasure, two is pure ecstasy, three can be pure disaster."

"Is that an old Lake District saying?"

"No. It's an old Barroway saying."

"Did disaster ever strike you on the third?"

"Too many times, when I was young."

"Poor Mr. Barroway."

She sat on the floor, looking at him. No flirtatiousness in the look, just a grave concern. Her wrapper had fallen slightly open and he could see the curve of her breasts. As he watched, a pulse started to beat at the base of her throat.

"No, never that. I am now a very lucky man."

Whether it was the mead, the moment, the man, or a combination of all three things coming together, Peridot did not know, but she felt her body move toward him, the rest of the room in shadow, the darkness pressing outside, the two of them bound together in this pagan firelight.

"You know what Violet once said to me? She said that I should sleep with you, that part of me really wanted to. Do you think that I do?"

He did not touch her. He sat quite still in his chair, watching the shadows flicker on her, deepening the cleft between her breasts. "I don't know. Only you know that. It's not for Violet or me to say. I have, as you doubtless know, desired you for a very long time." He saw the firelight halo her tousled hair from behind, as she put out her arms to him.

"Take me then. Hold me."

The robe fell open, and she brushed an arm against it, to close it.

"No, let it fall. Never—no, never between us. Don't you see? This far, life can match my curiosa.

It is ideal, it is perfection. All things—all desire, all lust, every act is possible in this best of all possible worlds, the world of what might have been. But the moment I actually touch you in lust, or love driven by that lust, it will shatter into a thousand pieces. Let it remain an image. The nearer I approach you, the further you will recede. The moment we touch we are finished. This, and only this, is possible between us."

She curled back, disbelieving, onto her haunches and then stood up in front of him. He spoke again.

"There is one thing. If you would let me. Take off your robe. Let me see your body, Peridot."

Just for a moment, she hesitated—she, who would have made love with him. Then, she let the robe fall.

Like statues, they remained standing for a moment. She, standing, light flickering like tongues over her pale skin. He, still in his chair, fingers contracted into its chintz-covered arms.

"Did Fairley ever paint you?"

"No."

"More fool he. Would that I could. You are a beautiful woman."

He stood up, and she wondered if he would take her, in spite of himself. Instead, he picked up the robe, wrapped it around her again, led her to her bed.

As he stood in the doorway, watching her already so close to sleep, he said, "Oh—and remember, Peridot. You are only a one-glass-of-mead woman. Two for you might well have spelled disaster!"

She smiled at him through the mists of approaching sleep, listening to the return of that cynical flippancy in his tone. "Thank you. You're very noble."

"Too noble. Oh, that is absolutely the right word for it."

He closed the door behind him. In the corridor, he leaned for a second against the wall, feeling the weakness in his legs.

"Mrs. Calderwood," he murmured out loud to the ceiling, "pray heaven you are back tomorrow. I am not sure I can make my thesis on lust and love hold true for me much longer than this one night."

Back in the living room, he picked up the bottle of mead once more. Holding it to the light, he said, "Fortunately I seem to remember that the end of my saying goes: that glasses number four and five bring pure oblivion."

He filled his glass with a steadiness he observed with detached admiration.

On the day that they were to leave, Peridot got out of bed very early in the morning. She finished the last of her packing and then slipped quietly out of the house. In the early morning mist, she walked along the narrow shore of the lake for the last time, listening to the sound of its waters. A water rat ran across the path in front of her and glided bonelessly into the water, making only the slightest ripple as his body parted the lake surface. At the edge of the little wood close to the shore a squirrel, cheeks bulging, darted up the nearest tree, taking something good to add to his winter hoard. For winter was now nearly upon them.

She heard a footfall behind her, the chink of a pebble against a shoe, and turned. Thomas Barroway came to join her, through the mist.

"You're up very early."

"Time was too precious to stay in bed. I wanted to say a last good-bye."

"I've changed my mind."

"I beg your pardon?"

"I'm not going to sell this place after all. You may have noticed that I did not spend much time in town arranging it. It is yours."

Words failed her for a moment, and then she said, "Forgive me, I don't understand. Do you mean—"

Testily he responded, "I mean what I say, I mean what I say. That much I did: The papers are drawn up. It's yours."

The tears that she had tried to hold on to came into her eyes. She struggled to hold them there, for she knew how annoyed he would appear if she let them fall. She understood that he hated shows of emotion because it made it difficult for him to control his own feelings.

"But why? It would have been—enough—if you had kept it and allowed me, perhaps, to make use of it."

"No. It is, if you like, symbolic. I have a weakness for symbols. So much more satisfying, often, than the reality they stand for. I cannot—rather, will not—give you my body. I refuse that between us. So, I give you this, another possession of mine. It is yours," he repeated.

She stretched out her hands, wordlessly, to touch him. In his step backward from her, she read that that was not what he wanted.

"I thank you, from the bottom of my heart."

"I know you do. But keep your heart. You will have need of it again."

"Will I ever?"

"Yes. You are back from no-man's-land. Just

make sure this time you are not misled by the body's messages."

"How does one do that?"

"I'm not sure. I used to be misled all the time."

The irony in the voice made her laugh, and a tear dislodged and fell down her cheek.

"I trust that is Scotch mist I see—or Lake District mist—that drips unbecomingly down your cheek."

"It is whatever you want it to be."

"Then mist it is."

"Very well."

Together, they turned and walked back to the house, not touching, but side by side.

London was reality. Sharp and shocking and frightening. London was a letter from Léon Costals, arriving at Bayswater to tell her that Violet was very ill again—had been, for some time.

> She would not let me tell you. She did not want you to see her like this. She wanted to get better, to have it again like Marienbad. Now that she is too ill to know what I do, I write to tell you. *Chère* Peridot, she is too weak to see you now. They will only let me see her occasionally. Her only chance is to be very, very quiet, in this good Swiss air. I repeat—do not come over now. It would be in vain. I will keep in touch with you. It helps me, to be able to write to you, the special friend of her soul. I will tell you when you can come. I promise that, if there is no amelioration, I will tell you before the end comes.

Before the end comes. The words tore into her like a knife, and she screamed out loud.

"No, no, it's not possible. No, Violet. You cannot leave me. I cannot be without you in this world. You must stay with me, forever and ever."

Barroway, who had rushed into the room on hearing her cry, took the letter from her and read it. He then took Peridot by the shoulders and shook her, roughly, sharply.

"Of course you can live. If death comes to her, she will have been given no choice. Do you intend to be defeated, too, so that you both go down together? Would Violet want that? She fought all her life for what she wanted."

She pulled away from him, still shaking, took the letter back in her hands. "I see, I see. I will be better, I promise. Just leave me now. Just leave me for a little while."

When he returned later, she was sitting, composed and pale, writing to Costals. "I have told him that I can come at a moment's notice. That if there is any thought at all that she will die, even if she is unconscious, even if she has not asked for me, he must tell me."

"He will."

"I know he will. He is a good man."

The next day brought one of those strange quirks of coincidence, those twists in life, that give one the feeling of a circle completed again. There were reviews in some of the morning's papers of Marcus Radcliffe's novel, *The Country Mouse,* that hailed it as a new classic. One critic even went so far as to call him "the new Dickens."

A morning of flashbacks, of instant recall: the greenhouse, with Marcus and Terence and Violet; the library with Marcus Radcliffe; the visit to his rooms before she went to Paris to visit Violet the first time. She remembered that she had said, "Will you sign a copy for me when it is finished, Mr. Radcliffe?"

And he had said, "Of course."

She could not find his name in the telephone book. She checked the name of his publishers in the newspapers, telephoned there and left her name, telephone number and a message for him to contact her.

Afterward, she was appalled at her temerity. Why should he want anything to do with her, even if he remembered her? She had never even gone back to see him after she returned from her first visit to Violet.

It was one of the first things that Marcus Radcliffe asked her when, to her surprise, he telephoned her that same evening. She told him exactly why she had not.

"Because Violet was happy, very happy and in the process of transferring from one man to another. I felt that it would only hurt you to tell you that. I was—embarrassed, if you like, to contact you with that information. Besides, you never took the initiative to ask me, so I presumed that was the way you wanted it."

"You're probably right. Thank you for being honest. Now—how can I help you?"

"You can sign a copy of your book for me, please—" She hesitated and he broke in.

"I promised you, didn't I? Of course. Why don't you come to dinner with me, and I'll bring a copy along?"

"That would be so nice but—I should tell you—there is another reason for my call. About Violet. It's not good news."

After all these years, she still heard the change in his tone.

"What's happened? Has she been deserted? Is she without money?"

"No, none of those things, far from those things, in fact. Worse, I'm afraid. She—may be dying. Let me tell you the rest in person. I don't like doing it this way."

The pause at the other end conveyed the shock she had given him.

Chapter Eleven

STRANGE. He was as she remembered him being the first time she had seen him, not as he was just after Violet. The Italianate grace of his body had returned. The vividness of the smile and the expression in his eyes were as they used to be. The spark that had caught and ignited her fifteen-year-old heart for that brief moment shone again from his face. He looked happy.

"The last time I saw you," he said, "I thought you looked like a blond Diana. Now, you look like a cross between a Renoir and a pre-Raphaelite painting."

"Heavens! What a strange beast that must make me!"

"Not at all. Pretty near to some people's ideal, I would say. I've been following your career, you know. You write very well—and I am glad to see you have regained your strength."

"You knew about Holloway."

"Yes. Your name was in the papers, naturally. I thought about contacting you or Barroway, but the course of your life seemed to be charted in very different directions from my own. And I do not believe in going back."

They were sitting in a small restaurant in Soho, reminiscent of some of the cafés that she and Violet had frequented in Paris. Radcliffe was obviously known here, and old friends and waiters stopped to congratulate him. When he introduced Peridot, a surprising number had heard of her, too. She had been out of circulation so long that she had forgotten the modest recognition that she had received. She did not realize her arrest had made such an impact.

"See, we are both famous now." He was smiling at her, with the crinkling of the corners of his eyes that had once bewitched her. Curling and twisting inside her, like the soft shoots of a young plant, she felt his charm begin to take hold of her again.

"Yes, I am taken by surprise. I realize that, until just recently, I had not read a newspaper in a very long time. Until yesterday, when I read the reviews of your book."

"I'll give you a copy afterward. I have one with me. First, tell me about Violet."

She had been dreading this moment. Her calm was only possible while she kept on with the other aspects of her life, did not allow her mind to drift to Violet, fighting for her life in Switzerland.

"Marcus, I've taken this—rather badly. So, if you please, I will tell you straight through what Costals told me, and also fill you in with what's happened in Violet's life, up to now. If you would like to know."

"Please, I would. Just carry on. Stop, if you have to. I'll just wait for you to go on."

He listened in silence. At one point, when she faltered and stopped completely, he took one of her hands and folded it gently in both of his, wordlessly. Peridot looked at the slender wrists, the long, strong fingers, and it occurred to her, even in that distraught moment, how very different they were from Barroway's hands.

When she had finished, he waited a moment, then poured her another glass of wine. "One consolation," he said. "Violet did all that she set out to do. I have seen her name and her picture in the papers, over the years. How old are you both, now?"

She found she could speak. "I will be thirty in January of next year, Violet in February."

"Great heavens. That makes me feel very old."

He paused, then said abruptly, "Another consolation. Violet would have hated old age, you know. The diminution of her powers. For women like you, thirty is often the beginning. For many women like Violet, thirty is often the end."

"I know that from her letters. She talked of withering and dying in her twenties. A premonition, perhaps."

"Perhaps. Or a genuine fear of the future, of growing old."

Curiosity impelled Peridot to ask, "Do you still love Violet? Do you still suffer when you think about her? Forgive my impertinence. There, you see—I would not have dared to ask you that even five years ago."

The sadness left his face, and he leaned back in his chair and smiled widely at Peridot. "No, nothing left. Most of the memories are now committed to paper and have therefore entered the realm of fiction. It's difficult to recall that any of them actually happened to me. I suspect, sometimes, that Violet is a figment of my imagination."

"There is someone else, then, who *is* real, to make those memories fade?"

He was serious again. "No, no one. Relationships of that nature seem to make life more complicated. I have eschewed them all."

She looked at him, puzzled. "Maybe I've misunderstood. You mean—there has been no one, since Violet? In nearly a decade?"

"Precisely. It has a wonderfully channeling effect on the creative drive. I doubt whether I could have written my book and done all the other work I have done without my celibacy."

She looked at him in disbelief. What an incredible effect Violet must have had, to turn this attractive man in his prime—who, reputedly, had adored women—into a dedicated bachelor. "I am not sure whether I believe you," she said.

Radcliffe shrugged his shoulders. "It really doesn't matter, Peridot. I don't preach or prate about it much. But it's true."

It was growing late. The restaurant was half-empty, their voices had fallen to a whisper. Peridot said, "I really must go home."

Radcliffe leaned across the table. "I'll take you back. Look—you must let me know about Violet. I know how much she means to you, even if she has passed, for me, into the realm of the unreal." He hesitated and then said: "I may be a celibate, Peridot, but I still love the theater, the opera, concerts. Much more fun to go with someone—will you be my winter companion?"

She thought how long it was since she had done any of those things. She thought of the long, dark tunnel that the winter was going to be, stretching toward—who knew what? Marcus Radcliffe had built a wall around himself, against the memories of Violet, but he would understand the ties that bound her to her childhood friend.

"Of course I will. I'd like that very much."

He signed his book, and she took it with her. She was not to bring herself to read it for a very long time.

They spent a great deal of time together in that strange, confused winter that took 1909 into 1910—the renewed spinster and the confirmed celibate. Their first excursion was to an Ibsen play. Since their meeting in Soho, Peridot had moved back home to care for her mother, who was ailing. This time, Thomas Barroway had supported her father's plea that she should go back, and told Marcus Radcliffe where to find her when he phoned for her at Bayswater.

The evening of their first night out together began in a mood of joint anticipation, sparkling with intellectual comment on the movements in modern theater. Peridot watched her companion using his slender hands expressively to press home a point and felt an incredible sense of release. Her mind started to unfold again, freed from the boredom of caring for an invalid mother and the torment of thinking about Violet's suffering. It was almost with regret that they broke off their conversation as the curtain rose for the first act.

During the second act, a remark was made onstage that reflected something Marcus had said earlier in the evening. Excitedly he put out his hand and pressed her arm, close to the elbow. To her utter surprise Peridot felt her heartbeat accelerate and her breath stick in her throat. Aghast, she turned and looked at her companion. His eyes were fixed on the stage and, a moment later, his hand had returned to his lap.

Twenty-four hours later Peridot could still feel his fingers on the soft skin of her inner arm and had forgotten which Ibsen play they had seen. The renewed spinster was falling in love.

It was a process, Peridot observed in wonder, with which she was not familiar. She had not experienced quite these feelings before. How many forms could this monstrous, hydra-headed emotion have? It was not the feeling Violet had described in Paris when she talked of d'Aulnay. It was certainly not whatever strange pull had nearly put her twice into Thomas Barroway's arms, nor yet was it the mixture of intellectual and sexual curiosity, and the novelty of being found attractive that had made Clive her first man.

Not her first man. This was her first man. Marcus, who had made love to her with his eyes in a library, and who had called her a "passionate intellectual."

He telephoned her at least once a week, and they went out together once or twice a fortnight. In between came news of Violet from Costals, and there were the constant demands of her mother. Peridot rode a roller coaster of emotions. She showed nothing to Marcus: he treated her as a colleague, and she was afraid of frightening him away.

Coming out of the opera one evening, he turned to her and said, "Peridot, let me take you out to dinner early next week. Talking over our mutual ideas at such long intervals is sometimes frustrating. This way we can develop them more fully."

Peridot prepared for that evening with a dedication worthy of her mother, or of Violet. She wore deep blue velvet that clung to her breasts and hips, piled up her hair and pulled tendrils around her face, as she had been shown in Paris, so long ago. She borrowed a fur cloak of her mother's, and she met Marcus on the steps of her home, as they had arranged.

Marcus had bent down to open the door of the cab, and as he looked up smiling toward her, she saw with a leap of joy the expression change in his eyes, the smile on his lips move to something she couldn't quite define. Then—click. Within seconds both reactions had disappeared, as completely as if a curtain had been drawn across a window.

The meal was excellent, the service superb. Her disappointment complete. And yet it wasn't, for she was with him, and he was still the witty, enormously clever and cultured companion whom she admired so much. Only, what she really wanted to do was to scream at him John Donne's lines "For God's sake hold your tongue, and let me love" and stop his talking mouth with kisses.

"Do you like the poetry of John Donne?" she asked abruptly. Marcus looked at her, surprised at the sudden change in the direction of their conversation. "Why yes, very much, though I haven't read any in years."

"Poetry for the passionate intellectual, I always feel."

His face lit up. "How true. I always feel like that about Racine as well."

"Venus toute entière à sa proie attachée."

"Oh, absolutely, although I find I tend more toward Corneille's plays in my old age."

He had forgotten. Just words. They meant nothing to him, nothing special. Peridot felt torn between wanting either to shake him by the shoulders and scream hysterically "I'm in love with you," or to put her head down on her baba au rhum and sob. She did neither. She smiled and said, "Talking of old age, it's my thirtieth birthday just after the new year. January six, to be precise."

"Heavens," said Marcus, "we must celebrate such a milestone. They're doing the *Enigma Variations* at the Albert Hall. We'll go for your birthday."

Enigma Variations. An excrutiatingly suitable choice for this maddening, enigmatic man, who could give her lubricious thoughts by the sound of his voice discussing the moral problems of Empire building, or the use of the diphthong in London dialects.

The birthday outing was to be the last such excursion of that winter. After the concert, he asked her back to his rooms. Peridot went, knowing only too well that his intentions were honorable. They were. He flung open the door and sang—briefly, lightly—"Happy Birthday to you," and she saw a cake with candles on a table decorated with flowers.

At last, at least, she had an excuse to cry. She put her hands to her face and sobbed like a thirteen-year-old rather than a thirty-year-old: for the demands made on her by her ailing mother, for Violet, for Marcus, for herself.

He held her awkwardly against him, laughing gently and patting her shoulder, saying, "Forgive me—is it something I sang, is it the thirty candles?" and she looked up and saw again a shutter open and close across the expression in his eyes.

* * *

A week later, the letter she had awaited so long came from Costals. It was quite brief:

Chère Peridot,
Violette is now back in France, in the country with me. We were able to move her last week. She seems so much better and keeps asking for you now. Please come. She seems so much better.

Regards,

Léon Costals.

Peridot went to see Thomas Barroway. As she stood on the doorstep saying her good-byes, he said, "Remember, when this winter is gone, with whatever it takes with it, there is always the Lake to go to. It has remarkable regenerative powers, as you know."

Barroway paused, then added, "It would appear, Peridot Sinclair, that you specialize in the attempted conversion of confirmed bachelors. Don't worry—with this one, you'll succeed. There's a ripeness about his time and yours that there was not for me."

Amazed, she said, "How did you know? I never said anything."

"You didn't have to. He must be the only one left who hasn't seen it in your eyes."

She spoke briefly on the telephone to Marcus, and within twenty-four hours was on her way to France.

The journey—cold, wet and lonely—did not bear thinking about. She got through it, her mind fixed on Violet, willing her to be all right, drawing every breath she breathed for her. She was haunted by

Costals's words, "She seems so much better." There was a feeling of incredulity about the repetition of them.

A lightening before death. That was it, that was at the back of her mind. Romeo and Juliet. "That which men call a lightening before death."

Pray God this was not. She, who thought she did not believe in a deity, did just that.

Costals's Mercedes awaited her at the Gare du Nord in Paris, a chauffeur and footman in attendance. The chauffeur handed her a note from Costals.

"You will understand why I did not leave her to meet you. She seems so well, but I will await you here. Léon."

Through the streets of Paris, well and sweetly remembered, but unfamiliar in their coat of snow; across the brown monotone—now white on brown-covered—countryside, with the tall poplars bending in the wind, to Costals's château. Neither the chauffeur nor the footman spoke. Peridot was only too glad that they maintained a well-trained silence.

There were fur rugs in the automobile, and as Peridot pulled them over her knees, a fragrance arose from them—essence of Violette. Violet laughing, pouting, shrugging a shoulder, sliding that exquisite body through life. Violet in the darkness of the barn at Brierley, eyes shining, telling her secrets of sex, of ambition, of power and success. The cherries glistened, swinging from Violet's ears, and Peridot could almost feel the pear juice trickling from her mouth again.

Words came back to her. "Be my friend. You teach me what you know. I'll teach you what I know."

Oh, Violet, you taught me so much. I taught you so little.

"I beg your pardon, madame?"

"It is nothing. Are we nearly there?"

"We have arrived, madame."

Costals was there, on the steps, as he had been the first time—thinner, haggard, but smiling.

"*Enfin*, Peridot. At last you are here."

Worry made her voice shake.

"Why? Is she weaker?"

"*Pas du tout*. The opposite. She looks so good. It is as if all is going better."

The room was ivory white and blue. A Wedgwood of a room. Hangings and bedcovers of Valenciennes and Brussels lace, a silk Chinese carpet, tone on tone of white and cream and bone, deep and pale blue silk on the bed, chairs and sofas.

A setting for a Violet who did not throb and pulse with peach and honey and rose any more.

But she was beautiful. A skin so white and delicate that you feared to bruise it by holding the thin hands; hair that seemed darker—almost black against the whiteness. And the eyes still blazed, like all the jewels of the earth come together in one perfect color that defied description.

She was sitting up, propped by pillows, her arms outstretched toward the door, and she was laughing as if she had not a care in the world.

"Perry, *ma* Peridot *chérie—amie de mon enfance*. You came! I will soon be better now!"

They were in each other's arms, hugging and kissing and crying together.

She was so frail, so incredibly frail. Peridot realized that when she held her. There was nothing to her, like thistledown, or a winged seed from a sycamore tree.

"Hush, hush. Do not undo all the good that has been done, Violet. I am so glad, so *glad* to see you! How you have frightened us all!"

"And myself not a bit, this time. But all will be well with you here—and my darling Léon. My two most precious people in the world!"

Peridot looked over Violet's shoulder toward where Léon stood at the head of the bed, behind Violet.

He was smiling, but she could see the tears brimming in his already red-rimmed eyes.

Gently, she put Violet back against the pillows.

"I am here, and I intend to stay for a long time. As long as you want. Now—*you* may be in fine fettle, but I am tired after that journey. So, I will go and change and I'll be back in no time. Rest until I come back."

Violet did not fuss or try to hold her. Peridot sensed she was glad to lean back, to be supported by the pillows once more.

"Good. Then we will have supper together. Like the old times. Darling Peridot."

Her eyes were already closing before Peridot left the room with Costals.

Outside the door, Léon turned and closed it. Then, he took Peridot by the arm, led her to a window seat in the long corridor and motioned to her to sit down.

"I will tell you what the doctors have told me, Peridot. She is dying. It will not be much longer. There was a slight improvement, and we got her back here, where she wanted to be. Now, she has you. Please stay with her. She has not very much more time."

Peridot stared out of the window, over that distant-horizoned countryside, across which she had once ridden while Violet sealed her bargain with this man.

As the tears started to roll down her cheeks—for the first time since she had read his letter to her about Violet's illness—he put his arm around her shoulders and held her shaking body against him, staring across the corridor into space, with his dry, agonized eyes.

Together again, they passed down that lonely little corridor that lay between the living of a life and the leaving of it. When Violet had the strength, they talked and talked of their childhood: of the barn, the house, the village and the river. They relived every episode again. The first few days of this shared space in time were filled with—"Do you remember?"

Costals was usually there, in the background or close to the bed, his eyes always on Violet, rejoicing when she smiled.

The first few days were peaceful, and Violet was well enough to be moved to a sofa in the adjoining dayroom, where she could see out of the window. Peridot played the piano for her, and Violet would lie, eyes closed, listening. She had developed a great fondness for Chopin and would ask for his nocturnes or polonaises, oftener than anything else.

For years to come, Peridot would find that the joy she had taken in the music of Chopin had disappeared. It was replaced by an agony that was transmuted, eventually, into melancholy, as the years passed. The joy, however, had gone, never to return.

For those first few peaceful days, the presence of death hovering in the room was an unspoken one.

Violet still said "When I am better" and "After this has passed," and wracked Peridot's heart.

"Yes, we will. Of course we will do that," she would say and grit her teeth until they ached, so as not to show her grief on her face.

One day, when Costals was out of the room, Violet asked about Marcus Radcliffe. "I have a little guilt inside me about him. Do you think he has forgiven me?"

"I know so. I saw him again, quite recently. He is a well-known author now. He has forgiven and forgotten, I know."

Violet pouted and a flicker of a smile crossed her face. "Oh, *chérie,* I hope not *entirely* forgotten. One does not like to feel that one is entirely forgettable."

Peridot smiled at this return to Violet the coquette. "In that sense, Violet, you will never be forgotten. He has immortalized you in a book."

She lit up, as Peridot had not seen her light up since her arrival. "Oh, how wonderful! *C'est chic, ca!* You have read it? He has done me justice?"

"Oh, yes, he has," Peridot said. "He has completely done justice to you. You have won more hearts."

How could she explain to Violet that she hadn't even read the book—and that the reason was she couldn't have borne to find in its pages Marcus Radcliffe's love for Violet.

Violet clasped her hands across her pathetically thin little chest. "That makes me happy. My final triumph."

The awful irony in those words echoed again in her ears that night. Violet's condition suddenly worsened. Peridot was awakened by Costals shaking her and saying, "Come quickly, Peridot. She is calling for you. She is coughing up blood again. I have sent for the doctor."

The agony of that terrible night was to drag on for another three days as Violet struggled to hold on to life. At one stage, the venerable doctor from Paris, who spent those three days with her, said, "She has nothing left—nothing physical left that is keeping her going. All she has left to fight with is up here."

And he tapped his forehead.

Peridot tapped her heart. "And here, doctor. And here."

"*Oui, mademoiselle.* Whatever is the seat of that incredible willpower—that is what is keeping this child alive now. There is nothing else left on earth we can do for her."

The worst—the very worst—was when Violet finally accepted that she was near the end of her life. She cried, weakly, holding on to Peridot's hand, her head supported on her friend's shoulder.

"Perry, Perry. You save me. Make them make me live. Remember what I said? How I wanted to be a white-haired old lady, full of wise sayings for the young? I still have so much to give! Make me stay here, Perry."

And Peridot held her and rocked her gently, while inside she wanted to rage and scream and hit out at whatever it was that ordained Violet's death.

Having exhausted herself with her emotions, Violet would then be torn again by another dreadful paroxysm of coughing and hemorrhaging.

The nurses and the doctor were there, but Peridot and Costals did everything for her during the last hours of her life. They barely left the room, and took it in turns to sleep on a couch under the far window, each saying to the other, "Be sure to wake me if it looks like—if the end may come."

Then, quite suddenly, the storm passed. They moved, one gray winter dawn, into a time of peace and tranquility, as if they had sailed together through the tempest into some quiet, protected haven. Violet slept on the bed before them, a truly deep and peaceful sleep. There was a smile on her lips. The doctor, who had been summoned from his room nearby, examined her briefly and joined them, where they stood by the window.

"The worst is over for her. She will slip very quietly from you now. I doubt that she will experience any more suffering, until the end."

Costals thanked him, then turned to Peridot.

"The time has come, I think, for me to send for the priest," he said.

Peridot closed her eyes. She felt them prick and sting behind her eyelids from lack of sleep. "Must you? I don't know that it's something Violet would want—the last rites."

Costals said gently, "Oh, no, my dear. Not the last rites. A wedding ceremony. You are to be the bridesmaid at a wedding."

From the bed, Violet called to them. They went over and Costals took her hands in his.

"*Chère* Violette, do not turn me down now. I have, over these last few months, quietly divorced my wife. I am a free man. Please, please, say you will marry me. I have a priest, I have a bridesmaid and I have a bride in white. All I want is your word."

There was love in Violet's eyes as she looked at him and in her smile.

"*Cher* Léon. What can I say? You have me at your mercy. Yes, I will be your wife."

She turned her head on the pillow, to look at Peridot.

"There now, Perry. I have found someone who will make an honest woman out of me."

Peridot allowed herself the luxury of tears in her eyes. "I am glad, Violet. But, you know, you are one of the most honest women I ever met in my life."

Violet considered this gravely, her fingers playing with Costals's sleeve. "You are right. I know, then, that I must be marrying for love."

The look on Costals's face was one of sheer, ineffable joy. He was hearing what he had wanted to hear for nine years. For him and for Violet, the ghost of Michel d'Aulnay was, at last, well and truly laid.

They fetched the priest from the village—a very, very young man, newly ordained, who told Violet it was his first wedding ceremony.

"Mine too," said Violet, smiling at him with delight from the froth of white frills and lace that Peridot had changed her into, with gardenias from the château's greenhouses clasped in her fingers.

Peridot watched the emotions flickering across the face of the young priest, as Violet wove her last web of enchantment about another man.

"Then, it is something we will both remember and take with us, on our pilgrimage, my daughter."

The great, violet eyes looked at him. "Is not my pilgrimage ending, father?"

"Oh, no, my child. It is just starting. Just imagine, the adventure is only now about to begin."

He could not have said a more perfect thing. Peridot rejoiced at the choice of thoughts that this young priest had given to Violet to hold on to. She watched the pleasure in Violet's eyes, as she turned to Costals.

"Just imagine," she repeated, "and it has been such a wonderful adventure, up to now!"

Peridot was bridesmaid, best man and father of the bride. She held the gardenias when Violet's hands grew tired; she gave the ring to be blessed and she gave Violet away.

The priest gave his final blessing to the couple and then stepped back.

"If it is permitted, I will stay," he said to Costals.

His presence felt right now. An atmosphere of peace and happiness had fallen over the room.

"Please, father, we would like that," was Costals reply.

So little time left together. What to say, to convey to Violet all she had meant to her, was Peridot's thought. "Violet, I love you. I—" Words failed her, as she had known they would.

Violet understood. The thin hand and the fragile wrist crept over the covers and held on to Peridot's strong square hand.

"No words to say it, are there, Perry? I know. *Je t'aime.* I love you. That is all there is to say. It says it all. *Je t'aime, Léon, mon cher mari.* My husband."

Then, Peridot remembered. How could she have forgotten—how could she nearly have missed telling Violet? She leaned over the bed in her excitement.

"Violet—something I have to tell you. Something good, something special. We share the same blood. You and I. My father's brother is your father. I told him about you, and he worked it out. You and I—both Sinclairs."

Incredibly, in her weakness, Violet started to laugh. A delightful, rippling, mischievous chuckle. It brought, in those moments of terrible sadness, laughter to the faces of those around her to hear it.

"*Tiens!* Who would have thought it! I really am a lady—*zut alors,* Perry, *quelle comédie!* We are something, we Sinclairs, *hein, ma cousine?*"

"Oh, we are, cousin Violet, that we are."

She and Violet, giggling together as they had in so many good times, as the eyelids started to droop, the hold on her hand to weaken. Once again, a supreme effort, the eyes opened, fixing Léon and Peridot with their deep, purple glory.

"*Dame aux Camélias,*" she was murmuring, as they bent low to catch her words. "Such a pretty death. Only—glad—it was—with style. Such fun—love—*j'vous aime.*"

She was twenty-nine, just thirteen days short of her thirtieth birthday.

It was on the brink of the twenty-fourth of January when Violet died. As she drifted into the sleep from which she never awoke, the young priest said the last rites. It now seemed right and fitting for him to do so.

Léon, who had been collected and in control up to the moment of Violet's death, finally collapsed from the appalling strain of the last year. Peridot took charge. She arranged the funeral, the burial. She took care of everything. She looked after Costals. She talked to him, cajoled him, persuaded him to eat. She wrote letters that had to be written: in France, to various friends—among them, Elise Damien; in England, to her parents, Thomas Barroway, Marcus Radcliffe.

It was she who supported Léon Costals at the moment when the first spade of earth is turned onto the coffin in the ground.

She had found a solution to the moments of weakness when she thought her strength would fail her. She talked to Violet, and Violet saw her through. For she found that it was not Violet's death that stayed with her during these last days in France. It was her gaiety, her toughness, her vitality. When she delved into herself, the precious nugget of Violet that she found was Violet's love of life, not her dying moments.

As she sat with Costals one night before she left, she said, "France will always be special to me, for it holds Violet beneath its soil."

"You would, perhaps, have preferred to take her back to her own country? I never thought."

"No, no. This was her chosen homeland. She should rest here. I will be back to visit her, but the best of her will always be with me."

"Come," said Costals. He took her to a large chest in the dayroom, next to the bedroom. In it, carefully wrapped and stacked, were the paintings that Violet had bought for herself: Picasso, Manet, Cézanne, Renoir.

"These are yours. She told me that. She loved them, you know. She once said to me, 'If my gift had not been beauty, I would have wanted it to be this.' I will see that they are packed and safely delivered to you."

From the pile, Peridot found the little harlequin.

"So sad in his party clothes. Not like Violet at all."

"Tellement gaie, ma Violette."

They both smiled together as, for a moment, the remembrance of her joyfulness filled the room.

"Remember that, Léon. Do not let grief make you forget that. You do wrong to Violet's shade, if you do."

She watched as he swallowed, blinked, fought for control. It was a beginning. She felt that her work was done. She could leave him now.

One last visit to the cemetery, to the flower-covered grave, the blooms shriveled and crisped with the cold, their colors still incongruously bright in the monotones of winter.

She could not, however, bring herself to feel that Violet was really there, under the cold, hard ground. It was the first intimation of immortality that she had ever had. It seemed to her as valuable a perception as if it had been put in the form of a theorem and proved a thousand times over.

She held it inside herself, where it was to warm her and give her strength many times in her life.

Essence of Violet, become essence of Peridot.

Peridot returned to England.

Irritatedly, Thomas Barroway contemplated the tall, elegant man on the other side of his desk.

"I presume this unexpected visit is about Peridot Sinclair?"

No half-shaven religious primitive, this one—like that young Fairley, peering through his study window so long ago—but the suave, man-of-the-world aura he carried with him couldn't hide from Barroway the sensual fervor this idiotic academic hadn't yet admitted to himself.

"Where's she gone? Her parents said she had disappeared and that you knew where."

"She's in the Lake District. On her own. Leave her."

"Good God—on her own! After what she must have been through—it's total madness!"

"On the contrary, it's total sanity. I repeat—leave

her. For a week or two. And if and when I give you the address and you go there, you'd better be very sure of your reasons for going. Or I'll have your head on a platter."

Radcliffe's pacings to and fro stopped abruptly. There was an almost comic look of surprise on his face.

"There, you prove my point. The damage you would have done. You've not thought it through at all, have you?"

"I didn't know until this moment that I had anything to think through," said Radcliffe slowly.

Up here, in this part of the world, there was snow on the ground, as there had been in France. Every now and then a few more snowflakes came to join what was there and freshen up the whiteness again. Will Barker had met her at the station and brought her to the lake. His wife was already waiting for them there. They had prepared the kitchen and the study for her to live in, with a bed in the study, close to the fireplace. They had stocked the larder with meat and eggs, milk and butter, bread, vegetables—enough to last one person for a week or two.

They did not seem surprised that she should want to be there on her own. They behaved as if it were the most natural thing in the world.

Then, they left her.

"Will'll come past of a Saturday morning for the market," said his wife. "If you need something, put the big basket out, with a list. If he doesn't see it, then he'll leave yer on yer own."

There were ice fragments on the edge of the lake. They crushed underfoot with the crisp tinkle of ice cracking in a glass of water. The water and shore birds came every day to snatch the crumbs she left on the front steps, swing on the pieces of fat she suspended from the chestnut tree in front of the house. Two squirrels broke their winter rest to carry these unexpected treats back to their store.

The house was sheltered, but the wind prowled and howled at night in the trees that surrounded it, bending the branches to brush the old stone walls, flicker their twiggy fingers against the windows. In the morning, the sun rose slowly, creaking from its frosty bed, peeling back cover after cover of winter-mist from its face.

After a week, the temperature started to rise very slightly and the ice disappeared. Against the warm south wall of the house, her walking boots uncovered a few snowdrops, those tried and true harbingers of the birth of another spring.

In a few days, the thin layer of snow had completely gone. Not spring yet—not really—but not winter either. A sort of waiting period in between.

Saturday came, and Peridot put out the big basket.

"All I need is milk and bread, please. I am quite well," the note said.

She heard the cart stop, the sound of Will Barker's boots on the path. He made no effort to see her, and she was grateful for that.

Nightfall, and the basket was returned. Some homemade scones had been added. That evening, Peridot took out Marcus Radcliffe's novel, which she had brought with her, and started to read it. She read all night, her bed pulled up close to the fire, the book propped on her knees.

She heard the birds first, before any sign of light announced the presence of the dawn. Outside the windows, two sparrows came down and squabbled loudly over the stale crumbs left from the night before. She closed the book, put it on the table beside her and snuggled down in the bed. There was a slight smile on her lips.

"It isn't really Violet at all," she murmured out loud. "Not just Violet. She is—Violet *and* me. And someone else, or something else, as well. But I think she is Violet and me."

She slept through the whole of the day and into the night that followed. Like the survivor of some terrible disaster who finally knows that she is safe at last. When she awoke, early, the following day, she felt like Rip Van Winkle, as if the missing day had moved her a hundred years away from what had preceded it.

"I feel as if I had been kissed by a prince," she said to a large pigeon, pecking through the grass in front of the house. "I feel as if I could start all over again."

The pigeon ignored her and carried on with his search. No princes came. So she used up the energy she had found by turning out the whole house in a flurry of excess vitality that lasted her through the week.

When Will Barker arrived the next Saturday, she greeted him on the pathway with the list in her hand and the offer of a cup of tea in the house, which he gladly accepted. They talked of farm prices, the weather and the countryside, and he promised to look in on his return in the evening.

The day behaved as if it, too, had been kissed by a prince. Soft spring breezes rippled the lake in the warm air, and the sun shone with a less watery light.

Peridot took herself hill walking, a knapsack on her back. She was out all day.

Coming home, she was tired. She had had no exercise for so long. She could feel her thigh muscles shake as she came down the hill, tired from their long, upward climb. The sun was low on the horizon and a great peace filled her. She started to sing.

Si le roi m'avait donné
Paris sa grande ville
Et il eut fallu quitter
L'amour de ma mie
J'aurais dit au roi Henri
Reprenez votre Paris—

From the bottom of the hill, somewhere by the lake, a man's voice answered her.

J'aime mieux ma mie au gai
J'aime mieux ma mie.

She stopped singing, leaving him to finish the refrain. A man of hidden talents he must be, if Will Barker of Barrowater knew that old French song.

As she came around the last corner of the track toward the foot of the hill, she saw the figure of a man, outlined against the dark spinney behind him. No pony and trap. No Will Barker. It was Marcus Radcliffe.

He wore tweeds, an open-necked shirt, hiking boots. There was a haversack on the ground beside him, and he sat on a large boulder by the water, flipping pebbles and twigs into the lake, watching her approach him.

Silly thing, her heart. Foolish, emotional thing,

springing up and turning cartwheels. Maybe it was just that she was unfit, that it was only the ache in her legs. But she saw the searching blue eyes, the smile that parted the strong mouth, the movement of his body as he stood up, and she knew that it was not. It had all started up again. Such a churning of emotions inside her—regret of the peace that he had now brought to an end and joy at seeing him again.

She opened her mouth to speak, and he put up his hand to stop her.

"First—you can send me packing if you want. I have a map to the Barkers' farm and good boots. So, if the last thing you want is company, feel free to send me on my way."

"Will Barker brought you here? How did you know—?"

"Barroway first, then Mr. Barker. With strict instructions from both parties to remove myself if not wanted."

"Well, at least, you will stay to tea?"

He grinned and picked up his haversack from the ground.

"In the wilds of the Lake District, the perfect hostess. Peridot, I would love some."

It became more than tea, for they were both hungry. While she cooked a simple meal for them both, he explored the house. Then, he helped her lay the table, and they ate in the kitchen together.

As they cleared up, he said, "Can you talk about it?"

"About Violet, you mean? Of course. I told you all there was in my letter, but I can talk about it."

She paused. "Just a moment."

She went over to the pantry and took down one

of the old, green bottles from a high shelf, picked out two glasses from the dresser.

"Let us have some of Mr. Barroway's mead, in the study."

Radcliffe laid and lit the fire for her with swift competence, and she sank gratefully onto the sofa, with her legs up. She felt very tired now.

With Marcus sitting in the chair opposite her, they sipped the mead and talked. Not facts—those, he knew—but emotions. What Violet had meant to her, the feelings they had shared and the feelings with which she was now left. He didn't interrupt, just listened.

When he saw that she had finished her glass of mead, he tried to refill it. Peridot put her hand over it.

"No. No, thank you. I only drink one glass."

"I'll have another, if you don't mind."

The conversation came naturally to an end. Peridot looked at the darkness outside.

"How will you go now?"

"I won't. Don't worry—only the Barkers know I'm here, and they will think nothing of it. After all, we are the gentry, and one advantage of that is that no one questions what you do. For better or for worse."

"But didn't you think that I might mind?"

"If you had, you would have got rid of me earlier. I'll sleep in the kitchen."

Of course. It would be easy for him. No one since Violet. No martyr either. He had even been quite joyful about it.

She withdrew, became dismissive. "I'm tired, Marcus. I think I would like to go to bed now."

Perfect gentleman that he was, he left her. She

heard him go outside, heard the sound of his boots on the pebbles.

In spite of herself, she drifted off into sleep, her tired body sinking gratefully into her feather mattress.

When she awoke during the night, she could hear rain falling on the roof, but not another sound. There was still a faint glow coming from the embers of the fire. He was here, under the same roof. Suddenly, she could bear it no longer. Too many unanswered questions, too much subterfuge.

She got swiftly out of bed while the resolution was still upon her, pulled a blanket round her and went into the kitchen. Marcus had taken a mattress off one of the other beds and put it on the floor, close to the range, and thrown some blankets over himself.

She went over and knelt down beside him, her hair falling over her face as she leaned forward to shake him by the shoulder.

"Why are you here?"

"What? I beg your pardon?" He rose groggily from sleep, his hair ruffled forward around his face. He looked absurdly young, the dim light hiding the gray in his hair.

She repeated, "Why are you here?" She watched the awareness return to his eyes—awareness of her and her question.

"Well, I told you. Thomas Barroway gave me the address and Mr. Barker—"

"No, not *how* you got here," she interrupted him. "But why."

"To see you." He said it simply now, looking straight at her.

"Why?"

"I wanted to. To see how you were."

"You have now. See—look how I am."

He looked. There was something a little less straightforward now in his eyes, that didn't quite meet hers.

"Will you go then? Now that you have seen me?"

The equivocation was now replaced by irritation. He ran his fingers angrily through his hair, making it stand up on end even more.

"For heavens' sake, Peridot, why are we playing semantics at this hour of the night?"

"Better to play with words than to play with emotions." Peridot paused, then said abruptly, "Why did you write about me and Violet, mixed together?"

His reply was gentle, kindly—an uncle responding to a favorite niece's inquiry. "Because you and Violet are part of my mythology. Just as I am part of my mythology. There was another element that came, I suppose, from my imagination alone."

Crouching on the floor beside him, she cried out, "I do not want to be part of anyone's mythology. Violet—that is different. Violet is—was—a legend, a mythical beast, a creature of an age that will not come again. But I am not a myth—I am flesh and blood! I am *real!*"

As if to prove her point, she thrust her hand out toward him, her fingers splayed convulsively. He met it with his own hand, sliding it under the palm and up to the elbow, where he held her firmly, pulling her in toward him.

"Peridot, I know, I know. No mythical beast ever had a heart that beat like yours."

She lost her balance and fell against him, pushing herself off from his body as if it burnt her.

"Then, leave me alone. It's all very well for you—if you choose to live like a monk for the rest of your life, that's *your* business. But I'm thirty now, and the thought of spending another half-century or so like this is not comfortable. So, go away and let me find someone who has *not* taken a vow of chastity—because of my best and dearest friend!"

She burst into tears, hiding her face in her hands. Through the sobs, she heard a strange sound. Looking up through her fingers, she saw that he was laughing. She was aghast at his lack of feeling. How dare he?

"So—I have taken a vow of chastity, have I? Because of Violet? Oh, Peridot, Peridot. There has been no one since Violet, because no one came along that I wanted. That's all. It took you, though, to make me see it. And Violet—Violet was unreality, a very dangerous form of addiction for me. When the addiction passed—and it did, you know—I thought my need for love had passed."

He was still laughing, softly, as if the true realization had only just dawned on him as he spoke. "But I was wrong. Oh, how idiotically wrong I was! At the risk of annoying you, or shocking you—because monks are not wont to say this sort of thing—I would like to kiss you, I would like to make love to you, I would like to marry you. Not necessarily in that order. You can choose the order. That is, if you choose me at all."

He started to pull her toward him again, but she, who had wanted him so badly, held him in check, taking in the smile that had devastated her at fifteen, and the expression in the eyes that she could at last read. She felt the laughter rise in her to meet his, as she stayed his hands that felt for her body.

"For *me*, Marcus Radcliffe, you'd break your vow of celibacy? Aren't you afraid that your source of intellectual inspiration will dry up if you expend all that precious energy on me? I thought you liked me for my mind, only my mind. Ah—"

Irony and clever repartee flew out of the window into the hills of Barrowater, as he pulled her under the blanket with him, stopping her mouth with kisses as she had so longed to do to him, his hands opening her wrap. She cried out in sharp, sweet wonder as her nipples rose against his hands.

"Kisses first, after such a long fallow period, darling Peridot—dear girl, I'd forgotten—I feel like some callow youth losing my virginity again. Dear God, I don't want to hurt you—but it's been so long and I want you so much—"

"Hurt me? Darling Marcus, you can only hurt me by doing nothing, by treating me as all gray matter again—with no body. I'm both, I discover—without both I am indeed nobody. If that's what happens, please hurt me, please!"

She covered him with kisses, pulling open the shirt he still wore to do so, feeling his hands move more surely, more firmly the length of her body.

"Vénus toute entière á sa proie attachée," she murmured. "I translated that for you once in my father's library. Maybe I fell in love with you then. It was so important to me, but when I quoted it to you in London a few months ago, you didn't remember. *That* hurt—that's what hurting is."

Thrusting his hand into her long fair hair, he pulled her face close to his.

"No more mind," he said. "No more talk, no more words."

The force with which he took her staggered her, but she rose to meet him: travelers together finally, after a long pilgrimage over a barren landscape, in the empty hinterland of the heart.

Through a tangled mass of hair she smiled at him, felt his hand against the curve of her thigh.

"You make a wretched monk, Marcus."

"Not at all. I was a pretty good monk, but it's made me a very poor lover."

"I'm not complaining, one bit. You look wonderful, feel wonderful, smell wonderful."

He pulled her close, brushed her hair back and kissed her ear.

"How little you know, poor innocent thirty-year-old. How low your standards are, how much I have to teach—"

Peridot put a hand firmly over his mouth. "Teach? Teach? Oh, Marcus, for God's sake hold your tongue, and let me love!"

This time it was slow. Love flowing and then ebbing, its rhythm carrying them toward the first light of day.

"Marriage then. I choose marriage. Having fought it before, I wonder why I would choose it now?"

Marcus shrugged, settled her more comfortably against his shoulder as they watched the first thin slats of light appear in the eastern sky.

"I could make smug noises, I suppose, about my persuasiveness or suitability. Don't worry, I won't. Could be realization. One day, it may be different—but today, one of the ways to liberty for a woman can be through marriage. To someone who recognizes his wife's freedom as an individual to pursue her talents. A partnership."

A partnership. It had a good sound to it. A triumvirate too. Violet was in there, somewhere, part of the fabric, part of the network of experience between them. Joining, not separating them.

"I feel as if I've just come through a long period of adolescence. At thirty, I think I've perhaps found the strength to admit that I need help, sometimes."

"We all do. Not just women. Parts of a whole. The whole being greater than its parts."

Without him she had achieved much. She felt that now. With him—what might she not accomplish?

Propping her arm firmly against his thigh, Peridot took a long, deep breath of the cool morning air that reached her through the old kitchen window. Together, they settled down to watch the emerging circle of the morning sun.

FROM NATIONAL BESTSELLING AUTHOR

All the passion, adventure and romance of 18th century England are woven into this bestselling trilogy by Laurie McBain, whose "skill at shaping characters and propelling the plot distinguishes her novels." ***Publisher's Weekly***

MOONSTRUCK MADNESS **75994/$2.95**
On sale now!
The book that captured the hearts of over 2 million readers is the explosive tale of the beautiful Sabrina and the dashing Lucien whose first bloody encounter grows into a turbulent, fiery romance.

CHANCE THE WINDS OF FORTUNE **75796/$2.95**
On sale now!
In *The New York Times* bestselling sequel, golden-haired Rhea, daughter of Lucien and Sabrina, is rescued from brutal kidnap by Captain Dante Leighton, titled-Lord-turned-pirate. Their fates converge in a quest for sunken treasure...and a love worth more than a thousand fortunes.

DARK BEFORE THE RISING SUN **79848/$3.95**
Coming in May 1982!
The final chapter of the trilogy follows the unforgettable lovers, Lady Rhea Claire and Captain Dante Leighton, on their return to Dante's ancestral estate in England, where they are thrown into a violent tempest of past and present that will test their love and set the course of their destiny.

Available wherever paperbacks are sold, or directly from the publisher. Include 50¢ per copy for postage and handling; allow 6-8 weeks for delivery. Avon Books, Mail Order Dept., 224 West 57th St., N.Y., N.Y. 10019.

McBain 3-82